LIE,
LIE
AGAIN

OTHER BOOKS BY STACY WISE

Beyond the Stars

Maybe Someone Like You

LIE,

LIE

AGAIN

A NOVEL

STACY WISE

LAKE UNION
PUBLISHING

Published by Lake Union Publishing, Seattle

www.apub.com

Amazon, the Amazon logo, and Lake Union Publishing are trademarks of Amazon.com, Inc., or its affiliates.

ISBN-13: 9781542022774
ISBN-10: 1542022770

Cover design by Laywan Kwan

Printed in the United States of America

*Dedicated to all those who inspired
the writing of this book*

AFTER

Monday, March 20

Sirens shattered the cool evening air with a piercing wail that rivaled a speed-metal concert. The bright lights of emergency vehicles spun dizzying circles through the sky, a frantic dance to the earsplitting dissonance.

Brakes squealed and doors slammed.

The sirens screamed to a stop at the apartment complex on Mockingbird Lane, and the night seemed to exhale.

Emergency workers streamed from the truck with rapid efficiency, their medical kits and blue latex gloves ready to work miracles. Only the onlookers, who wore the slack-jawed expressions of those who had seen a ghost, stood rooted to the ground, seemingly frozen in time, unable to look away from the body splayed facedown on the asphalt.

Sylvia stood between Riki and Embry, her arms crossed loosely at her chest. Their small semicircle was casual, like spectators at a parade. "Well, a body at the bottom of the stairs is sure to draw a crowd."

CHAPTER ONE

Before

Sunday, March 5

The world news section of the Sunday paper was spread across Hugh's otherwise pristine kitchen table. Sylvia dutifully skimmed the headlines. *Casualties! Crisis! Corruption!* Why couldn't they report good news? It seemed that paper sales would go up if they splashed uplifting headlines across the front page. She sipped her coffee and enjoyed the bittersweet tang of the powdered creamer she'd added. Hugh had introduced her to the chemical concoction. She'd initially mocked it, but now she was obsessed. Too much was probably deadly. She laughed to herself. The dreary news was clearly taking a toll. Doom and gloom. As much as she enjoyed her Sunday mornings with Hugh, she could do without the newspaper bit. But he loved his old-fashioned ritual, the familiar smell, and his eventual inky fingers. Trendy frameless glasses were perched on the tip of his nose, his half of the paper in a tight fold. Such a serious man. She liked that she had the power to make him smile.

He was absolutely perfect in an everyday-man sort of way. It was one of the things that made him so desirable. Would he be insulted by the everyday-man comment if she were to say it aloud? Words were funny. It was all too easy to misinterpret things when you weren't privy to the vast array of thoughts in the other person's head. She studied him as he read. Dark-blond hair, cool gray-blue eyes beneath the glasses. His lashes were stubby. There was really no nice way to say it, but on a man, stubby lashes weren't so bad, were they? They were thick and full and gave him an assertive look. A reliable look, like he'd be the one to give you tax advice or walk you through the process of setting up a wireless remote. Yes, everything about him was steadfast and sturdy. Hugh was the Volvo of men. She laughed to herself. He certainly wouldn't like that analogy. The man drove a Range Rover.

Meeting him had been a lucky fluke. He'd been wearing a wedding ring, and married men weren't her type. But he'd pulled up a barstool next to hers at the Vertigo, and a conversation began to flow as smooth as the red wine she sipped. The lights in the bar were dim and golden, and unlike the name suggested, the place had a gentle, old-Hollywood feel. When she'd asked how long he'd been married, he laughed and slid off the ring.

"It's a fake." He'd proceeded to twist what she realized was cheap metal into a tiny infinity sign.

"Fake? Why?"

He'd leaned forward, eyes twinkling, and spoken quietly, like he was letting her in on a secret. "Well, it's not like I'm fighting off women, but I've found that wearing a ring allows me to enjoy a drink without any weird vibes from a woman who thinks I'm hitting on her. Usually, I just want to talk." With a humble shrug, he added, "I'm a people person."

"And with the wedding band, you're Mr. Safe Guy, not Mr. Slick."

"Right." He'd tucked the crumpled metal into his pocket. "Does that make me sound crazy?" His smile was genuine, and Sylvia found herself grinning back.

She'd inspected his face. He had to be in his thirties—late thirties, so he couldn't be much older than her thirty-five years. Interesting that he was still single. "We'll call it a unique approach. How's that?"

"Fair enough." He'd lifted his drink to hers. "I'm Hugh."

"Sylvia." As they'd clinked glasses, a sudden certainty had washed over her. After all the thinking and plotting and planning, he'd simply appeared in her path like a lucky penny.

Later that night, in a dark corner of the Vertigo foyer, they'd pressed their bodies together and kissed like lovers. As she drove home alone, she'd laughed to herself, amused that she'd left the Vertigo with an acute case of vertigo. Because of Hugh. How long had it been since a kiss had left her dizzy?

Truth be told, it wasn't because he was an extraordinary kisser, though he'd been perfectly acceptable in that department. The excitement had stemmed from Hugh's infinite potential as a partner. He would be the one to father her future child. The two of them would make a beautiful baby together. A smart one too.

The baby-wanting was a fascinating new thing for Sylvia. When the calendar had landed on December thirteenth last year, quietly sliding her from thirty-four to thirty-five, her biological clock had transformed from the steady tick of a metronome's beat into a freight train doing doughnuts off the track. It was unusual for her to want something so badly. Sure, she could hook up with some guy and get herself pregnant, but there was risk involved. Bad genes, for one. And she wasn't interested in a baby with a side of herpes.

Her instincts had been right about Hugh. He was free of both. She smiled at him from across the table before returning her gaze to the headlines. One in the bottom corner caught her eye. "Mad cow disease was found in a cow in San Diego," she read aloud. "That'll do wonders for the meat industry."

"Huh?" He adjusted his glasses and looked at her.

"Mad cow disease," she repeated. "It says here that humans who consume the contaminated beef could be at risk of developing prion disease, which is . . . blah, blah, blah . . . Ah, here! 'A degenerative brain disorder that can quickly disable or kill its victims.' Well, that sounds delightful. Do you think the cows literally go mad?" She chuckled.

"Bumping into each other and mooing incoherently before they keel over? I mean, it's kind of sad but funny too."

"There's nothing funny about mad cow disease, though it's rare for humans to get it. If I recall correctly, they would have to consume infected tissue or some such."

Sylvia smiled. "It's rare? Do you see what you did there?"

He chuckled.

"Anyway, we should become vegetarians."

Hugh thumped his paper to the table and slid off his glasses, awarding her with an amused look. "We'll drink green juice and eat pounds of kale." A kitchen timer buzzed, and he stood. "Or we can indulge in buttermilk biscuits. They're vegetarian and they're ready."

"You are a prince among men. I'll get the butter and jam." As she took the jam from Hugh's tidy refrigerator, her mind trailed to the cows. How could a cow go mad? They didn't deserve to suffer that way, though some humans she knew might.

Well, even if Hugh thought she was joking, she was going to stop eating meat for the foreseeable future. Going mad by way of eating beef sounded dreadful. Sanity was something she treasured. Besides, it wouldn't be too difficult to give up meat. She was already faking it for the neighbors in order to avoid a repeat of the dreadful cheesy-beef-and-tater-tot casserole that Embry had brought over for no discernible reason several weeks ago.

"It's just the neighborly thing to do," Embry had explained in her syrupy southern accent when Sylvia had inquired as to the occasion.

"It looks delicious for the meat-eating crowd, but I'm a vegetarian. What a pity," Sylvia had responded, assuming an appropriately disappointed expression. "But you should enjoy it with your family. I'm sure it's Kylie's favorite!"

Kylie was three. And really, did anyone over three enjoy tater tots? Embry was sweet but dim. Hopefully she wouldn't get any bright ideas and show up one night with a quinoa-and-collard-greens casserole. Sylvia grimaced as she brought the jam and butter to the table.

Hugh transferred four of the biscuits to a plate, his hands tucked into large black oven mitts. "Here we are. Piping hot," he said as he delivered the biscuits.

Sylvia plunked one onto her plate and sliced it open with a knife, quickly slathering butter across the middle so it would melt into the doughy nooks. She began to spoon thick jam on top. "What is this? It's all coagulated." She laughed as she poked her spoon at the glop. "It looks like cat guts."

"Sugar-free," he said absently. "Lil—" He stopped abruptly and forced a cough into his closed fist. "Ahem. Wrong pipe. Anyway, what I was saying is, there have been a number of articles lately about how less sugar is better."

You almost said Lily. Sylvia stiffened but forced herself to soften her shoulders along with her expression. "Less sugar is better." She took a bite of gooey goodness, but it might as well have been tar. Her hackles were up. This was the third time he'd mentioned his ex in a week. *Lily.* That meek woman who walked as though her bones were healing from fractures. They had bumped into her a few weeks ago at a coffee shop. Hugh had stood to hug Lily when she'd timidly approached their table, her overcast eyes darting to Sylvia.

"Lily! What a surprise to see you. This is Sylvia, one of my coworkers." His tone had grown deeper, like he'd switched to his office voice. "We're having a quick briefing before we meet with Jeff."

Lily had perked up, though her eyes still looked like rain. "Oh, hi. Nice to meet you." Shifting her gaze back to Hugh, she said, "I decided to run out for a coffee, since Hunter is with my mom." She sounded apologetic, like getting coffee was a crime.

After she scurried away, Hugh tipped his head close to Sylvia's. "Sorry for lying about the work thing," he whispered, his stubby lashes fluttering. "She's an ex." He circled his finger next to his ear, indicating Lily was nuts. "If she thinks I'm dating again, she could very well do something desperate, like harm herself. Or me, for that matter. I don't want to feel responsible for her crazy."

"You've never mentioned a crazy ex-girlfriend."

He smiled. "I'm not supposed to, right?" Leaning back, he added, "At least, that's what I read in a magazine. It would lead you to think I have questionable judgment."

"Interesting theory. What makes her crazy? She seemed painfully normal."

He sat up straighter. "I'd rather not bad-mouth her. Besides, I don't have to worry about you. You're tough, not a fragile flower like—" He cleared his throat and sat up straighter. "Like I was saying, we should include the goal-analysis matrix in the report."

Sylvia shifted her gaze to the left, and there stood Lily, waiting for her coffee mere feet away. Hugh was good. Keenly aware. It was odd that he'd dated a woman like Lily. She looked like a flimsy scarecrow in her sloppy leggings and a peach tunic that nearly swallowed her. So very different from Sylvia, who never would've worn such an atrocious ensemble, even for scrubbing the toilet.

Hugh prattled on about goals and numbers and bottom lines while she nodded, still contemplating Lily. That shade was dreadful on her.

Hugh's expression suddenly relaxed, and his shoulders dropped. "She's gone. Sorry about the ramblings."

"Don't worry. I completely ignored every word," she said brightly. "By the way, who's Hunter?"

"That!" He'd rolled his eyes. "A Pomeranian. We got him together, but now he's Lily's. She treats him like a baby."

Hugh had scoffed about Lily a few weeks ago, but maybe he wasn't as over her as he'd claimed. It was mind-boggling. Sylvia had so much more to offer. And she was not about to stand for being second best. *Hell no.* She dipped a spoon in the jam and pulled it back out. Clotted red clumps hung from it. She laid the dirty spoon on her plate and jumped to her feet. "I have to go."

"But we just started eating."

Drawing her lips into a tight line, she said, "Sorry. You know how I love buttermilk biscuits, but I just remembered I'm supposed to meet with Belinda and Sarah. It's a work thing. I'll text you later." Her vagueness was purposeful. It was important he understood she'd lied. She checked his face for signs of frustration and smiled slightly at the way his thumb and pointer finger gripped his chin, as though he were trying to find the solution to a problem.

It's right in front of you, babe. Stop mentioning your ex, and we can move forward.

"I hate that you have to go. Can I see you next weekend?"

She took her plate to the kitchen and stopped to kiss him full on the lips. "Call me. I really do need to run. Bye." With a flourish, she swung her purse to her shoulder, grabbed her overnight bag, and left. She took a few steps, then stopped in the carpeted hallway of his apartment building.

Now what? Usually her Sundays were filled with Hugh. All day and into the night. But leaving had been necessary. *The only option,* she reassured herself as she started for the elevator. So what if she wouldn't see him for a week? He wouldn't see her either. It went both ways, didn't it? He would miss her when he was off in Vegas or Phoenix or wherever his job took him. Traveling for work was something that had sounded so glamorous until she met Hugh. Now it was only a drag. But she played it off as though it didn't bother her in the least. She was fun and carefree, after all. The opposite of Lily.

She rode the elevator to the lobby, deep in thought. As much as she wanted to believe she had the power in this relationship, a swing in balance was threatening, and it was giving her a stomachache. Strange. She was typically adept at keeping her feelings separate from her relationships. Some might claim it wasn't healthy, but for her, it was necessary. Better to cut a man off before he could do the cutting.

That said, she wasn't ready to sever ties with Hugh. But he needed a nudge in the right direction. If he mentioned Lily again, she would leave again. It would be like electric-shock therapy. He seemed like a fast learner. She certainly hoped he was.

CHAPTER TWO

Wednesday, March 8

Embry Taylor smoothed the paper napkin in her lap and watched her husband of four years tuck in to his plate of baby back ribs. It was the most relaxed she'd seen him in days. If only she felt that calm. What she'd learned that morning had her nerves sparking like live wires.

But she couldn't tell him. Not tonight. It'd be best to let the news simmer for a bit.

A smudge of barbecue sauce sat like a brushstroke on Brandon's chin, but he was enjoying his food too much to notice. His entire focus was on savoring every bite. Mindfulness in action.

That was important, wasn't it? Living in the moment. Being mindful. Ever since they'd moved to Los Angeles, she'd felt a shift in her thinking, as if the City of Angels were alive with real angels. Angels who whispered in her ear at night, prodding her with their silken voices.

Be present.

Think.

Listen to your heart.

She had done just that this morning. Those angels had stopped her from rushing out to Brandon and telling him what she'd learned. Persistent little things with their fluttery wings and sage advice.

Be calm. Just be.

Telling Brandon would relieve *her* stress, but what would it do to *him*? Send him right over the edge, that's what.

She exhaled and tried for a smile. It was their fourth anniversary. Reason to celebrate. They should be sipping fine champagne and laughing recklessly at their good fortune. But fine champagne wasn't their reality. Hollywood was to blame. If that fickle city had welcomed him with open arms instead of devastating punches, sharing the news right now would require a toast. How she wished things would change for Brandon. He was such a good man. Even with the voracious eating, he was the sexiest man in the restaurant. The sweetest too. Sometimes it was hard to believe she was the lucky one he fell for all those years ago. The first time she'd laid eyes on him in their crowded high school hallway, she'd dropped her folder and stood motionless as her papers had drifted across the slick floor. He was opening his locker in the bank next to hers, his firm teenage biceps flexing as he spun the dial. His dark hair fell across his eyes, and he brushed it aside before suddenly turning to her. All she saw was startling blue. Her heart hammered against her chest as he swept over to gather the papers.

"I think these are yours," he said, a captivating smile lingering on his lips. He straightened the papers before handing them to her.

She looked into his deep-blue eyes, and her legs became jelly. "Thanks," she said in an uncharacteristic whisper.

"You're welcome. I'm Brandon."

"Embry." Gathering herself, she said, "You're new here."

"I am. Maybe you can show me around after school."

That was six years ago. After four years of marriage and two babies, he still had the power to make her heart race. *That's what got us into this predicament,* she thought.

He swiped a napkin across his lips. "You're not eating much, darlin'. Is your burger okay?"

"Yes! It's good. Delicious," she added, taking a quick bite to prove it. "I'm just enjoying this alone time with you," she said around her food.

"Me too. We need more nights out, don't we?"

"That would be nice," she said. *But it's not going to happen.* Oh dear. That was true, wasn't it? An intoxicating cocktail of nerves and nausea shot through her stomach, and she reached for her mug of club soda. How long could she keep the news from him? It'd been only twelve hours, and it was scratching at her insides, begging to be revealed. She tried for a cleansing breath.

Inhale, exhale.

Better.

A hopeful smile lit his face. "I can't wait for the day I can quit my bartending job. I swear, if I never have to make another dirty martini, I'll die a happy man."

"I want that for you too," she said earnestly. "You work so hard for all of us. Maybe it's time I start doing something. I can work from home building websites. There was a time I was really good at it." *Hmm.* Her mind began gnawing at the possibility. *That just might be the answer.* He wasn't the only one who could make money.

"You don't have to. You're busy enough with the kids. Don't add more to your plate."

Too late. Her mind traveled back twelve hours to when she sat on the cold bathroom floor and watched the two pink lines appear on the pregnancy test. Baby Number Three. Up until that moment, she'd never once experienced absolute joy and absolute fear at the same time. Another baby! The pressure of one more mouth to feed! She clenched the napkin in her lap but responded with a smile.

He lifted his glass as his expression turned serious. "To you, Em. I love you more each day."

She touched her glass to his as their eyes locked. She knew he meant what he said with all his heart. It's why she'd said yes when she was only nineteen. "I love you, too, Brandon Taylor. And," she added, a sudden surge in her heart, "here's to our babies." She studied his face, hoping to see a glimmer of something that would reassure her that everything would be okay.

"To all of us." They clinked glasses again, but he quickly returned his to the table and reached for his vibrating phone. He slid it from the pocket of his jeans and held it up. "I've gotta take this. It's Adena."

She waved a hand at him. "Go on. It could be important." Adena was his agent and the direct link to his future success. To money in the bank and the end of their worries.

She watched, deep in thought, as he wove through the tables and exited to the parking lot. It seemed like just yesterday that she'd waved goodbye to her parents from Brandon's blue Ford pickup, the bed stuffed with trash bags holding all their worldly goods, the cab filled with wild dreams. She'd imagined she was Marilyn Monroe as her scarf blew in the breeze of the open window. Brandon was going to make it *big*. After all, he'd won the hearts of their entire town when he'd played Conrad Birdie in their high school production of *Bye Bye Birdie*. Next stop: Hollywood.

Hollywood. Magical and golden and brimming with opportunity.

Mama had run behind the truck as they'd rambled down the long driveway, waving furiously as though she'd been trying to flag down a coast guard helicopter from a sinking ship. "I want my invite to the Oscars next year! Don't forget about your family when you're rubbing elbows with Ellen," she'd shouted, a brave lilt in her voice as she'd wiped tears from her face.

Embry had laughed despite the lump in her throat. Mama was obsessed with Ellen. She fancied herself a modern woman, being that she openly *adored* a lesbian. She'd even taken to telling friends and strangers alike that she had no problem with gay marriage. "Whatever floats your boat!" she'd say as she passed the lemon bars at the community center bake sale or as she pointed to the cover of a tabloid while the supermarket clerk weighed her sweet potatoes.

Like her mama, Embry had thought they'd arrive to a land of endless possibilities. Embry squirmed in her chair, trying to get comfortable on the hard plastic. Brandon had been chasing his dream for four years now. Time had inhaled those years with virtually nothing to show for it. Oh, he'd worked as an extra in plenty of movies, but they'd come to learn that extra work was a long, dull stop on the road to nowhere. When he'd finally gotten representation after an agents' night in his acting class, they'd dusted off the bottle of champagne they'd received as a wedding gift and chilled it on ice. Embry was almost certain that was the night Kylie had been conceived. And Carson had arrived just seven months ago. Their precious baby boy with Brandon's blue eyes. Goodness! The next baby would arrive before he was even two. She reached for her soda water. The cool bubbles did nothing to calm the tumultuous nerves that rattled through her. Was it the timing of it all that was making her feel so unsettled? So guilty?

She shouldn't feel guilty. It wasn't like she was the only person responsible here.

Brandon strolled back in, and she smiled at the look on his face. "Tell me what that was about," she said as he resumed his seat.

"Remember how I put myself on tape for the soap last Wednesday?"

"Yes. It was *Days of Our Lives*." She smiled. "Memaw always said you'd be perfect on a soap opera. Brad Pitt got his start on one, you know."

"Is that right? Well, I thought nothing came from it, since a week has passed." Even though he tried to hide his excitement, the silly grin clung to his face. "I have a callback Friday afternoon. It's time I prove just how smart your memaw is."

Without warning, Embry's eyes filled with tears. She tried to blink them back, but one was already blazing a trail down her cheek. Swiping it away, she smiled. "That's amazing!"

He tilted his head and looked at her, the concern in his eyes palpable. "Why the tears, Em?"

"They're happy tears. I promise. It's really good news."

He raised a brow. "I'm going to get this one for us, okay?"

He thinks I'm crying because I'm afraid he won't get the part. Goodness, that couldn't be further from the truth. "I'm so proud of you." She lifted her hands, clasping them in front of her. "I'm just emotional because it's our anniversary, and I love you so, so much."

He touched a hand to her cheek. "I would marry you again today."

"I'd marry you again too."

He pulled cash from his wallet and smoothed one bill after another onto the plastic tray.

Laying his sexy gaze on her, he stepped from his chair and took her hand. "Since we're already married, let's skip right to the honeymoon."

Desire made her stomach flip as they rushed from the restaurant. *Everything will be fine,* she reassured herself. It had to be.

~

Riki McFarlan sat at the Taylors' kitchen table, a stack of graded papers piled to her right and ungraded papers on her left. A baby monitor hummed from its spot on the kitchen counter.

Carson had been asleep for two hours, so her ears were primed for his cry. A few hours was a long stretch for him, but he was such a sweet baby. And those blue eyes . . . they were so much like Brandon's. Riki's eyes were blue, but they were nowhere near as exquisite as Brandon's. His were violet blue, while hers were stuck somewhere between blue and green and totally expected with her light-red hair and the smattering of freckles across her nose. Hers blended. His popped. She twirled a pen in her hand and sighed. And then there was Embry. She was a doll—a great friend and one of the nicest people she knew. And she *looked* nice, too, like someone who'd be in a commercial for a foaming face wash that promised a pure and fresh clean. What would it be like to have flawless skin and a childlike pout that made her seem endlessly kissable? Not that Riki wanted to kiss her.

She just wanted to *be* her sometimes, late at night, when Riki imagined Brandon caressing her full breasts. Carson yelped, and she nearly fell out of her chair. She froze where she was, straining to hear more. *One alligator, two alligator, three alligator . . .* She counted fifteen alligators before she moved. The apartment was quiet, and she released the breath she'd been holding as she repositioned herself in the chair.

She grabbed her pen and focused on the page in front of her. Darcy earned 100 percent on her test as usual. Her mother would expect nothing less. Technically, the teachers weren't required to give spelling tests any longer, but Riki hated the idea of kids relying on spell-check for everything. She was arming them for future success. Drawing a smiley face at the top of the page, she moved to the next. Kenji had spelled *heat, seat,* and *treat* correctly, but he'd missed *cheat.* Riki circled the word and wrote the correct spelling next to *ceat* just as she heard Embry's tinkling laughter followed by a key turning in the lock.

The Taylors walked in, all smiles, and Brandon had an arm slung low on Embry's hips as he pushed the door closed. Riki busied herself with capping the pen and packing up her work so she wouldn't stare. "Hey, guys. Fun night?"

Brandon circled his arms around Embry's waist, and she leaned into him as he spoke. "It was nice, thanks. How'd my little rug rats do? Did Carson wake up?"

"They were both great," Riki said, relieved to discuss the business of bedtime. It gave her something to focus on besides Brandon. As hard as she tried, she couldn't stop her heart from breaking into a sprint when he walked into the room. "Carson had a bottle at seven thirty and was asleep by eight."

"Thanks, Riki. You're sure sweet to help us out so much."

She bit back her smile, trying to contain it, but it spread across her face. It felt like her cheeks were on fire. Was her blushing obvious?

She looked down as she shouldered her tote, wishing she could gain control of her reaction to Brandon. "Happy to do it," she said, forcing a detached tone. "See you soon."

"Wait!" Embry wriggled from Brandon's arms and rushed to the kitchen, taking a foil-wrapped plate from the counter and placing it in Riki's hands. "Death-by-chocolate cookies." She paused. "I usually don't bake with chocolate. I'm more of a fruit-and-butter kind of gal, but for some reason, chocolate appealed to me." She shrugged. "Anyway, I hope you enjoy them."

"Thanks. You make the best treats. You could open your own bake shop."

Embry smiled. "There was a time I was working on it. I was hoping to start with a stand at the farmers' market. I got my permit, but then Carson came along, and well . . ."

"Life got in the way," Riki finished. "And I'm going to have to carve out time for extra spin classes if you keep giving me cookies." She wouldn't let them pay her for babysitting, but nonetheless, Embry insisted on sending home-baked treats with her every time she watched the kids.

Brandon rubbed a hand down his stomach—the stomach that Riki knew was muscled to perfection. Every Saturday morning, she was reminded of that when he cut the grass shirtless. Apparently, the Taylors' rent was reduced thanks to his mowing skills. Whatever the case, if she timed it right, she never missed a viewing.

"Don't I know it? It's hard to resist the sweet stuff."

Her face flamed hotter. Was that a double entendre? Was he referring to her as the sweet stuff? The smile remained on his lips. It was too much. She veered her eyes to Embry. "Thanks again for these. They won't really kill me, right?"

Embry's hazel eyes grew wide. "Huh?"

"*Death*-by-chocolate?" When Embry still didn't get it, she added, "Poisoned cookies?"

She shook her head, laughing. "Goodness! I've never considered how strange the name is. Of course they're not poisoned."

"Right. Bad joke." Riki tried for a laugh, but it fell flat. "Yes, well, good night, you guys. I have an early morning. It's the jog-a-thon at school tomorrow. Bye!" She didn't wait for a response.

Once the door was closed behind her, she sped across the long driveway to her apartment, trying to escape the frustration that chased her. It would be really nice if she had an antidote for her body's response to Brandon.

But the truth of the matter was, he was a magnetic force she couldn't resist. As she unlocked the door, her bag slid from her shoulder, and she heard the rip of fabric. Shoot. She'd stuffed it too full, and now the strap was tearing at the seam. Tomorrow at school, she could staple it with the industrial stapler. Or maybe one of her students could do a creative duct-tape job on it. That was the hot new fad: duct tape. Her students had already gifted her with a wallet, a key chain, and too many bracelets to count. Today she was wearing one Chloe had made with sparkly pink tape.

Setting the cookies on the counter, she scrubbed her hands at the sink before lifting the foil and plucking one from the plate. She sank her teeth into it, and her eyes fell shut as the flavors teased her taste buds until they were wide-awake and begging for more. Embry worked magic in the kitchen, but the best Riki could do was plop premade dough onto a tray and end up with semiburned rocks. She shouldn't have made the dumb joke about poisoned cookies. Of course Embry wouldn't poison her. Embry wasn't the terrible person in this scenario.

The sound of Sylvia's TV buzzed from the apartment above hers. She couldn't make out the words, but based on the canned laughter, she assumed it was some dumb sitcom from two decades ago. Or maybe it was *Friends*. Sylvia loved that show. She looked like she could be Monica's sister, but Sylvia's figure was softer than Monica's thin frame. The dark hair and light eyes, though? Eerily similar.

Wiping the crumbs into the trash can, she washed her hands again and sank onto the sofa. She considered turning on her own TV but was too lazy to reach for the remote. Tonight had been draining. Guilt tried to settle in next to her on the sofa, but she shoved it to the floor. It wasn't like she'd done anything *bad*. She'd only looked at the shirts hanging on Brandon's side of the closet. She hadn't even touched them with her hands, only her eyes.

Her heart sped up in her chest. Jeez, she was like her own lie-detector test. Even though she tried to block it from her memory, her brain was eager to replay the scene in flaming color. There she was, pressing her face into a stack of Brandon's clean T-shirts, breathing them in and hoping for a trace of his scent. And then she'd rubbed his shorts against her wrists, transferring a touch of her perfume to them so when he took them from his drawer, he'd think of her. Guilt slithered from where she'd chucked it and began snaking up her leg, making her hands shake. What if they'd bought a nanny cam? She closed her eyes and tried to recall if anything new had been in their room, but her brain was like a freaking toddler skipping in circles and singing, *Who took the cookie from the cookie jar? Riki took the cookie from the cookie jar!*

Who me?

Yes you!

Not me!

We know it was you.

Oh, jeez. She needed to stop. This was getting out of hand. But in her defense, she wouldn't have considered the perfume bit if he hadn't told her she smelled nice the other day. When he made it big in Hollywood, he'd have to be a lot more careful about throwing compliments around like confetti. He'd end up with millions of women wishing they could be in bed next to him. *They* wouldn't care that he was married to an adorable girl with bubblegum lips, voluptuous boobs, and dazzling hazel eyes. She even smelled good, like she bathed in rose petals.

Riki sat up, her senses alert. That was it! She had been at the mall last weekend and had wandered into a shop that sold soaps, scrubs, and candles fragranced with scents that had her dreaming of Paris gardens and tropical vacations. A pale-pink candle had caught her eye, and she'd held it to her nose. Her brain had staggered in circles, attempting to touch down on what person or memory the scent conjured.

Now she knew. It was Embry.

She leaped from the sofa and jogged to her room. Sure enough, when she sniffed the candle, Embry filled her senses. She snapped the lid onto it, trapping the scent, and left her room. It had to be a coincidence. That's all. She wasn't trying to copy Embry. Rose was one of the most common scents. Besides, it wasn't weird for friends to end up trying one another's perfume or lipstick shade. Girls shared stuff all the time. Even bathing suits, although Riki would never do that. Way too much potential for serious germs. *But they don't share husbands! Way too much potential for* . . . Riki shook her head. For what? Poisoned cookies? *Shut up!*

She needed a distraction. It was late for a weeknight, but what the hell? She grabbed her phone and began scrolling down her text messages until she landed on Chris.

Hey. You awake?

She stared at the screen, not sure if she really wanted to see the dots that meant he was replying or not. He'd only be a temporary fix, like eating fast food when you were starving but then wishing you'd waited to have something better.

Yeah. You wanna come over?

Can you come here instead?

And now he was DoorDash. She bit her lip.

Yep. Be there in ten.

Her finger hovered above the screen before she typed a reply. Three kissy-face emojis. It was the right response. Cute. Simple. And she wanted to kiss him. She really did. It wasn't his fault she didn't want to tug on his lips with her teeth as she trailed her fingers down his naked chest, snaking them to the button of his jeans, making him beg for her, the way she dreamed of doing with Brandon. She set her phone on the nightstand and went to brush her teeth. As she squeezed toothpaste onto her toothbrush, the pesky voice of reason seemed to pop out of the bathroom drawer.

You're being stupid.

She slammed the drawer, but the voice refused to be quieted.

You'll lead him on.

You'll get hurt.

Well, so what? I'm allowed, she thought as she rinsed her mouth. She was only twenty-five, not forty.

Yet Embry was twenty-four. And married. And a mother times two.

Maybe this was a bad idea. She couldn't imagine Embry hooking up with some guy for comfort sex.

But she wasn't Embry.

And Chris wasn't just some guy. They were dating.

She turned her head down to brush the underside of her straight hair before flipping it back. It had become a habit, but not a very effective one. Her hair looked puffy, not full and luxurious like in the shampoo commercials. Not like Embry's. She ran the brush through it again, which got it right back to where she had started. Rowan, her older sister, had been blessed with a thick mass of chestnut curls, presumably from their maternal grandmother, though now Grandma Willet's hair was cut short and kept in place with half a can of hair spray. When she was little, Rowan had told her that Grandma Willet was the reason for the hole in the ozone layer. For years, Riki had felt a residual guilt that someone in her family had caused such damage to the planet, and she'd always made sure to pick up trash at the park and turn off all the lights every time they left the house. It wasn't until sixth grade, when her teacher taught an earth science unit, that she'd realized Rowan had been joking. How many other things had Rowan joked about that Riki had believed to be true? She looked at her reflection in the mirror. What would Rowan say about the thing with Chris? It'd be nice if they had the kind of relationship where they talked every day, eager to share even the most mundane details, but the truth was, they weren't close. It didn't help that Rowan was halfway across the world. She'd decided to travel all the way to Australia to get her master's degree in sustainability, whatever that meant. She'd probably say, "Seriously, Riki? Either you like him or you don't. Why the drama?"

But it wasn't so black-and-white in her mind. The ringing of the doorbell interrupted her thoughts, and she took a breath before opening the door.

Chris had his hands tucked in the pockets of his stiff jeans, attempting a cool stance. It was charming despite the forced effort. "Hi," he said, darting a kiss to her lips.

She took his hand and led him inside.

～

Jonathan parked half a block from the apartment complex, a good distance between the streetlights. Their glow was shrouded by heavy fog, but he couldn't be too careful. He didn't want the tenants to know he was back in town, crashing at Ma's old place for the night. Easing from his car, he tugged the hood of his sweatshirt into place and stole across the long driveway, keeping his head down as he crept to the second-floor apartment.

Shucking his sneakers by the door, he padded to the kitchen in his socks. Not that he cared about getting the floors dirty. This wasn't his place. He chuckled at the irony. Correction: this wasn't where he *lived*. And he didn't want the tenants below to call the police because they'd heard an intruder. As he filled a glass with water, he wondered if Ma had asked him to come back all those months ago so she could give him the paperwork for the complex. He wished she would've said more. But with her, it was always the dangled carrot, and he didn't have time for that.

When she'd asked him to come home, he'd been across the country in New York visiting a friend. She hadn't told him she was *dying*. It was a voice mail saying she wanted to see him about something important. How the hell was he supposed to know she was near the end? When he returned for the funeral, he found a note she'd left for him on the table by the door. In her annoyingly perfect handwriting, she'd written, *I wish you would've come around more. And I hope you find a nice girl.*

That's not a problem, Ma. He drained his glass, and a satisfied smile eased across his lips.

He was still riding high from his two-month luxury escape to Europe. How else was he supposed to process his mother's death? The Italian girls had been especially hospitable to the fine American man. Life was good. He could almost taste the salty air drifting up off the waters of Positano on the Amalfi Coast. Before long, he'd go back and rent a yacht. Hell, he could probably buy one. He'd cruise the waters with any number of gorgeous dark-haired females with satiny olive skin. A few details needed to be squared away with the apartment complex, and he'd go back. The tenants wouldn't be too tough to deal with. One had even brought him a casserole after Ma died. Too bad she hadn't offered to comfort him the old-fashioned way instead. That chick was hot. Married, but hot. Setting his glass on the counter, he crossed to the sofa and settled onto it, trying to get a clear picture of the blonde in his head, but the image was blurry. All he could see was her full lips babbling about the rent.

She'd insisted that Ma had given them a discount. That had knocked her hotness down a notch. Who'd she think he was? Santa Claus? He wasn't going to honor any alleged discounts. This was a business. And collecting the rent checks had become a hefty supplement to his fickle income. He smiled to himself as he thought about the piles of cash that would soon be his. Rent checks were one thing. But selling this place? He'd make a mint.

Ma had tidied things up nice and neat before her death, putting every last asset into a trust that transferred to him upon her death. Tomorrow, he'd meet with his real estate agent. The current climate for sellers in the area was sizzling hot. He could be a multimillionaire by the time the spring flowers had sprung.

CHAPTER THREE

Thursday, March 9

The alarm blared, startling Riki out of a deep sleep. She slapped at her phone, trying twice before successfully hitting the "Snooze" button. Chris pulled her close, tucking her body into his. "I wish it was Saturday," he whispered into her hair. "I want to stay in bed with you all day."

His words jolted her from sleepy to alert. They'd never stayed in bed all day. Not on a Saturday or any other day, for that matter. Was he imagining that they would sometime soon? Did guys fantasize about the future the same way women did? It should give her a feeling of security in their relationship, but it made her want to break free from his arms and run.

He trailed a line down her back with his finger. "Hey. I'm serious." He continued snaking his hand across her skin. His touch seemed to have hypnotic powers.

She shivered and softened into him. "About?" Her voice was husky with sleep, and it made her sound unintentionally sexy. She turned to face him and cleared her throat. "Sorry. Sleep voice. What are you serious about?"

"Wanting to stay with you all day." He readjusted the pillow under his head and closed his eyes.

Riki reached out a hand and rubbed it across his smooth buzz cut. She liked the way it tickled her fingers. *But I hate his haircut.* It reminded her of Geoffrey Kozinski, a neighborhood kid with a bully's swagger who'd taken to calling her Riki McHickey in middle school. She hadn't known what a hickey was back then, which had made him laugh even harder. Stupid kid. She tried to ignore the resemblance in their haircuts, but it was always there. Other things about his appearance were nice, though. He had good hands. They were big and capable with neatly squared fingernails. His eyes were interesting too—a dark contrast to hers—almost black, to be honest. She preferred soft brown eyes or even hazel ones. *Or bright blue like Brandon's.*

Stop! She wished she could poison the voice in her head, killing it once and for all. It was like her mind was a desperate addict, going back for more even though she knew better. She *knew* better.

So why had she closed her eyes last night and imagined Chris was Brandon? It was just so easy to do. Both he and Brandon were six feet tall, give or take. And his hands were so much like Brandon's. A casual observer wouldn't notice, but Riki had. It was in the way their knuckles knotted beneath the skin. It was in the square fingernails.

But it wasn't like she'd thought of Brandon the whole time. He'd only flitted in and out of her thoughts. Chris was a great guy. He'd been so sweet on their first date, holding doors for her and taking her hand. Throughout the night, he'd pegged her with compliments like Cupid with his arrows. It was nice until it wasn't—until she began to wonder if he was just another charmer. She'd told her friend Amelia, who taught second grade with her, about it, saying all the flattery seemed a little overkill, but Amelia had insisted he was probably smitten. "You're one of those weirdos who doesn't know how smart and pretty you are." Riki didn't know about that, but it felt good to believe that Chris's kind words were sincere. And since then, he'd been very consistent and reliable, calling when he said he would and not canceling plans. That was important. Relationships were supposed to be built on love and respect, not on the flimsy wings of butterflies.

He opened his eyes and touched her hand that was now resting on his head. She hadn't realized she'd stopped massaging. "What are you thinking?" he asked.

"Nothing." She tucked the covers to her chin. "I'm still half-asleep."

"So call in sick. Hell, call in sick tomorrow too. We need a long weekend." His voice was thick with suggestion. Simple enough for him to call in sick. He was a PA on a reality show. Or maybe even an assistant to an assistant. It seemed he didn't do much beyond fetching coffee. It was easy to have a slacker job when you were a trust-fund baby, but in his defense, he was still figuring out what his passion was. "Last night was amazing."

It *had* been amazing. There was something irresistible about his touch. His caress was intoxicating, as if he had secret magical powers. Sometimes when she closed her eyes and wasn't imagining Brandon, she believed that when she opened them, she'd see a man so gorgeous, he'd steal her breath. But in the light of day, lying next to him in bed, an inexplicable sense of loneliness washed over her.

With a flourish, she tossed the covers aside. "I can't. It's the jog-a-thon today. I have to shower."

His head flopped onto the pillow.

She headed to the bathroom. They could talk later.

When she emerged, she was freshly scrubbed, shampooed, and dressed in jeans and her light-blue Ocean Avenue Academy T-shirt. All the teachers were required to wear their spirit wear for the jog-a-thon. Ocean Avenue was so much different from Clover Street Elementary, the public school where she'd taught for two years before getting pink-slipped. It was a sad fate for too many new teachers whose positions were eliminated due to a lack of funding. It's why she'd been thrilled when she'd landed a position at Ocean Avenue. And Mrs. Fitzsimmons, the teacher Riki had replaced after her retirement, had left her with boxes of books, art supplies, and auction prizes. It was more than she could've dreamed of. Too bad no one had clued her in to the constricting strings that were attached to a private school.

Chris was perched on the edge of the bed, pulling his shirt over his head. She had the urge to sidle over to him and slip onto his lap for a last embrace, but she ignored it. "I have to run. Will you let yourself out?" she asked, gathering her purse and keys.

He stood. "I'm going now too."

She crossed to the door and lugged her work tote onto her shoulder, careful not to rip it further, stealing a glimpse at Chris as she did. His keys dangled from his index finger. He flipped them into his palm and closed his hand. "Are you okay? You seem jumpy."

She placed her hand on the doorknob and wished she were more skilled at masking her feelings. "I just don't want to be late. The jog-a-thon is apparently a big deal." She turned to peck his lips. "Thanks for coming over."

Tilting her chin up with his finger, he whispered, "All I want is to make you happy." When she didn't respond, he said, "And I'd like to continue giving you multiple orgasms on a regular basis if you're interested."

She bit her lip and looked at him.

"I know we haven't talked about being exclusive, but I'm kind of assuming we are, being that we're sleeping together. Were you worried about that?" He cupped her cheek with his hand, and she felt close to tears, but not for the reasons he probably imagined.

Touching his hand with hers felt like the right thing to do. "Kind of. Are you saying you aren't dating anyone else?"

"That's what I'm saying." He smiled, but she could see a hint of fear in his eyes. It was obvious he cared about her. "Are you seeing other guys?"

She playfully punched his arm. "No! Only you. Exclusively," she added with a grin.

"Good." His confidence restored, he pulled her close, pressing his body to hers. "I'll call you later. Good luck with the jog-a-thon thing."

He tapped the door twice and headed for the street where his car was parked. Riki went in the opposite direction. As she walked down the driveway toward the carport, she glanced at the Taylors' place. Through the big bay window in front, she could see a shirtless Brandon with Kylie in his arms. *Are they dancing?* As if feeling her gaze, Brandon looked over and smiled. He took Kylie's hand in his and waved it, the same way he sometimes did with the baby, and it caused the little girl to explode with giggles. In a quick swoop, he landed Kylie onto his shoulders, giving Riki an unobstructed view of his naked torso. Had he done that on purpose? Did he know the effect he had on her? Kylie gripped one shoulder with her little hand and waved frantically with the other, waking Riki from her daze. She'd literally been staring at him, unmoving. Lifting both hands, she waved back, blowing kisses as though she could see only Kylie. She licked her lips and tasted Chris on them before heading to her car.

Chris. He was her reality. They were exclusive. An official couple. It didn't matter that she sometimes wished Chris were Brandon. It probably happened with all couples. Chris probably wished she were a Victoria's Secret angel at times. He could very well imagine she was a different girl every single time they had sex. The point was, she liked him as a person. All the other stuff would come in time. Yes, this was the foundation for a solid adult relationship. She was twenty-five, after all, and it was time to banish the idea of fairy tales.

Fairy tales. She'd just started a unit on them at school. A common element was the monster, and with the way she had been thinking, she'd have to cast herself as the villain, not the princess. She shivered at the thought. That's not who she was. She held her arm out in front of her and clicked her key fob. The locks opened as if by magic. If only she had a similar clicker for her feelings. She needed to shut them down before they became so big, she lost control.

~

Riki cheered on her little joggers as they moved around the field. Two of the kids had given up on running and were plucking dandelions from the grass as they strolled along. She shaded her eyes as she watched Jeremy, one of the tiniest kids in her class, run with his arms flapping behind him as though he were trying to break through a barrier she couldn't see. His mother stood next to her. "My husband has tried to teach him to pump his arms, but he just doesn't get it."

"He will." Riki smiled as she looked on. "He's a great kid."

"Yes, he is."

Riki turned at the sudden sharp tone in his mom's voice.

Mrs. Tau continued. "Were you aware that he was shamed in class the other day?"

"What? No! When did this happen?"

Her lips formed a tight line. "It was during the nutrition lesson. Apparently, the docent asked what they'd eaten for breakfast. Jeremy raised his hand and shared that he'd had Cheerios."

Riki nodded, keeping an eye on her joggers. "I remember that."

"Well, her response could've been kinder. According to my son, she told him Cheerios aren't a good choice because they're processed. He said he'd added milk, thinking that milk is healthy because that's what I've always told him, but then she went on to lecture him about milk. She actually said if he used cow's milk, it made things worse, because cow's milk is meant for calves." Mrs. Tau turned to Riki. "Unbelievable. I wish he'd told her that her nut milk was meant for nuts, but of course, he would never think to say that. Our nanny said he wasn't himself all afternoon. I thought he was coming down with something and got out the thermometer, but he ran for the kitchen, where I caught him dumping the entire box of Cheerios into the trash. It was then that he finally told me what had happened. Poor kid. He'd gone the whole afternoon feeling bad. That woman was so focused on delivering her 'healthy eating spiel'"—she made air quotes with her fingers as she spoke—"that she didn't bother to check the students' reactions."

Here we go, Riki thought. The parents were worse than bickering children. "I'm really sorry. Now that I'm hearing it from Jeremy's point of view, I can see how upsetting it would be. When we're back in the classroom, I'll talk about how moving our bodies is healthy, and then I can transition it back to eating and how there are lots of healthy ways to eat."

"I really wish you would've taken more notice the day of. That being said, I know how difficult it can be to reel in some of the parents, especially ones like Cassandra Trainor." She stepped closer and lowered her voice. "Is she here?"

Riki scanned the line of parents that flanked the field. "I don't see her. Huh. She typically shows up for everything."

"It's probably best. I'm not sure what I would say to her. That woman knows how to get under my skin."

Cassandra Trainor was a little bossy, perhaps, but not mean. Well, not lately, at least. There had been a situation earlier in the year involving some alleged bullying of Darcy, her daughter. Alleged, because as it turned out, Darcy had been the one who was causing trouble with some of the other girls. As she recalled, Mrs. Trainor's reaction had been exaggerated. Riki hadn't taken it personally. She'd been warned about the hyper parents who were *always* right, even when they were proven wrong. "To be fair, I'm sure she didn't intend to upset Jeremy."

With a smirk, Mrs. Tau said, "That's to be debated. You don't know her the way I do. You're aware she sits on the board of directors, right? Everyone has to tiptoe around her because she thinks she owns this place."

A boom blasted the air, followed by a screech that caused everyone to slap their hands to their ears. They looked to see the principal, dressed in a brown sports coat and yellow shirt, fumbling with the microphone. "Sorry, Ocean Avenue families! A little bit of a technical problem here, but I've got it all worked out." He laughed. "I think," he said with another hearty laugh.

Riki wondered if anyone else thought he resembled the *annoying-but-meant-to-be-funny* uncle from an eighties sitcom she used to watch on Nick at Nite. She liked Principal Rosenkrantz—he was very supportive of the teachers—she just wished he wouldn't try so hard in front of the parents. He came across as a total clown.

"Thank you for coming to the sixth annual Ocean Avenue Jog-a-Thon! Let's give a big round of applause to all our *suuu*perstar joggers!"

Parents and teachers clapped and cheered. Riki whispered to Mrs. Tau, "Thanks again for filling me in. I'll keep an eye on things."

"If it happens again," she muttered, "I'm going to have a word with that woman."

Riki nodded and edged closer to her friend Amelia. "Can it be Friday yet?" she whispered.

Amelia laughed. "Right? It can't come soon enough. I bought some Girl Scout Cookies from one of my kids this morning. We can indulge at lunch."

"Can't wait," Riki replied.

As Principal Rosenkrantz led the students in a cheer, she clapped along, but her mind traveled to last night. The cheer reached a rowdy finale, and she stretched luxuriously, remembering how good it felt to have Chris's hands trailing down her back, teasing her as he dragged his fingertips across her thighs. She touched a hand to her cheek. *I can't think about that now,* she thought. *Not in front of all these kids.* But the fact that she had thought about it with such pleasure was a good sign. They would be a great couple. It could totally work. She was certain of it. She clapped and gave a loud whoop. The jog-a-thon was over. Thank God.

CHAPTER FOUR

Sylvia turned onto the long driveway of the fourplex on Mockingbird Lane, slowing her car to wave to Embry and Riki, who stood just outside the white picket fence that enclosed the small square that Embry laughingly referred to as her yard. Apparently, front yards were bigger where she came from. Bigger and cheaper.

Well, there's a price to pay for all this beauty, Sylvia thought as she rolled into her assigned spot in the carport next to Embry's ancient yellow Subaru. The window was down. Entirely irresponsible to leave a car window open. It was as good as asking for someone to steal your car. But nothing bad ever happened to Embry. It was like she walked with a protective cloud surrounding her, sheltering her and those darling babies from any harm. Some people were born lucky.

Sylvia wasn't one of them.

But no matter. She made her own luck. After gathering her purse from the back seat, she walked toward her apartment, not in the mood to join the neighbors' idle chitchat. Hugh had texted that morning saying he'd call at five thirty, and she wanted a minute to get ready. The week had been a busy one for him, so aside from some scattered texting, they hadn't had a chance to talk. It actually worked in her favor. He would be itching to see her, and she would tease him just enough to put a halt to any thoughts of Lily.

Embry flapped an arm, motioning for Sylvia to join them. "Hey, come on over. You're going to want to hear this."

She swallowed a sigh and walked toward them, her heels wobbly on the rough asphalt driveway. *This had better be worth it.* She still needed to change into something casual but sexy. Perhaps her thin scoop-neck T-shirt with her black-lace plunge bra. The perfect answer for understated sexy. And of course, she would need to reapply her lipstick. That was a must. As she neared Riki and Embry, she said, "What's this urgent news? Has Brandon become an overnight sensation?"

Embry tightened her ponytail assertively and leaned forward. It was hard not to like the woman, even though she wore rose-colored glasses on the daily.

"No, I wish that were true. It's Jonathan." She motioned toward the apartment above hers. "He's here, and he's been acting suspiciously. To be honest, I think he's been there all night. I swear I heard footsteps. It's like he's hiding out."

Riki leaned forward, her earbuds dangling at her shoulders. "He gives me the creeps." She looked at Embry possessively, the way a middle-school girl who wanted to lay claim on someone as *her* friend would. What was that all about? Sylvia wasn't a threat to their friendship. She watched with interest as Riki continued. "I was about to go for a run when Embry called me over. We decided we should ask what he's doing in Nadine's place. If he's going to rent it out, we should be informed, right?"

Sylvia studied Riki's earnest expression. Such a Debbie Do-gooder. The two were quite a pair. "He doesn't have to tell us a thing about his plans for Nadine's place as far as I know. But since he's here, let's ask. And I'll remind him about the broken step. It's ridiculous he hasn't fixed it yet, but then again, he's not the one nearly tumbling down the stairs every morning."

Riki nodded in agreement. "It's totally dangerous. If he doesn't fix it, you should consider filing a lawsuit."

Huh. That would be fun. She could imagine Jonathan turning beet red and hurling obscenities at her while she watched him calmly, like a parent waiting out a child's tantrum. "Interesting idea." Tapping a finger to her lips, she said, "Or better yet, I could lure him up with the offer of a nice glass of wine. I'll conduct an experiment to see if the busted step can hold his weight. Although I'd hate for him to fall to his death on my staircase just so I can make a point. That would be tragic."

Riki and Embry exchanged horrified looks. "Sylvia!" they said in unison. Once again, she was reminded of middle-school girls.

"You can't do that!" Embry said, her hand fluttering at her neck.

She laughed. They were so cute. Had she ever been that sweet and naive? Well, no. Probably not. She'd developed thick skin at an early age thanks to her fabulous childhood. Not many kids were fortunate enough to have sat on a precipice, watching as their treasured collection of rare childhood joys went crashing down in a sudden landslide, all before the age of ten. "Lighten up, ladies. It was a joke. Really," she added after a beat, knowing the emphasis would only cause them to wonder.

Embry's eyes suddenly went wide. "He's coming now!" She nodded toward Nadine's door, where Jonathan was exiting, a paper shopping bag in hand. *Blergh.* Sylvia wished Johnny Cat had taken his cat-shit self to Europe for good. Embry flicked a look at Riki and squared her shoulders. Was she afraid of him? For God's sake, the man was a complete idiot.

Jonathan neared, and Sylvia waved him over. "Well, if it isn't the man of the hour. We were just talking about you. Do you have a minute to chat?"

He scrutinized his watch. "Only a minute."

Because you're such an important asshole, Sylvia thought.

Embry crossed her arms. "What were you doing in Nadine's place?"

"Cleaning," he said without conviction. The way his lips flapped reminded Sylvia of a weasel. How fitting.

She eyed the shopping bag. "Cleaning? Or stealing from your dead mother?"

"She left everything to me, so I can't steal from myself." He reached into the bag and pulled out a book. A yellow Post-it Note was stuck to the cover. "Here," he said, passing it to Sylvia. "Mom must've wanted you to have this. I just found it."

Touching the note with one finger, she traced the swirly handwriting. *For Sylvia, with love.* She lifted the note and read the title. It was *Letter to My Daughter* by Maya Angelou, the book Nadine had wanted them to read together. Her eyes stung with the foreign sensation of tears. Only Nadine could edge into Sylvia's heart with such ease. "Thank you." She tucked the book into her purse and steeled her emotions. "While I have you, I'd like to remind you about the broken stair. It's lucky number seven." Batting her lashes, she added, "Let's not turn it into unlucky seven."

"Yeah, okay. I'm on it." He strode off, the bag sagging in his hand.

Sylvia sighed and exchanged a look with Riki and Embry. "He was only here to see what valuables he could get his hands on. It's surprising he hasn't been by sooner."

Riki touched her shoulder. "I know. He's a jerk, and Nadine was nothing but wonderful."

"Yes. He was horrible to her," Sylvia said, her voice flat.

They nodded quietly in agreement and said their goodbyes. Sylvia crossed to her apartment, trying to make sense of Jonathan's visit. She hated men like him. At best, he was a self-important loser. As she climbed the stairs, careful to skip the seventh, she checked her watch. Only five minutes to prepare for her call with Hugh.

He'd better not mention Lily again. She wasn't in the mood.

~

Sylvia curled onto the sofa, snuggling into the cushions as she sipped her rosé. It was such a trendy wine, marketed to elicit a Sunday-brunchy, breezy vibe. *It's pink and sparkly. Fun, fun, fun!*

How easy it was to condition the mind. She actually felt pink and sparkly and carefree. Although knowing Hugh would call any minute also had her feeling giddy.

Part of the excitement was that he was different from the other men she had dated. Trustworthy. An odd trait for a man. For any human, really. It was strangely nice.

The phone trilled, and she grabbed for it. Adjusting her shirt so a hint of her bra peeked out, she touched the screen to accept the call. Hugh's face popped into view. "Hey, you."

"Hey." He moved his head from side to side, trying to see her better. "There you are! Man, aren't you a sight for sore eyes."

"It's been so long, I was starting to wonder if you'd been struck down by mad cow disease," she joked.

"Very funny. How's the vegetarianism working out for you? Eating lots of rabbit food?"

She let out an exaggerated sigh. "Sadly, no. I should switch to that. I've had so much pasta this week, I'm probably going to gain ten pounds. But on the upside, I haven't eaten any meat, so I won't be going mad anytime soon."

A laugh burst from his lips. "A relief, for sure. I wouldn't want to see that happen." He smiled. "I've missed you."

As you should. "I've missed you too. How's Arizona?"

"It's hot. I—" A piercing cry sounded, and he froze.

"What on earth is that?" His phone went dark, and she wondered if it had fallen. "Hugh?"

He reappeared, looking flustered. "Sorry about that! I'm walking my friend's baby, and he started to cry."

"What? Whose baby?" She squinted at the phone, trying to get a better look.

"I ran into a college buddy at the meeting today. I had no clue he's a rep for us out here. Anyway, he invited me for dinner," he said breathlessly. "He ran back to get his phone and asked me to keep walking or else the baby would start to cry." A sheepish smile emerged. "Guess that didn't work out so well. But I found a pacifier, and he seems fine now. Right, champ?" he said in a sweet voice, clearly meant for the baby. He moved his phone down to reveal a stroller, but she couldn't see a baby because the sunshade was down. Seconds later, he was back, holding the phone close to his face.

"Why didn't you go back with your friend?"

"He ran. Literally. He said his wife would panic if she couldn't reach him."

"Oh. So you're just out walking? How will you know where to go?"

"It's very flat out here. I'm just walking in a straight line. He'll call me if he doesn't see me. No big." He wiped a hand across his brow. "Now, what's that thing you're wearing? What do you have going on beneath your shirt?"

"Just my after-work clothes. You know how I like to be comfortable." She tilted the camera to zoom in on her lacy bra, tugging at her shirt to give him a better view of her cleavage.

"You look great. I wish I could hop on a plane and see you."

She was about to tell him to do just that, but she suddenly had a view of the side of his face.

"Hey, man," he said to someone. His friend, presumably. "Yep. Okay." He turned back to her. "Sorry. I've gotta run. Joel just caught up, and we're going to dash to the store to pick up some basil for his wife. I'll call you later."

"Oh. Okay. Have fun." She pursed her lips and blew a kiss. "Talk to you later. Love you."

"Bye."

She shut off her phone and sank back onto the sofa cushions, her mind whirring. Had he been acting strangely, or was he simply stressed about caring for the baby? She'd seen the stroller. Heard him talking to another person, though she hadn't seen him. But Hugh wasn't a devious person. He wasn't up to anything.

More likely, he was concerned about keeping the baby happy and content. A very good sign, indeed. The time to bring up the subject of babies was rapidly approaching.

She'd been watching for clues and mentally logging them. In fact, when she commented on an article she'd read about the safety of Range Rovers a few weeks ago, he'd said, "Let's get matching ones. It'll be you and me and a house with a white picket fence."

So yes, family was on his mind.

~

Five hours had passed, and Hugh hadn't called back. After her glass of rosé, Sylvia had decided a relaxing bath was in order. She needed to chill. It wasn't odd that he hadn't called back immediately. He was catching up with an old friend. But a feeling of unrest nagged at her. It was that sense of losing control she'd first experienced on Sunday over the buttermilk biscuits. Her synapses began firing at once. She needed to speak to him tonight if she wanted to solidify their relationship.

"A virtual whirlwind romance," she had told her friend Belinda at work. They'd been in the office kitchen the morning after her third date with Hugh. It was there, huddled by the watercooler, that Sylvia had filled her in.

Over a candlelit dinner at his apartment, Hugh had looked at her with a moony gaze and said, *Dammit, Sylvia. What kind of spell have you put on me? I'm in love with you.*

She'd almost laughed. Of course he would fall under her spell. It was inevitable, really. Becoming what someone wanted was simple if you were observant enough. "I love you too. You're everything I want in a man."

How easy it had been.

And now, here she was, sitting on the sofa in her scoop-neck T-shirt, alone. No doubt she enjoyed the solo time, but eventually, this would have to change. It wouldn't be too difficult—a comment here about crowded airports, a word there about scratchy hotel sheets, and voilà—he would come to the conclusion on his own that the traveling was becoming tedious.

She hadn't wanted to call when he was still with his friend. That would've been obnoxious. So she'd waited. Now, with one finger, she clicked his name to make the call.

It went straight to voice mail. *Blergh.*

She should've texted in the first place.

Hey, you. Call me before you go to sleep. xo

It was hard not to stare at the screen, waiting for those three dots to appear. She flipped her phone facedown. A watched pot never boils and all that.

Minutes ticked by. She crossed the small room to the bathroom. If she got busy brushing her teeth, he'd respond. As she took her toothbrush from the medicine cabinet, her phone rang. She smiled at herself in the bathroom mirror. "Wish me luck," she said with a wink.

She padded back to the sofa and reached for her phone. "Hey, love. I was hoping to hear your voice before I slip into bed."

"Hey," he said in a hushed tone. "Sorry I didn't answer before. I was driving back to the hotel."

"You stayed at your friend's house for a long time. And why are you talking so softly?"

"Paper-thin walls in this hotel."

"I suppose it's good I'm not there with you. We'd wake everyone on your floor."

He breathed out a laugh. "Yeah. No kidding."

Sylvia pulled a throw blanket around her. "So how old is your friend's baby?"

"Uh, a few months?"

"Did you get to hold him?"

"Yeah. Cute kid."

She smiled into the phone. "I think you like babies."

"I hear they're great until they're teenagers."

"We should have one."

"What?" he asked in a loud whisper.

"A baby. You and I should have a baby. Start a little family of our own."

"Wow. Uh, I, um . . ."

She waited an uncomfortable second and laughed. "Oh, Hugh. Don't go all serious on me," she said playfully, even though his response had been less than desirable. Getting what she wanted would take strategy, patience, and perhaps, above all, a willingness to appear light-hearted and sunny. "I'm just throwing it out there. By the way," she started in a more somber tone, "I'm also thinking about getting a pet. Do you like cats?"

"Cats? I guess so. And about this baby thing, are you serious?"

She smiled at the frustration in his voice. He would think about babies all night long. Perfect.

"Just thinking aloud. We can talk more tomorrow. Sleep well."

"I'll try. We have a big presentation in the morning, but I want to see you when I get home. My flight will be in at four. How about you come by at five thirty?"

"I'll be there."

"Good night."

She let the phone fall to her lap as she reviewed their conversation. It had gone moderately well, all things considered. But the whispering had been annoying.

Well, there was a world of potential reasons for his actions. It wouldn't serve her to make something up. Better to store the tidbit and pull it out later if necessary. If there was one thing she'd learned, it was to always remain one step ahead.

CHAPTER FIVE

Friday, March 10

Embry unbuckled Kylie from the car seat and helped her out of the car before grabbing Carson's infant seat and the brand-new twenty-dollar sink plunger. The man at the hardware store insisted it would do the trick. "If it doesn't fix her up, bring it on back, and I'll give you a refund." She certainly hoped the stupid overpriced thing would work. Regardless, she would send Jonathan the bill. It was too bad the sink hadn't conked out earlier when she could've told him in person.

As it was, she'd woken to find the kitchen sink full of dirty water. Even after resetting the garbage disposal, it wouldn't drain. She'd fled to the hardware store with both kids in tow while Brandon slept, desperate for a solution. It was unsettling when anything was awry in her little haven. She hadn't even bothered to do her makeup. It wasn't like she'd see anyone she knew at the hardware store.

She hadn't considered she'd run into someone at the complex, but there Sylvia was, her heels clicking on the stairs. Of course she was dressed like an imposing businesswoman, which made Embry all too aware of how sloppy she looked. She waved half-heartedly.

"Good morning," Sylvia called. "You're out and about bright and early."

Kylie scampered across the driveway. "We bought a jabber!"

Sylvia glanced at her with a raised brow. "How nice for you! What is a jabber?"

"She means a plunger. My sink is clogged, and I went out and bought a sink plunger. I didn't know they existed, but the guy at the hardware store said to give it a try."

"Ambitious. It's only eight o'clock, and you've already been there and back?"

Embry held in a laugh. If she only knew how long days with kids really were. "Yes, we wake up early at my house." She flattened a hand against the loose strands of her ponytail. "Anyway, have a good day." She watched as Sylvia headed for her car. It was a little red convertible. What would it be like to be so free, to have no one but yourself to worry about? Sylvia was older than she was by a decade, but Embry felt like she was the older one, weighted down with a responsibility so big, she might topple beneath it. She snapped her gaze back to Kylie. Goodness! *Weighted down* sounded all wrong. Her children were a blessing. This growing baby was a blessing! Some people tried for years and could never have children. Shaking her head, she gripped Carson's infant seat and walked into her apartment, reminding Kylie to keep quiet so they wouldn't wake Daddy. He'd gotten home after three, which she hadn't been expecting. Poor thing! It wasn't uncommon for the bar to be booked for a special event, making it so he'd get home in the wee hours. He'd probably just forgotten to mention it to her. Heaven knows their lives were busy.

~

Sylvia sank into the seat of her car and blew out a breath. Sleep last night had been elusive. Her mind had been on babies—sweet little babies. She'd made a mental list of all the things she would need, and then she'd raked through lists of names when she knew she should've been counting sheep. It had all been so beautiful and exciting. Not stressful.

But seeing Embry looking positively haggard just now caused her enthusiasm to come to a startling halt. The woman was gorgeous, and she had a husband who adored her. A perfect life. What reason did she have to look so stressed? A clogged drain? Ha!

Well, it was entirely possible she had looked frazzled because she was a *young* mother, and her coping and management skills were still forming. There was no need to judge. True, Sylvia had finely tuned her coping skills years ago. Scraping through childhood had been a gift. It had taught her to be a survivor.

Perhaps Embry hadn't known the tiniest bit of stress until now.

But was there another reason her enthusiasm had wilted?

Yes.

Her mind was adept at blocking and tackling unwanted thoughts, but they would eventually seep in, working like a vaccine, giving her only a small amount of the bad so she was fully equipped to attack it head-on.

As she backed out of her parking spot, she felt the prickling beneath the surface of her skin. Realization settled in. It pained her momentarily, but she was quick to turn on her intellectual switch. No need to have any sort of emotion about the thought that was now flushed out and fully formed: Hugh had lied to her last night.

About what? She wasn't entirely certain. But she would get to the bottom of it. And she would either continue to reel him in or cut him loose. The father of her child would not be a pathetic liar. She refused to re-create the past for her future baby. Continuing onto the street, she reminded herself that Hugh was a simple man. A big, elaborate lie was beyond his skill set. But she was watching him.

At five o'clock sharp, Riki locked her classroom door. She lugged her tote to her car, knowing that it would most likely sit near her front door until Sunday. All she wanted to do tonight was curl up on the sofa with a bowl of cereal and fall asleep in front of the TV. But Chris had texted her during one of his many breaks, asking to see her tonight. She hadn't responded yet, which was fine, because he knew she couldn't use her phone while teaching. It was true she could've sent a quick text while her students had been at the library, but he wouldn't know that. She wanted to see him, but she needed some time alone before mustering the energy to be social.

As she drove down Ocean Avenue, a smattering of drops landed on her windshield. Was that *rain*? She flicked on her wipers and let them swipe before turning them off. But suddenly water was slamming the windshield. She gripped the wheel tightly with one hand and turned the wipers to high with the other. After hearing all winter that they were supposed to be deluged by the "storm of the century," they were getting a sudden downpour when it was almost spring.

She turned down the music and focused on the road ahead, anxious to get home, but she kept her foot light on the accelerator. The rain turned California drivers into maniacs. She could say this because she grew up here—she was one of them, but at least she was aware of it. The white Audi in front of her switched lanes, and she was now following a blue pickup truck. She licked her lips as she leaned forward over the steering wheel, anxious to see if the letters and numbers on the plate matched the ones stored in her memory. She hadn't tried to memorize the sequence; it had just sort of happened. It was hard to see through the rain-spattered windshield, but she could make out the last three numbers—428. Brandon's truck. She squeezed the steering wheel as she pulled into her driveway right behind him. Had he realized she was behind him?

They eased into their respective spots in the carport. His door opened, and a shiny black shoe appeared. She tried to ignore the increasing thump of her heartbeat. *It's only because I don't like driving in the rain.* Even though she willed herself not to look, she couldn't help but notice he was dressed in a black suit, and his dark hair was slicked back, revealing his impressive jawline. She waited, wondering if he would rush to his apartment without saying hi. But then his hand was waving wildly. It would be rude not to respond, not to mention weird.

She scrambled from her car and scurried to his truck, thankful for the cover of the carport. "Hi, Brandon," she called over the pelting rain.

"Hey there, Riki. Wild weather, huh?"

"Yes! It was so sudden. You look nice, by the way." Her smile felt like it had a life of its own, and there was nothing she could do to keep it from taking over her entire face.

"Thanks. I'm coming from an audition." He tugged on the lapel of his coat and stepped closer. "Not my usual look, is it?"

She placed her hand over her mouth as though assessing him and squeezed the wild smile from her lips. "You look great. What'd you audition for?"

He shoved a hand in his hair, and the thick silver band on his ring finger was a stark contrast to the dark brown. She let her gaze stay on it for an extra moment, seizing the reminder for her foolish heart that he was taken. "*Days of Our Lives.* It was a callback for a new character they're adding who's a mysterious millionaire. No one knows where he came from or how he made all his money." Flashing a grin, he added, "I don't even know if he turns out to be a good guy or a bad guy. They wanted me to play it like I was a tortured soul with an edge this time around." He managed a hurt look before letting his eyes fall into a sneering squint. "How was that?"

"Bravo! You're hired in my book." She clapped her hands, her ability to think rationally zapped by his pure magnetism. "You looked like a cross between James Bond and Superman."

His eyes lingered on hers as a smile tugged the corners of his lips. "Superman? Nah, I'm not as good-lookin' as that guy."

Is he flirting? Her mouth was so dry, she couldn't muster a response. Thankfully, he didn't seem to notice.

He nodded to the uncovered area beyond the carport. "Do you have an umbrella, or are you making a run for it?"

"I'm going to make a run for it. I have no idea where my umbrella is," she said seriously, coaxing her mind to stop lingering on the idea that he might be flirting.

"Same. Are you ready?" He lifted a brow and reached for her hand.

She inhaled sharply as their hands locked.

His eyes gleamed. "On the count of three. One, two, three!"

They tore down the gravel driveway, her heart tripping in her chest. All sense of reason washed away in the rain. She wished they could keep running, past the apartments and into the street, all the way to the ocean, where they could catch a boat headed for a Greek island and live happily ever after. It would be just the two of them.

But instead, he brought them to a stop between their apartments and dropped her hand. Rain dripped from his lashes as he looked at her. "You're soaked."

"So are you." She licked her lips, tasting rain on her tongue.

He laughed and grabbed her hand again, knitting their fingers together before lifting her arm. "Do, do, do, do, do-da-do . . . ," he sang.

She stood unmoving, mesmerized.

"Twirl, girl! Haven't you seen *Singin' in the Rain?*"

Unable to keep from giggling wildly, she spun as he held her fingers in his. "You're crazy!"

"You're the one dancing out here in the rain!" He twirled her again and again before he spun her to face him, his eyes bright with mischief. "I have to say, Riki, this was fun." He looked down at his wet clothes. "Hopefully not at the cost of my suit and your pretty pink shirt," he added with a sheepish grin. "I guess we'd better go on in and get dry."

"Yeah. Say hi to Embry," she said softly.

He jogged toward his apartment as she staggered to hers, feeling positively drunk. *Oh my God, oh my God, oh my God.* Guys like him should be banned from the planet. He must know his charm. It had to be obvious that women were rendered speechless around him.

She was supposed to be working on shutting off her feelings for him, and he was *not* helping. She forced herself to think of Embry. At this very moment, she was probably peeling the wet coat from Brandon's body and warming him with a tight hug. She'd press her breasts into his chest, and that would be all it'd take. He'd lead her to the shower, where she'd soap him up, tracing a line of bubbles down his naked chest.

On second thought, they couldn't do that. They had two kids to watch. Their sexy shower would have to wait until the kids were tucked safely in bed. By then they'd both be too tired to do anything but pull up the covers and pass out. As he drifted to sleep, would his subconscious mind toy with him, luring him to dream about the red-haired neighbor whose hand he'd taken in the rain?

She stood just inside the door and eyed the plate of cookies on the kitchen counter. If Embry could read her mind, she would hate her. And the truth was, Riki wouldn't blame her.

~

Sylvia capped her lipstick and smiled at her reflection in the large rectangular mirror. In less than an hour, she would be frolicking with Hugh. The light in the office bathroom was cruel, but it couldn't hide the fact that her teeth were simply perfect. She'd opted for braces six years ago. No one knew she'd once had the snaggletooth smile of a poor kid, and never again would she wear ratty hand-me-downs from that horrid neighbor girl with the slash of a smile that was entirely too large for her face, making her look like she was a descendant of Ernie from *Sesame Street*. New teeth and new clothes were an easy camouflage for her tattered past. She was the ruler of her queendom now.

Her lips were a vibrant coral. Mac Lady Danger, to be specific. It hadn't always been her go-to, but after Hugh called her lips enchanting, she realized she'd found her new signature shade. Her eyes looked strikingly pale in contrast to her dark hair and bright lips. They really were her best feature. Would her future baby have her ice-blue eyes, or would they be smoky blue like Hugh's? "Let's not get too far ahead of ourselves," she said aloud, still grinning.

The door swung open, and Sarah, her coworker, appeared. She darted her eyes from one sink to the next. "I could've sworn I heard someone talking in here."

"Nope. It's just me."

Sarah frowned and dipped her head to peer beneath the stalls. It shouldn't have bothered Sylvia, but it did. The woman always had to have her nose in everything. Including the toilets, apparently.

"Hmm." She eyed Sylvia's clothing. "You changed out of your work clothes. Fun plans tonight?"

Sylvia ran her fingers through her hair and turned to Sarah, who was clad in a musty-blue potato sack and brown clogs. *Quintessential Dowdy Sarah*, Sylvia thought. The woman dressed like she'd stolen clothing from a dead grandmother. "As a matter of fact, yes. I'll be spending the weekend at my boyfriend's place. How about you? Any big plans?"

She lifted her hands, palms facing upward, as if to say, *Who knows?*

Sylvia held back a smirk. Even Sarah's body language was frumpy. If she put in a little effort, she wouldn't look so drab.

"I might go over the Reebok proposal. It needs some fine-tuning," Sarah said.

Oh, for God's sake. Sylvia and Belinda had worked on the proposal for a good part of the week, and now Sarah was going to pretend she had something important to contribute? How very, very typical. By some degree of magic, Sarah had moved up in rank one month ago. It was truly a mystery how she had snatched the promotion. Everyone knew Sylvia had been the best candidate, and the way Sarah needled her with reminders that she was *in charge now!* was enough to make Sylvia want to poison the woman's coffee. But she plastered on a sweet smile and faced her. "No need. Belinda and I have thoroughly combed through it."

Sarah's mouth dropped into a pout. "Well, I'm going to have a look. If I determine it needs something, I'll go ahead and make the change."

"You do that," she said pedantically. "Be sure to tell Miriam it's your work product. You wouldn't want us to get credit for your dedication." *Or your shit work.* She widened her smile. *Kill her with kindness.* That's what she needed to do. Because otherwise, she would end up shoving her against the paper-towel dispenser and strangling her. On the upside, her job would be up for grabs. Something to ponder.

"Why are you looking at me that way? Do I have something in my teeth?"

"Not that I can see. My mind wandered for a minute. Anyway, have a lovely weekend." She breezed from the bathroom, leaving behind an utterly bewildered Sarah.

Thirty minutes later, Sylvia strode down the hallway toward Hugh's apartment. It was such a dark building—more like a dingy hotel than a home. But the inside of his apartment was white and bright and pristine. She had asked why he lived in an apartment when he could buy his own home. "I'm a minimalist," he'd answered with a shrug. "Besides, a home is for a family and should be chosen by a husband and wife together, don't you agree?"

The man made a solid point. She knocked and waited. How would he feel about a crib and a diaper-changing station? She closed her eyes and tried to picture it, but her mind strayed, only allowing the image of a toddler slapping a drippy red paintbrush across a favorite piece of art to play in sharp focus. Hugh wouldn't like that.

Well, like he said, a home should be chosen together. They would find one that suited both their needs and the needs of their future family. They could find the perfect house with the white picket fence he'd mentioned.

She rapped on the door once again, this time with more force, but was met with silence. No footsteps sounded, alerting her that he'd appear in a second. Well, this was annoying.

She flipped to his last text even though she knew she hadn't made a mistake. Five thirty was exactly what he'd written when he'd confirmed their plans that morning. It was 5:37 at the moment. Typing quickly, she wrote:

I'm here. Are you running late?

She skimmed her emails as she waited. A man dressed in running shorts and a T-shirt headed toward her. As he neared, she could see his hair was wet. So was his shirt. Good God. Who needed to exercise that hard?

"Got caught in the rain," he said with an awkward grin as he tugged an earbud from his ear. "I guess I should've checked the weather."

"I was literally outside just five minutes ago. It wasn't raining," Sylvia said, her brow raised.

"Yeah, I know. The clouds opened up. Freak storm. It felt like Hawaii out there." He wore a satisfied expression, as though knowing what Hawaiian storms were like made him special and unique. "Are you new here? In the building, I mean," he said, plowing a hand through his slick hair.

"Nope. Just visiting a friend." She motioned to the door. "But he's running late."

"I didn't know Sammy was back."

"Sammy? This is Hugh's place."

"Uh, no." He pointed to the apartment next door. "I live there. I'm pretty sure I know who my neighbor is."

"But I've been in this very apartment. It's Hugh's." She stood back from the door, reading the number. "Unless I got off on the wrong floor," she said, pressing a palm to her forehead. "Idiot move on my part."

He laughed as water dripped from his hair onto the flat carpet. "Don't worry. It's happened to me. What floor is your friend on?"

"Third. This is the second, isn't it? I'm impatient that way."

A perplexed look settled on his face. "Now I'm confused. This is the third floor." He pinched his wet shirt away from his skin. "Unless your friend is the guy who's been keeping an eye on his place. I just didn't know he was using it to entertain."

The way he said *entertain* was clearly meant to make Sylvia feel cheap. How rude. Hugh hadn't said a word about this not being his apartment. It *had* to be his place. His clothes were hanging in the closet, for God's sake. "Help me to understand. This apartment—number 305," she said, slapping the door, "belongs to someone named Sammy who is currently out of town?"

The guy looked to his own place as he flicked a hand down his shirt, causing water droplets to scatter. "Yeah. That sums it up. Call your friend." He gave her a helpless look. "Sorry, but I need to change out of these wet clothes. Good luck."

"Thanks," she muttered. What the hell was this? Was Hugh some kind of pathological homeless house sitter? She pressed his number on her phone.

No answer.

Probably best. She needed a moment to gather her thoughts. It could very well be that the wet neighbor was a lunatic.

She began typing.

Hey, babe. I waited for fifteen minutes, but I'm guessing you were delayed by the rain. Text me when you're here and we can meet up. xo

Before she left, she snapped a photo of the apartment door. There was no decipherable reason for it, but her instincts were leading her, and she wasn't one to ignore her gut.

As she rode down to the lobby, her eyes landed on the elevator buttons. The "P" glared at her. Why didn't Hugh ever park in the structure? She'd asked once, and he'd told her he made a habit of avoiding underground parking structures because of earthquakes. *An adorable quirk,* she had thought when he'd explained it to her. But was it a lie?

Strike two against Hugh. The lie last night and now this. Sylvia's pulse quickened.

There could be a perfectly logical explanation for all of this, she reassured herself. So what if Hugh was house-sitting? It wasn't like that was a crime.

But what if she hadn't looked at him carefully enough, given him enough credit? What if the guileless demeanor was an act?

She ducked her head as she darted into the rain. Her car was half a block away, and by the time she reached it, she was wet, though not as drippy as the man. Would it be worthwhile to sit in her car and watch for Hugh's arrival?

Hell no. Her time was more valuable than that. She would hit the grocery store and pick up something for dinner. Keep busy. Waiting and watching for him would only dredge up bad memories. An image of herself as a child, her face pressed to the window, flickered and waved in her mind. *Remember me? Do you see me here? I'm waiting, waiting, waiting.* The word echoed in her mind, but she quickly extinguished the memory. That was the past. Never again would she wait as fear scratched her to shreds. She'd rather tear out her own heart and scatter the broken bits.

CHAPTER SIX

Water dripped from Riki's hair as she tromped to her room to change out of her wet clothes. She wondered how it would feel to be the kind of person who didn't care that Brandon was married. Because if she was being honest, she wished she could be the one who was peeling his coat from him and soaping him up in the shower, the way she had imagined Embry doing. She closed her eyes and pictured the way his mouth had curved into a smile when he'd said, *Twirl, girl!* Jeez, he was hot. And it was obvious he liked her. *Not in a cheat-on-his-wife way,* her brain rushed to add. Her eyes snapped open. She couldn't be part of that. *Ever.* And he didn't seem like a cheater. But it felt really good to know that he thought she was cool enough to dance with in the rain. That maybe in another world where Embry didn't exist, he would ask Riki out.

Ugh! That was a horrible thought. She tugged off her shoes and tossed them to the floor. Embry was an amazing friend. The best. When Riki had moved in nine months ago, Embry had been like a ray of sunshine, stopping by with honey pops—homemade candies in the shape of beehives fitted on lollipop sticks—and a bottle of wine. She was sweet and funny and honest. And not someone she would betray.

She left her clothes in a pile on the floor and headed for the shower. Once she was scrubbed to a shine, she dried off with a fresh towel and put on her comfy flannel pajama bottoms and an oversize sweatshirt. The flannel was smooth against her legs—so much softer than the stiff jeans she'd worn all day with her *pretty pink shirt.* He'd really said that.

This wasn't easy. Maybe she could ask Chris to come over. He'd mentioned going out, but hitting a bar on a rainy night wasn't on her top-ten list of fun things to do. She turned on the TV for company as she headed to the kitchen. Before getting some cereal, she opened her laptop and sat at the table. Fourteen new emails popped up in rapid succession. The first was from Darcy's mother.

Dear Miss McFarlan and Room Fourteen Families,

I'm writing today in response to the letter that was sent home in the children's Friday folders about the leprechaun trap assignment, and I have some concerns. I'd appreciate it if you'd all weigh in.

I am not comfortable perpetuating this leprechaun lie. I don't mean to come across as harsh, but do you realize the damage that can be done? If we as parents lie to our children about something that's allegedly special and magical when they are at such a young and impressionable age, how are they expected to trust us in later years? Our children will find out about the lies one day, whether from another child, a movie, or maybe even a parent who has grown tired of keeping up with the charade. And where does that leave the child? Scared and confused. I strongly urge all of you to respond with your thoughts so we can make an informed decision about this "homework" assignment for our children. Miss McFarlan, I do hope you'll be open to our feedback.

Sincerely,
Cassandra Trainor

Riki glared at the screen. What the hell? First the Cheerios shaming and now this? She shook her head, wondering why anyone would make a big deal about a little green man.

This was supposed to be a fun project. The kids would bring in their traps on the sixteenth, and the "leprechaun" would leave plastic gold coins and some green glitter on St. Patrick's Day. He might even turn a few chairs upside down and scatter books across the classroom library. It had always been such a great event at Clover Street Elementary. She scrolled down, surprised to see that all fourteen emails had the same subject line.

Here we go again. How many times would she have to deal with utter nonsense? Thank goodness the end of the school year was nearing. As thrilled as she had been to get the job at Ocean Avenue Academy, *one of the finest private schools in Los Angeles*, according to their website, she had to admit she missed the public school system. So many parents had been grateful for all she did. But at Ocean Avenue, she couldn't read a story aloud without someone complaining that the book was too this, too that, or not enough. It was stifling. With a firm tap to her keyboard, she opened the next email.

Hi Room Fourteen Fams,

This is Jennifer Clarke, Payton's mom, weighing in. I love the idea of the leprechaun traps! It'll be fun for the kids! They enjoy believing! Sure, they'll learn the truth one day, but I plan on telling Payton when the time is right. I'll make sure she understands it's a fun legend, not some wicked lie I've concocted to confuse her. Let's be realistic about this. There's Santa, the Easter Bunny, the Tooth Fairy, and a few I'm probably forgetting!

For those of you who are interested, I've included some links to Pinterest for some fabulous trap ideas. My vote is to keep the assignment!

All best,
Jenn

Well, thank you, Jenn! Hopefully her enthusiasm and overuse of exclamation points would be contagious. Cassandra Trainor was inching her way to the top of the list of difficult parents. Riki pulled a sheet of paper from the printer and drew a line down the middle with another line crossing perpendicular at the top, forming a large *T*. On the left, she wrote *Sane Parents*. On the right, she wrote *Crazy Parents*. It was mean, but no one would see her list. And seriously, why did Mrs. Trainor have to get so bent? If a parent didn't want her kid to join in, she could have her skip the assignment. It was second grade, not Harvard.

After logging the first two names in the appropriate columns, she opened the next email.

Dear Miss McFarlan et al.,

Elliott Johanson, Dane's father, here. It strikes me that Ms. Clarke took a very cavalier attitude toward this serious discussion. Parenting done right takes thought and reflection. It requires time to consider what long-term effects our decisions can have. I, for one, believe Mrs. Trainor makes some valid arguments in favor of dismissing the assignment. Let's take a moment to weigh the pros and cons. I look forward to hearing additional viewpoints.

Best regards,
Elliott Johanson,
Senior Managing Partner
Johanson and Wolfe, LLP

Riki scrolled to the next email without adding Mr. Johanson to either side. At the moment, he seemed like a neutral party even though he came across as condescending.

By the time she'd finished the next twelve emails—another had come in while she was reading—there were five against, seven for, and three neutrals. Riki laid her head on the table and listened to the falling rain. Could she tell all the parents to shut up and get a life? She chuckled to herself. Probably not. Mr. Johanson would likely set up a conference so he could lecture her. *Teaching done right takes thought and reflection,* he'd start. Ugh. Maybe she'd call her own parents and get some advice.

The storm grew in strength, recruiting the wind to rough up some trees. She pushed her chair back and stalked to the kitchen. She couldn't think on an empty stomach. Lunch at school started at 11:48, and by now she couldn't even remember what her lunch had consisted of.

As she poured a mix of granola and Cookie Crisp into a bowl, it hit her. She'd run out during her lunch break to get an egg sandwich and an iced tea from Starbucks. There hadn't been time that morning to make her lunch. She added a little extra Cookie Crisp to her bowl and poured milk over it. Cow's milk. "Here's to you, Mrs. Trainor," she uttered before taking the first bite of milk-soaked cereal.

After the jog-a-thon yesterday, she'd talked to the class about food choices and had specifically called on Jeremy to share one of his favorite healthy foods. She'd held her breath as he answered, hopeful it would go well.

"Brussels sprouts," he'd replied.

"Wow, those are a great source of vitamins and nutrients. Good choice."

"I've never tried them, but my mom said if anyone asks me what I eat again, I should say brussels sprouts." His eyes shifted to Darcy before they darted back to Riki.

"Here's the thing, guys," Riki said, sinking into her read-aloud chair. "There are all kinds of healthy food choices. You know that fruits and veggies are always good, right?"

There was a murmuring of agreement.

"And beyond that, try to pick foods with ingredients you can read, or at least, foods without a really long list of ingredients. Easy peasy?"

"Easy peasy," they repeated.

"Look, I try to eat healthful foods. I like carrots and grilled chicken and salads. I eat eggs and yogurt and granola. But sometimes I want a Pop-Tart. And guess what? I'll have one, and I'll enjoy every chocolaty bite. And more important, don't let what someone else says make you feel bad." She looked at Jeremy, but he was busy twirling a pencil in his hand. "Okay, then. Questions?"

Brianne raised her hand. "What's your favorite kind of Pop-Tart?"

"The chocolate ones. And that's all we're going to say about Pop-Tarts." She'd smiled and stood. "Now, take out your math workbook and turn to page seventy-five."

If she hadn't made a quick transition, the kids would've turned it into a discussion of their favorite Pop-Tart flavors.

The sound of shattering glass rang through the steady fall of rain, followed by a sharp cry. She ran to the door and yanked it open. Sylvia was on her knees, holding her wrist, as curses tumbled from her mouth. A paper grocery bag lay next to her like a gutted fish with its entrails sprawled in a bloody pool. Riki held back the urge to scream. *It isn't blood,* she reassured herself, taking in a fractured jar of pasta sauce, its sharp pieces gleaming in the misty dusk.

Ignoring the rain and remembering too late that she wasn't wearing shoes, she rushed toward Sylvia. "Are you okay? What hurts?" she called, pushing her hair from her face.

Sylvia groaned and looked upward, the rain mixing with her tears. "My wrist." She held it to her body like she was cradling a baby. "I think I broke it."

"Oh no! Can you stand up? We need to get you inside."

"Yes. It's my wrist, not my foot," she said in a biting tone.

Sylvia wasn't mad at her—she knew that—but nonetheless, her tone stung. "Right." She led her into her apartment and pulled out a chair. "Sit. I'll get you some Tylenol. You shouldn't take Advil if you have a broken bone," she said, selecting a water glass from the cupboard.

"I thought you were a teacher, not a doctor."

"I've broken my ankle, my wrist, and my elbow. Clumsy kid. Or weak bones. Anyway," she said, returning from the kitchen with water and two pills, "take these. I'll pick up the groceries and clean up the glass. The urgent care should still be open. It might be a better option than the ER—less wait time. It's probably packed tonight with the rain." Without listening for a response, Riki pulled off her socks and stepped into her Ugg boots before grabbing a broom and dustpan from the tiny hall closet. Her clothes were already wet, so she didn't bother taking her umbrella, which she was surprised to see was propped in the corner of the closet.

As she swept up the mess, Embry appeared, huddled beneath a kid-size umbrella. She was wearing old Levi's and a Duke University sweatshirt. The sweatshirt must've been a gift from her older brother. Riki had heard all about him—the Duke University graduate and doctor. "Is everything okay over there? I heard some shouting a minute ago."

"Sylvia slipped. She thinks she broke her wrist. I'm going to run her to the urgent care once I get this cleaned up."

"Oh no! Do you need some help?" She turned back to grab a look at her apartment. "I can sweep that real quick. Carson's in the playpen, and Kylie's watching a show we just started."

"Thanks, but it's okay. Go back in with the kids. We'll be fine."

"If you're sure. Send me a text if you need anything at all. We're here."

Riki swept up the mess, careful to avoid stepping on the broken glass. If Brandon had been home, would he have rushed over to help? He was probably already out bartending by now. Riki had often wondered where he worked, but she'd refrained from asking. It was better to not know. The way her slippery mind worked, she'd end up an alcoholic, ordering drink after drink just so she had an excuse to sit at his bar. With a final sweep, she collected the last shards into the dustpan and walked them carefully over to the trash area.

She returned to find Sylvia with her cheek pressed to the table. The rest of her face was drained of color, just like the diluted marinara sauce. Riki's gut reaction was to leave her undisturbed, but her sense of duty kicked in, as it always did. "Are you ready to go?"

"I'll drive myself. You don't have to babysit me. I'm fine."

"Not a chance. I'll get my keys." She rushed to her room and tore off her wet clothing for a second time today before swiping a towel across her damp skin and wriggling back into a pair of jeans and slipping on a hoodie.

As she was about to leave, she grabbed two books from her shelf—*The Devil Wears Prada* and *The Da Vinci Code*. Either would suffice to keep Sylvia's mind off the pain. They were old, but she'd saved her paperback copies because they were two of her favorites. She'd read whichever one Sylvia didn't want.

"Okay, are you ready?" she asked, collecting her umbrella from the closet.

Sylvia sighed. "I suppose. Let's go."

~

The drive to the urgent care took only ten minutes, but it felt like the last stretch of a long road trip. Rain poured down and sloshed against the tires. Sylvia was silent the entire way, staring at the blurry windshield as if her force of will could get them there faster. Maybe it was the pain, but Riki got the feeling she was uncomfortable for an entirely different reason, which in turn made her anxious. Her attempts at small talk crashed and burned.

It had to be the pain. Sylvia was always pleasant. That was such a weird word. *Pleasant.* Nice but untouchable. That's exactly how she thought of Sylvia. It was like living below a famous person—not a movie star but a news anchor—someone who had an air of intelligence and commanded respect. Maybe it was because she was older and always looked so polished and professional. She had been very welcoming when Riki moved to the complex. Not like Embry, but perfectly nice. And after all this time, she didn't know her nearly as well as she knew Embry. Riki tried to recall what Sylvia did for a living. Was it marketing? Something like that. Regardless, she worked at a place that made boxes for shoe manufacturers and pizza conglomerates. But that was the extent of what she knew. She didn't even know if she had any family nearby, and Riki had told Sylvia all about her own mom, dad, and sister on their first meeting. Had she been so eager to talk about herself that she'd failed to ask Sylvia any questions? Her face grew hot. She really needed to figure out how to be a normal human being, not a clunky, awkward rendition of one.

Sylvia finished checking in at the front desk and took a seat next to Riki. "Thanks for the ride. I'll Uber home."

"I'm happy to stay with you." She reached into her purse and took out the paperbacks. "Look. I even brought books for us."

A sadness crossed Sylvia's face, making it look as if she might cry, but it disappeared so quickly, Riki wondered if she'd imagined it. Probably so. She was always so contained and pleasant. There was that word again.

"I'm fine. I'd rather wait alone, if you don't mind."

"Oh. Um, okay. Do you at least want a book?"

"I have my phone. I'm fine. Really."

"Okay." She fumbled to put the books back into her purse. "If you need anything at all, you know how to reach me. The rain may make it hard to get an Uber, so please call if you need a ride after all, okay?"

Sylvia only nodded and remained in the waiting-room chair, her arm tucked into her body and her eyes glued to her phone.

Riki checked her own phone to make sure her ringer was on and saw three new texts from Chris. *Shoot.* She should've called him before they left.

So sorry! My neighbor fell and I took her to the urgent care. Can we do something tomorrow?

She watched the screen as the three dots appeared.

NP.

That was it? He couldn't even write out *no problem*? Oh well. She couldn't take his short response as an indication of anger. Maybe he was in the middle of something. Besides, it was nice that he responded quickly. She replied with a smiley face and tucked her phone back into her purse. As she drove home, rain slammed against the windshield, and she had to strain to see through the watery mess. She couldn't help wondering why Sylvia would want to be alone. If the roles were reversed, she would've been begging Sylvia to stay. Well, not begging, but she would've immediately accepted her offer to stay. It's what you did for a friend. And there was no chance she'd said anything that could've upset her, because they had hardly exchanged five words tonight. No, this was just strange.

Maybe she felt nauseated and wanted to be alone for that reason. Riki could certainly understand that. No one wanted to feel like they were going to barf in front of someone else.

She pulled into her parking spot and watched as the wipers shucked water from the windshield before she shut off the engine. The rain slammed the ground outside the safety of the carport. Flipping up her hoodie, she jogged down the driveway and turned left instead of right.

She rapped lightly on the door—just three times in case the babies were sleeping—and swept water from her sleeves as she waited. Footsteps sounded, followed by the rattle of the bolt lock. Embry opened the door, her curious expression replaced with a warm smile. "Riki! Come in. You must be freezing! It's an absolute mess out there." She peered past her. "Is Sylvia with you?"

"No, she's still at the urgent care." As she followed Embry to the kitchen table, she stole a quick look to see if Brandon was nearby, even though she knew he was out bartending. "It was so weird. I offered to stay with her, but she insisted I leave," she said, peeling off her hoodie and smoothing her damp hair.

"What on earth? Why?" She handed Riki a kitchen towel and motioned to a chair at the table.

"I don't know. She didn't say much." She took the seat Embry offered. "I would hate waiting by myself at the urgent care, but then maybe I'm a wimp."

Embry laughed and sat across from Riki. "You're not a wimp. Far from it. Sylvia's just different. She's lived alone the entire time we've been here, and that's coming up on four years."

"That could be it. I just felt bad for her."

"I don't think she has any family nearby. She's never mentioned them, and honestly, it seemed Nadine was more family to her than anyone." She stood, tightening her ponytail. "Where are my manners? I'll make us some tea. Peppermint or lemon?" she asked, already putting the kettle on the stove.

Riki watched Embry, her ponytail dancing softly at her neck as she took two tea bags from a countertop basket. She was so easy breezy with everything. And so invigorating to be around. Riki wished she could be more like her. But the truth was, she often felt stiff and robotic in social situations. But Embry was like the sun, shining on even the sorriest little sprout. "Peppermint sounds great. Thanks." A messy stack of papers sat on the table, and next to it was a professional-looking photo of Brandon. Riki spun it with one finger so she could see it better. "Wow. Is this his acting picture?" she asked, only slightly aware of the awe in her voice.

"Yeah. He had an audition today, but they already had his headshot. He must've forgotten to put that one back in his work folder," she said as she placed two teacups on the counter before turning to the stove top.

Riki slid the picture closer and realized there were two stuck together. Her pulse raced. *Could I?* Without giving it another thought, she swept the top headshot into her purse, sliding it under the books while Embry poured hot water into the mugs. She swallowed hard. "Yeah, I ran into him when I got home from work. He mentioned *Days of Our Lives*. That's so cool."

"I hope he gets the part. It's been a struggle." Her voice was brimming with frustration as she brought the teacups to the table.

Riki met her eyes and nodded. "I can imagine." She sipped the hot tea, but Embry held up a hand, stopping her. For a fleeting second, Riki wondered if she was going to snatch the cup and throw the hot liquid in her face. Had she seen what Riki had done?

"Wait on that a sec. I almost forgot the best part." She flitted to the kitchen and returned with a plate of honey pops.

Riki's eyes sprang wide. "Yum! I love when you make these," she said, relief flooding through her as she realized Embry didn't know after all. *But that doesn't change the fact that I'm now a thief.* This was bad. Terrible. It wasn't like she could return the photo, claiming it fell off the table and into her purse. Any reasonable person would know that was a fat lie. So she would keep it. *And if I'm smart, I'll burn it.*

"They are good, aren't they?" Embry said, taking a lick. "Kylie and I made them this morning. I'm struggling for ideas to keep her entertained," she said, her eyes downcast as she slowly swirled her tea. "I feel like I'm a terrible mom half the time." When she looked back up, her eyes were glossy.

"You're an amazing mom!" Riki rushed to say as she stirred the honey pop in her tea. Seeing Embry upset tore at her. "I'm always so impressed with how patient and sweet you are with your kids." She covered Embry's hand with her own and squeezed. "They're really fortunate to have you as their mom. And Brandon is lucky too." Saying the words aloud was cleansing. In her heart, she knew both Brandon and Embry were lucky to have each other. They were perfect together. She was the one who was terrible, not Embry. "What's making you feel this way?"

Embry pressed a hand to her face and shrugged. "I don't know. Maybe it's the baby blues." She attempted a laugh. "Or sleep deprivation. Carson isn't a great sleeper, as you know."

She nodded. "I'm here anytime you need help, okay? With anything. I'll watch the kids so you can rest, or I'll go to the store for you, or whatever. Happily, okay?"

She sniffed. "Thanks, Riki. I'm sorry for complaining. I'm sure I'm just tired."

"I should let you get some sleep. I'll check in tomorrow." Riki stood. "Thanks for the tea."

"Always a pleasure," Embry said, standing to hug her. "Good night. And thank you."

Riki hugged her back. As she did, her nostrils filled with the sweet scent of roses. If Embry had been the one to take Sylvia to the urgent care, she would've walked away smelling like a rose while Riki itched for a shower. It wasn't fair. She dropped her arms and fumbled for a smile. "See you later." She slipped out the door and into the driving rain. As she sped toward home, her thoughts lingered on Embry. She made being a mom look so easy. It was strange that she had come so close to crying tonight. Was she experiencing postpartum depression? Riki didn't know much about it, but she knew it existed. Could it come on seven months after having a baby, though?

She gripped the sleeves of her sweatshirt in her fists. What if it was something even worse? Had Embry seen Brandon dancing with her in the rain? She hadn't even considered it at the time. What if Kylie had been looking out the window and asked what Daddy was doing with Miss Riki? Her face burned. She reached her apartment and let herself in. Leaning against the door, she squeezed her eyes shut and, without warning, an image of Brandon crashed into her mind. He looked at her, a half smile on his face. "It was sure nice dancing with you, Riki. You're a real sweetheart." And he skimmed a hand across her cheek before pressing his lips to hers.

She flung her eyes open. *No!* She couldn't think of him that way. What the hell was wrong with her? She was acting like a desperate addict. That description fit too well. She was addicted to her feelings for him. Was this how alcoholics felt when they vowed not to take one more drink, but the beer or whatever was *right there*, close enough to grab, yet doing so would only send them down a dark rabbit hole of despair? Because nothing good was coming from these mixed-up feelings. Nothing whatsoever. She set her purse on the table and took the stolen headshot from it. Brandon's eyes appeared to be staring right at her. It was a wonder he wasn't a major Hollywood heartthrob yet. How would Embry feel when he did make it big? She would have to endure watching him on the big screen, making out with any number of beautiful actresses. Was that what had made her sad tonight? The thought of Brandon kissing a soap star? That's all they seemed to do on soap operas—kiss, marry, and, well, murder. She stuffed the headshot back into her purse. She'd have to find a good hiding place for it. Or better yet, she should sneak it into the back of Brandon's truck so it looked like he'd dropped it. That was the best way to go. If she kept it here, she'd probably start talking to it like it was real.

CHAPTER SEVEN

Well, it was only a sprain. Sylvia almost wished for a cast instead of the ridiculous brace that made it look like she had a robotic arm. A cast would suggest a real injury—one that warranted her reaction to the pain.

But maybe the pain was phantom, transferred to her wrist from the unsettling feelings that twisted through her. Hugh hadn't responded. No text, no call. Nothing. She stared absently at the wall. Her eyes slid onto a puddle that spread across the kitchen floor. Had she inadvertently knocked over a glass? She stood to investigate where the water was coming from. A trail trickled down from the window. It was open just a crack but apparently enough to create a flood. Just what she needed! Grabbing a rag with her good hand, she awkwardly began mopping up the spill. It was her fault for leaving the window open, but she wanted someone else to blame.

She pushed the window closed and chucked the rag into the sink, where it landed with a thud. It had been years since she'd witnessed a storm like this. Maybe even decades. If this kept up, the damn stair would only get worse. She picked up her phone and clicked on Jonathan's number. He was the perfect recipient for her anger. But after four rings, his voice mail came on. The idiot. He was clearly screening his calls.

At the beep, she began speaking. "Hello, Jonathan, this is Sylvia in apartment D. You said you would do the repairs, and yet my stair is still broken. As it is, I've already had a nasty fall on the wet asphalt. The cracked stair will only worsen in the rain, and I'm certain you don't want me to take a tumble and break my neck. That would create quite a mess for you, wouldn't it? I would be dead, so I suppose it wouldn't matter to me, but nonetheless, I suggest you get right to it." That should do it. The man was an imbecile, but he wouldn't want a dead body on his hands.

She stared out the window at the slamming rain. What a fun-filled night it had been. Sliding onto her favorite spot on the sofa, she flicked on the TV. She scrolled through the channels distractedly, her mind occupied by Hugh once again. What the hell was going on with him? As she had waited at the urgent care, worst-case scenarios raced through her mind. Car accident? Hit by a bus in the crosswalk? Or something even more tragic?

Even though there were signs posted all over the urgent care waiting room prohibiting phone use, she had ignored them. If anything was urgent, it was finding Hugh. She had called all three of the area hospitals, and no Hugh Martin had checked in to any of them.

As she had waited in that horribly sterile place that reeked of antiseptic and bleach, she realized she knew nothing about Hugh except his name and address. That and the type of car he drove. When she'd asked to friend him on Facebook, he'd laughed and said he was a dinosaur. "I don't do social media. I'm happily existing in the Dark Ages. Don't wake me from the dream."

How delighted she'd been with his quirks. "You make a good point. Social media sucks." And that had been the end of it. She should've asked more questions.

None of this would've seemed strange if that drippy little man hadn't insinuated that Hugh was some kind of squatter. He was a wealthy man, for God's sake.

Leaning forward, she popped the cap off the Tylenol bottle and took two more. It'd been a good five hours since she'd taken it last—plenty of time to warrant another dose. She certainly didn't want to OD and have to go back to a medical facility. Dreadful places. Being at one hadn't helped her peace of mind. She pulled a throw blanket across her lap. Riki had been right, though. The urgent care was much easier than the ER.

How strange that she had brought books with her, as though Sylvia were a child. Maybe it was because she was a teacher, and that was how she dealt with emergency situations. She could picture Riki scooping up an injured child from the playground. *Come along, honey,* she'd say. *Let's go get you a nice book to read, and we can put a nice ice pack on your head.* Nice, nice, nice. That seemed to be her favorite word. She was an odd one, that Riki. Embry and Brandon were from the south, so their gooey sweetness was easy to understand. But Riki? It was like she was from another universe, as if Mary Poppins herself had raised her. Or more likely, nice parents. Though Jonathan had had a wonderful mother, and he was a dick.

Sylvia grimaced as she thought of the sadness that had always flooded Nadine's eyes when she spoke of Jonathan. It had been quite a surprise that Sylvia had befriended a woman older than her own mother. Nadine had invited her in for a cup of coffee and homemade cookies when she'd turned in her rental application. "I like to get to know prospective tenants. There's only so much a credit report shows me," she'd said, her eyes bright.

Sylvia's radar had gone up, and she'd nearly left. The thought of having coffee and cookies with an old woman who smelled of cupcakes wasn't on her agenda. But Nadine's warm smile and *I-won't-take-no-for-an-answer* aura had lured her to the table. She was curious about this woman who seemed so at ease with herself. The coffee was strong and the cookies were sweet, and as it turned out, not unlike Nadine herself.

Tightening her gaze on Sylvia, Nadine had said, "I like you. And one of the great things about having this old place paid for is that I can charge whatever I want for rent. I don't need much. I'd rather find tenants whose company I like than those who can pay me a hefty check every month." She'd tapped the table with a finger. "My son heartily disagrees, but I'm the one living here." She'd met Sylvia's eyes. "If you can promise to help me carry the odd package of bottled waters up the stairs, maybe join me for a cup of coffee now and again, I'll let you tell me how much rent you're comfortable paying."

The offer had been too good to pass up, so she'd said yes on the spot. Oh, Sylvia had assumed she'd help with groceries every time Nadine asked, but she'd planned to avoid the coffees and chats. She wasn't one for scheduled commitments.

But week after week, she'd found herself looking forward to her visits with Nadine in a way that was entirely foreign to her. The woman was sharp as a tack. Funny too. They'd laughed like old friends. Sylvia was the one who had taken Nadine to all her doctors' appointments. Jonathan had been strangely absent until the end. Then he'd wanted to put her in a home. He'd called it "one of the best assisted-living facilities," but Sylvia knew it would be a prison for Nadine.

"How about I check in on you, just like I do now, and if the time comes when you need more help, we find a devilishly handsome young man to be your nurse?"

Nadine touched the back of her hand to her forehead and gave Sylvia a dramatically exaggerated sigh. "Be still my beating heart. I do believe that's the best idea I've heard all week."

"It's settled." With wide grins, they shook on it.

And then the universe decided Sylvia had been rewarded with Nadine long enough. Though they had been concerned about Nadine's heart, it was a ruptured brain aneurysm that had taken her life.

She should've known happiness like Nadine was fleeting. Good things had a shelf life. That had been shoveled and dumped into her heart with painstaking regularity. Was her time with Hugh up too?

She stood abruptly. The blanket fell to the floor, and she dropped it back onto the sofa before marching to the fridge and selecting a half-full bottle of wine. Yanking the cork out with her teeth, she spit it into the kitchen sink. For a moment, she considered drinking straight from the bottle, but she wasn't her mother's daughter. She set it on the counter and took a glass from the cupboard. Pouring with her left hand was a bit of a challenge. On the upside, her left arm would get a workout like it hadn't seen in ages. The pour was a heavy one, but that was for the best as well. *Where are you, Hugh?* she wondered as the wine slid down her throat. Even if his plane had taken a detour halfway across the country, he would've been home by now. Something wasn't right.

She was treading a very fine line between worry and anger. A small voice in her head begged her to tiptoe away from the anger—to leave it quietly before she woke a sleeping monster.

CHAPTER EIGHT

Saturday, March 11

Dear Room Fourteen Families,

I hope you're all enjoying this rainy weekend! I wanted to take a moment to address the concerns some of you have about the leprechaun traps. As I stated in the letter I sent home, this project aligns with our unit on fairy tales and folklore. Nonetheless, I understand this assignment upsets some of you. I respect your feelings on the matter and want to create a situation that is acceptable to all of you. Therefore, I'm making it optional. If your child would like to participate, great! If not, that's great too.

I received some emails that weren't part of the chain, in which parents expressed concern that some of the nonbelieving children might tell the "believers," for lack of a better term, that the leprechaun isn't real. To sum things up, they fear this will lead to discussions they aren't prepared to have about other mythical figures. They want to protect their children's beliefs for a few more precious years.

For those of you who would prefer to have your child skip the assignment, I'm asking you to please discuss the importance of not sharing the "cold hard facts," as one parent put it, with the students who are participating.

With best wishes,
Miss McFarlan

Riki hit "Send" and closed her laptop. She'd had enough of the leprechaun discussion. What she needed was a dose of reality, of home. She picked up her phone and dialed her parents' number.

"Hi, hon! You're up bright and early for a Saturday."

"Hi, Mom! You know me. Once I'm up, I'm up."

"I wish your sister would wake up earlier. I have to wait until four our time to reach her. Speaking of which, have you checked in with her lately? She said she hadn't heard from you."

Great. Even from Australia, Rowan was tattling on her. "I texted her a few days ago, but she never got back to me. It takes two to communicate." She tried to keep the edge from her voice, but she couldn't stand that Rowan always put a spin on things. If they hadn't talked, it was Riki's fault. If Riki was worried about something, she was just being dramatic. A problem had occurred? Must be Riki behind it. *Everything* was her fault.

"Well, she made it sound like you hadn't tried. Maybe she's just missing home. We all need to make the effort to show her how much we support her and miss her."

"Mom, she's doing fine. Look at her Instagram posts. She's literally having a blast."

"Well, I just worry. Australia is so far away. And with the time difference, it's hard. Anyhoo, in other news, a tree fell onto Grandma's car last night when lightning struck it. Is it still raining down your way? I saw on the news the rain was coming down hard in LA."

"What? Is she okay? Was she in the car at the time?"

"Oh, she's perfectly fine. She was in the house watching *Wheel of Fortune* when she heard the boom. It happened just as she'd figured out the bonus-round puzzle—before the contestant, I might add. I keep telling her she should audition for the show. She'd win, you know. Anyway, the tree fell smack on the hood of the car. Grandma said it was a blessing. Ever since the news stories about the acceleration problem with Toyotas came out, she's sure it can happen with any foreign car. She said she wants me to look at Lincolns with her. She likes the one in the Matthew McConaughey commercial."

"Of course she does. What does Grandpa think of that?"

"Oh, you know Grandpa. He'll go along with whatever she says. Whoa, hang on, hon. Greg! *Gregory!* The oven mitt is on fire! Can you grab it before you burn down the house?"

"Mom! What's going on? Do you need to go?"

"Hmm? Oh, we're fine, dear. Your dad just left the oven mitt too close to the burner, and it caught fire. He's making us southwestern omelets. I told him not to make mine spicy. You know how he is with the hot sauce. Between you and me, I think he's destroyed his taste buds. Anyway, it's the third or fourth oven mitt he's burned in the last month. I'm happy he's taken up cooking, but I'll tell you what, I bought a little handheld fire extinguisher a week ago just in case."

"Good call."

"Yes. Come to think of it, I'll order one for you. I'm sure they have them on Amazon. Most likely for less than I got mine."

"Thanks, Mom. That sounds great. So back to Grandma, you're sure she's okay?"

"Perfectly fine. Like I said, she was inside. The city is sending someone out to haul away the tree. You should call her, though. I'm sure she'll want to tell you all about it."

"I will."

"All right, dear. It was good talking to you. Your dad says hi. He's waving me over so I can try the omelet." She lowered her voice. "I'll let you know how it is. Let's hope it's better than the chicken piccata he made."

Riki laughed. Now that her dad was semiretired, it was like her parents had sipped from the fountain of youth. Or a fountain of fun. Even though her mom complained, Riki knew she was endlessly amused by her father's antics. "Good luck. I love you."

"Love you too. Daddy's blowing kisses. Okay, bye!"

"Bye."

She hung up and stared out the window, feeling more alone than ever. Was it because her parents sounded like they were having a ton of fun without her? It would be nice if they could at least *act* like they missed her. Like they couldn't wait to see her, the same way they couldn't wait for Rowan to come home. Her mom even had a calendar with big *X*s on it, crossing off the days until her greatly awaited return.

And come to think of it, her mom hadn't even bothered to ask how she was doing. It was becoming all too common, like she always just assumed everything was fine. *It's because I spend so much time faking that everything is fine,* she thought. Well, no one liked a complainer. It was easier to plaster on a smile and pretend. She turned her lips up, trying for one, but she knew if she were to look in the mirror, she would look like a demented clown.

The rain was falling at a slant. It was too wet outside for Brandon to mow the lawn. Not that she would've watched today. She decided late last night that she was going to approach this Brandon thing the way someone would go about quitting smoking or cutting carbs. One small step at a time.

She forced herself to block him from her mind's eye and instead pictured her mom and dad in the house she grew up in, enjoying Saturday-morning omelets, but strangely enough, she was at the table with them. A lump built in her throat. Maybe that was the real reason for her loneliness. It'd be nice to have someone to spend the rainy Saturday with. A family of her own. Maybe she would call Chris later and see if he wanted to come over tonight to make pasta with garlic bread. He was a good guy. Everyone liked him. And it would be a perfect night to stay in and enjoy dinner with a movie, especially since it hadn't worked out last night.

But as soon as she imagined him in her apartment, his wallet on her counter and his socks in her bedroom, she started to feel like she needed some air. She stood and filled a glass with water. Maybe she shouldn't call him. She wished she knew how good relationships were supposed to feel. The sex was easy—she knew she liked that part with him. But what did it mean that she never wanted him to stick around, and when he was away, she felt lonely? Was there something wrong with her? She thought about this, reviewing all her past relationships as though flipping through a yearbook.

She skipped right past her high school boyfriends—well, all two of them—because they had been more like friend-boys whom she'd seen movies with or gone to dances with in big groups. College brought her first real boyfriend, Darian. He had quickly and efficiently broken her heart. After they dated for a few months, he was ready to move on to his next conquest, the pretty exchange student from Germany. Following that, she'd dated only a few guys very casually.

Her heart stung as she remembered how Darian had brushed the hair that fell toward her face as they'd stood under the big shade tree in middle campus.

"You're so sweet," he said. *"We've had some good times."*

"We've had some great times." Riki stood on tiptoes to kiss his lips. *"It'll only get better."* Her mind had raced ahead, sprinkling rose petals along the path that led to an altar and a pretty white gown.

He stepped back, his eyes darting to the tree, the sky, and finally back to her. *"I don't think so. This is where it ends, Riki. I've met someone else."*

"Oh."

That was all she could say. She didn't scream or yell or beg for him to stay. She didn't ask who it was or where he'd met her. In that moment, she froze. And he left her there, standing under the tree, all alone.

She shook her head. That was a long time ago. *I shouldn't even care anymore.*

But it still stung.

She'd never walk into that kind of pain again. Chris wasn't like Darian. He wouldn't suddenly drop her for someone new. So why was she feeling so hesitant with him? The answer rippled to life like a Technicolor picture right in front of her, but she blinked it away. *Don't hide from it. You know you want it all,* a little voice said.

Ha. Not everyone could have it all. Well, Embry and Brandon seemed to have it all, but they were different. She would settle for fine. It was safer that way.

~

Brandon moved across the room with Carson in his arms, pausing to peer out the window. The baby pressed his hands to the glass, leaving tiny smudges that Embry would have to scrub later, while Kylie pranced about wearing her Supergirl cape, using a spatula as a magic wand, turning anything in her path into a toad or butterfly. Embry wasn't quite sure what the criteria was, but if Kylie waved that wand at her, she'd request to be cloned. Heaven knows she could use an extra pair of hands.

"It's too wet to bother with the lawn," Embry snapped as though it were foolish to even look outside. She folded another towel into a perfect square, and he inched closer to her.

"I wasn't planning on it. I can see it's wet."

"Sorry." She flapped a dish towel to straighten it. "I'm not mad at you. Carson had a rough night, and I'm tired. Everything is bugging me right now." She added the towel to her pile. At least that was nice and orderly.

His brows shot up as he tucked his arms across his chest. "Everything? Including me?"

"No." She waved a hand toward the sink. "I'm scared of the sink now. The thing has a life of its own. And I'm going to have to return the plunger. It did nothing more than put a bandage on the stupid problem."

"Did you call Jonathan?"

"I left a message. The man never answers his phone. It's annoying."

"It is annoying. If he doesn't get back to you by Monday, we can call a plumber on our own and bill him. In the meantime, we can survive a few more days, right? We'll pretend we're camping," he added with a wink.

"No thanks! You know I hate camping."

His cell phone rang, and he shifted the baby to check the number. He met Embry's eyes and passed Carson to her. "It's Adena. This is it."

Embry nodded and held the baby close, watching Brandon as he rushed to the bedroom and closed the door. She squeezed her eyes shut, making a wish. *I hope he gets it,* she thought. *He has to get it.*

"Mama, why you close your eyes?" Kylie asked. "Ba boo!" she shouted, waving the spatula in front of her. "You awake!"

"You got me, sweetie! I'm awake now," she said. "Will you wave your wand and make some good luck for Daddy?"

With a flourish, she twirled in a circle and waved the spatula so hard, it flew from her hand, landing with a clatter near the door.

Laughter spilled out of her. "That was big magic, Mama. Daddy has a whole bunch of good luck," she said, spreading her arms wide.

"Thanks, Ky." She pressed her face into the bundle of baby, and Brandon came back into the room, his eyes bluer than she'd ever seen them. She wanted them to be happy tears, but she knew better. It was in the stiffness of his shoulders and the tightness of his jaw. He locked eyes with her and shook his head.

She covered her mouth with a shaking hand and hurried Carson to his swing, barely stopping to fasten the straps before sweeping her arms around Brandon. There were no words to make this better. He'd put every last egg in this basket. She knew a little piece of him was dying on the inside. His agent had all but promised he'd land this part after yesterday's audition. *The casting director loves you! She wants this for you so badly.*

Embry had wanted it even more. For Brandon. *For the baby.* She wished she could change history, but no amount of wishing or positive thinking could make things different. Brandon wasn't a working actor; he was a waiter by day and a bartender by night. She shuddered a sigh into his shoulder. "Maybe we should think about going home."

He took her by both arms, holding on to her as if to steady himself. "What?"

"It's a thought," she said, taking a step back. "Money is tight, and we don't have any family out here. And . . ." Tears pooled in her eyes. "And I—"

"And what? You don't think I can do it? Is that what you're saying?"

The sharpness in his voice stung, and the urge to spill the baby news hovered on her lips. What would he say if she just tossed it out there and let him deal with it? What sweet relief that would bring. But it wouldn't be fair to him. And no matter what, she couldn't help but put his feelings first. It was what you did when you loved someone.

She shook her head. "No! I'm not saying that at all." Softening, she added, "I just want to do what's best for us. That's all."

"Dammit, Embry. What do you think I want? Do you know how I feel every time I have to tell you I didn't get another goddamn part?" He violently slit the air with his hand. "Not even a stupid costarring role that any asshole can book. I'm failing you. There's always someone taller, shorter, more southern, less southern. They always want someone with a bit more or a bit less. I'm never the one." He shoved a hand in his hair and turned away.

Embry threw a protective glance toward Kylie, worried that she'd heard Brandon swearing up a storm, but she was busy wandering the room, tapping her spatula to the books on the shelf as though anticipating their coming to life. Satisfied Kylie wasn't listening, she touched her hand to Brandon's shoulder. "You're not failing us. The whole Hollywood thing is like getting picked up by a tornado and tossed around until you're sick. But you will land."

He shrugged her hand off and spun to face her. "How do you know that? Truth is, you don't."

"I'm only trying to be supportive, Brandon. You don't need to act like a jerk," she whispered harshly.

"You know what?" he snapped. "Maybe you're right about going home. I'll start working at my daddy's gas station. I can see it now—going from pouring drinks for desperate divorcées to rotating tires on trucks." A rough laugh fell from his lips, making his handsome face turn ugly. "Talk about a success story."

"You don't have to be sarcastic."

"Oh, I'm not being sarcastic. Isn't that what you want? To go home? I'm telling you my options there. And you can get Kylie all prepped to go out on the pageant circuit. It'll be a dream come true for your mama."

Her hand burned with the foreign desire to slap him. She balled it into a fist, afraid she might actually do it. "Don't you bring my mama into this. She's been nothing but your biggest fan."

He stormed past her. "I need to get some air." Grabbing his keys from the hook in the kitchen, he yanked open the door and let it slam.

Embry collapsed into a chair. She stared at the spot where Brandon had stood. They'd never once fought like that. Not when she'd backed the car into a pole at Costco or when Brandon had fallen asleep while watching the kids and Embry had returned home to find Kylie drawing purple marker all over a sleeping Carson's hands. Her husband was falling apart before her eyes. She could feel his despair in her bones.

If the going gets tough, the tough get going. It's what her auntie Boots used to tell her all the time when she was a teenager. Boots wasn't her real name, but Embry had called her that ever since she could remember. When Embry was first learning to talk, she couldn't pronounce her real name, Ruth. Her daddy had laughed and said, "It sounds like she's saying *boots.*" The name stuck, and it had managed to create a special bond between the two. Auntie Boots was her daddy's aunt—her great-aunt—but Embry liked to think of her as her very own. She had a never-ending supply of great stories and solid advice. And if she were here now, she'd tell Embry to take matters into her own hands. *If your finances are a worry, get out there and find a way to help.*

There it was again, the idea that she could earn some money too. She'd find a way. The blood of generations of determined women flowed through her veins, after all. It was up to her now.

CHAPTER NINE

Sylvia sat up in her bed, adjusting the pillow so it supported her back, and flicked the cap off the bottle of Tylenol, washing two down with water from the glass on her bedside table as she glared at the stupid brace. She'd be better off amputating her wrist and purchasing a pretty hook. She could find an antique that would not only be functional but could double as a unique piece of statement jewelry. And it'd certainly come in handy. When someone annoyed her, she could use it as a weapon.

Hugh was to blame for her injury. If she hadn't been busy trying to mentally pinpoint his location, she wouldn't have tripped. She tried to release the anger. Maybe he was suffering in a gutter somewhere, the victim of a hit-and-run that had left him with severely broken bones. Or he could've been captured by disgusting drug dealers who were too stupid to have gotten the right guy. She hoped that was the case.

She tapped her phone to life and pressed "Recents." Hugh's name was at the top of the list. She had tried calling him four times in the course of six hours last night. A brewing rage sat across the room, ready to slam into her if he didn't pick up this time. Thunder boomed outside, as if the universe shared her frustration. She touched his number and held the phone to her ear. If he didn't answer, she would call the police.

One ring, then two. She held the phone in a death grip. Three rings. "Hi, Jeff!" It was a woman's voice.

A cold rush ripped through Sylvia. Who the hell was Jeff? And why was a woman answering Hugh's phone? "Uh, no Jeff here. Who's this?"

"Oh!" She sounded surprised. "Sorry. This is Lily. Hugh's bathing the baby, and the caller ID said 'Jeff Ulrich, Global Consulting,' so I answered. This must be Krista."

The room swayed, and Sylvia grabbed a fistful of sheets. *Hugh is bathing the baby?* As in *their* baby? She forced herself to focus. To think. "Yes, I'm calling from Jeff's phone. We're planning a surprise party for him, and I'm making sure we have all the right contact information," she said in a steady voice.

"Oh! How fun. Do you need an email address?"

Bile rose in Sylvia's throat. Her hand crept to her mouth, and she landed her feet on the floor, ready to bolt. "No, I'm texting invites." Her hollow voice was better suited for planning a funeral than a party.

"Great. I won't say a word. In fact, I'm not going to mention a thing to Hugh. He doesn't like anyone touching his phone, but since I know Jeff, I figured it was fine. Husbands," she added with a laugh.

"Husbands," Sylvia repeated. "Bye now." She let the phone slide from her hand and beelined to the bathroom.

After rinsing her mouth with Listerine and splashing cold water on her face, she was ready to address the facts.

Hugh wasn't stuck on an airplane. He wasn't in a hospital, a jail cell, or a shallow grave getting pounded by rain. He was married with a baby. Perhaps the saddest of all possible outcomes.

She wanted to scream but clamped back the desire. Her teeth scraped against each other as she ground them until they felt loose, an old habit she'd tried to overcome. It was astounding that her teeth hadn't fallen out due to the amount of time she'd spent clenching and grinding them as a child.

Hugh had led her down a pretty pathway that had dead-ended in asphyxiating quicksand, a silent killer. The more she struggled against the news, the faster it would swallow her alive. She had to face the truth like the survivor she was: Hugh was a liar. A married daddy, and a motherfucking liar.

Her eyes burned with rage. It took every ounce of restraint to stop herself from picking up the phone and hurling it at the wall.

Don't kill the messenger.

True, true. It was never the messenger's fault.

Hugh, on the other hand, was guilty. She stood and pulled her nightshirt over her head. It felt symbolic, like shedding the skin of her former self—the Sylvia she had allowed Hugh to see. How unfortunate that he hadn't seen her angry. It would've been helpful if he'd at least had a glimpse. But alas, he'd only known happy Sylvia. Happy, buttermilk biscuit–eating Sylvia. She'd enjoyed the newspaper, just like him! And the powdered creamer? A brilliant grocery-store find!

He had done absolutely nothing to anger her.

Up until now, that is.

She smiled. Actually, he was an idiot to have introduced her to powdered anything. It was all too easy to add a little something to it. Rat poison, perhaps. Shake to mix, and *voilà*! Powdered creamer turned lethal.

Fun to think about, but she wouldn't poison him. It was impossible to torment a dead man. No, she really needed to keep him alive.

The question was, what did he hold most dear? That would be the quickest path to his demise. Her mind traveled back to the night they'd met, and it landed on his fake wedding ring. Odd, but genius in its ability to allow him to hide in plain sight. A lot of thought and energy had gone into protecting his image. And his wife.

He wanted to look like a good guy.

So bit by bit, she would make him look bad. It wouldn't be too difficult to create the illusion that Hugh was becoming unstable. He was so polished and perfect that people would thoroughly enjoy his downfall. Oh, they'd talk about it in whispers, claiming how sad and surprising it was. But that talk would quickly shift to all-knowing smirks. *I saw it coming. It was only a matter of time. If it seems too good to be true . . .*

As for Lily, it would be unfortunate for her to learn that her darling spouse was a cheater. But she needed to know. Lily would unwittingly act as Sylvia's right-hand woman. *Literally,* she thought with a laugh.

What would Lily do? Sylvia closed her eyes and imagined her pale hand wielding a kitchen knife. Would she go to that extreme? *Could be.* After all, Hugh had said he didn't want to be responsible for her crazy. *Well, Hugh. Guess what? Now you are.*

She could almost see his face, fraught with fear, as his lies scurried toward him like roaches at night. It was hurtful that he'd lied to her again and again as though it was nothing. But she wouldn't dwell. Never did. Old wounds became armor. Why she had stripped herself of that armor for Hugh was beyond her understanding. It wasn't something she did. But his lies had been so pretty. Shiny little things that she had run to like an eager child.

A cold chill shook her as she imagined herself as a little girl, her face open and trusting as she watched her dad smile before putting a finger to his lips and tiptoeing backward through the door. "Cover your eyes with both hands. Count all the way up to fifty," he'd said in a whisper, and she'd eagerly played along.

But what if she hadn't? What if she had run after him instead, claiming she didn't want to cover her eyes? Would he have lifted her into his arms and nuzzled her neck as he had done so many times before?

She wouldn't know. She had followed his rules.

The scars that he'd left had healed into a very tough skin. Untouchable.

So Hugh hadn't *hurt* her. Not really. She would never truly fall for someone. *He was only a pathway to my future,* she reminded herself as she wiped away an unwelcome tear. *One pathway of many.* But he'd proven to be slippery. Deceitful. And for that, he would pay.

Oh, he would pay dearly.

Too bad, so sad.

There was nothing Sylvia hated more than a liar.

CHAPTER TEN

Glancing at the clock, Riki wondered if it was too soon to check on Sylvia. But it was almost eleven, so it should be fine. And the rain had subsided to a gentle mist. She pulled up the hood of her sweatshirt and headed to Sylvia's apartment. The doormat was red with the words HOME SWEET HOME, printed in white font.

She tilted her head after knocking, listening for footsteps, but the door suddenly swung open without a sound. Sylvia stood in front of her, wearing a faux-fur robe and a darling pair of gray bunny slippers with ears that stood up. *Kate Spade,* she thought, noting the gold spade charm in the center of each. Only Sylvia would wear designer slippers.

"Hello, Riki. Or should I call you Florence Nightingale? What brings you out on this fabulous day?"

"Hi, I just wanted to see how you're doing. I was worried about you last night."

Sylvia smiled without showing her teeth. Her eyes were bloodshot, as though she'd been up all night. "Oh, that's sweet of you. But I'm fine. It was just a sprain."

"What a relief."

"Indeed."

She shifted her feet, waiting for something more. Seconds ticked by, and the silence became too loud. "Okay. Well, let me know if you need anything."

"I will." She smiled again, but it didn't reach her eyes. In fact, if Riki were to simply go off the look in her eyes, she'd say Sylvia's arm hurt a lot worse than she was letting on.

Riki turned to go, but Sylvia's voice stopped her, and she spun around. "Thank you for taking me last night. I'm pretty sure I failed to say much yesterday. I wasn't myself."

"It's okay," she rushed out. "I figured you must've been in a lot of pain."

Sylvia nodded. "Yes. It was a double dose. My boyfriend stood me up last night. I was thinking about him when I slipped. And then," she said, staring off in the distance, "just this morning, I discovered that he's married. Married with a baby. What kind of disgusting human being cheats on the mother of his child?"

Riki's mouth dropped open. "I don't even know! That's awful. What an asshole!"

Sylvia narrowed her gaze like she was zeroing in on Riki's thoughts.

She blinked, trying to block the piercing stare, but she couldn't escape it. *Oh, jeez.* Had Sylvia caught her ogling Brandon the other morning when he'd waved? Or had she somehow witnessed her staring through the window on a random Saturday morning? Riki shifted her feet and looked at the brace on Sylvia's wrist, trying to think of something else to say.

Sylvia finally answered. "Yes, that's what I was thinking. What an asshole. Apparently, he lives in a mirrored bubble and can only see himself. He clearly wasn't thinking about his child when he was busy seducing me. What a terrible role model for that poor baby." She clamped her lips into a flat line and inhaled through her nose. For a second, Riki wondered if she would explode, but instead, with a sad smile, she closed the door.

Riki shivered and started down the stairs. This was a big, glaring sign that she needed to get control of the feelings she had for Brandon. She was becoming paranoid. Sylvia hadn't said any of that to warn her. It was because she was completely freaked out right now. Her boyfriend was married!

Riki's mind lingered on Sylvia's vacant expression. It was like every emotion had seeped right out of her. As she touched the next step, her shoe skidded, and she slipped. Frantically, she grabbed hold of the handrail. *That was close,* she thought as she continued down, careful to avoid the seventh step. The last thing she needed was to fall in the rain like Sylvia had.

~

Jonathan eased to a stop across from the apartment complex and killed the engine. He exited his car and jogged over to the car parked in front of him, where a man was looking at the property with interest.

"Hey, Pat. Good to see you, buddy. Thanks for coming over on a wet Saturday."

They shook hands. "No problem at all. So this is it?" He pointed to the complex. "Ten fifty-four Mockingbird Lane?"

"Yep. There she is. It's a twenty-thousand-square-foot lot. Big for this area."

"Sure is." He nodded authoritatively. "Not a bad location either. I have a couple of contacts who are looking for development properties. This place could be interesting to them. Then again, we may find a buyer who wants to keep it as an investment property."

Jonathan nodded. "Right. And your boy Dave said he'll come over tomorrow to do the few repairs, weather permitting. Thanks for connecting me with him."

"No prob. He's a good kid." He crossed his arms and turned to Jonathan. "It has the potential to go quickly with the way the market is at the moment. That can change in an instant, but I think we're in a good position with this one. Let me know when you want to pull the trigger, and I'll get things rolling."

Jonathan held back the urge to do a victory punch to the air. He forced a serious look. "I'll keep you posted on my decision. The old place has been in the family for years. It's going to take the right price to get me to part with it." *Ha! I can't wait to dump the place and the nagging tenants.* But the harder Patrick had to work to convince him to sell, the harder he'd work for a stellar selling price.

"What about leases? Do you have any tenants with a lease, or are they month to month?"

He nodded assuredly, as though he'd expected the question. "The tenants won't be a problem."

They shook hands once again, and Patrick drove off. *Leases.* Shit! Why hadn't he thought of that? If any of the tenants came up with some grand idea about him paying out their lease when he needed them to move, they had another thing coming. He wasn't about to part with his hard-earned cash. With any luck, Ma had kept handwritten notes that he could easily destroy. He smiled. Maybe her refusal to use technology was a blessing after all. Shoving his hands in his pockets, he turned back to his car. He'd figure it out. Always did. And if the place didn't sell right away, he'd figure that out too. Hell, he could set the place on fire and collect the insurance money if it came to that. Of course, he'd do it when the tenants were out and about. No need to harm anyone. He chuckled to himself. It'd be easy to tell them he had to tent the place for termites. Accidents happened, after all.

CHAPTER ELEVEN

Riki opened the door to Chris, his hair glistening with raindrops. "You don't have an umbrella?"

"Nah. It never rains."

She laughed as he stood dripping on her welcome mat. "Stay there. I'll bring you a towel." She took a bath towel from her linen cupboard and tossed it to him. "I think you might need to break down and get an umbrella. Every time I think it's over, it starts up again."

He wiped off his jacket before pressing the towel to his face and ruffling it across his hair. "Guess I'll have to stay where it's dry until the storm passes."

A finger of dread scratched down her spine as she imagined him staying all weekend. Only until tomorrow—Sunday—but still. What if he stayed late on Sunday? Or even until Monday morning? Using the towel, he drew her into a hug, and the bad feeling vanished. What was wrong with her anyway? Would it be this way with any guy she dated?

This time, fear didn't scratch—it clawed. Maybe she was someone who preferred solitude, and no one would ever feel like the yin to her yang. It's possible no guy could ever be the one. What if she grew old all alone? How would she feel with no one there by her side when the inevitable happened?

She swallowed the sudden lump in her throat. *Don't be dramatic and stupid, Riki.* She stepped out of the hug and looped the towel over her arm. "I'll hang this in the bathroom. There's beer in the fridge if you want one." *And plenty of girls out there who aren't secretly a mess, if you'd prefer one of those.*

"Thanks."

Chris was sitting on the sofa when she returned, a papier-mâché panda in his hand. He held it up. "What's this ball thing for?"

She plopped next to him. "It's a panda, not a ball."

"Really?" he asked, spinning it from one side to the other. "A panda?"

"Yes. We're doing an endangered-animal unit next month for Earth Week, and I'm having the kids make papier-mâché animals to go along with their reports." Taking it from his hands, she said, "This little guy is my example. I spent a few hours making him the other day."

He circled an arm around her shoulders and frowned. "Wow. It's . . ."

"Is it that bad?" she asked as she placed it back on the table.

"It's something. The good news is, your kids won't feel like theirs suck because the teacher's looks so much better."

"Thanks a lot. Mrs. Fitzsimmons left her sample behind, but it was all dull and dusty. Even so, maybe I should just use hers."

"No. Don't. I hated it when my teachers made these amazing projects and mine looked like crap."

"Thanks, I guess?" She playfully touched her shoulder to his. "Do you want to order pizza? It's kind of too wet to go out, don't you think?"

"It's not that bad, and some of the guys are meeting up at the Lantern for drinks and appetizers. You love seeing everyone."

Do I? Or did he just want to believe that? She didn't even know his friends all that well. But then again, most girls would jump at an offer to go to a cool gastropub with their newly official boyfriend, wouldn't they? *Yes, Riki, they would.* That's what Rowan would say, and she was probably right. Rowan was always giving her advice on how to "act normal." To be fair, sometimes it was helpful. Mostly, though, it was annoying, and she wasn't in the mood to follow Rowan's advice. She turned to Chris and patted his leg. "If you want to hang out with them, you should. I'm not up for it."

He placed his hand on hers and sighed. "I'd really love for you to go with me. It's Saturday night." Tapping his thigh against hers, he smiled and said, "Come on."

She struggled to come up with the right words. He was Mr. Personality, and she was a homebody. *Which is exactly why I need to push myself,* she thought. *I'll end up a complete recluse with an apartment full of cats.* Not that she had one now. But she could see the path in front of her, and it was littered with cats. Or maybe she'd heard it enough from Rowan to start believing it was a real possibility. "Okay."

"Really? You'll go?"

She leaned forward to kiss him. "Yes. I'll go. Give me a few minutes to change, okay?"

"Awesome. I told them we'd be there in thirty."

She started to say something but instead headed for her room. What if she'd insisted on staying home? Would he have thrown her over his shoulder and strapped her in the car? She couldn't imagine Brandon making assumptions about what Embry wanted to do. She sighed. It wasn't fair to compare Chris to him. But it was like thoughts of Brandon had hijacked her brain. Maybe she could set up a point system for herself, and once she racked up enough points—earned by not thinking about Brandon as anything but her friend's husband—she could buy herself a reward. Something she'd been wanting, like a new tote for her school things.

She pulled a black turtleneck sweater from the back of her closet and tugged it over her head. Her jeans were fine, she decided, and she slipped on a pair of black leather boots. They probably weren't waterproof, but she didn't have anything else to wear besides flip-flops and sandals.

She brushed her hair into a low ponytail before putting on tiny gold hoop earrings and dotting rosy lipstick onto her lips. Done in less than five minutes. She smiled at her reflection. The low ponytail looked good. Usually, she wore them higher, but this was a fun change. It looked more sophisticated. Pretty.

When she emerged from her room, Chris stepped close to kiss her cheek. "You look gorgeous."

"Thanks." She took the umbrella from the hall closet and shrugged into her coat. "Let's go." Did he hear the lack of enthusiasm in her voice, or had he made up his mind that she *loved seeing everyone*? It was like he was adding traits to her along the way that didn't really belong. Although it was possible he was just being encouraging, in the same way her parents used to tell her she *loved* going to her dance classes, when in reality, she'd dreaded them. Brandon, on the other hand, was the perfect dance teacher. *Twirl, girl.*

~

The Lantern was nestled between an art gallery and a juice bar near the beach. Not too many years ago, trash, weeds, and empty storefronts had lined the street, but some entrepreneurial soul had come in and revitalized the entire area. The trash was gone, and the weeds had been replaced with wooden flower boxes and pretty herb gardens. There wasn't a vacancy on the whole block. It always amazed Riki how quickly things could change.

Chris's friends were seated around a center table. She'd met them all before—Calvin the production assistant, who looked like Steve Harrington from *Stranger Things* with his poufy eighties hair; his girlfriend, Shannon; and Eddie, Liam, and Rob, the single trio. Interestingly enough, Liam had a date tonight. The girl next to him had an athletic build and wild dark hair that was capped with a red cashmere beret. She looked chic and cool, which only made Riki feel extra awkward in her plain jeans and basic boots.

A chorus of hellos sounded as Riki and Chris pulled up chairs and wriggled off their coats. Was Liam excited about this new girl? Did she know he had the reputation of a player, or was she happily unaware, drawn in by his cool charm? Maybe she was already imagining what their babies would look like. She was dark while he was fair. Her genes were surely dominant, unless she had some recessive genes in her DNA that would match up with his. She'd wondered that about Chris and had been intrigued when she finally saw a picture of his parents. They both had dark-brown eyes like his. Swarthy, like a pirate.

So that would mean if she and Chris had babies, they would probably have dark-brown eyes. Which was fine. Brown eyes were cool. But she would be the different one in the family—the one who didn't match. Would it be strange to look into her baby's eyes that were so unlike hers? *Oh, come on, Riki!* She couldn't believe she cared for even a second about what color her future kids' eyes would be. She should be worried about the important things, like heart health and whether cancer ran in his family.

Chris passed a mug of beer to her, and she took a sip. What the hell was she thinking? If Chris knew she was imagining their children, he'd probably down his beer and ask out the first girl he saw.

Or would he? It was equally easy picturing him bringing over boxes so she could move in with him. She shivered at the thought.

So why was she planning babies with the guy? He kept a hand on her leg as he talked with Eddie and Rob. It felt nice. Protective.

Liam's date—Evelyn, she learned—sat opposite Riki. She was originally from Wisconsin. It was the first thing she told Riki upon their introduction, although Riki could've guessed she was from somewhere else because of her accent. Somehow, it made her less intimidating when she went on to say that she came out here to work in the industry.

"My neighbor did the same thing," Riki told her. "He and his wife moved here about four years ago. He's been trying to make it as an actor."

"Oh, that's tough. I wasn't exactly sure what I wanted to do before coming to LA, but I ended up getting an internship with one of the writers on an HBO series. Now I'm the assistant to one of the other writers, who's kind of a big deal. It's been great." She laughed. "Aside from the fact that I work a million hours a week and make nothing. But one day." She reached for her glass. "Right now," she continued, "we're working on a pilot. It's a legal drama with an ensemble cast. My boss wrote it and is directing. We're getting a lot of early hype. Sandra Bullock is already attached to the project. She's playing a hard-core district attorney."

"Really? That's awesome! I love Sandra Bullock."

"Me too. So what's your neighbor like? We're still casting five series-regular parts, three of which are guys."

"He's awesome. Totally handsome, for one, but not in an aggressive way, if that makes sense." It was fine to talk about Brandon this way. If she could help him get a lead to an audition, she would. She would do it for any friend. So yeah, this was fine.

Evelyn nodded. "Yeah. More Chris Hemsworth, less angular model guy?"

"Exactly." She smiled. "He's in his midtwenties, has dark-brown hair and exquisite blue eyes. Seriously. Like if Bradley Cooper and Alexis Bledel had a baby." She pictured his face, and her heart began racing. "If his eyes don't kill you, his body will." She lowered her voice. "Clinically speaking, that is. Anyone would say that about him," she rushed on, more for her own benefit than Evelyn's. No need to deduct any points. She could do this.

Evelyn laughed. "I get it. Does he have any acting experience, though?"

Her face reddened. *Duh. She meant acting-wise.* "He's done some small things here and there, but he hasn't booked anything big yet. I know he will, though. He has an irresistible vibe about him." Riki blamed the warmth she felt on the beer. Her mug was surprisingly half-empty. "He's southern, so he has a charm that comes naturally."

"Really? The show is set in Louisiana, so he could be right. I'm happy to get his headshot and résumé to the casting office. The casting assistant and I have bonded." She rolled her eyes. "That sounds so cheesy, but it's true. We save each other from sinking into the fiery pit of industry bullshit on an hourly basis."

"It's that bad?"

"Worse. But good too. It's hard to explain. What do you do for work?"

"I teach second grade."

"That must be so fun."

"It is." She searched for something else to say about her job, but having this safe conversation about Brandon felt too good. "Do you want me to have my neighbor email his stuff directly to you?"

"Sure. I'm assuming he has an agent, right? Because if not, we should forget it. There's no way someone without representation will get anything."

She pictured the headshot she'd taken. *Stolen.* It was still in her purse. She really needed to do something with it. But at least some good had come from it—she knew he had an agent, because his résumé was attached to the back of the photo, and centered at the top in bold was the name of his agency. "Yeah. He does."

"Awesome." She pulled her phone from her purse. "Give me your number, and I'll text you so you have mine."

As she recited her number, Chris turned, a smile on his face. "Making new girlfriends?" He pecked her cheek.

"Yes."

Evelyn smiled. "You know it." She finished typing and glanced at her phone. "Got it. I'm sending you my number now. You can have him text me directly or whatever is easiest. The pilot is called *Baggage*, by the way."

Chris's smile faltered, but he covered it with a laugh. "What's this you guys are up to?"

"Oh, nothing major. Her boss is doing a pilot, and I told her about my neighbor."

He swigged his beer. "The hot guy with the even hotter wife?"

"Yeah."

Chris looked past Riki to Evelyn. "I think this one has a crush on him. I might, too, but don't say anything." His laugh came from his throat, not his stomach. Riki bristled but joined in the fake laughter.

Evelyn smiled and tucked her phone into her purse, using it as an excuse to turn back to Liam. She was clearly adept at easing out of a conversation.

"You're going to connect her with your neighbor?"

She shrugged. "Yeah. It's worth a shot. They've both been so nice to me that I'm happy to help them if I can."

He fingered her ponytail. "You're even twinning with Embry now. Every time I've seen her, she's worn her hair like this."

For a split second, it felt like the room grew silent before roaring back to life with chatter. Riki's face burned. She hadn't meant to copy Embry. Jeez, she hadn't even realized she'd done it! She was only trying something new. Something to make herself feel pretty. Her cheeks grew hotter as she pictured Embry's smiling face. Attached to her earlobes were tiny gold hoop earrings. *I copied that too.* Sliding a hand down her ponytail, she glared at Chris. "Don't be ridiculous. So does most of the longhaired female population."

"Touchy! I'm just teasing you." He lifted a brow. "But you do kind of look like her tonight. Just saying." His voice took on a playful tone, but a darkness crept around the edges. "I've also seen how you look at her husband. It's cool, though. He's married, and I'm the one you're sleeping with, so I'm not jealous or anything." He leaned in to kiss her neck. "Do you want to get out of here?" he asked in a gruff whisper. There was no faking the intent in that, and her insides sizzled.

She needed to go. She wanted to get lost in Chris, to let him have her fully and completely, washing away the sticky feelings of guilt that she could no longer deny. She only hoped she could keep her focus on him when they were in her bed. Because closing her eyes and imagining he was someone else would make things worse. "Yes. Let's get out of here." She moved her lips close to his ear. "And you have exactly thirty seconds to strip down once we're back at my place."

The surprised smile that lit his face was the relief she needed.

As they stood to leave, Calvin bumped fists with Chris. "We're going to Mammoth next weekend for some skiing. My boss has a place we can use. You guys want to join us?"

Chris looked to Riki. "We're in! Riki loves to ski, right, babe?"

"Um, I've been a couple of times, so I wouldn't say I love it, but it'd be fun to try again." She forced a smile but wondered if he'd gotten her confused with some other girl he'd once dated. She'd never said she liked to ski.

"Cool." Calvin grinned. "I'll count you two in."

Once they reached the warmth of the car, Chris said, "I think Eddie is your biggest fan. He was like, 'Dude, you're so lucky.'"

"Wow. And I thought Eddie didn't like me. He didn't say a word to me, and I've met him a bunch of times."

Chris gave her a pensive look. "It's the opposite. I think he likes you too much, so he ignores you."

"Really?"

"What? Are you going to tell me you think Eddie's hot now?"

"No! I mean, he's a nice enough guy, I guess, but no." She touched his cheek. It felt like the right thing to do. "I like you."

"Sometimes I need to hear it."

"I like you, Chris." It was true. She *did* like Chris. He was confident and outgoing. Funny too. And he made her feel special. Well, sometimes. The skiing comment rippled back to her mind. But that could've been his own excitement talking. *Or maybe he doesn't even really know me.* Was that true? That she just fit the mold on the outside and he didn't really care about the inside?

"So I can officially call you my girlfriend? I know we kind of talked the other day, but I want to be sure." His nerves filled the space between them as he waited for her response.

With each passing second, his unease seemed to grow, filling Riki with a power she hadn't felt before. One more second and she would be invincible. It was alluring and terrifying and gross all at once. Wanting to escape the confusion, she uttered, "Yeah. Now let's get home so you can keep your end of the bargain." The lusty shadow of her touched her lips to his, nudging them open with her tongue while her bewildered heart rattled in her chest, overlooked and alone.

~

Embry lay on her side in the bed she shared with Brandon, listening as he quietly slid off his shoes. Her arm was cramped, but she didn't dare move and alert him she was awake. Usually if she woke when he came home after a long night of bartending, she'd whisper to him, and he'd slide into bed next to her. But tonight, she only wanted sleep. The afternoon had been a long one, and she still hadn't come up with a plan to make any money. She was exhausted from trying.

Brandon's jeans fell to the floor, and his shirt softly followed. The water in the bathroom sounded, and she knew he was brushing his teeth. Seconds later, footsteps padded toward the bed. Keeping her breathing steady, she waited for the covers to shift, but there was only silence. Was he checking his phone? Stretching?

As she strained to decipher what he was doing, his voice sounded through the dark—a husky whisper that swept across her.

"I'm so sorry, baby. I was an asshole, and I know it." The covers shifted, and she felt his weight next to her. He kissed her cheek. "I love you, Em. Always. I hope you know that." He wrapped his arms around her, and she softened into him. *This is what matters. In the end, it's all that matters.*

CHAPTER TWELVE

Sylvia turned up the volume on her TV until it was loud enough to drown out the sounds of the teacher wailing like a wet cat in the apartment below. And that boyfriend of hers. For God's sake, he sounded like a fat football player grunting through his last set of jumping jacks. If they kept this up, she might be inclined to call the cops to file a noise complaint.

She poured herself a hefty shot of vodka and reached for a lime from the bowl on the kitchen counter. With a sharp knife, she sliced it into quarters before squeezing the juice into her glass.

The first sip went down like fire, but a smooth warmth followed, reaching all the way to her injured wrist. The pain was significantly reduced. It wasn't because of the miraculous healing powers of vodka. She was certain of that. It was because of the body's capacity to focus on the sharpest pain, causing any other suffering to all but disappear. The stabbing pain was the blade in her back. Or heart. She couldn't really pin down where the knife had entered.

Sliding her laptop to the table's edge, she brought it to life. It was time to do some investigating. Using one finger, she typed the name Hugh Martin into the search bar. The profile for a dead composer popped up. *Huh.* How sad. *Hugh Martin is dead,* she thought with a smirk. Scrolling down, she searched further, skimming the results.

Nothing.

"Oh yeah, Hugh? You can't hide from me," she whispered to the screen.

What had Lily said his company name was? Global something. *Think, Sylvia.* Global Imaging? No, that couldn't be it. He was a consultant of sorts. At least, so he'd claimed. That was it! She chuckled to herself. *Global Consulting.* She typed the name, and the company website appeared. There, in the top left-hand corner, was the employee directory tab. *Here goes.* She clicked on it and scrolled down until she saw his picture next to his name. *Hugh M. Pacheco.* So it appeared he'd used his middle name as his last. Clever. He wore a crooked smile in his photo, as though someone had said something funny to encourage him to laugh. His eyes were warm and friendly. *Oh, Hugh,* she thought. *Why did you have to do this?* He looked so affable in his picture. Reliable. Well, this was one more bit of evidence that not everything was as it seemed. Hugh had created an alternative persona for himself for the sole purpose of getting what he wanted. Sure, she had adapted her likes to his, but where was the harm in that? No one suffered by her pretending to enjoy the Sunday paper. And she really had come to like the powdered creamer, strangely enough.

Reading the company address from the website, she copied it down on a sheet of paper. Next, she googled his full name. Just as she suspected, a different address from the one she knew appeared. If she was calculating correctly, it was less than a mile from her apartment. How terribly convenient. It would make her first visit that much easier.

CHAPTER THIRTEEN

Sunday, March 12

Embry was off to do the weekly shopping despite the fact that it was pouring rain and despite the fact that they should be at church. She flicked on her turn signal as the wipers screeched and squealed across the windshield. The noise made her want to cover her ears and scream. She couldn't help but feel annoyed that Brandon hadn't changed them even though it hadn't rained in ages. It was his job to deal with the cars and the yard, and it was her job to do the cleaning and shopping. It was how they'd decided to split up the work. She was doing her part, sweeping crumbs from the corners of the kitchen and scrubbing the bathroom faucets to a shine. But there was nothing she could do about the smell coming from the broken garbage disposal. She gripped the wheel and told herself she was being petty. "Breathe, Embry," she whispered.

She inhaled and exhaled. *Better.* Getting angry about things beyond her control was fruitless. But honestly! Sometimes she wished she could fall to the floor and bang her fists like a toddler. A good old-fashioned tantrum would do wonders. All this mindfulness crap was only making her shove down her feelings. One day she'd explode.

No, no, the angels whispered. *Inhale, exhale.* It took practice. She could do this.

A feeling crept around inside her, darting this way and that, making it so she couldn't pin it down. *What is it?* She focused on the road ahead, wishing she had someone to talk to. She couldn't call her friends back home because they'd faded into watercolor renditions of close friends. Time and distance had washed away the vibrancy. She'd tried to make some friends at the Mommy and Me class she'd joined when Kylie was first born, but that had been flat-out bizarre. They'd made her feel like a freak of nature, being that she was the only twenty-one-year-old mother in a sea of thirtysomethings. *You got married at twenty? I didn't even know who I was at that age.* Or one of her favorites, *Must've been a cinch for you to lose the baby weight. I was a rail in my twenties. Now it takes a lot of hard work.*

She knew the other moms didn't mean to make her feel like an outcast, but after months of being the token zoo animal, she'd stopped going to the meetings.

The feeling she'd had earlier banged its way to the front of her mind. Thinking about the other moms had made it reappear. She remembered the conversations where they'd openly shared their fears about losing their identity. They were no longer Janelle or Jodi or Christine; they were only so-and-so's mom. Was that happening to her? She didn't bother answering. The knowledge sat inside her like a stone. All that she had been was slipping from her grasp, and her own husband, the man who loved her for her spunk and spirit and spontaneity, hadn't seemed to notice.

She shook her head, trying to dislodge the guilt she suddenly felt. Goodness, she loved being a mom. Mommy. Mama. All of it. She wouldn't trade that for the world. Becoming a mother was the best thing she'd ever done in her life.

But was there room for more?

She pulled into one of the many open parking spots. Knowing it would be impossible to remain dry while getting the kids from the car, she slid an arm through her baby carrier and fastened Carson into it before helping Kylie unbuckle from her car seat.

Flipping up the hood on Kylie's pink slicker, she took her hand. They'd gone no more than five steps before Kylie found a puddle to stomp in.

"Kylie! Don't do that. You got my jeans all wet."

She looked up at her with big blue eyes. "Sorry, Mama. I dry you off?" She brushed her hand along Embry's leg, not aware it wasn't helping.

Embry sighed. "It's okay. Let's get inside. I'll let you pick the cereal." She moved as fast as she could, keeping a hand pressed to Carson's back so he wouldn't get too jostled.

As they entered the store, Kylie spun in a circle. "Mama, I'm dancing like Daddy and Miss Riki!"

A chill that had nothing to do with the cold ran through Embry. "What do you mean, Kylie?"

"They dance and dance in the rain, Mama! Just like me."

"When? Where?" The questions tumbled from her lips.

Kylie only shrugged and clomped in a giddy circle, clearly enjoying the squelching sound her boots made.

Embry took a breath and tried to reassure herself that kids sometimes got things wrong. *But sometimes they get things perfectly right.* With a shake of her head, she said, "Stop that right now, Kylie. We need a buggy."

"I drive one too?"

"Not today."

"Why?"

"Let's go find the bread. Stay close to me." Her voice was clipped, but the vision of Riki and Brandon having a good old time in the rain together had her head spinning. Carson spit out his pacifier and whimpered. His tiny body stiffened against her chest before he let out a big wail. She exhaled as he cried and forced herself to focus on what was in front of her. Letting her imagination run wild wouldn't help matters.

"Shush, shush," she said, fishing her hand between the baby carrier and his warm body to find the pacifier. She stuck it back in his mouth and kissed the top of his head as she walked toward the carts.

Another woman was already there, wrestling one from the row. "Finally!" She turned toward Embry. "Pesky things, aren't they?" Three children stood patiently near her. The youngest looked to be about five. The mother's face softened as she smiled at Embry. "Oh, what a sweet baby. I miss those days." She tousled her son's hair. "My baby is almost six now. Treasure these days, because before you know it—" She snapped her fingers. "They're gone."

Embry nodded. She'd heard that before, along with, "The days are long, but the years are short."

"And so you know, it does get easier."

Embry wanted her to keep talking. She wished she could pull this woman aside for a cup of tea while their children played. She had so many questions. Sure, she'd read plenty of books, but here was a woman who seemed to have it all together. Her kids were clean and polite. She, too, was clean and polite. "Thanks for sharing that. It's a good reminder."

"Oh, you're welcome." She smiled at Kylie. "It's such a sweet time. Okay, we're off to battle the cookie aisle. Happy Sunday!"

"Happy Sunday," Embry said softly, watching the kids trail after their mom as she headed for the aisles like a pro.

She pushed her buggy slowly, lost in thought.

"Mama, I ride?"

"Sure thing, honey." She scooped Kylie up, careful not to bump her into Carson, and placed her in the cart. As she steered to the bread aisle, tears filled her eyes. Was she treasuring these days enough? Or was she so worried about Brandon and his career that she was only halfway present? She plucked a loaf of generic whole wheat from the shelf and dropped it into the front of the cart. Kylie began singing "Part of Your World," from *The Little Mermaid*, in her darling, wobbly voice, and tears rippled from Embry's eyes. She swiped them away quickly, not wanting her daughter to see her crying.

"I love your singing, Kylie girl. You make me so happy."

As she paused to check her list, she was surprised to hear someone saying hello.

She looked up to see Sylvia.

"I thought that was you," Sylvia said.

"Oh! Hi." She brushed a hand across her hair, hoping she didn't look frightful. "My goodness, how are you? Riki told us about what happened."

Sylvia appeared to be studying her face, which clarified that she must look a mess. "She told you about my wrist or something else?"

Embry frowned. What else would she have told her? "Your wrist. You fell in the rain," she added. Did Sylvia think she and Riki were gossiping behind her back?

"Yes. Well, it was only a sprain. I have to wear this clunky brace for a while, but it's better than a break." She glanced past Embry to the cart, eyeing Kylie's pink slicker, neon-yellow tutu, and froggy rain boots. "You look very stylish today, young lady."

"I have my tutu," Kylie announced proudly. She took the tulle in her hands, pulling on it for Sylvia to see.

"I noticed. It's very bright." She turned back to Embry. "Are you okay? You don't look well."

Embry fluttered a hand to the pendant at her neck. "Yes, I'm great. It's just—" A lump crept to her throat, lodging itself into place, making it so she couldn't talk.

"It's just what?" She cocked an eyebrow, and for a moment, it reminded Embry of a look her mama would give her, even though Sylvia was much younger than Embry's mom.

She flattened her hand to her chest. "I'm pregnant." It came out in a whisper, but as soon as the words escaped, Embry wished she could breathe them back in, hiding them inside her where they were supposed to stay.

"You're pregnant? Again?"

Embry nodded. "Yes." She gripped the heart pendant in a fist. "I can't believe I told you." She lowered her voice to barely a whisper, hoping to prevent Kylie from hearing, but she was too busy taking off her boots to listen. "Brandon doesn't know yet."

"Oh my. Why not?" She lowered her voice. "Not his?"

"No! Of course not. Why would you think that?"

Sylvia lifted a shoulder in a casual shrug. "It just popped into my head. People cheat."

"Well, I don't! And I haven't told him because I don't know how to yet. It was unexpected." She met her eyes with a pleading gaze. "Please don't say anything."

Sylvia's expression reminded Embry of the pictures in her old Raggedy Ann book where the doll had come to life and, upon hearing her mistress walk into the room, made a quick, slightly creepy change back to stillness. "Well, I'm sure he'll be thrilled."

"Yes, you're right. I'll tell him soon. It's just the acting thing, um—well, you know. Anyway. Please let us know if you need anything. We were so sorry to hear about your fall."

"In the scheme of things, I'm lucky. Very, very lucky. Lots of people don't survive falls like that," Sylvia said in a clipped tone. She took a jar of strawberry preserves from the shelf. "Have a good day. And congratulations."

"Thanks. And remember not to say anything. I just—"

She laughed and mimed locking her lips. "I'm a vault. Your secret is safe with me."

Embry smiled as she passed her. She kept the grin plastered to her face until she had turned the corner and was in the next aisle. It was then that she exhaled loudly. *This is bad.* How could she have told Sylvia before Brandon? It was all wrong. If she hadn't seen that woman at the entrance who made her feel hopeful about the baby, and if Sylvia hadn't reminded her of her mother for that split second, her secret would still be locked up tight.

"Mama, I get cookies?" Kylie was pointing to the bag of Oreos on the shelf. Normally, she would roll right past them, saying, *Next time, sweetie.* But today she said yes.

"Here you go."

Kylie gripped the bag in her little hands and brought it to her nose, inhaling plastic more than cookie, Embry assumed. "I love these, Mama. You're a good mama."

Embry tousled her hair. "You're my sweet girl."

~

So Embry was pregnant. Sylvia gripped the jar of jam and slammed it to the ground. Glass shattered near her boots, and the jam sat in grotesque clumps. It reminded her of Hugh and his sorry, sugar-free, cat-gut jam. She stepped around the mess and headed to the front of the store, where she found a clerk, easily identifiable in his red T-shirt. "Excuse me, but there's a broken jar in aisle seven. A child must've knocked it from the shelf." She rolled her eyes. "Kids these days."

"Yeah, no kidding," the young clerk said. "I'm on it."

She steered her cart to the opposite side of the store, but suddenly, the thought of shopping seemed overwhelming. Embry was pregnant with her third child. Unexpectedly, no less. *Lucky, lucky Embry.* And Sylvia had been ghosted by a married motherfucker. She gripped the cart handle, steadying herself from another imminent fall. A voice from within sneered, *Toughen up, you pathetic loser.*

With a determined stride, she abandoned the cart and fled from the store. The rain beat the earth relentlessly. After popping open her gigantic golf umbrella, she marched into the chaos. It wasn't like she would get wet. She was suited in the proper rain gear. She crossed the parking lot while the rain pelted the black umbrella. *Ha,* she thought. *Not even close.* She stormed toward her car, but as she neared it, her steps slowed. Was she ready to drive home and sit with Embry's secret?

Shaking her head, she tromped toward the coffeehouse across the lot. The café was warm and dry and smelled of freshly baked blueberry muffins.

This was better. A lovely barista with a tattoo of a broken, bleeding heart on her inner forearm took Sylvia's order. *How obvious, wearing her heart on her sleeve like that.*

Sylvia chose a table in the corner, setting her number in the center. Most of the other tables were filled. There was a group of young people with books spread out, and another with two women, their foreheads nearly touching as one spoke in a rapid whisper, her eyes darting after every few words as though she were checking for eavesdroppers. Sylvia wished she were closer so she could listen in. It always fascinated her to hear what other women talked about. Were they sharing secrets and pinkie swearing they'd never tell? And upon leaving, they'd rush to call another friend and spill the beans? Pretty little betrayals.

Directly in front of her was a father with his young son. The boy looked to be about two. He had a shock of blond hair that clearly hadn't been brushed that morning. She scanned the man's left hand for a ring. It was there, all right, bright and shiny. Had his wife allowed him to leave with their son looking like a street urchin? Maybe they had fought, and he had grabbed the small boy and left, barely missing a well-aimed frying pan that was careering across the room toward him.

On the other hand, it could be that she was a businesswoman who was finalizing an important project for Monday, and she was relieved to have her husband take their son out for some Sunday fun.

The man stared at his phone screen, scrolling now and then to read more of whatever was so enthralling. And that sweet little boy held a white plastic fork with a determined grip, and after two tries, he stabbed a piece of watermelon. Her hands quivered with the desire to clap. He put the food in his mouth and chewed. Sylvia wanted to shake the man. *Are you seeing this? Do you even know what's going on right in front of you, you big idiot? Your son—your own flesh and blood—just succeeded. And you missed it because you're too goddamn busy.* As if her wrath had drifted across the room and snatched him by the neck, the man turned, meeting Sylvia's eyes. "Your son is adorable," she said loudly, pointing.

The man nodded. "Thanks. He's a great kid." He set the phone on the table and spoke to the child. *Surprise, surprise.* Well, at least she had done some good today. Maybe that would make up for hurling the jar of jam to the floor, though it had felt undeniably satisfying to break something. Great, in fact. Maybe she was on to an idea here. She could open a newfangled type of recreation center where members would gear up with helmets and padding. As part of the membership, they'd be given a giant bucket of rocks, the kind that crack and break, that they could chuck at a concrete wall. She closed her eyes and imagined the place. Companies could have retreats and trainings there. Maybe even holiday parties. It would become all the rage. She laughed at her pun, unintended as it was.

A server arrived at her table with a warm blueberry muffin, the butter and jam on the side, exactly as she'd ordered it, along with a vanilla latte. A heart was swirled into the foam. How sweet. Must not have been made by the girl who took her order, or there would have been a slash down the middle. Sylvia picked up her knife and drew a zigzag down the center of the heart.

Cutting the muffin into two halves, she spread a healthy dollop of butter on each side, allowing it to melt into the bread. Then she added a thick layer of strawberry jam and took a bite. She closed her eyes again, this time to savor the deliciousness. Warm blueberry muffins would definitely be served at her rec center. God, she was on a roll! She could call it the Wreck Center—a place for the emotionally wrecked. She could already see the waiting list. It would be pages long.

As she sipped her latte, she contemplated how she would spend the rest of her day. A trip to the mall was in order. She needed a special gift for a special little guy. *Hunter.* How could Hugh say his own son was a Pomeranian? He'd even laughed about it. And then he'd said Lily was the crazy one. A sick individual, indeed. He wouldn't like what Sylvia had planned. But really, he should've known that playing with someone's emotions like that was dangerous. But alas, it was a risk he'd chosen to take. He'd started this game, but she would finish it.

CHAPTER FOURTEEN

Riki tucked herself into Chris's warm body and listened to the rain drum the ground outside. The gentle beat soothed her mind.

She sighed contentedly and ran a hand along his forearm. From his steady breathing, she knew he was still sleeping. How she wished her body would allow her to sleep in. But now her brain was booting up, and seconds later, it was humming at full speed as her to-do list started taking shape. She slipped out from under Chris's arm and tiptoed across the room to the bathroom. After washing her face and brushing her teeth, she wound her hair up in a messy bun and padded to the kitchen to make coffee. It was ten—early for a Sunday morning—but not too early to text Brandon about the pilot. She knew he worked the breakfast shift on Sundays. Embry had complained about it openly, lamenting the fact that her family couldn't go to church together.

Hey Brandon! I wanted to let you know I met the assistant to a writer/producer who's doing a pilot called Baggage last night. It's set in Louisiana, and they're currently casting! She said you can have your agent send her your headshot and résumé, and she'll get it to the casting office. Let me know if you're interested, and I'll send you her number. Say hi to Embry and the kids. :)

She hit "Send" and set her phone aside, ignoring the desperate little voice that wanted her to hold the phone in her hands and watch for his reply. Instead, she grabbed the tote that she'd abandoned by the door on Friday afternoon.

She woke her laptop and began scrolling through her emails. Only three relating to the little green man had rolled in. That wasn't so bad. The first one was from Mrs. Trainor.

Dear Miss McFarlan,

Thank you for excusing Darcy from the project. However, I think you've created a bigger problem. Now you are asking us to tell our children to LIE to the other kids in class. I really don't mean to harp on this, but you're putting me in a very uncomfortable position. If we can't get this resolved, I'm going to have to take this to Principal Rosenkrantz.

With best wishes for a positive resolution,
Cassandra Trainor

What the hell? These parents were such a pain. Why couldn't they just let her do her job? She tapped the tabletop with her pen, thinking about how she would respond, when Chris wandered from her room looking dazed. He planted his hands on the back of the sofa and shook his head. "Damn. Why'd you get up before noon? It's Sunday."

"The rain woke me, so I figured I might as well get some work done. I made coffee if you want some."

"Nah." He stretched his arms above his head and yawned. "I need more than just coffee. Do you want to hit Millie's Diner?"

No, no, I do not, she thought. She hated the bacon-y smell of diners. The stench clung to her hair and seeped into her skin, making it feel like she'd bathed in grease. To top it off, there was no escaping the syrup. Sticky droplets sat on the table or hid on the menus, waiting to attack her. Diners were swarming with germs, and she avoided them at all costs. "I'm not up for a big breakfast, but thanks. And I really need to work today. Some of the parents are all bent because I asked the kids to make leprechaun traps. Like that's a crime."

"Are you kidding?"

"No. It's irritating."

"Tell them to fuck off."

"I'd get sued for harassment or libel or something. And being that it's my first year, I'd end up fired. So yeah, bad idea."

"Don't let them get to you."

She smiled. "I'll try not to. They're just bored rich people who can get over it, as far as I'm concerned. Thanks for coming here last night."

"I'll call you later, okay?"

Just go! The thought was like a sudden flame in her head, but she immediately extinguished it and stood on her toes to kiss his cheek before he left. As she returned to her spot in front of her computer, she tried to focus, but the words on the screen blurred in front of her. Why was she so eager for Chris to go? It wasn't a good sign. With a sigh, she began typing a letter to the principal.

Before she had a chance to proofread her work, her phone buzzed, and her heart kicked up a notch as she saved the letter as a draft. With her focus on the leprechauns, she'd actually forgotten that she'd texted Brandon. She grabbed her phone and looked at the message.

> That's so cool. Thanks, Riki. Everyone's been talking about this pilot. I'll owe you big-time if I get this audition. Send me her info and I'll have my agent get my stuff to her today.

She gripped the phone and read it again. It was amazing how a tiny typed message could have such a profound effect on her body. It felt *good*, like the stomach-droppy feeling riding roller coasters gave her. And really, was it so wrong? No one knew. It wasn't like someone was going to sit her down in an interrogation room and quiz her on how she felt about her neighbor. She kept her feelings carefully guarded, and she would continue to do so. But here, alone in her apartment, it was fine. She closed her eyes and let her mind drift across the driveway and into his apartment. Embry and the kids didn't exist. He was just a lonely, single, aspiring actor . . . No, scratch that. In her fantasy, he would be a fellow teacher. Maybe a college professor. The thought of him having to do racy nude scenes with a gorgeous actress was gross. She shook her head and imagined him opening the door to her as a smile lit his face.

"Come on in, sweetness. Let me warm you up."

She would fall into his arms, and he would press her up against the door as his greedy lips found her neck. "Oh, Brandon," she whispered aloud. "Don't stop." She drew her hand to her neck and slid it down her throat.

Beep!

The sound of a text made her jump from her chair. What was she thinking? Well, she wasn't. She looked at the text.

Thanks again! :)

Only two words. Not necessary, really. Her mind sped ahead, leading her down a forbidden path. *He sent that second text to prolong our conversation.* It would be so easy to write a little something more. She could add a question and keep things going. *But guys like challenges.* So she'd leave it. Let him wonder. And she could fantasize that he was checking his phone every few minutes, wishing she'd respond. If she thought about him enough, would he *feel* it? She sighed. It didn't matter. But she was going to keep thinking about him all she wanted. In private. It wasn't hurting anyone. And she needed it. If she ever found someone like him—a guy who managed to make her feel comfortable and roller-coastery at the same time—she would marry him. *So much for my point system.* She had only just started and was already failing. Well, maybe it just needed fine-tuning. It was okay to dream about him in private, but when she saw him in person, she had to think of him as just another guy, nothing more. She could manage that. It would be fine.

~

Sylvia stepped off the escalator and headed for the grand entrance of Tiffany & Co. A bulky guard stood near the door, as unmoving as a statue, though more like a fat Buddha than a Michelangelo. She breezed past him. He seemed bored, even though his shift had presumably recently started. Wouldn't it be fun to sprint through the store acting like a criminal just to see how fast he could move? But no, she wouldn't do that. She smiled at the salesclerk (or maybe she preferred to be called a diamond expert) and paused to admire a case that could've been filled with stars, it shone so brightly. It was true that nothing compared to a Tiffany diamond. She strolled to the area where baby items were displayed, and while she had envisioned something silver and timeless for Hugh's baby, it was the earthenware elephant bank that caught her eye. It was creamy and white, adorned with tiny green polka dots. Perfect for baby Hunter. And even more perfect for Hugh. Sylvia could almost feel the fear that would chill him when he saw the gift. He had often joked that she had the memory of an elephant. So yes, this was the ideal gift. It would make Hugh sweat and Lily wonder.

She turned, and the saleswoman was right there. Slow day at Tiffany's, apparently. "I'd like to purchase the elephant bank, please."

"Oh, it's precious, isn't it? I can't wait for my daughter-in-law to get pregnant so I can buy one for her. It's perfect for either sex."

"Yes. It really is. I'd like it wrapped too."

"Certainly. It'll only take a minute."

"Thanks. I'll just browse a bit while you get it ready." She slipped her wallet from her purse and passed the woman her AmEx.

Now Sylvia could stroll freely without people watching her. They had her card, so it wasn't like they'd worry she was going to break open a glass display case and make a run for it, her pockets sagging with sparkling diamonds. Maybe in another lifetime. She smiled to herself. She would actually make a good jewel thief. No one would suspect her.

The woman returned with a big blue bag and receipt that Sylvia promptly signed.

"Enjoy."

"Thanks. I'm sure my dear friends will be thrilled."

Five minutes later, she was back in her car. She took the coastal route the entire way home, enjoying the brief glimpses of the gray ocean as she headed south. The sea churned, restless and angry, like it was trying to escape the very earth that contained it. *How much we have in common,* Sylvia thought. The sun battled the clouds, making a valiant effort to dry out the wet morning.

By the time she turned onto the long driveway, feeble sunshine was flickering on the wet asphalt. Squinting, she slowed her car but had to stop midway. A ridiculous truck fit for a hay-hauling cowboy was blocking the drive. *Blergh.* Did this monstrosity belong to a friend of the Taylors? As much as she wanted to pound her fist to the horn and hold it there until the guilty party appeared, she put her car into park and shut off the engine. No need to be rude to the neighbors' friends.

To her surprise, a young man stepped out just as she did. Tucking a strand of his longish sandy-blond hair behind his ear, he greeted her with a lopsided grin. "Hey there. I'm blocking your spot, aren't I?"

She studied him unabashedly. She knew from experience the effect that her piercing blue eyes had on men. Anyone, really. "Indeed. Who are you?"

He flipped his keys in his hand. "Dave. I'm here to fix some stairs and a garbage disposal. Do you know anything about that?" he asked, the smile still hanging on his face. Sylvia knew he believed his charm would allow him to leave his giant vehicle exactly where he'd parked it.

"As a matter of fact, I do. The stair is right up there." She pointed toward her apartment. "It's the seventh. And the garbage disposal is Embry's in the bottom unit across the way. She was having trouble with it on Friday."

"Coolio, Julio."

This guy looked more like a surfer than a handyman. She raised a brow. "You spoke with Jonathan, I presume?"

"Yeah, yeah." He dropped his keys into his pocket. "He knows my dad." Nodding as though this explained everything, he added, "My dad's a real estate agent, and he's helping him with selling the place."

Sylvia forced her expression to remain neutral. *Jonathan is selling the place? This is absurd.* A lesser woman would've flinched at the news, but Sylvia knew better. The smaller the reaction, the more Dave would spill. "Oh."

"So yeah, I'm helping out with a few things before it goes on the market. Making a little extra moola." He rubbed his palms together. "I'm a screenwriter. Starving until I get my big break."

"Right. I understand." She softened her gaze, allowing her eyes to work their magic. "So is your dad one of the big real estate agents in town? Would I recognize his name?"

"Probably not. His name is Patrick Sharp. He does listings in Santa Monica and Venice, but he's not like the über-successful dudes on the reality shows. Bummer."

"I'm sure he does just fine. So are you Dave Sharp?"

"Yeah."

"I'll be sure to keep my eye out for your name on the big screen."

"Right on. Thanks!" He wiped a hand across his smile. Oh, how easy it was to flatter people. "So, uh, do you need me to move my truck, or is it cool to leave it there?"

She waved a hand. Suddenly, the parking situation didn't matter. "It's fine."

"Cool." He shifted his gaze to her car. "She's a beauty," he said in an awed tone.

His reaction was no surprise. People loved classic Ford Mustang convertibles. Hers was a snappy candy-apple red. It evoked a feeling of *fun, fun, fun!* In reality, she should drive a heavy semitruck loaded with something toxic. Something she could mow Jonathan down with. Who the hell did he think he was to sell Nadine's place?

"Sixty-eight?" he asked, clearly impressed. He was cute. Not that she was looking. It was merely a fact. Besides, he was in his early twenties—practically a child in man years.

"Precisely. Good eye. The doors are unlocked. Feel free to take a look inside if you like."

"Awesome!" He opened the passenger door and passed her the Tiffany bag before sliding in. "How long have you had her?"

"Three years."

Sinking into the soft leather seat, he smiled. "You're so lucky." Popping up, he added, "I could sit here all day, but I've got shit to get to. Thanks for being cool about my truck." He flaunted a smile again. As he stepped out of the car, something tumbled to the damp ground. He grabbed for it and passed it to her. "Sorry. I didn't see it there."

She slipped the Tiffany bag to her good wrist and took the small black camera case from him.

His brow furrowed. "Is it okay?"

"I'm sure it is. The case is padded."

"Phew! I'm here to fix stuff, not break it. I'll just grab my tools and get to work."

"Thanks." Once he turned toward his truck, she looked at the camera in her hand. Dave had proven to be a virtual treasure trove. Her insides quivered with excitement. The camera had to be Hugh's. He'd brought it when they'd gone to the horse races the week before last. Had it fallen from his pocket? Did he even know it was missing?

As much as she wanted to scroll through the pictures right there in the middle of the driveway, she needed to do this in private.

Once inside, she took Hugh's camera and linked it to her laptop with the cord that had been tucked in the case. *Download all items?* it asked.

"But of course. I'd love to," she said aloud as she clicked *yes.*

And just like that, his entire collection of photos started their voyage to her laptop. A dialogue box popped up, alerting her that thirty minutes remained. "No rush," she said to the screen. "I have all day." She opened a new tab and typed *Patrick Sharp* into the search bar. In seconds, she had his phone number and email address, and she typed them both into the notes section of her phone.

Of course Jonathan would find a way to wreak havoc on her home life. Bad things always came in threes. First her wrist, then Hugh, and now Jonathan selling her home. She wished a Wreck Center actually existed. Shattering something—or someone, for that matter—would be quite satisfying right now.

But she would be fine. *It's about being three steps ahead at all times,* she thought. It was that simple. Nothing could break her. She was a survivor. Her dad had made damn sure of that. Tears made her vision blur, but she squeezed her eyes shut, refusing to let them fall.

Sylvia's knees rested on the stained blue corduroy sofa as she stared out the living room window counting cars, telling herself the fifth one would be her dad's car. And then the tenth, the fifteenth . . . the thirtieth. But theirs wasn't a busy street. The thirtieth car never came. And her dad's dented blue Chevy never did either. She waited until the streetlights flickered on. Fear ate at her little body as she wondered what had happened.

She counted to fifty, just like he'd told her to. Usually when they played hide-and-seek, she counted only to twenty, but today, he'd said fifty was better. She skipped from her small room to the tiny family area, calling,

"I'll find you, Daddy!" after those fifty seconds. But he wasn't in any of his usual hiding places.

After shouting for him, she cautiously stuck her head outside to look in the tiny garage. His car wasn't there anymore. She wasn't supposed to leave the apartment, so why would he drive to a hiding spot?

She thought and thought. Her dad had to run errands a lot. Maybe someone had called him and needed him right away, and he'd left, forgetting all about the game. She decided that must've been what happened, so she crept onto the sofa to wait. When it started to get dark, her stomach ached with fear. She picked up the phone to call the number her mom had made her memorize after the divorce. It was the pager number she used at the hospital where she was a nurse. She wasn't supposed to call it except in an emergency.

She tapped the buttons for her dad's phone number followed by the tic-tac-toe sign, then hung up, just like she'd practiced, and climbed back onto the sofa. She pressed her hands and face to the glass, straining to see in the darkness. There were no neighbors to run to, because she didn't know the neighbors. This wasn't her home. It was the apartment her dad had moved into after the divorce. Her mom hated it. "It's in a shitty part of town," she'd said. The side of her mouth would twitch up in disgust, instantly injecting anxiety into Sylvia's veins.

By the time her mom called back, Sylvia could speak only in sobs. Her mom said so many bad words, it made her cry even harder. She hadn't meant to make her mom angry. Her mom told her to stay put and she'd be there as soon as she could. Sylvia was too scared to leave the sofa. She desperately wanted Grizzly, the bear her dad had won for her at a carnival, but worry kept her rooted to the spot on the saggy sofa. She counted six tiny brown holes on the corduroy cushion.

The sky had grown black by the time she heard the pounding on the door and her mother's voice. She ran for the door, asking who it was even though she knew it was her mom. When she unlocked the bolt, her mother charged in, grabbing her and checking for injuries. Sylvia melted in her mother's arms. But too soon, her mom released her to stalk toward her dad's room. A wild cry emerged from her, and Sylvia peeked in from behind. The closet door was wide open, and nothing remained but a few plastic hangers. He was gone.

"Did he say anything? Try to remember, Sylvia. What did he say? Where did he go?"

"We were playing hide-and-seek. I looked and looked, but I never found him," Sylvia sobbed.

Her mom pulled her into her arms. "It will be all right now," she said.

Everything else was a haze. She couldn't remember packing her things. The only memory that stayed was hugging Grizzly to her chest on the ride back home. Her dad's face was now a blurry memory. She didn't try to sharpen the image in her mind. Blurry was better.

She stood and moved to the kitchen to make a cup of tea and some buttered toast. Her laptop had dinged, alerting her that the pictures were loaded, but she wasn't prepared to look at them just yet. It'd be best to do it with a little something in her belly. It felt like hours had passed since the blueberry muffin. As she reached the bread box, she remembered she didn't have any bread. Why had she run from the grocery store like a maniac? She should've stayed to finish the job. So what if Embry was pregnant? It didn't affect her in the least. She pulled some crackers from the pantry. Funny that she had saltines but no bread. She should probably offer them to Embry. Poor thing had looked rather green this morning. As she nibbled a cracker in the middle of the kitchen, an idea struck.

Why hadn't she thought of this sooner? Well, no matter. She would text Embry with her request tonight. Finishing the cracker, she dusted her hands on a kitchen towel and took a swig of water before resuming her spot in front of her laptop. Showtime!

She started with the most recent. How many photos had he taken at the horse races? Scrolling through quickly, she came upon pictures of the two of them at Christmastime. There they were, standing in front of the giant tree at Disneyland. She'd looked so festive in her red-wool Kate Spade coat with the cute bow at the collar. He wore the creamy fisherman's sweater she'd found for him. She sped past the photos she recognized until she reached one she didn't.

Hugh was pictured standing proudly next to an adjustable bed where a hospital-gown-clad Lily lay with a freshly born baby in her arms. She studied the photo with interest. It was fascinating that women lost all sense of vanity after childbirth, allowing others to photograph them when they looked like they'd just plowed a field barefoot in the blazing sun. Every picture she'd seen on Facebook or otherwise was essentially the same. If she were to have a child, she'd be certain to apply a touch of makeup before any photos were taken. It's not like the baby would change in the first fifteen minutes of life. No need to show the world that she'd been through a tough ordeal.

A knock sounded, and she darted her eyes to the door. Flipping her laptop shut, she crossed the room and peered through the peephole. *Dave.*

"Is it all fixed?" she asked as she opened the door.

"Uh, no." He looked legitimately disappointed, as though he had really tried. How cute. "All I could do was tape it up." He shrugged. "I had some bright-orange tape, but it's not caution tape or anything. It's a bigger fix than Jonathan described. I'll let him know he needs to get someone else out here."

"Well, thanks for trying. Hopefully the garbage disposal will be straightforward."

"Yeah. No kidding. See you later."

"Bye."

She closed the door and sighed. Leave it to Jonathan to cheap out on repairs. Resuming her spot in front of her laptop, she wondered what she would do with the photos. They could be of some use. The camera, too, for that matter. *Huh.* Maybe her luck was taking a turn for the better.

CHAPTER FIFTEEN

Monday, March 13

Before sunrise, Embry set the plastic container outside her door, just as Sylvia had asked. She tried not to think about how odd the request had been. While drying dishes last night, she'd received the text from Sylvia, asking to meet between their apartments for a quick chat. Even though the rain had started up again, she'd sloshed outside with the hood of her jacket up, praying fiercely that Sylvia wasn't going to ask if she'd told Brandon the baby news yet. The expression she'd worn as she stood there in the grocery aisle had been downright strange.

"Hi there," Sylvia said from beneath her massive umbrella. "Did Dave the repair guy fix your garbage disposal today?"

Couldn't she have texted that? Embry shivered. "Um, he did. It's fine now," she said stiffly, bracing herself for questions about the baby.

"Lucky you. Sadly for me, Dave couldn't fix the step." She raised a brow. "Which means I'll have to call Jonathan again. For two reasons."

Embry reeled in her desire to demand she just get to the point already. "What's the other reason?" She wondered why Sylvia was being so cryptic. And the look on her face was a little scary, to be honest.

"Are you aware that Jonathan is putting our place on the market?"

"What? No! He's going to sell this?" She nearly dropped her umbrella and scrambled to tighten her grip.

"Apparently so. Dave told me. His dad is Jonathan's real estate agent."

"What on earth? What does that mean for us?"

Sylvia shrugged. "I wouldn't know. But I'll find out. It doesn't sound good." Embry wanted to ask more, but Sylvia continued before she had the chance. "There's one more thing I wanted to talk to you about." She paused to take a breath. "I have a favor to ask of you." She almost looked embarrassed, which was unusual.

"Sure. Do you need help with dinner? Is your arm bothering you?"

"No, no." She smiled. "I'm building up the muscles in my left arm, which isn't a bad thing, I suppose," she added, lifting her umbrella higher. "I called you out here because I have a situation with my job." She smiled that uncomfortable smile again. "We're randomly drug tested, and I have some inside information that it's going to be tomorrow." Embry felt her eyes grow wide, and Sylvia shook her head. "Oh, don't look so worried. I'm not a druggie, but with my wrist, I've taken several Vicodin that weren't prescribed to me for this injury." She frowned. "They told me to take two Motrin and to rest it, as if that would do the trick. The bottom line is, I'm worried I'll be written up. This is going to sound bizarre, but will you pee in this cup first thing in the morning and set it outside your door?" She clumsily fished from her coat pocket a small plastic container like the ones Embry used to pack grapes or Goldfish crackers in for Kylie.

Embry rushed to take it, not wanting Sylvia to drop it in the rain. A reflex, not a sign of her willingness to comply, but a wide grin spread across Sylvia's face. Embry struggled for words. "I, um . . ." She could picture her grandmother, pointing her polished cane at her as she said, "For crying out loud, say no, young lady. When in doubt, you always say no." Well, Embry didn't have any trouble saying no, but this request was so disturbing, it left her uncharacteristically speechless.

Sylvia's lips snapped into a tight line before she spoke again. "Look, I can't afford to lose my job, especially with the uncertainty surrounding the sale of our apartments. I'm hoping I can trust you to not say anything, the same way you're trusting me with your secret." She'd raised one eyebrow just slightly, and Embry could feel the threat hovering in the air.

"I'll help," she muttered, wishing she could throw the stupid cup and rush inside and tell Brandon about the baby right there and then so she didn't have to go along with this stupid plan. But instead, she smiled sweetly and said, "I wouldn't want you to get written up at work."

Sylvia nodded. "Leave it on your porch, and I'll pick it up before I go to work. I told you once, and I'll say it again: I'm a vault." She repeated the locking of her lips before turning back to her apartment.

Nightmares about getting written up by a police officer for urinating in public had knocked Embry from sleep throughout the night, and she practically jumped out of bed at dawn to fulfill her promise. After that, unsettling thoughts had chased her all morning until a call from her brother had given her some sweet relief.

Brandon walked in with Kylie lying flat across his arms. "Vroom, vroom!" He swooped her near the ground. "And the airplane has reached its final destination." He landed her on her feet as she giggled. "Go kiss your mama. She looks tired."

Kylie scrambled to sit in Embry's lap and placed her hands on both cheeks. "I love you, Mama." She touched her nose to Embry's and patted her hair. "My pretty mommy," she said before hopping down from her lap.

Brandon tousled her curls. "Smart girl." He turned to Embry. "Was that your brother who called? It sounded like he was asking for a favor." He unbuckled Carson, who was frantically swiping his Cheerios from the tray of his high chair, and lifted him out.

Embry stood to fill her water glass with ice cubes. *He's not the only one asking for favors, though his wasn't completely bizarre.* She sipped the cold water. It was strange, but she couldn't seem to get enough ice water during her pregnancies. She hoped Brandon wouldn't notice, but then again, maybe it would be easier if he put all the clues together instead of having to tell him. Maybe she could even act like she'd started to wonder, too, and they could take a pregnancy test together. Facing him, she said, "Yeah, that was Evan." She swirled the cubes in her glass, then sat back at the table. *Notice the ice, Brandon!* But he only looked at her with a raised brow. "He asked if we could watch Gracie."

"His dog? That's kind of a lot for him to ask, don't you think?"

Embry frowned. How could you place a limit on what you'd do for family? She would donate a kidney for her brother. Watching his dog was nothing in the scheme of things. "It'll be fine. You know how much he hates to ask for help. He wouldn't have done it if he wasn't in a bind."

"It'll be fine?" he asked as his eyebrows shot to his forehead.

"Yes, it'll be fine. He'll leave us with plenty of food. It's not like it'll cost us anything. Anyway, I already said yes."

"You didn't think you should run it by me?" he asked with a forced smile. "What if I don't want to watch a dog? It's going to poop all over the yard, and it'll need walking—"

"So I'll pick up the poop. And I'm more than capable of walking a dog." She threw him a look. This new short-temperedness had her nerves on edge.

"That's not the point!" His voice was sharp, startling Carson. He set the baby in the swing and spun to face her. "I'm already stressed enough. I don't want to add a goddamn dog to the mix, okay? Tell him we can't. Say I'm allergic."

"Brandon Taylor, you watch your mouth. And no, I won't lie to my brother."

"This is unbelievable. Do you have any idea how much pressure I'm under?"

She lowered her voice, hoping to calm him. "I get it. But Evan said it'll only be for a few weeks. His dog walker got a full-time job, and instead of finding someone new, he asked if we'd watch her until he moves down here."

"Can't a neighbor watch the dog? I'm serious, Embry. I can't handle any more change right now. I was counting on the soap. Adena led me to believe it was a done deal, and I'm not getting any younger. Can't you understand that? I'm working my ass off, and I can barely make the rent."

"I get it. I really do, baby. All I want to do is help you, but I can't say no to Evan."

"But you'll say no to me. That's just great," he snapped before storming into their bedroom and slamming the door behind him. The clanking of his dumbbells sounded. Well, it was better than him taking off in his truck, she reasoned as her eyes filled. She sank into the chair and covered her face with her hands.

"Mama! Carsie is falling! Hurry, Mama!"

She jumped from the table and rushed to Carson, who had tipped forward in the swing and was hanging on by only one strap around his chubby leg. In a fluid movement, she scooped him up and held him close. If he had fallen, goodness knows what could've happened. He could've broken a tiny bone or gotten a concussion. There was a plush rug covering the wood floor, but still. What if he'd hit his fragile little head? And all because Brandon hadn't bothered to buckle him in. She bit back the desire to call him in so she could yell at him. Instead, she kneeled down to where Kylie was. "You're such a good big sister. Thank you for helping Carsie." Wrapping her free arm around Kylie, she kissed her forehead.

Standing, she said, "Your uncle Evan is going to bring his dog to stay with us next week. Will you be a big helper with Gracie too?"

"No doggie on couch." She shook her finger and spoke in a tone that mimicked a grown-up.

"That's right, sweetheart. The dog stays on the floor. We can take her on walks and play with her. It'll be fun, right?"

She clapped her hands. "She come over today, Mommy?"

"Not today. Next week on Tuesday."

"I get a water bowl for her," she said, scurrying toward the kitchen.

Maybe she shouldn't have told her about Gracie just yet. Kylie didn't have a grasp on time. Well, with any luck, her enthusiasm would get Brandon on board. She kissed Carson's head again and hugged him close, wishing the morning had gone differently. Maybe it *was* time to consider moving back home. She shivered. The baby news might be the final straw.

But he wanted more kids. Eventually. When the time was right. *Damn, Embry. We've gotta be more careful.* That's what he'd said after she'd told him about Carson. But he'd brought her a carton of strawberry ice cream along with a bouquet of flowers from the market that day.

With all that was going on now, she couldn't dump more pressure on him. He was already near a breaking point. For heaven's sake, he was only twenty-five. Most guys his age were still single and whooping it up. And here he was, pushing the boulder uphill trying to make it in Hollywood, all while working to provide for his family. She felt a little sorry for him, but dammit if he hadn't acted like a jerk. She tried to swallow back her anger, but her stomach churned violently. She fumbled to set Carson on his play mat before racing to the bathroom. Kylie's potty seat was on the toilet, and she tossed it aside before retching into the bowl. Sweat beaded across her forehead, and she released a tiny breath, hoping it would calm the raging volcano that was her body. As though an angry alien were trying to escape from her belly, clawing at her esophagus and kicking her intestines, she was sick again. She stood frozen, hoping the stillness would cause the nausea to subside. Counting to ten, she attempted a breath and waited. Her body remained quiet. It was over. She flushed and replaced the potty seat. She washed her hands and rinsed her mouth. Twice. And then she went to retrieve Carson, who had rolled his way next to the sofa.

As much as she wanted to feel sorry for herself, there was no time. She had to get Kylie to the Mom's Morning Out program in fifteen minutes. Brandon usually took her, but apparently he wasn't going to today. She placed Carson in his infant seat and clicked the buckles before poking her head through their bedroom door. "I'm taking the kids," she said flatly. "Kylie has her school."

Brandon set a dumbbell on the floor and turned to her. "Huh?"

"I'm taking Kylie to class."

He yanked out his earbud. "I can't do it. I'm in the middle of my workout."

She closed her eyes, willing herself to stay calm. "I didn't ask you to do it. I told you I'm doing it, just like I've been doing everything else for the kids lately."

He gaped at his dumbbells, as though they would commiserate with him. *How dare my wife call me out on my crap!* Was that what he was thinking? "I'm not going to argue with you anymore. If you want me to take her, just ask."

"Don't worry about it. I'm on my way out." Even as she said the words, she was hoping he'd insist, taking both kids so she could lay her throbbing head on a pillow. Just for a few minutes. Maybe sip some bubbly water. But he didn't. She closed the door and clambered outside with the children, understanding for the first time the old expression about the fine line between love and hate. She knew in her heart she didn't hate him. Of course not. But she hated how he was acting.

As Embry stepped onto the long driveway, she looked up to see Riki loaded down with her work bag. Goodness, she seemed to have a never-ending stack of papers. Embry smiled as Riki jogged toward her.

"Hey! Good morning, Em. Hi, Kylie. Hi, Carson."

Embry couldn't help but return her smile. Riki was always so cheery. Brandon had commented on it once. *That girl's always smiling. Have you noticed that? I don't think she's had one bad day.* Her smile dropped from her face as she recalled Kylie's words from yesterday, but she quickly shook the bad thoughts away. Ky was three. And besides that, Riki would never make a move on her husband. "Good morning. Off to school?"

"Yep," she said, fumbling with her purse. "I'm totally running late. Fingers crossed there's no traffic," she added with a laugh. "Now if I can only find my keys." She yanked her purse open wide, and something familiar caught Embry's eye.

It can't be. She stepped closer, not even trying to be subtle about looking into Riki's purse. "That's Brandon's headshot! Why do you have it?"

"Huh?" The color seemed to drain from her face. "What? Where?"

"In your purse." She pointed. "It's right there."

"Omigod! Right!" She slapped a hand to her forehead before taking it out and handing it to Embry. "I meant to return this to you guys, but I honestly forgot all about it. I'm thinking it must've gotten mixed in with my papers when I babysat. I found it in a pile of spelling tests. Funny, huh?"

Embry took the photo. "Yeah. Funny," she said without humor. "Thanks for returning it."

"Sure," she said, still digging in her purse. She lifted her keys. "Found them! I better run. Have a great day!"

Embry shuttled Kylie to the car, her mind still tangled in the conversation. Had Riki been acting weird, or was she just flustered because she was running late? Probably the latter. And she was probably embarrassed that she'd accidentally taken something from the apartment. Riki was a nice person. *Very* nice. But seeing Brandon's photo in her purse coupled with Kylie's comment was making her stomach ache. Embry knew Riki thought he was handsome. Everyone did. It was just something she accepted. But she would not put up with someone coming after him, and especially not a trusted friend. That would hurt more than she could bear.

～

Sylvia sat at her kitchen table with a mug of hot coffee and pressed "Play" on the video she'd made. The pregnancy test sat on her kitchen counter.

A blur of pink washed through the window as a dizzying euphoria coursed through her. Maybe she should've set the video to music. It would've been such a nice touch. Delight settled in her belly as she watched the first pink line appear followed by the magical second line. She sighed happily, her body limp with joy.

It had been so easy. She'd dipped the stick in Embry's pee, but of course hadn't needed to record that, because presumably, she had peed on the stick in the privacy of her own bathroom. Hugh wouldn't expect her to document that on film.

She'd placed the stick on a paper towel on the kitchen counter and used time-lapse video to capture the moment. It had felt so real, happy tears had formed in her eyes as she'd watched the two lines appear. Would Hugh tear up when he saw the video? Or would beads of sweat form along his hairline as his stomach rumbled and lurched? The father of two babies. Irish twins! Oh . . . she would have to use that in her message to him. Not today. No, she had to carefully construct her plans. First things first. And then she'd blast him with the delightful video. It would be a veritable kick to the crotch.

～

Riki sprinted up the steps to campus, her pulse racing. How could she have forgotten to move the headshot? She reviewed the conversation in her mind. Embry had believed her. Jeez, she hoped she'd believed her. She adjusted her tote and hurried into the main quad.

"Riki?"

She pivoted to see Principal Rosenkrantz approaching with long strides.

"Good morning!" She smiled, hoping he wasn't going to comment on her tardiness. As he neared, she noticed his eyes were all squinty, making him look angry. *Shoot! But it could be the sun,* she thought.

He gave her a brief nod, the stern look remaining on his face even though he was now in the shadow of the building. "I'd like to have a word. My office, please."

Why would he need to talk to her about being late in his office? It would make her even later . . . *Oh, crap!* She hadn't sent the email. It was still sitting in her drafts folder. "Sure," she said, forcing a smile. This was so not how she wanted to start her day. If she were at her old school, Principal Griffin would've had a laugh with her about the ridiculousness of the email complaints while they brainstormed solutions over a box of chocolates. Principal Griffin had a secret stash for such occasions.

As she walked into the office, she scanned the wall. It was lined on one side with tissue-paper butterflies made by a kindergarten class and limericks written by a first-grade class on the other. *I wonder if a parent complained about the butterflies,* she thought bitterly. And weren't limericks rude? How dare they teach precious children about this ugly form of poetry at such an impressionable age! She followed the principal past Ms. Harper, his assistant, into his large office.

He motioned to the tiny plastic chair that sat opposite his desk, and she sat. It was kid-size, and she immediately felt at a disadvantage.

"Do you know why you're here, Miss McFarlan?"

She crossed her legs, trying to get comfortable, but they were too long for the stupid little chair. "Is it because of the leprechaun-trap assignment? Mrs. Trainor mentioned she might email you."

He nodded solemnly. "It is. How would you evaluate your handling of the situation?"

At least he wanted to hear what she had to say. Hopefully he recognized how silly Mrs. Trainor's complaints were. She leaned forward. "I think I handled it well. Quite a few parents chimed in after Mrs. Trainor's initial email, and I logged their opinions on whether they wanted their child to participate or not." She hesitated as she recalled her list and hoped he wouldn't ask to see it. She'd have to make a new version without the current label of "Crazy Parents." Should she tell him she meant to send him an email, or would that make her sound flaky and forgetful?

Definitely flaky. She straightened. "I thought making the project optional was a good solution."

Principal Rosenkrantz listened with his hands folded on the desk as she spoke. Very casually, he leaned back and rubbed his chin. "Mrs. Trainor told you she would bring this to my attention. Did it occur to you that you should've alerted me?"

Heat sprang up Riki's neck, and she was certain her face was scarlet. *Great.* She was going to be written up because she'd forgotten to do something *over the weekend.* "Yes. I should've emailed you," she responded, her tone flat.

He squinted and appeared to be holding his breath. He looked like an angry toddler ready to burst. "But you didn't. And that's a problem, Miss McFarlan. A big one. You know I'm very supportive of the teachers here. However, when I'm bombarded by a couple of irate parents first thing Monday morning, and I haven't a clue as to what it's about, it puts me in a very awkward position. Do you understand?"

"The Trainors came to see you this morning?"

"Mrs. Trainor and Mrs. Johanson came to see me. They were waiting outside my office when I arrived. I didn't even get the chance to have a cup of coffee." He said this as though it were an equal outrage. "Mrs. Trainor made claims that with your 'flip response'—that's a direct quote, mind you—you invited an opportunity for the matter to take an argumentative turn, causing her to feel that she was getting bullied by other parents. Mrs. Johanson came in support of her. She and her husband were both extremely upset by your response."

"What? My response was to let each family decide if the project was right for their child."

"Well, that's not how they see it." He sighed. "And please keep your emotions in check. I've already had to deal with excited parents." He pushed a stack of papers across his desk toward her. "Mrs. Trainor printed these out for me. I've highlighted the emails you might not have seen."

She picked up the top page. It was the first one Cassandra had sent. Looking to Principal Rosenkrantz, she took the entire stack, skimming through them, trying to decipher what he was talking about. When she reached the fifth page, her breath caught in her chest. She hadn't seen this. Oh no. *Shit, shit, shit.* She'd gotten so caught up in the text from Brandon, she hadn't sent the email to Principal Rosenkrantz, let alone read any new ones that had come in.

From Janelle's mom:

> Are you kidding me? Please tell me this is an April Fools' joke a month early.

And from little Jeremy's mom:

> First you call my son's diet crap, and now you're calling us a bunch of liars because we choose to follow some sweet traditions? I think you need to mind your own business and keep your mouth shut.

Riki looked up from the emails to see the severe look on Principal Rosenkrantz's face. "As I'm sure you can see, she has a point. Things escalated. And something you should keep in mind is that Mrs. Trainor and both Mr. and Mrs. Johanson sit on the board of directors for Ocean Avenue," he said, enunciating each word for emphasis. "To refresh your recollection, Elliott Johanson is a prominent attorney. The last thing this school needs is a lawsuit."

"They threatened to sue?" Her voice was fit for finding a spider crawling on her arm, not someone who was keeping her emotions in check. She swallowed and tried again. "I'm sorry, but how could the school be blamed for this?"

His lips turned down, making him look like a droopy dog. "Oh, I'm sure they could find a way. It might get thrown out, but it would be a mess for me, and I don't like getting caught in a hornets' nest." He folded his hands on the desk once again, the picture of a composed principal. "Now, I've fixed the problem for the moment. I've reassured both moms that you and I agreed together that the other parents acted in an inappropriate fashion. Like I've said before, I'll protect my staff, but it's hard to when I'm not in the loop. I led them to believe that we chatted over the weekend about this and that you were equally concerned for her." He pinned his gaze on her. "Do you understand what I'm saying? We talked this weekend."

Riki felt like she'd been sucker punched. Her principal had to *lie* for her? And he was asking *her* to lie? This was ridiculous. Not to mention, he'd be watching her like a hawk for the rest of the school year. Another mistake and she'd be sent to talk to Ms. Hammacher, the head of school. This was bad. She blinked hard and forced herself to think of Disneyland, the beach—anything to stave off tears. Crying in front of her principal would only make things worse.

"Yes," Riki said in a quiet voice. "Where do we stand with the traps? Can I just cancel the project altogether? Had I known it would cause such an uproar, I never would've planned it."

"Oh, don't cancel it now. Mrs. Trainor is on board, and Mrs. Johanson followed suit. As upset as they were about the bitter reactions, they've decided to rise above the fray. They suggested we turn it into an art contest. That way, it takes the focus off the leprechaun, but the kids have something to work toward. To be honest, I thought it was a brilliant solution."

Riki tried to look relieved. "Great. That sounds like a fun idea. Um, what is the prize for the contest? Did Mrs. Trainor have some suggestions?" *Or demands.*

"We'll leave that up to you. I'm sure you can come up with something wonderfully creative."

"Okay. I'll get right on that." She stood. "Thanks for taking the time to fill me in. I appreciate your support."

"You're welcome. Have a good day."

She turned and rushed for the door. Only six minutes remained until the bell rang—hardly enough time to get everything squared away for the first lesson, but she trailed slowly to her classroom. Chris had said to tell them to eff off. That wasn't what she needed. She wanted reassurance, understanding. If Brandon were here, he'd look at her with those sincere blue eyes and draw her into a hug. She could almost feel his lips in her hair, whispering words of support. He'd take her hand and say, *Twirl, girl! Cheer up.*

No! Stop, stop, stop! She slapped a hand to the side of her leg. Her tote slid from her arm and crashed to the ground, the stapled strap torn and dangling. *Shit! This day just keeps getting better.* She grabbed the bag by the one good strap and headed to her classroom. She hadn't even come close to earning enough points to buy a new one. It was so difficult. *He* made it difficult. Maybe she could force herself to picture Principal Rosenkrantz when she saw him. That would shut her feelings off in two seconds flat.

CHAPTER SIXTEEN

Embry straightened the HOME IS WHERE MY HORSE IS throw pillow where it sat on the sofa. It was made of a soft blue chambray with embroidered letters that resembled lassos. Auntie Boots had given it to her before they'd headed for California. *Don't forget where you come from, baby girl,* she'd said.

"I haven't forgotten, Auntie Boots." She abandoned the cushions and sank into a kitchen chair. "But I might have lost a little bit of the girl I was." A lump formed in her throat as she picked up her phone. Just one touch on the screen, and it would ring Mama. But what would she say? *Hi, Mama. Everything's going great here. Brandon can't get an acting job to save his life, and he's clomping around like a poked bear, we're near broke, and I'm pregnant again!* A tear rolled down her cheek. The truth was, she wouldn't be able to get that many words out, because as soon as she heard Mama's voice, she'd surely burst into gaspy sobs. She rested her head on the table and tried to focus on three good things. *I have two healthy babies and a roof over my head. And I have a wonderful husband who's . . . falling apart on me.* No! She hadn't meant to let her mind go there. The whole point of the exercise was to think positively.

But what if the Hollywood struggle was slowly destroying the bright-eyed man he'd been? No amount of positive thinking could fix that. Life had seemed so sparkly and glamorous those first few months here. But when they actually went to the city of Hollywood (which was part of a humongous entity everyone referred to as "LA"), she'd struggled to find the right words. It was only when they'd passed Grauman's Chinese Theatre on the historic Walk of Fame that Embry had yanked on Brandon's hand in delight, pulling him toward the handprints in the cement. "Can you picture getting your handprints done here one day? We'll throw a big party at the fanciest hotel and invite everyone!"

His smile lit his entire face, reflecting off her wide grin. They were so deep in their own world, their minds full of fantasy, that it was easy to overlook the trash on the streets and the run-down buildings. It had simply been a part of the landscape—weeds among flowers. She should've paid closer attention. Hollywood was a farce. But it had Brandon clenched in its greasy claws. As far as Embry could tell, he didn't mind the scratches it left behind. He just kept going back for more, no matter the cost. Her mind wandered down a dark road. It'd been there before, but she was always quick to turn her thoughts around. Today, she didn't.

What if Hollywood wasn't the only appeal? His class was full of actresses, each one more beautiful than the next. Brandon was an outgoing person by nature. Playful and friendly. An image of Riki's face when she caught her with his headshot this morning rippled in her mind, but once again, she shook the thought away. Riki wouldn't do anything. She wasn't that kind of person, but what if a grabby actress took his friendliness for something more? A burning sensation wafted through her, igniting her cheeks. He wouldn't act on it. Of course not! He *loved* her.

But what about the recent moodiness and his short temper? Was that a sign of him thinking the grass was greener with another woman? And the night he'd come in so late, he'd whispered to her, *I love you, Em. Always. I hope you know that.* It was the *always* part that played over in her mind. *Always* meaning even when he was—

She shuddered, shaking the thought away. Good Lord! Brandon was *not* a cheater. But even as she tried to focus on what she knew, her thoughts scurried to gather evidence to the contrary. There *had* been the late nights and extra acting classes. Were those real or a cover? She scrunched her hands into tight fists as she pictured Brandon on their wedding day. His smile had been so big, it'd reached all the way up to his eyes. There'd been tears of joy too. Those kinds of feelings didn't just up and disappear, did they?

She pounded a fist to her leg. All these harebrained ideas had to be hormones coupled with flat-out fear over having a third baby. She could barely manage two kids. How on earth was she going to manage three? Kylie needed her attention all the time. And Carson was twenty-four seven. She sank to the kitchen floor and clutched her knees to her chest, burying her face in them.

If Brandon was acting weird, it was because of the soap. It had been his big chance, and it was gone. He'd be a bartender and brunch server forever, struggling to make the rent month after month. *He's never going to stop making martinis with an extra stupid olive,* she thought. That was the kind of frustration that could drive a man to the edge. But she wouldn't let him fall. She'd do whatever it took. They'd made promises to each other, and she wasn't about to break hers. If the finances were causing him to worry, she'd find a way to help. And if it were something else . . . well, she refused to let her mind go down that road again.

She smacked the linoleum floor with her hand. It was an ugly shade of yellow, but it was the cleanest floor in town. She knew how to clean. That was something. Maybe she could become a housekeeper. It'd be easy enough to bring Carson along. She could set up a playpen and he could . . . She smacked the floor again. That wouldn't work. Her eyes roamed the kitchen, searching for something. Anything. She needed a lifeline.

A stack of mail sat on the counter next to one of Brandon's Hollywood magazines. Standing, she flipped it open and landed on a page near the end. It was filled with classifieds. She skimmed down, reading ads seeking wedding DJs, dog groomers, and guitar players. Her eye was drawn to one in all caps: CHARACTERS NEEDED FOR BIRTHDAY PARTIES! JOIN THE FUN AND HONE YOUR SKILLS! *Huh.* Maybe she could dress up as a Disney princess and work the party circuit. But those costumes looked tight and uncomfortable. Not unlike those terrible pageant dresses she'd worn to make her mama happy. How dare Brandon suggest they get Kylie on the circuit? He'd said it only to rile her up.

She sighed. Something had to give. Besides, no one would hire a pregnant party princess. The door rattled, and Kylie burst in with a large piece of green construction paper in hand, followed by Brandon. "Mama! Look," she said, waving the paper near her face. "I make a pot of gold!"

Embry took the paper. "Wow, sweetie. This looks great. How did you get the gold pieces to stick?"

"We used glue, Mama!" she said, throwing her hands in the air as though using glue was reason to celebrate.

"I have just the spot for this," Embry said, tacking it to the refrigerator with a ladybug magnet. "There. It looks perfect."

Kylie beamed. Brandon, who had lingered near the door, approached the kitchen slowly, a hesitant smile on his lips. "Hey, darlin'. I thought it might help if I brought Ky home and saved you the drive. I know we're a little early, but . . ."

She drew her eyes to him and kept her voice light for Kylie's sake. "That's okay. Thanks." The urge to say more sat on her tongue, growing more and more bitter by the second. It seemed he was trying, but she wanted him to say the words with a proper apology. Didn't he know that? She stood waiting, wishing he could read her mind, but his expression was blank. Shaking her head, she said, "I should go check on Carson. He'll be up any second."

"Right. Okay. I'll help Kylie with a snack."

She walked stiffly toward their room. The baby wasn't awake yet. It had been an excuse. Waking him wouldn't do any good. She stopped and turned. "Hey, Ky, why don't you go potty and wash your hands before we get your snack, okay?"

"Okay, Mama!" Kylie sang. "I go potty like a big girl!"

"That's right!"

Once Kylie was out of earshot, Embry spun toward Brandon, her hands on her hips.

"Are you okay?" His voice was a shadow of its usual hearty baritone. The man hated confrontation. So did she, for that matter, but sometimes it was necessary.

"I'm fine." She nodded firmly and crossed her arms in front of her. "And I'll be even better when you apologize for being a jerk this morning. It's time we kick the elephant out of the room."

His mouth fell open, but he quickly clamped it shut, and a half smile emerged. "There is an elephant in here, isn't there?"

"I'm about ready to poke it with one of my wooden spoons." The sound of the flushing toilet punctuated her words. "If you have anything to say, you'd better hurry. Little Miss will be out in a minute."

"Way to use our daughter to put me on the spot." She started to speak, but he stopped her. "No, you're right. I'm sorry. I've been really stressed and feeling like—"

"Mama! I wash my hands for two whole minutes."

Embry met Brandon's eyes before smiling at Kylie. *More like ten seconds,* she thought as their opportunity slid away. "Good job. Now, do you want some apple slices or peanut butter and crackers?"

She clasped her hands and grinned. "I have a cookie, Mama?"

"No. Apples or crackers?"

Carson's cry rang out, and Kylie stomped a foot. There was no way she and Brandon could talk now. The conversation would have to wait until the kids were in bed later that night, and by then, he'd be out working. So it would happen at some unknown time in the future. Or, more likely, never. It would sit in a heap, and they'd keep dumping more unfinished conversations on top until they caught fire.

"I'll get him," Brandon offered, already in motion. As he passed Embry, he whispered in her ear. "I really am sorry. I love you."

"I love you too," she murmured before heading to the kitchen. Her eyes wandered to the door, and she felt a strange pull, a need to escape. How would it feel to just walk out? Not for good, but to just go on a walk alone with her thoughts? Brandon did it all the time. Well, he left for work, but still. He could come and go as he pleased, and she felt like she always had to ask permission because of the kids. Why did she always ask? He was their parent too. As he emerged with a crying Carson in his arms, she knew it was now or never. "Since you're home now, I'm going to run out for a bit. I have a few things to do." There! She'd done it. Statements, not questions. She pecked a kiss on Kylie's head. "See you later, alligator."

"After a while, crocodile!" she echoed back.

"Wait a sec, Em. Where are you going?"

"To the store," she said quickly, even though she had no idea where she was going. And it would be strange to say she was taking a drive down the street.

"Right. Okay. Will you be back before one? I have to leave for work by then."

"No problem." She grabbed her keys and purse from the table by the door and left. Halfway up the driveway, she broke into a jog. She was really doing this! How long had it been since she'd gone anywhere besides the market without the kids in tow? *Too long.*

Ten minutes later, she found herself in the grocery store parking lot. *Good Lord.* She should've driven down to the beach to look at the ocean. But finding a parking spot was always a nightmare, and too many people clogged the boardwalk, beeping their bike horns and nearly running folks off the path with their wild Rollerblading. But the grocery store? It was like she had a homing device directing her here.

Well, there were other shops in the center. Her eyes wandered from one store to the next as she walked. There was a nail salon, a dry cleaner, and a smoothie bar. *Ha!* That's just what she needed—a kale smoothie. How very Los Angeles. The next shop was called Soul Candy. Well, that sounded nice. She peered in the window, expecting to see a variety of chocolates, but was surprised to see it wasn't a candy store at all. The shelves were lined with crystals in all shapes and colors. A sign that hung from the door said, COME IN AND SOOTHE YOUR SOUL. It was almost like the angels of Los Angeles had led her here, nudging her inside.

Bells chimed as she entered, and the scent of lavender filled her nostrils. She closed her eyes and inhaled. It felt like the mindful thing to do. A couple stood in front of a book display directly to her left, and she drifted to the opposite side of the store. The shelves were packed with tiny labeled bottles of essential oils—clary sage, orange blossom, and juniper berry. She carefully lifted the clary sage sample and sniffed. Without warning, a wave of nausea swept over her, and she rushed to replace the jar before covering her nose and mouth with her hand. *Oh no, no, no.* She couldn't barf in here. "I'm fine," she whispered as she slowly exhaled.

A woman with sleeves of tattoos that were all the more colorful against her pale skin crossed to her. "Are you okay, miss?" she asked in a melodious voice.

Embry nodded. "Just overwhelmed by the scents."

"Ah, here," she said, waving a small wooden bowl full of coffee beans under her nose. "Breathe in deeply. It will cleanse your olfactory palate."

Embry recoiled at the bitter smell, praying she wouldn't gag. "I can't," she uttered, covering her mouth with a hand.

"Ah, you have a sensitivity. Take some small breaths and smell your own skin."

Embry didn't know whether she wanted to laugh or cry at the suggestion, but she found herself trying it nonetheless.

"Keep breathing. It'll pass." Her serene smile seemed convincing, so Embry tried to just breathe. "There you go. Good now?"

It took Embry a second to realize the woman had actually been breathing with her. It was strangely comforting but also totally weird, though the nausea had completely passed. "Yeah. Thanks. I should go," she mumbled.

"But you didn't get what you came in for."

"I don't know why I came in."

The serene smile returned, and her eyes—the color of the tigereye rocks Embry had seen on a shelf—lit up. "I like to say that what we're looking for is always in front of us. We just have to *see* it. Look around and let me know if I can help with anything."

"Thanks."

The woman seemed to float to the other customers, and Embry stared straight ahead. *If what I'm looking for is right in front of me, let me see it,* she thought with a heavy dose of skepticism. The angels whispered in her mind. *Be calm, just be.* Well, she'd come all the way here. Closing her eyes, she turned in slow circles, stopping halfway through the second, and opened her eyes. She took in the shelf before her. On it sat stacks of paper-covered soaps shaped like honeycombs. Tiny bees were printed on the packaging along with the words HOMEMADE WITH LOVE IN SANTA MONICA, CA. So she needed soap? *No, bees! That's what I need,* she thought with a laugh. Below the soaps were jars of honey—clover, wildflower, and amber. Maybe what she needed was a nice cup of tea. Shaking her head, she left the store and headed toward the market. She might as well do what she told Brandon she'd set out to do.

CHAPTER SEVENTEEN

Sylvia tromped into the restaurant bathroom. It'd been only ten minutes, but she needed a break from her lunch mates. The plan had been to dine with only Belinda, but as they'd waited for the elevator, Sarah had trotted over and invited herself. Sylvia practically lost her appetite as they walked the two blocks from the Stone-May building to the restaurant. And yet Belinda managed to proceed as though they were all great friends, and wasn't this *fun*? It didn't matter that they'd had numerous private discussions about Sarah's presence being like nails on a chalkboard. And now Belinda was faking it for Sarah's sake. That was the problem with people today. They were so worried about being nice or politically correct, they blurred the truth all damn day.

She peered at her reflection in the bathroom mirror. Perfect makeup, as always, but it wouldn't do now. She dug eye drops from her purse and squeezed a few into each eye, blinking rapidly. They were meant to counteract redness, but they had the opposite effect on Sylvia, causing her eyes to burn. She swiped a finger beneath her lashes, making sure to smear a little mascara. Better. And to think there was a time she hadn't had to fake tears. *You had it rough, little one, but I'll protect you now.*

She relined her lips and filled them in with Mac Lady Danger. Now that her wrist was no longer squawking in pain, it was relatively easy to use her fingers. She pressed her lips together, making a smacking sound. Hugh used to tease her that his shirt collars were smeared with her lipstick. The dry cleaner near his office couldn't get the stains out to his satisfaction, so he'd always left his shirts with her to clean, claiming her dry cleaner was better. *Liar. I wonder what his shirts are stained with now,* she thought. *Lackluster Lily?* Dropping the lipstick into her clutch, she inhaled deeply. It was time to rejoin the ladies.

Belinda set her menu aside when Sylvia returned and tapped it with a frosty-blue fingernail. "The server popped by, but I only ordered waters. I wasn't sure if you—" She stopped abruptly and inspected Sylvia's face. "Are you okay? Your eyes are all watery."

"I'm fine, thanks," she said in a husky voice that didn't sound fine at all.

"You look like you've been crying," Sarah offered in an awed voice. "Does your wrist hurt?"

"It's allergies. I'm perfectly fine. Now, what were you saying about ordering?" She smiled broadly, knowing it looked too big to be real.

"Right," Belinda said. "I was saying I didn't order for you because I didn't know if you were in the mood for your usual or not." She slid off her reading glasses and tucked them into their case.

Dowdy Sarah peered over her menu, and Sylvia was reminded of an owl. "What's your usual? I haven't paid attention to what you order here."

Her voice was so gentle, it was hard to be annoyed with her. She was clearly worried by Sylvia's appearance. "The half-salad, half-sandwich combo. I get the spinach salad with blue cheese instead of vile goat cheese, and the grilled chicken sandwich with added tomatoes on sourdough."

"Wait, I thought you said you were now a vegetarian."

"Yeah. That didn't last."

"Oh. Well, I think I'll try the combo too." Sarah leaned in, as though ordering the same thing as Sylvia made her an ally. Maybe the woman thrived on other people's sorrow. It wasn't uncommon, but that didn't make it any less strange.

"Great." She smiled and flagged the server with a flick of her hand. He appeared in seconds, and they placed their orders. "May I also have a Hangar One Mandarin on the rocks? Thanks."

"Sure thing." The server looked to the other two. "Ladies? Anyone else want a drink?"

Sarah tittered a small laugh. "We've never had cocktails at lunch!"

Belinda smirked. "Right? But we just turned in the Reebok proposal. A celebration is in order." She smiled at the server, tucking her thick golden hair behind her ear. "I'll have a glass of the house sauvignon blanc."

Dowdy Sarah fiddled with her menu, nervously rubbing the top between her fingers. The woman was going to give herself a nasty paper cut. "I'm afraid I'll end up drunk if I get a drink."

"Better not, then," Sylvia said with a patronizing glance. She turned to the server. "Just the two of us will imbibe."

Sarah frowned. "On second thought, may I please have a strawberry daiquiri?"

The server's expression didn't waver, but Sylvia could tell he was laughing on the inside as he walked away.

"How cute! I haven't had a daiquiri since—well, I can't remember. Must've been back in high school."

Sarah shrugged. "I haven't had one since my trip to San Diego last spring, but I do enjoy them."

"San Diego? Is that when you went to see your sister?"

"Yes! I'm surprised you remember."

How could she not? Sarah had rambled on for weeks about traveling to see her twin for their twenty-eighth birthday. Her parents would be there too. Yay! And Grandma and Grandpa. Yippee! A big, happy, disgustingly sweet family. Clearly, they were hiding something. No family could get along that well.

As if sensing Sylvia's unrest like a dog before a thunderstorm, Belinda tapped the table with her hand. Her eyes shone with intensity. "Ladies, I wanted to have lunch today because I need advice."

Ooh . . . maybe she wasn't changing the subject for Sarah's sake. Sylvia sat back. "Fire away. I'm all ears."

"Well," she said slowly, "I'm considering signing up for an online dating service, but before I do, I need the scoop. Have either of you done online dating?"

Oh, sweet, darling Belinda. Sylvia knew she'd been frustrated with her lack of dates. But online dating? It was rife with possibility. There was no doubt about that, but it could present a risk for someone as trusting as Belinda.

"I did. It has to be three or four years ago now." Sylvia looked to the ceiling and sniffed. A quick reminder that she had been crying. "Maybe five, but who's counting? On the upside, there's an endless supply of men. The question is, do you have the stamina to weed through them?"

Belinda frowned. "I don't know. I suppose so. It has to be better than dating no one."

"Oh, you must meet lots of men. You're so pretty and smart." This from Dowdy Sarah. She was so eager, it made Sylvia's teeth ache.

Moving past her words like she was swerving to avoid roadkill, Sylvia said, "It also creates a situation in which it's easy for people to misrepresent who they really are."

"Blech. Like the guy who posts a great picture, and when you meet up for the date, you realize he's the sweaty bald one in the corner who leers at you like he's been locked in a men's prison. I've read all about that," she said, adjusting her napkin in her lap. "Hence, my need for advice."

Sylvia's mind drifted back, trying to pin down the name she'd used. Buffett was the last name. That was easy to remember because she had researched it so thoroughly, but what was the first name? She still had the gorgeous Prada handbag William had given her. They'd been out for an alfresco lunch in Beverly Hills and had decided to walk along Rodeo after. Sylvia had squealed and taken his hand, pulling him into the store to see the purse up close. A salesclerk had stepped over, crooning about the beauty of the bag. How easy she'd made it for Sylvia to slide into the role of the shopper, the moneyed one who could buy whatever she desired. She'd smiled at the salesgirl and asked to see it in taupe. That had sent the girl scurrying to get her what she wanted. When she'd returned with it, Sylvia simply nodded and started to take out her wallet. She had been deliberate about the process, knowing if she didn't act too hastily, William would slip his Amex Black Card from his wallet and pay.

As if she were a mind reader, he'd done just that. "Let me get it for you. It can be my one-month anniversary gift for you."

"No, no," she'd said softly. "You don't have to do that." She'd touched his hand reassuringly, and that was all it took.

"I insist."

Shortly after that, William had started asking too many questions, so she wiped her burner phone and dumped it in a trash can outside a Chinese restaurant on Lincoln. It had taken only thirty minutes to remove her fake social media profiles and *voilà*! Carrington—that was the name—Carrington Buffett had vanished. No one had been hurt in the process. William had enjoyed her company, and she hadn't made any promises, the way Hugh had.

Dowdy Sarah interrupted her thoughts. "Sylvia, did that ever happen to you?"

"Hmm?" What was she even talking about? Thankfully, the server arrived with a tray of drinks. Once he left, Sylvia raised her glass. "To finding you a nice man, Belinda." They clinked and sipped. As Sylvia placed her vodka on the table, she said, "I suggest trying to find someone you already have a connection with, whether he's a friend of a friend, someone you meet at the gym, or even someone who's browsing the same section of a bookstore."

"I agree." Sarah quickly sucked on her straw as though she'd said something scandalous.

Sylvia offered a kind smile. "Really? Did you meet your beau that way?" She never used the word *beau*. It was a buttoned-up, old-fashioned word, but she thought Dowdy Sarah would respond to it like a dog to a bone.

Sarah took another sip and blushed. "Sort of. He's not someone special yet. I have my eye on him, though. He works in the accounting department."

Accounting. *Oh, hell.* Sylvia had forgotten to make her car payment. She'd have to do that once she got back to the office. Or not. There was a fabulous pair of Jimmy Choos that had been marked down to nearly nothing at Nordstrom Rack. Well, nearly nothing for Jimmys. And it wasn't like someone would tow her car if she missed a payment. She could make a quick sob-story phone call. People really did love to help. And the shoes were amazing. They practically had her name on them.

She took a swig of her vodka and enjoyed the burn in her throat. Belinda was asking Sarah questions, and Sylvia thought she'd probably need another vodka before lunch was over.

"He's handsome in a nice sort of way, like he'd be a good listener. He looks friendly, is what I'm trying to say, I guess." Sarah looked from Belinda to Sylvia, silently asking permission to continue with her cute-boy story. When they said nothing, she plowed on. "And when I saw him a few Fridays ago, he was wearing a short-sleeve polo shirt, and his arms . . ." She smiled and covered her mouth with a hand. "Oh my gosh, you guys. His arms are like Tim Tebow's, and I thought, I want to meet him, like, meet him and date him."

"Clue a girl in. Who is Tim Tebow?"

"Heisman Trophy winner? Great quarterback in college. He's played for the Broncos and the Jets." The server returned bearing a tray full of food and, apparently, an endless supply of sports facts.

"Who knew?" Sylvia said with an artfully raised brow.

Sarah blushed again as the server walked away. "Do you think he heard me?" she whispered.

Sylvia rolled her eyes. "He was responding to me, so no, probably not."

"Right. Good. Um, his name is Sal Mendel."

"I'm stuck on the short-sleeve polo shirt. Why is he wearing that to the office?"

"Casual Friday."

Sylvia smirked. "I don't do casual Fridays. If I'm at work, I'm dressed for work."

"Well, you have the clothing for it. You always look so polished."

"Thank you." A sign to buy the shoes if there ever was one.

"You should try to meet this Sal guy," Belinda said. "Let me know how it goes. Maybe he'll have some nice single friends, right?"

"Yes! It'd be so fun to double-date."

Sylvia set down her fork. "Now that I think about it, you really should stay away from the internet. One of my friends went out with someone who'd said he was a specialist at Apple. Turns out, he worked at the Genius Bar. Can you imagine? I suppose he could've fixed her iPhone in a pinch. But that's what I mean. People can lie so easily on the internet and pass it off as truth." *Although they can do that in person too,* she thought.

"You're right. I was just trying to be open to all the available options."

"Well, if you decide to do it, I'm happy to help you set up your online profile, but consider yourself warned."

"Thanks."

Sarah leaned forward, clearly eager to rejoin the conversation. "Speaking of men, how was your weekend with your boyfriend?"

Sylvia finished her vodka and set the glass firmly on the table. "It was awful. He vanished for a few days."

They both turned to her, their mouths hanging open like carps. "What?" Sarah whispered.

"Yeah, fill us in. This doesn't sound good," Belinda added, her eyes wide with concern.

Sylvia spun her empty glass in a slow circle. "He wasn't at his place when I arrived on Friday. When I was standing outside his door, his neighbor, who I'd never met, came home and told me that Hugh doesn't live there. Someone named Sammy, who has been out of town, does."

Sarah's shoulders caved in around her. "Oh my. He's gay?" she asked in a small voice. "Is Sammy his boyfriend?"

Belinda shot her a look. "It sounds like he's using someone else's apartment and calling it his own. Isn't that right, Sylvia?"

"Indeed. Although at the time, I presumed his neighbor was mistaken. I thought something terrible had happened. When I still hadn't heard from him by Saturday morning, I made one last attempt to reach him before I planned to call the police and report him missing." She took a deep breath. It wasn't hard to fake her distress. The wound was still fresh, though now it burned with a need for revenge.

"What happened? Did you reach him?"

"He didn't answer. But his wife did. He was busy bathing their baby."

"He's married *and* a dad?" Sarah squeaked, quickly jerking a hand to her mouth and darting her eyes left and right to see if anyone was listening. "That's terrible!" she said in a whisper.

Hugh's unsuspecting face popped into her head, and Sylvia frowned. "Isn't it, though? He piled one lie on top of the next."

Sarah nervously tugged a strand of limp hair and leaned forward. "That's why you went to the bathroom. You don't have allergies! You were crying."

Sylvia turned an unblinking gaze on Sarah, holding it until it looked as though she might regurgitate her strawberry daiquiri. "Wouldn't you?"

"Oh! I'm sorry. I didn't mean that I wouldn't have cried. I don't know what I would've done."

"Forgive me if I'm on edge. I confronted him with the truth, as anyone would in my situation, and instead of offering me an apology, he made threats." She shook her head. "I'm sure it's nothing. He won't act on any threats, right?" she asked with a forced laugh. She'd learned a long time ago, the more she denied something, the more others would insist.

Belinda placed a comforting hand on hers. "You can't be too careful. What is he saying?"

She shrugged. "That he'll kill me if I tell his wife."

Sarah gasped hard and began hacking. Good thing she didn't have a slug of daiquiri in her mouth. She would've sprayed it across the table.

"I would go to the police," Belinda said firmly once Sarah's coughing fit ended.

"What can the police do? To be honest, I just want him to go away. Ignoring him is really the only solution."

"I disagree. Take action. Far too many women don't realize how dangerous an ex can be until it's too late."

Sylvia flicked her gaze to Belinda. "I really appreciate your concern. Seriously. But I'd rather not think about it anymore. I didn't want to tell anyone, but I have to admit, telling friends I trust helped more than I would've imagined. And I would appreciate it if you will both keep this to yourselves." She looked from Belinda to Sarah, her expression somber. *That should do it.* Simple reverse psychology. Sarah would surely engage Belinda in a whispered conversation later, once they were alone. *We should help Sylvia! It's so sad.* And without Sylvia feeding them the words, they would come to the conclusion on their own that she had dated a very bad man. Two witnesses locked in, but she needed more. The neighbors would suffice, but it would be smart to have another. When accusations were hurled at him, they would come from all directions. It made things that much more believable.

Sarah slurped the last of her daiquiri, and her eyes looked a little wobbly as she lifted her face from her straw. "I won't tell a soul."

"I'm here, okay?" Belinda said calmly. "You can count on me to help in whatever way I can. Angry men can be dangerous."

"I suppose so." She nodded, her head swimming with thoughts. "Thank you. Really. It means a lot to me."

Thirty minutes later, they trailed back to their building. Dowdy Sarah had earned a new nickname—Tipsy Sarah. How one sugary cocktail could hype her up was a mystery, but Sylvia seized the moment. "You should go talk to the man from accounting when we get back. Ask him a question about what he does. Men love to talk about themselves. And you look so cute in that green dress. It's a great tone for your skin." She didn't mention that it looked like something that had been packed in mothballs.

"Really? Do you think I should?"

"Sure! Why not? Maybe he'll even suggest a Saturday matinee."

Belinda gave her a stern look. "I'd wait until the end of the day. You wouldn't want to interrupt his work, right, Sylvia?"

"Probably true." She smiled innocently at Belinda. "Very good point. And you wouldn't want him to think you're a lush."

That earned her another look from Belinda, but Tipsy Sarah was blissfully unaware, teetering ahead like an excited child at Disneyland.

~

As Sylvia sat behind her computer, the name Sal Mendel played in her mind. She clicked on the company website and typed his name into the search bar. His profile popped up immediately, along with a photo. Sylvia blinked. How had she never seen this individual before? He had a wonderfully friendly face, just as Sarah had said, and a full head of sandy hair, a square jaw, nice lips, and an unassuming nose. A great candidate for an ally indeed. She set her phone timer for fifty minutes.

That would give her enough time to finish her report, brush her teeth, and touch up her lipstick. And a few extra minutes to hatch a plan that would end with a visit to the second floor, where the accounting department was located.

Fifty minutes later, with a manila folder in hand, Sylvia headed to the elevator bank. She was armed with old invoices for orders that had already been delivered, but she planned to feign ignorance and say she wasn't certain they'd gone through accounting. Maybe she could save the company hundreds of thousands of dollars! It was a bit of a stretch, but she could sell it. When the elevator arrived, she stepped in, taking a deep breath as it ascended.

The doors opened on the second floor, and a man stood waiting. He slapped a hand to the door to keep it from closing. *Holy shit.* It was him.

"Are you getting off?" He raised a brow, waiting. "It's the last stop."

She shook her head and stepped back. "Sorry, no. I was coming up from the parking structure and passed my floor. I guess I'm distracted." She was distracted all right, but she'd let him think it was a personal problem, not a thwarted plan.

"In that case, I'll ride down with you." He pushed the button for the lowest level of the structure and looked at her. "Back to the first floor for you?"

"No. I left something in my car," she said with a sheepish smile. "P2, please."

She pressed a hand to her cheek. Her cell phone sounded with a text alert, and she took it from her pocket. UPS had just delivered her package. She'd found a great vintage Chanel dress on eBay and had actually won the auction. She'd chalked it up to beginner's luck.

Wait! This could work. Smacking her phone against her leg, she closed her eyes for a moment and released a small breath.

"Are you okay?" His brown eyes filled with polite concern.

"Fine," she rushed. "Mostly." She lifted her phone limply. "My ex can't seem to stop from sending harassing texts. I should be used to it by now . . ." She bit down hard on her lip. "Sorry. I'm sure you didn't want to hear all that. Ignore me! I'm perfectly fine." The doors opened at P2, and she plastered on a brave smile. "Here's my stop. Have a good afternoon."

She stepped out of the elevator and headed toward her car, congratulating herself on the quick thinking. If he wanted to make the leap that the texts were from her boyfriend, so be it. But she hadn't said that, now, had she? How she loved semantics.

"Hey, um, excuse me?"

She turned. Well, God bless Lady Danger. She had caught him checking out her lips as she bit them. "Yes?"

"I didn't get to introduce myself." He held out a hand. "I'm Sal Mendel."

She carefully moved the folder to her bandaged hand and shook his. Their first contact. "Sylvia Webb. I work in the marketing department. How about you?"

"Accounting." He grinned. "Less creative than where you are, but I like it."

She tilted her head and smiled, taking in his sincere brown eyes. "But it appears you get to leave early. That's a perk."

"Not really. I have a dentist appointment."

"Ooh. Good luck with that."

Her phone beeped again. The timing couldn't have been more perfect! She looked at the screen hesitantly and quickly shut it off.

"Was that him again?"

She sighed. "When is it not?" Technically, she hadn't lied. It was a second reminder from UPS.

Sal studied her face, and she opened her eyes wide, hoping she looked brave and fragile all at once. It's why she kept her hair glossy black. The contrast with her crystal-blue eyes was dramatic: severe yet sweet.

"I don't mean to butt in, but you could block him."

"Good thinking. It might come to that." She smiled again. "I'm happy I got off on the wrong floor. It was really nice to meet you, Sal."

"Nice to meet you too." He fished his wallet from his pocket, and Sylvia noticed the muscles contract beneath his shirt as he did. Tim Tebow had nothing on him. Of course she'd known exactly who Tebow was. "Here's my card, just in case you ever need anyone. In accounting or for whatever. I'm your guy."

"That's sweet of you. Thanks."

He turned to the elevator, and she walked slowly to her car before heading back. It was nice that Sal had offered his card. Now she had more information. He wasn't wearing a ring. She'd noticed that when he'd held the door open for her, but he could have a girlfriend. Nonetheless, he would work as her final ally.

For a moment, she wondered what it'd feel like to be someone who could let things slide. Maybe it would be relaxing, like a warm bath in lavender-scented water. But all she knew was plunging into ice-cold water and righting injustices. Revenge had always been a close friend, but now it had *become* her, encompassing her entire being, thanks to Hugh. Well, she couldn't give him all the credit, now could she? A memory flickered to the forefront of her mind.

It was her second year at college, and she was using the computer at the library, since she couldn't afford to buy one of her own. The essay she was writing on government corruption required focus, but her mind traveled to her dad. It had been a long time since she'd thought of him, but the past few nights, he'd crept into her mind, scaring her from sleep.

She couldn't remember the dreams. Not exactly. But memories—frightfully real memories—pushed and shoved, trying to reach the front of her mind. A tiny voice pleaded with them to go away. But they were persistent, like a desperate concertgoer who elbowed her way to the stage for a front-row opportunity.

The memory slammed into her.

They'd stopped in front of an apartment that had red graffiti on the walls. "Get in the back seat and lay down behind the seats. Don't move until I say so. I'll be right back." The car door banged shut.

She did as he asked, wondering what kind of game this was. The floor mat was scratchy against her face, and it was hard to breathe in the tight little area behind the driver's seat, but she was afraid to move her head to gulp some fresh air. The car began to quake, and men who looked like the living dead pounded on the windows and rattled the doors. She tried to disappear beneath the seat and squeezed her eyes closed, silently calling for her dad. His voice sounded from far away. Yelling and cursing. The men scattered, and her dad slammed into the driver's seat, turning around to yell at her. "Next time you don't hide good, I'll let them take you." Tears spilled down her cheeks as she looked at him. "I'm joking," he said when he saw her tears. "It's a joke, Sylvia. Just don't fucking move next time. These are bad guys. I'm doing them a favor, and if I mess it up, they'll kill me."

Her own father had taken her on his drug runs.

That day in the library, she'd set aside her paper and googled him. A flurry of Mick Webbs appeared, but she kept scrolling until she landed on a link with his picture, and she opened it. *Gabrielle Pine, best known for her pop hit "Carry Me," marries Mick Webb, eleven years her senior, whom she met in rehab.* The article had been two years old. Sylvia inspected the photo. There her dad was, smiling stupidly under an arch of pale-pink roses and creamy-white hydrangeas with his young wife. Sylvia had never heard of her, but after a quick search, she learned that the woman was rich. In photo after photo, she appeared in flashy designer clothing. There was really no explaining why she would go for someone like her father, except for their addiction connection. Had he told her he was a dad? A sharp pain had throttled through her, and she deleted the search. He'd been clean and sober for years, and yet he'd never bothered to look for her. It wasn't just the drugs that had kept him away, like her mom always claimed. *He just didn't want me.*

That was the day she'd decided she would never look for him again. Her protective mind had rescued her, erasing the memory of him until he was nothing more than a shadow.

She would never allow anyone to break her again. Stepping back into the elevator, she pushed the button, and it jolted up. How symbolic. There was nowhere to go but up. Hugh would not take her down. No one would.

CHAPTER EIGHTEEN

Riki opened the door and latched it to the stop at the end of the school day. She peered outside and spotted Mrs. Trainor clad in a long black sweater that overwhelmed her slim figure. Her arms were crossed at her waist, and her posture sagged, as though the weight of the sweater, or perhaps the world, were too much. Dark sunglasses covered half her face. Riki pretended she hadn't seen her and turned back into the classroom.

"All right, kiddos, let's see which table will get to line up first." The kids scrambled to straighten their pencil boxes and books, and the sound of chairs scraping the floor rang through the room. They were no longer expected to place their chairs on their desks after a student— before Riki's time, thank goodness—got a fat lip when her chair fell off the desk. She'd heard all about the uproar that had caused. "Okay, I see the Dolphin table is sparkling clean. Thank you, Dolphins! You may line up."

Group by group, Riki sent the students to gather their backpacks and line up near the door. Typically, Riki followed them out at the sound of the bell, but today she hung back—a watchful eye on the children, of course—but the thought of conversing with any parents caused her head to ache.

Little arms slid around her waist, shaking her from her thoughts, and she looked down to see Penelope.

"I love you, Miss McFarlan!" she sang before skipping to her mom. More kids rushed by, including Darcy, who also paused by the door to hug her.

Riki patted her back. "Have a good afternoon, kiddo. Your mom is waiting outside by the round table."

The last student left, but before she could swing the heavy door shut, Mrs. Trainor held up a hand. "Miss McFarlan!" She advanced toward the classroom, the heels of her black-suede knee-high boots clicking against the blacktop. Mrs. Trainor probably had an Instagram account titled @MommyFashionista.

"Hello, Miss McFarlan. We need to chat for a few minutes. I've sent Darcy home with our nanny." She shifted her glasses to her head, revealing perfectly applied eye makeup, as though she'd just returned from an afternoon at Sephora.

Excuses to avoid talking with her swamped Riki's mind. *I have to use the restroom. It's our staff meeting day. I haven't wiped down the tables yet—think of the germs! I don't want to talk to you!* But she smiled politely and invited her in. "Of course." She held the door open. "Have a seat."

Mrs. Trainor sat at the horseshoe table, landing her supple leather purse on a chair with a thud. Her expression was pinched.

Stealing a look at the clock before she sat, Riki said, "I'm assuming this is about the email conversation?"

"How astute of you. Surprising, being that you acted with such carelessness this past weekend."

"I'm really sorry about—"

She held up a hand. "I'm going to stop you right there," she said, her eyes brimming with anger. "Susie Johanson and I had a chat with Gerry this morning, but I need to get a few things off my chest with you."

Riki nodded pleasantly even though she felt like fire ants were crawling along her skin. Mrs. Trainor was on a first-name basis with Principal Rosenkrantz? Talk about a red-flag warning.

"I know you came from a public school, but this is a private school. Do you understand me? A private school," she said, drawing out the words.

Riki swallowed in an attempt to moisten the desert that was her mouth. "I understand that. It—"

"There are social dynamics here," she said pedantically. "If a parent, someone who pays large sums of money for their child to have a positive experience here, emails you with a concern, you should address the issue."

"And I did just that."

"No, you didn't do just that," she repeated with a snap. "What you did, Miss McFarlan, was to allow the conversation to turn into bullying. There's a fine line."

"But I—"

"Do not interrupt me. I've defended you all year to parents who claim you're too young, too inexperienced, and, frankly, too careless. I understand what a nasty group they can be." She pursed her lips, making her look more like a duck than an imposing power mom. "But this was unacceptable."

Riki wondered if it would be *unacceptable* to tell Mrs. Trainor it was time for her to leave. She bit down on the inside of her lip to keep from saying a word. And maybe to keep her focus on the sting so she wouldn't burst into tears at the insults. Inexperienced and careless? That was simply untrue. She knew all her students by heart—their strengths and weaknesses, their friendships and struggles. But she couldn't try to explain all that to Mrs. Trainor. Riki had the strange feeling Mrs. Trainor might attempt something unexpected, like pulling a knife from the sleeve of her sweater and stabbing Riki's hand if she dared to correct her.

"You're right," she said. "I handled it inappropriately, and I'm very sorry. Principal Rosenkrantz and I talked at length over the weekend," she said, crossing her fingers beneath the table, "and we are dedicated to resolving this positively. We chatted this morning about the contest you suggested, and we both think it's a wonderful solution."

"Well, like I've said all along, I'm here to help." She riffled manicured fingers through her hair. "I'm glad you were able to take ownership of the mistakes you've made. It's difficult for new teachers, but it's also tough for us parents. We want to do the very best for our children. It's why we made the choice to have our children attend private school."

"I understand. Thank you for coming to see me."

Mrs. Trainor offered a condescending smile as she gathered her bag. "You're welcome."

Riki waited until the door clicked shut behind her before she slumped back into her chair, her thoughts scattered across the table in front of her like the pieces of a jigsaw puzzle. Only three months until summer break. She could do this. As she moved a stack of noun worksheets toward her, her phone trilled with a text. Brandon's name appeared on her screen, and her foul mood vanished.

Hey, Riki. Great news! They asked me to audition for one of the leads on Baggage. Thanks a million for hooking me up.

She began typing.

You're welcome! I'm so happy for you. Let me know how it goes. I'm rooting for you! :)

Aw, thanks. You're the sweetest. Also, will you not mention this to Em? I don't want to get her hopes up.

Riki reread the text and told her heart to chill. *Sweet* was clearly a word Brandon used a lot. That's all. It wasn't his subtle way of telling her he loved her. She closed her eyes and tried to center her thoughts. It was getting harder, not easier. She told her mind to picture Principal

Rosenkranz, but all she could see was Brandon's smiling face. He winked at her. *Now we share a secret, sweetie,* she imagined him saying. She shook her head and began typing.

I won't say anything. I'm excited for you!

She stared at her phone as she waited for his response, half wishing he would respond with a little heart and half wishing he wouldn't respond at all. "I really wish I didn't like you so much, Brandon," she whispered. "And I hope you get the part."

A rattling sounded outside the classroom, and her eyes sprang open, jolting her back to reality. She stood abruptly and grabbed her phone, shoving it into her pocket as George, the grandfatherly custodian, wheeled his cart past her room. He always started on the far end and worked his way to Riki's. It wasn't because he was saving the best for last. George wasn't harboring secret, loving feelings for Riki. And *she* certainly didn't engage him in conversation because she had a crush on him. She was only being polite, just like Brandon. After moving her chair, she began pacing around the table. "Riki, it's fine for you to like Brandon. Fine!" she hissed. "It's impossible not to," she muttered. She blew out a breath and pushed her arms forward, as though shoving a heavy door closed. "But I have to stop trying to find clues that he likes me," she whispered. "It's making me crazy," she said, gripping her head. "I just need to stop. Please let me stop."

Her phone sounded again, and she walked slowly to the table to retrieve it.

Thanks, sweetie. You're awesome.

She sank into the plastic chair. "You're awesome too, Brandon. But you're killing me," she said aloud. "Killing. Me."

CHAPTER NINETEEN

Tuesday, March 14

Even though the rain had finally stopped, the world was soggy. The air was heavy and thick like a pregnant woman ready to give birth. Waterlogged newspapers sat on driveways, turned to pulp. *Why can't people bring them in?* Sylvia wondered. *They'll only end up in the storm drains. Or they'll sit so long, the sun will bake them into crunchy piles until someone finally scoops them up and dumps them.*

She parked directly in front of the house and strode to the stately front door. A flock of birds flapped above, testing their wings after the soaking they'd received. *How beautiful,* she thought. A good sign, indeed. But upon a closer look, she realized they were pigeons. *Flying rats,* as she called them. Dirty little creatures.

Well, it was true that anything could appear beautiful from a distance.

She rapped the ornate knocker against the door and stood back to wait, the pale-blue bag in hand. Hugh was at work already, but that was part of the plan.

Moments later, a timid voice called, "Who is it?"

"Sylvia Webb." She added a friendly lilt to her voice that mimicked Embry. "I'm a coworker of your husband's, and I'm here to drop off a baby gift. A little late," she added with a laugh.

The door opened, and Lily's hand fluttered to her chest. "Hi. I recognize you. You were with Hugh at Coffee Zombie a while back."

"That's me. I'm sorry I'm so late in getting this to you." She handed her the Tiffany's bag. "I've been traveling for work . . ." She waved a hand. "I don't have to tell you. Hugh has to do a lot of traveling too, doesn't he?"

"Yes. He certainly does." She raised the bag with a delicate hand. "Thank you for this. Would you like to come in for a minute?"

Sylvia knew she'd asked only to be polite. She was probably holding her breath, hoping she'd decline the offer and claim she had to rush off to work. Sylvia nodded. "I'd love to."

Lily's lips formed a little O before she spoke. "Okay. Um, follow me." They reached the living room, and she hesitated. "Why don't you have a seat on the sofa? Would you like some water or maybe some coffee?"

Sylvia took a seat on the pristine white sofa and wondered if she was the first guest to grace its cushions. "Water would be nice. Thank you. Your house is lovely," she called as Lily retreated to the kitchen. *Lucky Lily, living in a beautiful home that should belong to me.* Once she was out of sight, Sylvia slid her driver's license from her pocket where she'd stashed it and placed it on the sofa, nudging her purse on top of it. That done, she assessed the room. A canvas print of Hugh and Lily hung above the fireplace. Canvas prints were so popular right now, but they looked tacky, in Sylvia's opinion. A silver frame would be so much nicer.

Lily returned from the kitchen holding two glasses filled with ice water, the Tiffany's bag dangling from her wrist. Her hands looked pale, as though they belonged to a ghost. She passed a glass to Sylvia with a tentative reach. Was it possible she knew? Or was she just a timid little bird? Sylvia watched as she sat across from her, checking for signs.

Lily took a coaster from a wooden box and placed her glass on it before taking the bag from her wrist. "Can I open this now?"

"Yes. Please do. It's just a little something."

She lifted the elephant from the box, and her eyes lit up. For the first time since Sylvia had arrived, Lily appeared to exist in bright color, not in faded shades like a flower whose petals had been bleached by overexposure. "Oh, it's perfectly perfect. Thank you so much. Elephants are good luck, aren't they?"

"They sure are. I rather like them. And their ability to remember is fascinating. I just read an article about it." She smiled. "Though this one is simply cute. It can't remember anything," she added with a laugh.

"The baby's sleeping, but we can take a little peek if you'd like."

"Are you sure?"

Suddenly confident, Lily stood. "Of course. I try not to worry too much about keeping the house silent when he's napping so I can do what I need to do. Besides, they say babies like white noise. Do you have children?"

"No. Not yet." She faked a breezy tone, though her blood boiled as she followed Lily down a hallway lined with photographs that she quickly studied. Little details were important to remember. You never knew what you might find.

"Okay, here we are." She turned the knob quietly and crept in. Apparently, all the talk about noise was just for show, but nonetheless, Sylvia followed silently. A mural covered one wall. It was all pale-blue skies and puffy clouds. *How adorable.* Lily had probably painted it herself. She looked like someone who would be artistic. A red-and-blue airplane soared across one wall, towing a banner with the name HUNTER printed in puffy cloudlike letters. The crib was made of a dark wood and centered against the adjacent wall. Lily walked toward it and peered down. "Here he is. Little Hunter," she whispered.

Sylvia placed both hands on the side of the crib. A baby boy with a shock of dark hair and ruby lips lay on his back, his arms above his head as though he'd just called *Touchdown!* The hollow spot in her heart dissolved to ashes, but that didn't stop relentless flames from licking the wound with scorching swipes. He was supposed to be *her* baby. "He's beautiful."

"Thank you. We call him our miracle baby. We weren't sure if we could conceive." She set the elephant on the dresser. "It's perfect here," she whispered, and motioned for Sylvia to follow her out.

Weren't sure they could conceive? Sylvia's hatred for Hugh uncoiled, and she had a venomous desire to strike something. How could Hugh have cheated on his wife, annoying as she was, when she had just given birth to their miracle baby? They reached the bedroom door, and as though sensing their departure, the baby woke with a tiny cry. Lily swept back into the room, brushing past Sylvia.

Well, look at Little Miss Supermom.

Lily cooed to her baby, gathering him in her spindly arms. Amazing those arms could bear such weight. "Look who woke up."

Sylvia leaned into the door for support. "What a darling baby. He's precious."

"Would you like to hold him while I fix a bottle? You can sit in the rocker there." She carefully deposited the little bundle into Sylvia's arms.

Surprised as she was, she held the baby close and sank into the upholstered blue rocker. As Lily left the room, Sylvia inhaled the sweet scent of powder and baby. Anger and affection battled for space inside her.

Anger at Hugh.

Affection for this tiny little life.

This life that should belong to her, not Lily.

She slid her hand into her pocket and reached for her phone. The least she could do was capture the moment. She extended her arm and snapped a selfie. Just her and the baby. She smiled to herself, tucking her phone back in her pocket as Lily returned with a bottle.

"Here we are," she sang in a whisper. "Would you like to feed him?"

Without responding, Sylvia reached for the bottle and gently held it near the baby's lips. He knew just what to do. Oh, this gorgeous little human. So much life was ahead of him. Had Hugh considered his son when he was making promises to Sylvia?

No. No, he hadn't. He'd been thinking only about himself and his needs. How had she allowed herself to fall for a man who was so like her own father? It was disgusting. She wanted to destroy everything around her—to become a human wrecking ball that could crush Hugh with a devastating blow. Jonathan, too, for that matter. He hadn't given his mother a second thought as she had faced her final days.

Hugh didn't deserve his perfect family. The only thing he deserved was pain. As little Hunter suckled eagerly, Sylvia knew the time was right. She bit down on her cheek until she felt tears form in her eyes. And then she uttered a muffled sob. When Lily didn't react, she let her shoulders shake, and she began faking a good cry.

"Oh my! Are you okay?" Lily reached for the baby, but Sylvia tucked him closer to her body and continued to sob.

It sounds so real! She dipped her head low and rocked forward and back, forward and back in the soft blue chair. She didn't dare steal a look at Lily, but the woman had to be alarmed. This performance was one of her better ones. Shuddering out a breath, she kept her head down and continued to rock. "Such a sweet baby," she whispered. "So perfect." She stole a look at Lily's sickly pale face.

"I'll take him now. You should have some water," she said, her voice steady and firm, as though channeling a hostage negotiator.

Sylvia continued rocking slowly, knowing each second she didn't return little Hunter was torture. Was she a potential kidnapper? Crazy?

"It's just so hard to believe," she whispered. Lifting her eyes to Lily, she rattled out a raspy breath and said, "I'm so sorry for bursting into tears. You must think I'm a lunatic."

Lily extended her arms desperately. All sense of calm had vanished. "No! It's okay. Can you—"

Sylvia sniffed. "I've had a very difficult few days. Perhaps I'm not ready to reemerge into the real world just yet." She stood and passed the baby to Lily, who nearly crumpled with relief. Sylvia touched her arm to steady her.

Cupping her hands protectively around Hunter's warm little body, Lily said, "Do you need to talk about it?"

She lifted a shoulder in a sad shrug. "My boyfriend disappeared." She snapped her fingers with her good hand. "Just like that," she said in an empty voice. "He made me think we'd get married and start a family. But then he vanished. After fearing the worst—that he was dead in a ditch somewhere or kidnapped by terrorists—I discovered something else. He can't marry me because he already has a wife and child."

Lily's eyes went wide. "That's horrible." She studied Sylvia's face, clearly searching for something to add.

Sylvia nodded. "Horrible," she repeated. "It sickens me to think that I didn't suspect a thing."

Lily stood before her, clinging to her baby. Was she afraid Sylvia would try to take Hunter and make a run for it?

"I should go now. I'm already late for work, and I need to pull myself together."

"Oh, of course! Let me walk you out. Is there anything I can do?" Her rushed enthusiasm made Sylvia inwardly giggle. Poor Lily had probably been one step away from dialing 911 and reporting an intruder.

She shook her head bravely and continued down the hall. As they reached the front door, Sylvia said, "Thank you for letting me meet Hunter. He's just perfect. And tell Hugh I said hello."

"Of course. I'll tell him as soon as he gets home tonight. And thank you for the gift. It was so thoughtful of you. Um, take care of yourself. I'm so sorry about . . ." Her voice drifted, as though saying the words would somehow infect her perfect little family. How sad that they were already infected. She just didn't know it yet.

CHAPTER TWENTY

Sylvia rode the Stone-May elevator to the lobby and stepped outside into the weak sunshine. Lily's words from earlier that day rang in her head. *I'll tell him as soon as he gets home tonight.* It had been nagging her, prodding and poking, but the importance of what she'd said hadn't settled in until moments ago, creating a veritable *aha* moment. It was why she'd left her desk to make a private call. It was important she do it now, before Hugh left work for the day. Two benches flanked the expansive entrance to Stone-May, one of which was vacant, and she settled onto it.

She pulled the slip of paper with Hugh's office information from her pocket and dialed the number. When prompted, she touched the first three letters of his last name. A thrill shot through her when a robotic voice said, "For Hugh Pacheco, dial fourteen." She tapped in the numbers and held the phone to her ear.

"Hugh Pacheco." He sounded so confident. *Not for long.*

"Hugh! I'm so relieved to hear your voice. Thank goodness you're okay!"

There was a long pause. She was fairly certain he was debating whether to hang up or not. He cleared his throat. "Sylvia. I'm fine. I, uh—"

"Oh, thank God. I honestly didn't know what to think. Just as I was about to call the police and report you missing, I realized I should try you at work. I only wish I would've thought of it yesterday. It would've saved me another day of worry."

He squeezed out a tinny laugh. "I, uh, lost my phone. I left it in the restroom at the airport. Someone found it, and it's being shipped back to me."

"You're very lucky."

"Yeah. Hey, I've got—"

The hell you're getting off this call. She talked over him in a husky voice. "Needs? I know. I was so excited to see you on Friday that I went out on my lunch hour and popped into this darling shop and bought some new lingerie. The panties are a silky lace—really nothing more than a wisp of red fabric. And the bra matches. I couldn't wait for you to see me in them and to feel you tear them off."

He cleared his throat, and Sylvia went in for the kill.

"Even though I left your place, I was so desperate for you when I got home, I stripped down to just my panties and lay on my bed." She continued in a voice dripping with desire. "And then I slid my hand into my panties . . . and *ooh!*" She uttered a soft moan of pleasure. "It felt so good, but all I could think about was you. It's going to be a long week. I wish I could see you today."

"Fuck. You're getting me hard, and I'm at work." She heard the rustling of papers. "Can you meet me in a half hour?"

"A half hour?"

"Yeah. I'm getting out of here right now."

"I'll leave now too. And, Hugh?"

"Yeah?"

"I can't wait." She ended the call. That should do it.

∼

Thirty minutes later, Sylvia stood outside the apartment she had once believed was Hugh's. Before she could knock, the door swung open. Hugh was clad in only black boxer shorts and a big grin. Well, well. Wasn't he the eager beaver with the promise of sex?

Holding back an acerbic laugh, she said, "Hey, handsome."

"Hey, yourself. I'm glad you called me." He frowned. "How'd you get my office number, by the way?"

She let her eyes go wide. "You must've given it to me at some point. It was in my contacts."

"Oh, right."

Before he could ask anything else, she dropped her purse to the floor and unzipped her dress, letting it fall to the ground. Stepping over it, she took his hand and led him to the bedroom, knowing he would be panting over the sight of her in high heels and black lingerie. She didn't own anything red, nor was there a darling shop near her work. The closest thing to a shop near her office was Target.

Once inside the bedroom, she eased her hands under the elastic band of his boxers and stroked him. He reciprocated, though she felt nothing. Well, maybe a hint of disgust, but she had a job to do. Pushing him onto the bed, she peppered kisses down his chest while he worked his fingers on her.

With a couple of well-timed moans and a yelp of pleasure, she had him just where she wanted him. "Condom," she whispered, reaching for the one she'd stashed on the nightstand moments ago. She tore it open before sliding it onto him.

He plowed into her, pumping furiously while she stared at the ceiling and uttered fake purrs of pleasure. With any luck, it wouldn't take long. *Ticktock, ticktock.* She arched her back and groaned. That earned her a hearty grunt from Hugh. She knew the end was near, and he moved faster before slumping onto her, panting like a dog. *Finally.*

"Good thing you wore a condom," she murmured in his ear. "You wouldn't want me to get pregnant, would you, Hugh? Two babies would be one too many." She grazed her teeth across his tender earlobe before adding, "Your wife would hate that."

As though he'd been poked with a hot cattle prod, he sprang from her and slammed his back to the headboard. "What the fuck, Sylvia! I don't have a baby! What are you saying?"

She sighed heavily and eased toward him, gently dragging her nails along his arm. "But you do. And maybe a second on the way. The condoms we've been using are long expired." Her voice was a throaty whisper. Pressing a hand to his shoulder, she leaned close to his ear. "There could've been holes in them. But don't worry." She pinned him with her gaze. "We'll know if they worked or if they failed very soon. I'm already five days late."

He rolled off the bed and landed on his feet as though he were a ninja escaping the bad guy, though he was far less graceful. "You're pregnant? What the fuck!" He began popping around the room, causing his parts to *flap, flap, flap*. "I think you're making shit up! You're just angry that I didn't call you all weekend. I told you, I lost my phone!"

Sylvia held in her laughter. "Oh, Hugh. I'm not making things up. But you are. We both know Hunter is a baby, not a Pomeranian."

His face grew so red, she wondered if a blood vessel might burst. "How do you know that?"

She raised a brow and smirked before whisking past him to get her discarded clothing. What a pathetic creature he'd turned out to be. Pulling up the zipper of her dress, she considered what to say next.

He slunk out of the bedroom, a robe cinched at his waist. "Where are you getting all these ideas?"

She sneered at him. "Do you think I'm stupid, Hugh Pacheco?"

His eyes sprang wide at the mention of his real name, but he ran a hand across his mouth, presumably stifling the need to shout. "You're crazy. You don't know what you're talking about."

She fluffed her hair and laughed. "Okay."

"Okay?" he asked, losing bluster.

"Sure. I'll play the crazy one, and you can be you," she said with a too-wide smile. "That can be your story. Give my best to Lily. Sammy, too, when you talk to him. Remember, if at first you don't succeed, lie, lie again."

He lurched toward her, his face rapidly growing darker. He looked like a fat summer plum with bulging eyes. Not a pretty sight. She opened the door and quietly stepped outside.

A crash sounded behind her, but she didn't bother turning to see what he'd thrown. Poor Hugh. He'd messed with the wrong woman.

With any luck, Lily would show him the earthenware elephant tonight. Would hearing it was from Sylvia send him over the edge? Maybe he would break down and confess everything to his unsuspecting wife. Sylvia closed her eyes and imagined Lily hurling the elephant at his head. *Huh.* Maybe her gift would be a smashing success.

CHAPTER TWENTY-ONE

Wednesday, March 15

Embry pushed her jogging stroller along the winding path that led into the neighborhood park. Carson was strapped to her body in the baby carrier. Before she knew it, the new baby would take his place, and he'd move to the jogger while Kylie would have to walk.

The sun was gentle, casting a hazy glow through the filmy clouds. Spring was just around the corner. She smiled to herself. Not that it mattered much. Southern California didn't seem to recognize seasons. The rain they'd had over the weekend was the most weather she'd seen all year. "Okay, Kylie bear. We're here. Hop out."

"You bring my scooter, Mama?"

Embry clicked the brake into place and stepped around to help Kylie unbuckle. "Not today. You didn't want to bring it. Remember?" As she said the words, she chastised herself for not packing it anyway. One of the wonderful things about this park was the meandering path that looped up and around the perimeter. "Let's go play on the slide," she said with an enthusiasm she didn't feel.

Kylie pressed her hands to the seat and stiffened. "No, Mama! I want my scooter."

Touching a hand to Carson's little body so he didn't topple as she leaned over, she reached an arm to help Kylie out. "Come on, sweetie."

Kylie kicked her feet. "No! I no go!"

Carson wailed as though his sister had kicked him, not the air, and Embry took a breath. Kylie burst into tears. *I'll look back and laugh at this,* she reminded herself. *This is just a tiny moment in time.* But goodness! Another mom rolled up with an infant stroller, and Embry wheeled to the side of the path to allow her some room. Of course, *her* baby was sleeping peacefully.

The woman offered an understanding look and smiled at Kylie. "Those are very pretty shoes you have on."

Kylie froze, clearly surprised that this stranger had spoken to her, but she quickly resumed her crying.

"Toddler fun!" Embry whispered, punctuating her words with a tight-lipped smile. She gave the woman a conspiratorial glance and said in a loud voice, "It's such a nice morning that I thought a trip to the park would be fun! But it looks like we'll have to head back and get ready for a nap," she added with exaggerated remorse for Kylie's benefit. Some days it felt like she was fighting an uphill battle in psychological warfare. This toddler business was exhausting.

"Oh yes," the woman said, moving her stroller back and forth with one hand. "I understand about the napping. I've recently started coming here every morning to walk the pathway. My son loves to nap in the stroller," she said, nodding at her little bundle of blue, "and he gets very crabby if he doesn't get a good nap."

"No nap!" Kylie said, throwing her arms across her chest.

"Well, if you don't want a nap just yet, I suppose we can stay and play for a little while," Embry said with false hesitation.

"Playing at the park is a lot more fun than napping," the woman added, her eyes shining.

How sweet of her to play along so easily, Embry thought. "It sure is." She glanced down at Kylie, who had her lips pursed in a frown.

"Do you live nearby?" the woman asked.

"As a matter of fact, we do. Just a few blocks away on Mockingbird Lane, which, come to think of it, is a strange name, being that I've never once seen a mockingbird in the area. Only crows, pigeons, and seagulls. Nuisances. Anyway, how about you?"

"We're about a mile away. I drove here," she said, almost apologetically, as she continued to gently move her stroller back and forth. "This is the closest park to us. But you live on Mockingbird Lane," she said with interest. She took a card from her pocket and read it. "Any chance you're near 1054?"

Embry stiffened. How would she know that? What if this woman were part of a crime ring, luring unsuspecting moms to trust her? She'd seen plenty of strange things on the local news. But then again, there wasn't much to steal from her place. A thief would scoff at their archaic TV. Well, just in case, she would ask the questions. "Why?" she said with a sweet smile. "What is that?" She motioned to the card in the woman's hand.

The woman flipped it to show her. "It's a driver's license. Do you know Sylvia Webb?"

"She's my neighbor." It was impossible to hide the surprise from her voice. "Did you find that here?"

"No, she stopped by with a gift yesterday and must've dropped it. Can you give it to her for me? It'll save me the trip."

Kylie thumped her feet against the jogger. "I go play now, Mama!"

"Hold up, Ky." She turned to the woman. "Sure, I'd be happy to. She actually lives in the same complex as me." *Of course this woman isn't part of a crime ring. She's just another mom at the park.* "I'm Embry, by the way."

The woman reached across the jogger to shake her hand. "Lily. So nice meeting you. Please give Sylvia my best." Stealing a look at Kylie, who was inching down the seat of the jogger, she said in a timid voice, "I was thinking about her all day yesterday. How is she?"

"You mean her wrist?"

"No." She frowned. "She hasn't told you about—"

Embry stiffened as she recalled the odd request. What if Sylvia *had* been written up at work? "Told me what?" she asked in a measured tone.

"I don't mean to gossip," she started, lowering her voice to a whisper, "but she found out her boyfriend is married with a baby. You didn't know?"

Embry clamped a hand to her mouth. This was terrible. Why hadn't she said anything? "I didn't. That's awful."

Kylie's feet touched the ground, and she stood. "We go now, Mama?"

"One sec. How about you dash over to the big tree next to the bench and back, and then we'll go play?" She watched as Kylie clumsily began skipping across the dewy grass.

"Sorry. I know you need to go with her. And I hope Sylvia doesn't mind I told you." She gave her a quizzical look, as though she was trying to work something out in her head. "The way she blurted it out made me think she was telling everyone. She was really upset. Crying," she added, her eyes wide. "But maybe she felt more comfortable telling someone she doesn't know well. She works with my husband, and we've only met twice."

"Wow. I had no idea that she had a boyfriend. What a horrible thing to discover." She pocketed the license and thought back to their conversation on Sunday night. Why hadn't she said anything then? "I'll be sure to give this to her." She wanted to ask more questions, but Kylie was back.

"It was really nice meeting you. And you," Lily said, smiling at Kylie, who was loping around the jogger. "I don't know many other moms. It can be lonely."

"Well, if you're ever visiting Sylvia, stop by and say hi. We're across from her in the lower unit."

"I'd like that. Bye." Lily started down the path as Embry followed Kylie, her hand firmly against Carson's back. It was only ten past eight in the morning, but she felt like she'd been up for hours. *That was the strangest thing,* she thought. It was hard to imagine Sylvia crying in front of anyone. She was always so contained.

Kylie came to an abrupt stop and plopped onto her bottom, pulling her foot to her lap. "I take off my shoes, Mama."

"Let's leave them on, okay? No bare feet at the park. It's the rule."

But the shoe was already off, and now she was busy peeling her white sock from her foot. She threw it above her head and laughed. "Look, Mama! No shoes, just like Carsie."

"Carson doesn't have shoes on because he always yanks them off. Now put your sock back on."

It was too late. She had already scrambled to her feet and was running for the play structure, wearing only one shoe.

Embry sighed and picked up the discarded sock and shoe. What was she going to do once Carson started walking? Buy leashes for her children? She pushed the jogger to the far side of the path and stepped on the brake bar before following Kylie, who was busy climbing onto a big wooden fire truck.

Should she insist she put on her shoe? She tried to remember what she'd read in the parenting book, but her mind was fuzzy. It was hard to operate on such little sleep. Well, it was a battle she didn't feel like taking on. Score one for Kylie. Carson stirred in his carrier, and Embry bounced a little, hoping he wouldn't start to fuss.

"I drive it, Mama! Wee-ooo, wee-ooo," she sang.

"Are you going to put out a fire?"

"Yes, Mama!" She began making a loud siren noise again.

Embry glanced across the park at the play structure. "Do you want to swing?" she asked hopefully. Anything to put an end to the constant *wee-ooo, wee-ooo.* She was going to end up with a migraine.

Kylie didn't answer, but she jumped down from the truck. "I go potty, Mama!"

Embry glanced at the driver's side of the truck. Relief spread through her at the sight of a dry seat. Kylie only meant she *needed* to go. "All right." She swooped her up with her left arm and began jogging toward the bathrooms. Who needed to work out when she was running with a heavy kid in her arms and another one strapped to her body? She didn't bother with the stroller—it wasn't like someone would run off with it. As they reached the restrooms, three teenage boys sidled to the back of the building, trying to look like they belonged. But it was a regular old Wednesday, and Embry knew they were supposed to be in school. A burst of smoke trailed them as they stuffed their vape pens in their pockets. Embry scowled.

Kylie wriggled in Embry's arms once they were inside. "I get down, Mama!"

Embry lowered Kylie to the ground, reassuring herself that her daughter wouldn't die from stepping barefoot on a dirty bathroom floor. And it was just the one foot that was bare. Kylie began tugging at her stretchy cotton leggings, but it was too late. The puddle Embry hadn't wanted to see was now surrounding Kylie's feet. Tears pooled in Kylie's blue eyes.

"I sorry, Mama. I go pee-pee."

Embry wanted to shout curses at the top of her lungs—not at Kylie but at the situation. At the stupid teenagers and the dirty bathroom floor. And at the park designers who had made the brilliant decision to put the bathroom too far from the play structure.

Deep breaths.

"It's okay, honey. The important thing is you let me know that you had to go, and we tried to make it on time. Accidents happen." She lifted her with both hands under her shoulders and walked her to the sink area. "We'll wipe you off as best as we can."

"Okay, Mama."

A burst of love flowed through her as she reached for some paper towels. She'd felt it before, like a sudden ripple, as though her heart had actually expanded, but it was strange that it was happening now, as she wiped pee from her daughter's pants. Maybe it was because she felt guilty for having wanted to shout at the world. It really had been an accident. "Okay, I think that's the best we can do for now. Let's get your shoe off. I'll rinse it in the sink, and we can wash it at home."

Kylie nodded and handed her the wet shoe and then the sock.

Embry scrunched her nose as she held the sock with two fingers. "How about I toss the pee-pee sock?"

Kylie laughed and plugged her nose. "Bye-bye, pee-pee sock!"

Embry flipped it into the trash can. "Bye-bye!" She rinsed the shoe and wrapped it in a paper towel that might as well have been a piece of paper for how absorbent it was. "All right," she said, facing Kylie. "I think our visit to the park has come to an end. Let's get our stroller and go home. I'll just grab a few more towels to put under you so the seat doesn't get wet."

As they headed home, Embry looked at her watch. It was only eight thirty. Goodness! They had done a lot of damage in just twenty minutes. When Brandon took the kids out, he always came back smiling and happy, acting as though it were literally a walk in the park to spend a few hours with them. Would he have just told Kylie to strip down and pee on a tree? *Yuck.* That was a gross idea. He'd better not be doing that. But what was it? *Annoying,* that's what it was. Maybe he should stay home with the kids and she could work. *Then I won't have to worry about all the pretty girls he's meeting.* Oh, that sounded awful. He was chasing his dreams, and she needed to be supportive of them.

He would do the same for her. She didn't know exactly what her dream was at the moment, but she knew there was something more. It didn't have to be a party princess or something from the back of a magazine. She had plenty of skills, and if she could just find a way to make some money, having a third baby wouldn't seem so overwhelming. And she wanted this baby with all her heart.

Her mind drifted to the woman with the colorful arms and the angelic voice. *I like to say that what we're looking for is always in front of us. We just have to see it,* she'd said.

Well, I'm going to keep my eyes open, Embry thought as she rolled into the driveway.

Carson's limbs stiffened against Embry's body, and he let out a wail.

"Mama, tell Carson he's too loud!" Kylie slapped her hands to her ears.

Embry clicked the stroller brake with her foot. "Climb out, Ky. Let's get you inside." She purposefully ignored the complaint. Kylie was right, though. He was loud. She closed her eyes and inhaled. *Breathe in, breathe out. This is only one moment. It will pass.*

Carson's cries grew in strength. She unfastened the carrier while silently counting to ten. "I'll get you a bottle, Carsie. Hang on." Her voice was calm even though in her mind she was screaming. She focused her attention straight ahead. It always helped if she could mentally distance herself from the stress. The honey bear sat on the kitchen counter, left out from breakfast. It looked like the bear was smiling at her. Or maybe laughing. *Don't you laugh at me,* she thought. *I'm doing my best!*

With one hand, she made a bottle, which Carson grabbed for as though he hadn't eaten in days. She set him in his high chair, making sure he was strapped in, and went to help Kylie. Her mind tried to imagine a third baby in the mix right now, but she squeezed the thought from her head. One step at a time.

She found Kylie in the bathroom, naked on the fluffy blue rug, using a baby wipe to clean her legs. "Oh, sweetie. What a great job! You're getting yourself all cleaned up."

"I'm a big girl, Mama!"

"Yes, you are. I'll get some fresh clothes for you. Toss the dirty ones in the tub, and I'll rinse them before washing them, okay?"

She nodded as she scrubbed the wipe across her foot. Embry checked on Carson before returning to Kylie. All was well. Everything would work out just fine. Once Kylie was dressed, they walked to the kitchen together.

"Ky, do you want some juice?"

"In my sippy cup, Mama! The green froggy one."

"Okay." She took it from the cupboard and smiled to herself. Frogs today, and who knows what tomorrow? The girl changed her mind like the weather.

"Hello, honey bear," Kylie sang. "Honey, honey, honey, you are so yummy!"

"Are you talking to the honey bear?"

"He's right there, Mama!" She pointed.

"Oh, I know. I forgot to put it away after breakfast." She shook her head and turned to grab it.

"We make honey pops today, Mama?"

She stopped where she was and looked from the honey bottle to Kylie. "What'd you say?"

"Honey pops, Mama. We make them? I love them so much."

The woman's words were in her head again. This time, loud and clear: *We just have to see it.*

"Honey pops," she repeated slowly, but her heart began to race. The honeycomb soap and the cute little bees in the store yesterday—had they been signs she hadn't seen? "That's it, Kylie! That's it!" She smiled down at her and drew her into a hug. "We'll make a whole bunch of them today. Mama has an idea." Her mind zipped ahead like watching a movie in fast-forward. It was all so clear now! She'd been perfecting the honey pops recipe since Auntie Boots had first taught her how to make them when she was only nine years old. People gobbled them up every time she made them. What's to say she couldn't earn money from selling them? Hart's Honey Pops. That's what she would call them, in honor of all the strong women in her family. She could almost see them here now, cheering and clapping as she took her first step toward this shiny new idea. Or maybe it was a discarded dream that she could breathe back to life.

CHAPTER TWENTY-TWO

Sylvia parked her car across the street from Sammy's place. How quickly she'd been able to categorize it as *not Hugh's* in her mind. Picking up her phone, she dialed the number listed on the sign outside the sprawling apartment complex, but before she could connect, her phone rang, and Hugh's name appeared.

She slid her finger across the screen. "Hello, Hugh. I thought you would've called last night."

"I couldn't! You came to my house?" His voice was a desperate plea. *Wow.* He'd uttered only a few words, and he was already losing his shit.

She yawned. He was such a bore. "I did. I'm surprised you couldn't smell little Hunter on me when we were making love. Hang on," she said, tapping on her photos. "I'll text you a picture of the little guy with me." With one finger, she sent the photo to Hugh.

"Stop it! Do you hear me? This has to stop!" he spat.

She held back a laugh. "Stop what? Feeding your baby or sending you photos? You're not being very clear, now, are you?"

"Stop contacting Lily. Stop coming to my house. All of it. I'm telling you right now!" His words were slow and measured, as though he were trying to gain control. "If you—"

"Wait!" she interrupted, infusing her voice with excitement. "Hugh? Can you hear it?"

"What are you talking about? I don't hear anything."

"You have to listen carefully!" Her voice was fit for a mother delighting in her child hearing Santa's reindeer on the rooftop. "Do you hear it?"

"Hear what?" he snarled. Poor guy wasn't having as much fun as she'd hoped.

"It's the sound of your world shattering around you," she said cheerily. A laugh rose from her throat, and he went silent, just as she knew he would. There was nothing more unsettling than hearing someone laugh at a serious situation. *Is the person nervous? Caught in a lie? Deranged?* Yes, a perfectly executed laugh was an effective tool. "You played me for a fool, Hugh, and now it's my turn to play. Isn't this fun?"

"You're crazy! What the—"

"Oh, I'm sorry." She assumed a pitying tone. "I get that it's probably only fun for me, not so much for you. But you've had your good time, haven't you?"

"We're done." His voice was a seething whisper. "And if you dare come to my house again, I'll . . . I'll have you arrested!"

"Okay," she sang. "We'll see how that goes. I hear the police aren't big on arresting visitors, but okay."

"Shut up! I could kill you right now!"

"Oh, Hugh. Now, that's something that'll get *you* arrested. And besides, I'm like a phoenix. I'll rise from the ashes. Nothing can kill me."

"I don't even know you anymore. You're a fucking cockroach."

She ended the call and ignored the unrest in her belly. Hugh deserved this. He had worked hard to gain her trust, only to light a match to it and watch it burn. The man didn't deserve even a moment of sympathy. No, she wouldn't hesitate. The smart thing was to forge ahead with her plan and allow him to suffer.

Her phone buzzed with a text, and she glanced at it.

> Don't ever call me again!!! I'm serious, Sylvia. Bad things will happen!!!

"Ooh. Bad things will happen," she mimicked. "Yes, they will, Hugh. I'll just go ahead and save this text so I can use it later. No one likes to be threatened by an ex, Hugh. But you keep them coming," she whispered. "Keep them coming. I'll destroy you with your own words."

She closed her eyes and tried to clear the noise from her head. The clock was ticking. She pressed "Recents" on her phone and tapped the number. This time as it rang, she wasn't interrupted.

"Management. This is Brian," a man's voice said. He sounded bored, like he'd spent too many hours staring at a crossword puzzle or, more likely, inane videos on his phone. Lucky for him, she would rattle him from his stupor.

"Hi, Brian. This is Lily Pacheco. My husband and I have been keeping an eye on Sammy's place while he's been out of town, and I've locked myself out." She faked a girlie sigh. "I popped out to my car for a second to get the window cleaner that I left behind, and of course I left the keys inside," she added with a laugh. "It's been one of those days. Would you mind opening the door for me?"

"Last name of the tenant?"

"Gilligan." That hadn't been too hard to find, thanks to the internet.

"Hang on. Lemme check." There was a pause and the sound of tapping on a keyboard. "Got it. Unit 305. I'll meet you there."

"Thank you!" She took the grocery bag filled with household cleaners from her car and walked toward the lobby elevator as she checked her watch. It was her lunch hour, and she needed to get in and get out.

By the time Brian arrived, she was outside Sammy's all-too-familiar door.

"Hi. Can I see your ID?"

Blergh. She hadn't thought of that. Tapping a hand to her head, she said, "Oh, this really isn't my day. I have the cleaning products, but I've left my purse in the car. I'll run down and get it." She let the bag drop from her hands, and bottles clattered to the floor. "Shoot! What a mess."

He bent down to help her gather the fallen items. "Don't worry about the ID. You've got your hands full." He smiled as he picked up the window spray. "And it's not like you can vandalize a place with Windex."

She laughed. "Right? I'll scrub the windows to oblivion."

He unlocked the door, and Sylvia eagerly scrambled past him, a single key hidden between her fingers, and she swooped to the floor, letting the key appear in her palm. "Look! I found it!" she said. "I must've dropped it on my way out."

"Okay. So you're all set?"

"Yes. Thank you."

"No prob."

Once inside, Sylvia locked the door and headed for the bedroom. Pulling the covers back from the bed, she arranged the pillows and fluffed the duvet, making it look rumpled from play. Satisfied, she stripped off her clothes and took the brand-new burner phone from her purse. It had been fun using Lily's name and Sammy's address on the contract. Should it ever be found and traced, every indication would be that Hugh had purchased it. Of course, she'd already created some sexy conversations between the burner and her own phone. It was so easy to make the texts sound like Hugh's. All she had to do was copy what he'd already sent. Coupled with labeling it *Hugh's Phone* in her contacts, all signs pointed to him.

Next, she fished out the selfie stick. They were admittedly obnoxious but, in this case, necessary. She positioned herself on the bed, posing in a satiated sleeping position, and began snapping photos, taking care to keep her face out of the shot. The idea was to make it look like someone else had taken the photos while she slept. Angling the stick just so, she made sure to capture the intricate spiderweb tattoo that covered a two-inch space across her left hip. The spider's legs were elegant, and its body was a bold, multifaceted, bloodred ruby. Best to get a shot with that little beauty. Scrolling through her work, she smiled. These were perfect.

The sound of a cell phone ringing cut through the quiet. She froze. *What the hell?* It rang once more, and she realized it was coming from the en suite bathroom. Through the closed door, she heard a man's voice say, "This is Sammy."

Had he been on the toilet this entire time? *Shit!* She quickly straightened the pillows, grabbed her clothes, and crept on tiptoe to the kitchen. His voice grew closer. There was nowhere for her to hide, short of ducking into a closet, but she wasn't about to trap herself all day. Running naked into the exterior hallway wasn't going to work either. She wriggled into her panties and fumbled to fasten her bra as she heard him say, "Later, man." The bedroom door opened.

She was still half-naked, but she could work with this. *Here we go,* she thought. "Hugh? Is that you, babe?" she called. She stood near a kitchen chair and turned as Sammy appeared. "You're not Hugh!"

"What the fuck!" he shouted, backing into a strange, lowered stance, like he was readying to pounce.

"Who are you?" she screeched, covering herself with her arms. "Where's Hugh?" she asked, infusing panic in her voice.

"Who the fuck are you? This is my apartment!" He moved from his squat stance and shoved a hand through his hair. It fell to his shoulders in curly dark waves. He wore rock-star skinny jeans that hung low on his hips. Typically, shirtless men were attractive, but Sammy looked like a tall ten-year-old who hadn't reached puberty, although he had a scraggly beard that he probably thought made him look edgy and cool. In a pinch, she could take him down, even with the sprained wrist.

Sylvia slid her dress over her head and grabbed her bag and purse. "I'm not sure what kind of clever criminal you think you are," she said, backing away, "but if you take one step closer to me, I'll scream."

"I'm not going to hurt you. You're the intruder," he muttered. "This is *my* apartment. Call Hugh."

"Oh, I will." She rushed through the door and resumed a normal pace as she walked to the elevator. Well, that hadn't gone exactly as planned, but at least she had her photos. And information. Now she knew exactly why Hugh had decided to ghost her when he did. His love nest was no longer available.

CHAPTER
TWENTY-THREE

Jonathan rolled into his mom's old parking spot and strode to the hot blonde's apartment, a tattered briefcase in hand. It wasn't his—he'd found it in Ma's apartment tucked in the back of the hall closet—but the prop would make him look more authoritative. Imposing. With any luck, he'd be able to get them all to sign the papers he'd stuffed in the case. He reached the door and rang the bell.

"Mama! Someone's at the door," a whiny voice said from inside. "I open it?"

"I'm coming, sugar."

He rolled his eyes and tapped his foot. How long did it take to open a freaking door?

Finally, she swung it open. He offered a wide smile, even though the sight of her with a baby on her hip and her ponytail askew was enough to make him vow to never get involved with a woman who wanted children. Kids turned hot chicks into hot messes. "Hello, Elizabeth."

"It's Embry."

"Shit. Right."

She glared at him. "I have small children here," she said tightly. "I'd appreciate if you'd keep that in mind when you speak."

"Yeah. Sorry about that." He straightened. "I wanted to make sure Dave fixed the garbage disposal to your satisfaction."

"Yeah. It's working now."

He waited for a thank-you, but she continued to glare. *Ungrateful bitch.* "Good. Another quick thing," he began, shifting his briefcase so he could open it. "I need you to sign this paper for me." The less he said, the better. With any luck, the baby, who was now grabbing at her shirt, would act as a distraction.

"What am I signing?" she asked, gently removing the baby's hand from where he'd nearly pulled it low enough to reveal her bra. "Does this have something to do with you selling the place?"

Jesus Christ! He swallowed wrong and coughed into his hand. "What do you mean?" he asked, recovering.

"Dave told us. The handyman?"

"Right, right." *The idiot.* He wasn't ready for the tenants to know just yet. That would only create complaining and questions he couldn't answer. Rolling back on his heels, he said, "It's always a possibility, I suppose. Dave can fix things, but he clearly can't differentiate hypothetical from reality," he added with a smirk. "This page is just confirming that you're on a month-to-month lease. It allows you to leave whenever you want. At the end of the day, it's for your own protection." He nodded as he handed her the paper. It was something he'd found on the internet on an attorney's website.

"Fine. Will you hold Carson for a sec?" she asked, offering the baby to him.

The things he had to do to get what he wanted. Tentatively, he took the baby and held it under the armpits while she scribbled her signature across the line with the pen he'd generously offered. At least she was quick about it. She handed the paper to him and reached for the baby.

"Thanks. Let me know if that garbage disposal gives you any more trouble."

She closed the door without a word. *Whatever.* He'd gotten what he wanted. One down, two to go. *Bam!* He grabbed his briefcase and crossed the driveway. Something bright orange on one of the stairs caught his eye, and he picked up his pace. *Shit.* He'd forgotten about the message Sylvia had left. What had Dave been thinking, taping the step like that? He climbed the stairs and stopped on the sixth, reaching out his foot to tap the seventh. *Huh.* It actually felt pretty darn sturdy. Grabbing the railing, he put some weight on it and smiled. Totally fine. If it could hold his weight, it could hold hers. Traipsing up the rest of the stairs, he knocked on her door. When she didn't answer immediately, he jammed his finger against the bell and knocked once more.

Not home. He took another document from his briefcase and slid it under her mat, leaving a corner sticking out, before jogging down the stairs.

As he reached the ground, the girl from the lower apartment pranced out, dressed in black leggings and a tight little top. She'd be totally hot if there were a little more to grab on to. "Hiya! I was just about to knock on your door."

"Oh. Is something wrong?"

"No, no. We're good! I was just checking on a few things, and I have a paper for you to sign." He opened his briefcase, snapping the locks with a flourish. "Here we are. If you can just sign at the bottom, I'll be out of your hair and you can be on your way. Jogging?"

"Uh, yeah. I'm going for a run."

"A run. Not a jog. You're fast," he said, pumping his fist. "Good for you. Keep that heart healthy, right?" He openly stared at her chest. It was where her heart was, after all, and if she was going to prance around in a tiny top, he could look.

She skimmed the page as he waited. "Uh, I'm on a year lease," she said, handing the page back to him. "This doesn't apply to me."

Dammit! He raised his brows and smiled, covering his annoyance. "It's your lucky day. This allows you to leave whenever you want. Consider it a gift."

Her face scrunched up in confusion. "I don't know. I feel like I should ask my mom and dad about this. You can leave it with me, and I'll let you know."

"Um, I think you're not understanding me. I need you to sign it now."

A red car zipped by, and she motioned to it. "Sylvia just got home. Let me ask her." She took off ahead of him.

By the time he reached the carport, he was tempted to shove the pen in her hand and force her to sign. And the stupid girl was already whispering with Sylvia. Sucking in a breath, he said, "Hi there! Has she filled you in?"

Sylvia was wearing a tailored dress with sexy high heels. That woman looked like she knew her way around the boardroom and the bedroom. He rewarded her with a charming smile, but she glared at him. "Are you selling the complex?" Before he could answer, she said, "Dave, the stair-repair genius, says you are and that his dad is your real estate agent."

"Well, Dave's dad and I are old friends. I'm not going to lie. We've tossed the idea around, but like I just finished explaining to Emily across the way, Dave gets confused easily." He tapped his head. "Nice enough kid, don't get me wrong, but there's not too much going on upstairs. This document has nothing to do with that. It's giving you freedom from a lease."

"Or making it so you can raise the rent at will, I presume?"

"No, no. I wouldn't do that. California has rules and laws that protect renters." He had no clue what they were, but he assumed there must be some type of law in place. He'd seen the lawyer's website that was full of information, even if he hadn't read it word for word.

"Are you sure? I don't want to do anything rash."

He stepped forward and gave her his best puppy-dog-eyes look. "Trust me," he said, drawing the words out in a way that always worked like magic. "You'll be better off."

She bit her lip but took the page. "You're sure?"

"One hundred percent. You're golden with this."

"Okay, I trust you," she said with a warm smile. It was pretty obvious she was attracted to him by the way she'd angled her breasts toward him. And then she took the pen and signed!

Bam, bam!

She passed it back to him and gave the runner a supportive look. "Riki, you should sign too, even though you're still on a lease. Jonathan wouldn't do anything to screw things up for us."

She grabbed the paper and balanced on one leg as she signed the page using her thigh as a table. Fit little thing.

He took the document and folded it. *Done and done.* "Thank you," he said. "And I checked your stair, Sylvia. It's fine. Held my weight and all. You're good."

"Well, that's a huge relief. Thank you so much."

"You know it!" He turned to leave, holding back the desire to cheer. He was one step closer to megabucks. *Cha-ching!*

~

Embry held Kylie's hand tightly as she marched up Sylvia's stairs with Carson in her arms. "Careful, hon," she said as they avoided the bandaged step. She knocked, wishing Brandon were home so she could do this without the kids.

Sylvia swung the door open, looking annoyed. "Let me guess. Jonathan wanted you to sign something about the lease?"

Embry nodded. "Yes. He was downright pushy about it, but we're not on a lease, so I figured it didn't matter one way or the other. Did you sign?"

"He thinks I did, but I didn't sign my own name." She smiled. "Sylvia Browne, renowned psychic," she said, rolling a hand in front of her like royalty, though with the brace, she resembled a royal robot.

"I thought she died a long time ago."

"Well, yes, but he won't know that. He's an idiot—he thought your name is Emily. It'll take him a while to figure out I signed the wrong name. Riki is now the amazing Ricky Ricardo. She was all too happy to sign a fake name when I suggested it to her. Apparently, Jonathan was leering at her and trying to force her to sign. I've never seen her that upset about something. Makes me hate Jonathan a little more than I already did."

"Oh. Goodness, I wonder if I shouldn't have signed."

"I'm sure it's fine. My bigger concern is that he's lying about selling. I think he told Dave the truth about it. That could leave all of us scrambling to find a new place to live."

"I know! Nadine never would've done this. I'm trying to stay calm, but it's got me worried."

"Yes. I'm thinking if people come look at it, we can tell them how awful it is. You know, the rats in the trash area and the faulty wiring."

"What? There are rats?" She stole a glance at Kylie and gave her hand a reassuring squeeze.

"No, but we can tell prospective buyers there are."

A smile lit Embry's face. "Oh! Right. And leaky pipes."

"Exactly."

Embry shifted her feet. "So the other reason I stopped by is because I met a woman at the park who knows you."

Sylvia frowned. "Who?"

"Lily." She looked upward before returning her gaze. "Shoot. I didn't catch her last name, but she gave me your license. She said you left it at her house yesterday." Embry handed it to her.

"Thank you." Sylvia looked amused, as though she really *were* psychic like Sylvia Browne and had predicted the entire thing. "How did she know you're my neighbor if you just met her?"

Embry shrugged. "That was kind of strange. We were just talking in passing, and I mentioned we live on Mockingbird Lane. That's when she asked if I know you. Is she not a friend of yours?"

"She's a relatively new friend. A colleague's wife."

"Oh." Embry's face burned, and she grappled with whether she should tell her more. But she had to. It was the right thing to do. "Um, there's something else I need to tell you. Is it okay for Ky to go in and arrange the magnets on your fridge while we talk?"

"Always. Come on in, young lady," she said, stepping aside so Kylie could pass. "You know where it is. I bought a new one the other day. See if you can find it." She smiled as Kylie darted into the kitchen, then turned back to Embry. "What is it?"

"Well, it's something Lily told me, but I feel obliged to share it with you."

"Okay. Fire away."

Embry shifted Carson to her other arm. "She asked how you were, which is fine. I assumed she was talking about your wrist, but then she went on to say you were upset about finding out your boyfriend is married and a dad. Is that true?"

Sylvia turned her gaze to the ground, and Embry wondered if she'd said too much. "Sadly, yes," she said quietly before lifting her eyes. "Disgusting, isn't it? It was quite a shock. And to think that he's blaming me."

"That's awful. Why?" Embry whispered. She seemed to have swallowed her voice. This was horrible. She couldn't imagine what Sylvia must be going through.

"Who knows? I thought I knew him, but I'm seeing a side that's . . ."

She waited, searching Sylvia's face. "That's what?"

"Scary. I feel so stupid saying that. I'm probably imagining it. I'm sure it's fine."

"Sylvia, don't downplay it. My favorite aunt always said you should listen to your gut. Is there any way I can help?"

"I don't know. He's made threats. He's worried I'll tell his wife. That seems cruel, though, doesn't it? Why hurt her?"

Embry's eyes went wide, and another chill shot through her. "I would want to know if Brandon cheated on me! I'd strangle him and then run him over with my car."

"He's not the cheating type, though, is he?"

"No! Of course not. It's just horrible that this guy lied to you." Embry's heart raced as a hideous thought edged its way in. *Brandon could be the cheating type if he wanted to.* How could Sylvia remain so calm? If it had been her, she'd have punched a hole through the wall by now, and she wasn't even a violent person.

"Indeed. If I could go back in time and change things, I would." Tilting her head, she said, "You really think I should tell his wife? How would that work? Do I invite her over and tell her over a nice cup of tea? Is that what you would do?"

Embry felt herself frowning. Why did Sylvia keep turning this back to her? Was she trying to give her a hint about something? "I have no idea what I would do if I were in your shoes. But wait. You *know* her?"

"We met recently, though he told me she was an ex-girlfriend. He also said she was unstable, which, as it turns out, probably isn't true." She crossed her arms in front of her chest. "Anyway, if I do tell her, maybe you can be there too. I wouldn't want her to kill the messenger. It'd be less likely for her to hurt me with a witness."

Embry's hand fluttered to her lips. Why would Sylvia want *her* there? It was all too strange. "I would just have her meet you at the police department if you're worried she'll hurt you. Although that would be weird, wouldn't it? Oh, I just don't know. What a mess."

"It sure is. I'm going to buy some pepper spray. And if you see anyone lurking around, please let me know."

Embry nodded vigorously. "We'll definitely keep our eyes open. It's okay to tell Brandon, right?"

"I suppose, but I really don't want to worry anyone unnecessarily. Maybe I'm making too much out of this. I'll be just fine."

"You have the right to be worried, Sylvia. Anyone would be." She peered inside and called for Kylie. Suddenly, she couldn't wait to leave. "Thanks for letting her play with the magnets."

"Anytime."

Embry headed down the stairs and tried to work out what was bothering her. Something wasn't right, but she couldn't put a finger on it. Then again, she hadn't been sleeping well because of the pregnancy. There was plenty on her mind. Sylvia was a capable person. That much she knew. She seemed like the type who would always land on her feet. But nonetheless, Embry was going to keep an eye out for her. And an eye *on* her.

CHAPTER

TWENTY-FOUR

Thursday, March 16

Riki grabbed her purse and keys from the kitchen table as she made a mental list of the tasks she needed to complete that day. *Tasks.* That's what it boiled down to now. Just one year ago on the sixteenth, she'd been so happy. The memory was bright in her mind. She and the rest of the first-grade team at Clover Street had used glitter and bits of green paper from the three-hole punch to sprinkle across the students' tables after school. They'd even bought plastic gold coins and sparkly shamrocks. The kids had been giddy when they'd walked in the next day.

She might've been feeling a little giddy this morning if Mrs. Trainor hadn't sent an email at 6:17, requesting a meeting for 7:30. Did she honestly think Riki could drop everything and rush to meet with her before school on a busy Thursday? *Of course she does.* It was her world, and Riki was just living in it. *Ugh.*

If it had been anyone else, she would've responded and set something up for the afternoon. But she'd decided to ignore the email. She could respond at snack break, or lunch, or after school. As she crossed the driveway, she stopped short. A For Sale sign was standing tall in the middle of the Taylors' yard. She should've known. Jonathan had asked them to sign the paper because he'd known all along he was selling. Sylvia had said he was up to something, and she had agreed, but she'd hoped he was just smarmy, not a full-on liar. She jogged toward the sign and snapped a photo of it before opening the little plastic box and taking a flyer. As she skimmed the page, her mouth dropped open. Jonathan was selling the entire complex for $3.5 million. Was he delusional? She shook her head and continued reading. UNIQUE FOUR-UNIT INCOME PROPERTY IN A WORLD-FAMOUS BEACH NEIGHBORHOOD. GARDEN-STYLE BUNGALOWS WITH HARDWOOD FLOORS AND OCEAN BREEZES. A PERFECT PROPERTY FOR OWNER-OCCUPANTS OR THE IDEAL SPOT TO BUILD YOUR OWN DREAM HOME.

Build a dream home? That meant her home would be bulldozed. She shoved the sign, but it didn't budge. Would it be illegal to take an ax to it? Even though the asking price was astronomical, there were plenty of people in Southern California with gobs of money.

Stuffing the flyer in her purse, she stole a look at the Taylors' apartment. Had they seen the sign already? She imagined Brandon's truck packed with furniture and Embry's yellow car jammed full of suitcases. The thought of not having them as neighbors was enough to make her want to cry. In a quick move, she grabbed the stack of flyers and ran for her car. Jonathan could try to sell the place, but she wasn't about to make it easy for him.

~

Sylvia breezed through the door of the Coffee Cart. A piping-hot blueberry muffin and a nice caffe latte were in order after spotting the dreadful FOR SALE sign when she'd opened the shutters early that morning.

Dave had been right. And Jonathan? Well, he'd proven himself to be a liar in addition to a self-important loser. Her mind had roared into gear as the sun came up, and she'd skipped washing her hair so she could leave early. Lucky for her, the trip to the convenience store where she'd purchased a second burner phone had taken less time than planned, leaving a solid twenty minutes for a well-deserved morning treat.

Once her order was in, she chose a table in the corner. The place wasn't crowded, but the morning crunch would hit soon. She closed her eyes and leaned into the wooden chair, letting the sturdiness of it support her as she reviewed her plans. Did it happen like this for other people? *Ha! No way.* She was smarter than the masses. She opened her eyes, and a man standing in line caught her attention. He was waving his hand back and forth as though washing a window. Or to knock her out of her daze and get her attention. She squinted, trying to figure out who it was under the black-and-yellow jacket. He looked like a giant bumblebee. She gave him a confused look but returned the wave anyway.

The man approached her table, and now that he was inches from her, Sylvia knew exactly who he was. He had a number in his hand, so she knew he was staying. She took a satisfying breath, marveling at how her luck continued to grow.

"Hi, Sylvia." He waved awkwardly. "It's Sal. From the elevator?"

"Of course," she said, her tone warm. "You're out and about early."

"Yeah. My Thursdays start at the crack of dawn." He pointed to her wrist. "What happened?"

How lovely that he'd noticed! She met his eyes slowly, as though she were trapped and didn't know whether or not she could trust this person in front of her. *Like a cornered animal.* And then she smiled brightly. A big, happy, *I've-never-been-better* smile. Because she was a brave soul. "Oh, this." She lifted her wrist limply. "It was like this when we met. My jacket must've covered it. Anyway, it was . . . well, it was a fall." She tucked her wrist close to her. "A clumsy move."

He shifted his feet and tried for a smile.

He didn't believe her. She knew by the way his body sagged and his eyes narrowed, like he wanted to hurt the person responsible.

Sometimes it was too easy to make people wonder. She motioned to the empty spot across from her. "Have a seat if you'd like. Unless you're meeting someone, that is."

He pulled out the chair and set his number on the table. "Thanks. I'd love to." As he draped his jacket across the chair back, he said, "I just dropped my daughter at my ex's place. That's why I'm here so early. My ex wants her by seven thirty every other Thursday morning, which is a struggle for a number of reasons. It's tough leaving her after spending a few days together. I end up coming here and loading up on carbs and caffeine before work on drop-off days. Do you have kids?"

She sipped her latte and imagined it was a calming serum. It was like the universe wanted to make sure she never forgot she wasn't a mother. "I don't." She smiled. "Never been married and no kids."

He nodded. "Divorced and one kid. She's seven." His face lit up and fell, all in a matter of seconds. "It sucks not being able to see my little girl every day. At least I have shared custody."

"Do you live here? In Venice?"

"No. Santa Monica. My ex lives here."

A server stopped by the table with a large cappuccino and a blueberry muffin, plucking the number stand as she left.

"Excellent call on the muffin." She lifted her own from her plate and inhaled the sweetness. "Yumm. I could exist on this smell alone. Real estate agents understand this, you know. They bake muffins or cookies the morning of an open house. When prospective buyers walk in, they don't want to leave. It works like magic." *I suppose the reverse is true too,* she thought. Maybe she could wrangle some skunks over to Mockingbird Lane if Jonathan decided to hold an open house.

"Sounds sneaky." He smiled as he peeled the paper from his muffin. "I'm addicted to this place. These are like crack for me."

She knew right then and there that he'd never had experience with drug users. No one who had would make a joke about addiction and crack the way he just did. She didn't blame him, though. He hadn't lived it.

"The coffee is wonderful too," she said, sipping hers.

"I was thinking about you after we met." He smiled. "As I was sitting in the dentist chair."

"Oof. That's not a good thing. You're going to associate me with pain."

"I don't mind the dentist. I actually like the taste of the stuff they use to polish my teeth." He leaned back in the chair, stretching, as if prepping to say something important but wanting to give the impression of being casual. "I was wondering how long you've been dealing with your ex." His eyes shifted for a moment but then focused back on her. "I know how upsetting it can be. I've been there. Well, with angry texts, at least."

"Really?" She placed her good hand beneath her chin and leaned forward a touch. Enough to say, *I'm listening.*

He ran a hand through his hair. "Yeah. When I was going through the divorce."

"Which was how long ago?"

"Three years now. Things have finally settled down, but it was hell for a while. And when you got those texts, it brought it all back. I felt for you. I probably sound intrusive. Maybe I am." He laughed. "I sometimes think it's my job to protect anyone who's getting bullied by an ex. And one day, if anyone dares to hurt my little girl—watch out. I'll kill them with my bare hands."

What a lovely sentiment. An idea floated above her like a soft cloud blocking the glare of the sun, but she left it to hover. No need to make any snap decisions. She moved her eyes to Sal's. "You're quite the protective one."

He shook his head. "I just have a knee-jerk reaction to certain things, and that's one of them. So while I was sitting there in the dentist chair, I was angry with myself for not trying to help. It's funny that I ran into you here today. I'd already planned to track you down in the marketing department." He held up his hands. "And if I'm sticking my head in where it's not wanted, I'll back off. I just wanted you to know I'm here to help if you need it." He glanced at her wrist but shifted his gaze quickly back to her eyes. He knew better than to pry. Lovely man.

"Thank you. But I'll be okay." She looked away from his probing brown eyes, urging her mind to work quickly. "Here's the thing," she stated slowly. "It was my fault too. I discovered he was married. And," she said, taking a breath, "he has a baby. A brand-new baby."

"Oh, shit. What a prick."

"That's a nice description of him." She smiled before soldiering on. "He was afraid I'd tell his wife."

"But you didn't?" His eyes were wide.

"No."

"Why?"

"Why, indeed," she said. "Karma?"

He laughed a big, genuine, contagious laugh.

She blinked innocently. It was a look she'd mastered over the years. "What? You don't believe in karma?"

"Yeah, no. I don't know." He grinned. "I like you. You may think that's weird for me to come right out and say, but after my divorce, I promised myself I wouldn't dick around ever again. I like you and would love to take you to dinner. Are you free tomorrow night? I know it's last-minute, but I have my daughter back Saturday morning."

She looked at him from beneath her lashes. "I don't know."

He shifted in his chair and looked down, just as she hoped he would. The trick was to make him worry her answer would be no. It would make her ultimate yes that much sweeter. Holding up her bandaged wrist, she said, "This is what happens when I venture out in the rain. Are you willing to take on that kind of responsibility? I mean, I'm insured, but there's a risk involved."

He laughed again. "I'll take the risk. I'll valiantly protect you. But it could stop raining for good by then, you know."

She nodded. "Very well, then. It's a date." With a bright smile, she capped her coffee and stood. "I'd better go. Maybe I'll see you at work."

"Bye, Sylvia."

She could feel him watching her as she walked to the door. It was nice to know that he liked her already. To be fair, she liked what she knew about him too. Though in the scheme of things, it didn't matter. He would only serve as a means to an end. The idea she'd had earlier was now glimmering brightly. It was time to get what she wanted.

~

Riki hunched over her phone, typing quickly. It was only 8:05—twenty minutes before the school day officially started—and with any luck, Sylvia or Embry would respond right away.

> Hi, guys, did you see the sign? Jonathan full on LIED to us about selling the place. I should've known. Do you think he's going to force us to move? I'm trying not to freak out.

She held her phone in hand, watching for a response. The door suddenly swung open, and she looked up to see Jeremy shuffling in, holding his leprechaun trap in both hands as if it were a special cake in a pink bakery box. Mrs. Tau followed, wearing a proud smile. "Hi, Miss McFarlan! Is it okay if we leave his project here before he goes up to the blacktop? He worked so hard on it, and I'd hate for it to get broken up there."

"Sure," Riki said, walking toward them. "I told the kids yesterday they could drop them off here before school starts." She smiled at Jeremy. "Wow! I love the way you added a second story with the smaller box. That must've taken you a long time." Her phone trilled with a text alert. She itched to check it, but this was more important at the moment.

Jeremy beamed and gently touched a finger to the top of his project. "It's the trap part! The stick holds it up right here, and when the leprechaun touches the stick, it'll fall and trap him!"

"That's so cool! Excellent creativity. Go ahead and set it on the horseshoe table. At the end of the day, I'll have all of you bring your traps to your desks."

He eased his masterpiece onto the table, careful not to topple it. That's what the project was all about—allowing the kids to feel proud of something they'd made.

A clattering sounded outside, and seconds later, Mrs. Trainor burst into the classroom hauling a red wagon burdened with a wooden contraption rivaling a Barbie Dream House. It was green and glittery with a flagpole perched on top bearing the Irish flag.

Darcy followed, a stuffed whale in hand. "Be careful, Mom."

"I've got it, hon. Don't worry." She stopped by the horseshoe table. "Whoa. This was quite a challenge to get up here. But we did it!"

Jeremy stood back, his eyes wide. "That's your leprechaun trap?"

Darcy shrugged. "Yeah." She pointed to Jeremy's, whose trap suddenly looked very rudimentary. "Is that yours?"

He shoved his hands in his pockets and nodded. "It's kind of small."

Mrs. Trainor wore a condescending smile. "Darcy's has a very elaborate trapping feature," she said, hoisting the leprechaun palace from the wagon. "Shoot. This is heavy. Can I have some help, Darcy?" Her voice had a sudden edge.

Darcy rushed to her side, but not before the trap wobbled from Mrs. Trainor's hands and crashed into Jeremy's trap, tumbling it to a chair before it toppled to the ground, where it landed in two pieces.

"No!" Jeremy screamed as he and his mom scrambled to collect the broken parts.

"Whoops! That didn't go as planned." Mrs. Trainor checked to make sure Darcy's trap hadn't suffered any damage. "Good news. It's okay." She straightened her already pristine sweater. "This leprechaun business is going to be the end of me." She frowned at Jeremy, whose face was wet with tears. He held a piece of broken trap in his hand. "Don't worry about that. I'm sure Miss McFarlan has some tape. Actually, I have some double-sided tape in my purse from when I fixed Darcy's bow this morning. If you have some glitter, Miss McFarlan, we can spruce up Jeremy's little trap and make it look even better."

Who does she think she is? Riki balled her hands into fists and counted to ten.

Mrs. Tau's mouth fell open. "It was great how it was! An apology would be nice."

Waving a hand, she said, "Oh, I'm sorry. It was an accident."

Riki exhaled and looked at Mrs. Tau. Her lips were now pressed together so tightly, Riki started to wonder if she was still breathing. But her nostrils flared, and Riki released a breath. The chatter of kids broke the strained silence, and three more students bustled in, their homemade traps in hand. At this point, she wouldn't have a second left to chat with Embry or Sylvia. Well, it wasn't like she'd be evicted today. But her mind was already charging ahead. She could practically hear Chris say, *No big. Move in with me.* Her face flushed, but she forced a smile at the students. Just because Chris owned a two-bedroom condo, it didn't mean he'd use her potential homelessness to push their relationship forward.

"Where do we put these?" Penelope asked, shaking her from her thoughts. "My mom said to make sure it goes on a flat surface."

"Right over here, sweetie. There's plenty of room on the table."

"Plenty of room if you didn't make a McMansion," Mrs. Tau muttered under her breath.

"Excuse me?" Mrs. Trainor snapped.

"Look around you. None of the other kids brought in giant traps made out of wood." She leaned closer, her hands braced against the table. "And aren't you the one who complained about them in the first place? Now you need to one-up everyone else so your daughter can win the big prize?" Her voice rose to a higher octave as she straightened. "You should be ashamed of yourself."

Jeremy's lip quivered as more kids filtered into the classroom, weighted down with backpacks and colorful traps made from shoeboxes, milk cartons, and Popsicle sticks.

"Hi, guys," Riki said in a rushed voice. "Traps go on the table, and put your backpacks on the hooks. Then head right out to the blacktop."

Spiteful laughter fell from Mrs. Trainor's lips. "Maybe *you* should be ashamed of yourself. Or do you take pride in being a cyberbully?"

Mrs. Tau lurched forward as Riki gasped. She grabbed for the lanyard that hung from her neck and blew hard into the whistle. "Ladies, stop!" she shouted with more force than she'd intended. The room grew quiet. Riki cleared her throat and smoothed her shaking hands down the front of her pants. It was up to her to regain control, even though she wanted to run from the room and never look back. In a calm voice, she said, "Okay, kids. You can go to the blacktop. I'll meet you there in just a minute."

Around her, students stood frozen, their traps and backpacks trembling above their designated spots.

"Let's go, everyone," she said in a cheerful voice, hoping to ease the tension. They scrambled to set down their traps and rushed from the room in clusters. Jeremy had wrapped his arms around his mother's leg, his face pressed to her hip.

"Ladies, this is absolutely not the place to battle it out. You're scaring the students."

Mrs. Trainor took the handle of the red wagon and glared at her. "I'd greatly appreciate it if you would refrain from talking to me like I'm a child. I'm not the one who raised a hand. That was Mrs. Tau." She touched a finger to her lips. "Oh, wait. It doesn't matter who started it. You just blame everyone!" she snapped. "I'd suggest you go back and refer to some of your teaching books. By the way, it's not professional to ignore emails. But don't worry, Mr. Rosenkrantz was able to chat with me." Riki's heart skidded around in her chest as Mrs. Trainor breezed out the door.

Riki heaved a sigh and looked at Mrs. Tau and Jeremy. "I need to apologize to both of you. That shouldn't have happened. I . . . I, um—"

Mrs. Tau held up a hand and gazed wearily at Riki. "Not your fault. I'm sorry for losing my temper. That woman drives me crazy."

"She broke my trap." Jeremy sniffed.

Riki kneeled in front of him. "She did. But I'll help you fix it during our morning work packets. I have plenty of tape and glue, okay?"

He nodded, and his mom kissed the top of his head. Riki snuck a look at the clock as she stood. "I really have to get to the blacktop now."

"Right. Sorry about all this," she said as they moved to the door.

"It certainly wasn't your fault." She patted her pocket. "Oops, I need to get my keys. I'll be out in a sec," Riki said, rushing back to her desk. She grabbed her keys and phone and headed for the door. The bell rang seconds before she reached her line, but Amelia had her eye on both classes. "Thanks," Riki said. "It's been quite a day already."

Amelia rolled her eyes. "It's been quite a year," she muttered. Stepping closer, she said, "Just so you know, I overheard some parents talking outside our classrooms the other day. They were saying you encouraged the kids to eat Pop-Tarts. I guess one of the kids went home and reported that you said they're fine to eat and that you like the chocolate ones. I'm sure it didn't happen that way, but I thought I should give you a heads-up."

Riki shook her head. "One of the moms shamed a kid for eating Cheerios, so I was trying to explain that there are all kinds of healthy foods and that it's okay to eat junk food sometimes."

"Yeah, I get it. But you know how second graders filter things. They hear what they want." The final bell rang, and Amelia said, "Just be careful. You really don't want to get the parents riled up. They wield a lot of power."

"Right. Thanks." As Riki waited for her turn to walk her students to the classroom, she stole a glance at her phone. The first text was from Sylvia.

I'll call Jonathan today. This is maddening.

I know! I can't even think about how much it would cost to move. There has to be something we can do.

Riki began typing.

I took all the flyers. I don't know if it'll help, but it felt good. I can't stand Jonathan! Sylvia, your idea about inviting him up to your place is sounding better and better. I'm not sure I'd rush to help if he trips on your busted stair.

They would know she was kidding. She didn't really want him hurt, but jeez! It was insulting that he had lied to their faces. As she was about to slide her phone into her pocket, it beeped again. She glanced at it, a half smile on her face as she imagined Sylvia's response. As she read the screen, her eyes grew wide. It wasn't Sylvia. The message was from Brandon.

Hey, I got a callback! I'm going in for the producers later today. I still haven't told Em, so don't say anything, but I had to tell you. This is awesome! You're awesome! I'm freaking out right now, lol. :)

She felt like time stopped as she reread his words. It was right there—he'd called her *awesome* again. And he'd said, *I had to tell you.* She didn't even try to slow the thrill. It hit her like a building wave, and she would ride it all day long.

Way to go, Brandon. I knew you could do it. You're amazing!

As she sent the text, her anger for Jonathan surged. The last thing Brandon needed was more stress on the day of his big callback. He needed positivity and support. Well, one way or another, she would stop Jonathan from selling their place. At this point, she didn't even care if he got hurt in the process. With the way he'd acted yesterday, he deserved whatever bad things happened to him.

~

Sylvia settled in at her desk and opened her phone to a search page. She tapped in *Sal Mendel, California.* God, she loved the internet. So much information at her fingertips. Several choices appeared, but it took only seconds to find the Sal Mendel with the pleasant brown eyes. He certainly wasn't careful with his personal information. He'd purchased a house in Santa Monica seven years ago for $430,000. It was a two-bedroom, two-bath home on a three-thousand-square-foot lot. A homeowner and an advocate of good dental health. What a responsible man.

She clicked on his Facebook profile and found he had a public account. It appeared that Mr. Sal Mendel graduated from Arizona State University with a business degree. He was originally from Fullerton, California, and his most recent post was from two weeks ago, so he was clearly active, but not a pathetic habitual poster still seeking approval from people he knew in high school. She saved the photo from his post to her desktop so she could analyze it without the risk of liking it.

He was at a golf course centered between two other men. Both were relatively attractive, with genuine smiles and bellies that stayed firmly behind their belts. A man whose gut reached down toward the crotch of his pants looked so sloppy. If anyone needed shapewear, it was the beer-bellied men. There were no females lingering in the background, but then, it looked like this was a boys' outing. She went back into Facebook and read the two comments. *Looking good, boys. Nice to see the old gang back together.* That was from a man named Danny Saunders. The next was from an Yvette Mendel Rodriguez. *Great photo!*

So, she thought. *He has a sister.* She clicked on Yvette Mendel Rodriguez, but her profile was private. Smart woman. Closing out of the page, she tucked her phone into her drawer and resumed working. She had all the information she needed for their first date.

CHAPTER
TWENTY-FIVE

Embry scooped Carson from the portable changing table and hugged him close, breathing in his baby scent. There was nothing she loved more. "Kylie, grab a sweater so you can go to the park with Daddy before lunch," she said as she walked to the kitchen. She knew she was rushing them out, but she was eager to do some research on how to get her honey pops into stores. With that sign outside, she was more determined than ever, and once she had everything all set, she would tell Brandon.

Kylie slunk by the master bedroom door. "Daddy's not going."

"Why? It's not raining."

She shrugged and sank to the floor as if her entire day had been ruined. Embry shifted Carson to her other hip and walked past Kylie into her bedroom. "Brandon," she started but then stopped. His hair was slick, and his face was freshly shaved. The jeans he wore looked new, as did the button-down shirt.

"Hey, darlin'."

"Where are you going?"

"I thought I told you. I picked up the midday shift at the restaurant." He patted his jeans for his wallet and headed for their closet, riffling through coat pockets.

"You didn't tell me." She watched as he grabbed his keys and stuffed his wallet into his back pocket. It didn't escape her that he was avoiding looking her in the eyes. "Are you not working tonight?"

"Uh, yeah, I'm still going in tonight, but I picked up an extra shift." He looked past her to Kylie, who had her back against the doorjamb and her feet pressed to the opposite side. A half grin emerged, and he winked at Embry. "Hey, sugar bear. Can I have a big hug before I head out?"

She lifted a shoulder and let it drop.

He scooped Kylie into his arms and blew a raspberry into her tummy, causing her to burst into a fit of giggles as she wriggled and squirmed. Goodness, it was so easy for him to get that girl to laugh. But Embry knew, sure as the sun, that once he walked out the door, she'd be left with a little girl who didn't understand why her daddy wasn't taking her to the park like he'd promised. He gave Kylie a big kiss on the cheek and set her gently on her feet.

"I'll try to stop by before I have to head out to the bar tonight, okay?"

Embry nodded and held Carson close.

"And don't look so worried," he said, following her gaze to the sign in the yard. "Just because it's for sale doesn't mean someone will buy it right away. It's all going to work out. You mark my words," he said, kissing Carson on the cheek. "Bye, baby." He gave Embry a meaningful look and left.

She squinted after him, trying to decipher what that look could've meant. It hit her like a sock to the gut. He'd lied. *Great acting, Brandon. I saw right through you.* What was it with people today? First Jonathan and now her own husband. She looked to Kylie, wondering if she could pile the kids in the car under the guise of running an errand so she could follow him. But his truck was already rambling down the driveway, and she'd have to work magic to get the kids buckled in the car fast enough to catch him.

She kissed Carson again, getting comfort from his sweet baby scent. Oh, for heaven's sake. Brandon wouldn't lie. And he certainly wouldn't cheat on her, would he? Oh, she was scattered! Ever since Sylvia had told her about her cheating ex-boyfriend, she'd become absolutely paranoid. That look could've meant anything. Heaven knows they had unfinished arguments lying around the house. Life had charged on, and they'd left them in piles on the floor, stepping around them as though they weren't there.

She startled when she realized Kylie was calling her. "Oh, sugar. I got so caught up in my thoughts, I didn't hear you. What do you need?"

An assortment of Tupperware containers was lined up in front of her on the linoleum floor. She tapped one with a wooden spoon. "Listen, Mama." In her sweet little voice, she warbled out a song. "I love my daddy. I love my mommy, too-ooh-ooh."

Embry smiled and clapped as her eyes filled with tears. These pregnancy hormones were causing her to get choked up at the drop of a hat. She had to figure out a way to tell Brandon soon. It was getting harder and harder to keep her tears at bay. "I like your song, Kylie. Will you sing it for Daddy when he gets back?"

She nodded solemnly. "I miss my daddy."

I do too, she thought, but she smiled brightly. Letting Ky see her upset wouldn't help a thing. "He only just left. And you'll see him soon. Now, how about you play some songs while I rustle up an early lunch. I'll make some nice soup for us. Do you want Nemo or Olaf?"

"Olaf." She looked up at Embry with her thick-lashed eyes. "You know what's sad, Mama?"

"What's that?"

Her lips formed into a pout. "We don't have Moana soup."

She smiled. "I don't think they make Moana soup."

"It's very sad."

"Maybe they will one day. You never know."

She just shook her little head, and Embry's heart squeezed. What if this wasn't about the soup? What if her sweet girl was sad about something else?

"Mama, Moana only gets sippy cups and underwear."

She almost laughed but held back. Kylie was clearly taking this to heart. "You're right. But she has some really nice cups. Do you want to use yours with lunch? Give your froggy cup a break?"

She clapped her hands, dropping the spoon in the process. "Oh yes, Mama!" She pattered over and kissed Embry on the cheek. "You're the best mama in the whole world."

At that moment, Carson wailed. Embry looked at Kylie. "Your brother doesn't seem to think so. What do you say we go get his pacifier?"

But Kylie was already prancing over to retrieve it from his crib. She returned, and in her singsong voice, she said, "It's all right, Carsie. It's all right. *Shh. Shh.*" She plunged the pacifier into his mouth, but he wriggled his head and screamed louder.

Embry quietly tried the pacifier again. "Thanks, Kylie. You're a good big sister. He's a little fussy, isn't he?"

"Oh, Mama. He's a mess."

This time, Embry did laugh. *Aren't we all?* she thought. *Aren't we all?* Maybe if she embraced the messiness of her life, everything would seem easier. "Hey, Ky? After lunch, would you like to watch a movie? You can sit on the sofa with Cuddle Kitty like a big girl." Usually Embry or Brandon sat with her, because they'd vowed never to use the television as a babysitter, but today, she was making an exception. Just because Brandon's schedule had changed, it didn't have to mess up hers.

Her eyes grew wide. "I watch *Moana*?"

"It's a plan. I'll be at the table doing a little work, okay?"

"Carsie watch too?"

"No, sweetie. It'll be his naptime then." *And I'll start to make things happen.* The sign outside stood like an unwanted visitor, but she would use it as motivation. *If the going gets tough, the tough get going.*

Thirty minutes later, Kylie had eaten her soup and was settled happily in front of the movie with Cuddle Kitty, her favorite plush toy. Embry made a list of ingredients she would need and checked the prices online. It would be a gamble to buy in bulk, but she was going to make this happen. *Make it happen or go broke trying.* At least she'd saved the box of printable business-card paper she'd bought years ago. It'd be easy enough to make an eye-catching card on the computer to go along with the pops. The more professional it looked, the better. If there was one thing she could say about herself, she was creative. And a perfectionist when it came to aesthetics. She would get these pops into a store one way or another. *Go big, Embry. Go big.*

CHAPTER
TWENTY-SIX

Riki pulled into her spot in the carport, and her eyes flashed to Brandon's truck. He was home. She wondered if he'd gone to his audition yet. The heady feeling she'd had earlier rushed her as she walked to her apartment, growing in strength with each step until she felt like it would sweep her from her feet. It couldn't be all one-sided. She lifted his spirits too. He'd called her *awesome*, after all. He was always happy and smiling around her, wasn't he? She dropped her bags on the table and floated to the kitchen. Maybe she could do a test, like ask him to come over to help with something totally boring. If he was happy and laughing while doing it, she would know for certain that he liked her too. It wouldn't change anything—it wasn't like she would suddenly start pursuing the guy. But it'd be nice to know if someone as perfect as Brandon could be attracted to her. If anything, it would give her hope that other equally amazing guys could like her. She glanced around the kitchen, wondering what type of task she could manufacture. *Not much in here.* She walked to her bedroom and turned on her floor lamp. As dim light filled the room, she knew exactly what she would ask him.

One of the bulbs in the ceiling fixture had been burned out since she'd moved in. She'd tried changing it herself, but her step stool wasn't tall enough, and reaching out to Jonathan had resulted in annoying silence. And after the way he'd looked at her yesterday, she wasn't about to invite him into her bedroom.

She grabbed her phone and began texting.

Hey! I have a situation and would love your help! Are you around?

Seconds passed, and her armpits began to tingle with nerves. Maybe this wasn't a good idea.

With a sigh, she walked back to the kitchen. She looked up when she heard a knock at the door.

She opened it, and a smile leaped to her face. "That was fast!"

"I was just walking out to get the mail, so I figured I'd come over."

"Thank you! But first, have you gone to your audition yet? I've been dying to hear about it."

He reached a hand to high-five her. "Thanks for asking. I've been dying to talk about it." He nodded to himself and met her eyes. "It was good. Real good. I know better than to get my hopes up too high, but the casting director asked a lot of questions. They had me do the scene a few times, which is a great sign. If you're not right, they're quick to tell you to go."

She squeezed her hands together. "I hope you get this! I can't imagine that they wouldn't love you."

"From your mouth," he said with a chuckle. "Now, what is it I can do for you?"

She grinned. "I need your legs."

His lips struggled to fight a smile. It made him look positively adorable. "Say again?"

"For the ceiling light," she explained as his expression shifted to neutral. "Even with the step stool, I'm too short to change the bulbs. And calling Jonathan again isn't an option."

"Yeah, I don't want to see that guy's face. I might end up punching it." He shook his head and laughed. "All right. My legs are yours for the taking. Show me the way."

Her face flushed hot. "Follow me. It's the one in my bedroom." Did he hear her voice quiver over the word *bedroom*? Was he stumbling behind her, wishing he could rush her and throw her down on the bed, while his loyalty to Embry was grabbing his ankles, tripping him up? She cleared her throat as she crossed the threshold. "There it is," she said, pointing to the ceiling light.

"Right where I would expect it to be," he said with a smile. "Your apartment is just like ours, minus the extra room we have." He glanced around her room, and his eyes landed on her bed. It was made up as usual, her pretty pale-yellow duvet looking like a sunny cloud with an array of fluffy pillows positioned perfectly at the headboard. "Man, your bed looks like something out of a magazine. I'd never want to get out of that thing. Look at all those pillows."

She forced a shrug, even though her insides were dancing. *You can test it out.* "It is pretty awesome. Sometimes I want to lie in it all day and never leave." She bit her lip as she watched him. Was he fantasizing too? She stepped forward. All it would take was a gentle hand on his back. His perfectly muscled back that was burned in her mind's eye. What would it feel like to run her fingers across his skin? Her heart banged against her chest, pushing her forward. She was doing this. Just one touch. That's all. Just one. And if he responded, so be it. Her eyes landed on a bulge in his back pocket as she took a step. She paused, trying to determine the shape. *A pacifier.* She bit down hard on her lip and drew her hands into fists. *What the hell am I thinking?*

He clapped his hands together and turned to her. "Okay. Where's that step stool you mentioned?"

"Right there." She pointed a shaky finger. "I'll grab the light bulbs."

He set up the step stool and positioned it beneath the light. "Okay, lady. Stand right next to me, and I'm going to pass you the cover in a sec."

"Sure." She held tight to the package of light bulbs and forced herself to focus on his shoes. *It's just Principal Rosenkrantz on the step stool,* she tried to tell herself. But her body mocked her mind, sparking with the electricity Brandon created.

"Here you go," he said, passing her the glass cover.

She set it on the ground and took the bulbs from the packaging.

"Trade?" He handed her one bulb and then another as she gave him the new ones. His arms reached above his head as he worked, which resulted in his shirt riding up, revealing a glimpse of his perfectly muscled stomach. If anything could be in a magazine, it was his abs. They were cover-worthy.

Her eyes drifted to the bulge in his back pocket, and her heart slowed. He was such a good dad. How many guys would carry their son's pacifier in their pocket? *It's the most attractive thing about him.*

"Okay, I'm ready for that cover." He pointed to where she'd laid it on the floor.

"Right." She handed it to him. "Thanks so much for doing this. I really appreciate it."

"Anytime. Want to flip the switch and make sure they all work?"

She flicked it up, and the lights went on. "Yay! You did it."

He swiped his hands together as he climbed down. "Mission accomplished."

"I owe you one."

"Nah. That's what friends are for, right?" He touched a hand to her back as he followed her from her room. If he knew how his touch affected her, he would pull it back like she was on fire.

"You guys are the best," she said, stepping ahead to open the front door. "I couldn't ask for better neighbors." She said it more for herself than for him. If he knew what she'd almost done, he'd . . . *he'd gently move my hands away and tell me no.* That was the thing about Brandon. He was always kind. No matter what.

"All good. I'll tell Embry you said hi."

"See you later." She closed the door behind him and pressed her hands to her face. *I love you, Brandon. I love Embry too. And I'm an idiot. Maybe I should drop everything and move to Australia,* she thought. It would solve everything.

∼

Embry peered through the window to see what was taking Brandon so long at the mailbox. He'd been acting strange since he'd gotten home from the extra lunch shift, and now it was just about time for him to leave for the bar, and he was taking ten minutes getting the mail. But he wasn't at the mailboxes. She frowned. Had he left for work without saying goodbye? Motion at Riki's apartment caught her eye. Brandon was smiling as he walked out her door. Embry could feel the color draining from her face. *What is he doing at Riki's?*

Her mind raced to the day she'd met Lily, who had strangely told her about Sylvia's cheating boyfriend. What an odd thing to tell someone you'd just met. And when Embry had returned the license, Sylvia had kept asking her what she would do in her shoes. It had struck her as odd that day, but she'd brushed it aside. What if Sylvia had recruited her friend Lily to "accidentally" bump into Embry? Sylvia knew they often went to the park in the mornings. Embry tried to remember if she'd said hi to her on that morning. But would Sylvia have created such an elaborate scheme to hint that Brandon was cheating? Well, she'd concocted a harebrained plan to get out of drug testing, Embry thought. But why wouldn't she just come right out and tell her if she suspected Brandon and Riki were having a fling?

Her heart slammed to a stop at the thought. He would *never*. Would he? The door rattled, and he walked in.

She forced a steady voice. "That sure took some time."

"Huh?" He set the mail on the table. "Oh, yeah. Riki texted me and asked me to help her change some bulbs on a ceiling light. She couldn't reach them."

"Oh!" Of course it was that simple! But she itched to sneak his phone and read the text. She squeezed her eyes shut, hating that she couldn't just trust what he said. "How is she?"

"Who? Riki?"

"That's who we're talking about, right?"

"She's fine, I guess. You talk to her way more than I do. She seemed okay, though. Why, is something going on with her?"

"No, I just was asking after her in general." *And trying not to lose my mind,* she thought.

CHAPTER TWENTY-SEVEN

Friday, March 17

Friday was finally here. Riki had jumped out of bed early, eager to get her day started. With all the drama surrounding the trap projects, she wanted to prove to the parents that it would be a wonderful day. She gently turned three of the traps on the Penguin Table upside down, as though the leprechaun had outsmarted them, but she was careful not to damage the traps. *Unlike Mrs. Trainor.* Her classroom phone rang, and she rushed to answer it. "This is Riki."

"Hey, it's Amelia. Do you have some green glitter I can use? I can't find any in the supply room. The kindergarten team must be hoarding it again."

"Yep. I couldn't find any either, so I picked some up the other day."

"Awesome. I'll be right over."

She turned a few chairs to their sides as she walked across her room. Amelia breezed in, clad in a bright-green dress and a shamrock head-band. "Whoa. You went all out," she said, eyeing the butcher-paper pathway dotted with tiny green footprints that led into the room and up the wall.

Riki grinned. "Cute, right? I saw it on Pinterest. I stayed late yesterday to do it."

"I should've done that, too, but I was so annoyed after school, I just blew out of here. Dylan's mom is making me crazy."

"It just takes one to ruin your entire day."

"No kidding." The shamrocks bobbled above her head as she spoke. "It's frustrating."

"If they'd just let us do our jobs and not get all bent, life would be so much easier," Riki said, straightening her own headband.

Amelia eyed the paper. "How'd you make the little footprints?"

"I dipped my fingers in green paint and kind of hopped them across the paper." She tilted her head, looking at them. "They look a little bit like alien feet, but I tried."

"They're awesome. You're so creative."

"Ha. Have you seen my papier-mâché panda? Chris thought it was a ball." Riki turned to her. "We're official now, by the way. As of last week."

"I thought you had been for a while."

"I mean, I guess we both weren't dating anyone else, but he wanted to make it officially official." She carefully tipped another chair to its side. "We're leaving for Mammoth with some of his friends this afternoon. It'll be our first trip together."

Amelia turned to her. "Why do you sound nervous about it?"

Because I almost tried to seduce my neighbor yesterday, and I've never traveled with a boyfriend? Instead, she said, "I don't know."

"Of course you know. What's up?"

"It's just—" She straightened a stack of papers on her desk. The traveling would be fine. It wasn't like they were going to Europe. They weren't even going on a plane. They were driving to the mountains. But if something went wrong, there was no escape. *Nothing will go wrong!* she chided herself. It was all going to be just fine. And she hadn't done anything to clue Brandon in on her feelings. She'd backed away from it.

But it still bothered her that she felt so strongly for Brandon when Chris was the guy she was with. "Um, how do you know when it's right? Like, does everything line up, or are there still things you wonder about?"

"Depends on what you're looking for, I guess. For me, I'm having a great time with Wes. He's fun to hang out with, and I think he's hot. But will I marry the guy? Probably not. But I'm not looking for that at the moment, you know? It boils down to what you want."

She made it sound so easy. And really, it was. So why did Riki have to make it so complicated? If only she could be as laid-back as Amelia. She could picture her flying down a mountain on skis and having a beer with the guys after. But she saw herself sitting on the chairlift, afraid to get off, faking confidence. She wondered if everyone faked it sometimes.

~

Sylvia cracked the car window as she sat in the Stone-May parking lot, her newest burner phone in hand. How she adored these gadgets. They were just so *convenient*. This one had a postage stamp stuck to the back—a reminder that it was strictly for calls to Patrick Sharp.

She glanced at her watch. Only twenty minutes left of her lunch hour. She typed Patrick's number. The phone rang twice before he answered.

"Patrick Sharp here."

"Hi, my name is Ann Travis, and I'm calling about the property you have listed on Mockingbird Lane in Venice."

"Yep, that one just went on the market. There's a lot of versatility with the property."

"That's the impression I got when researching it. I'd like to come take a look. Is there a time that works for you early next week?"

"I'll let you know up front that we're only considering serious inquiries. The seller doesn't want to waste his time."

"Nor do I," she said, copying his supercilious tone. "I own several income properties on the Westside, and I'm always scouting for good investments. Google me if it makes you feel better."

"I apologize. It's been a busy morning with calls from people who saw the sign and want to know if one of the units is for rent. They can't even read. Anyway, you said your name is Ann?"

"Yes. Ann Travis." She rattled off the number for the burner phone. "I'm out of town until Monday night, but I can be available Tuesday morning."

"How about Tuesday at noon? I'll meet you there."

"I'll see you then. Have a good weekend." She ended the call and smiled. Of course, she would cancel the meeting at the last minute due to a delayed flight, but she would talk numbers big enough to keep him salivating. And more important, good old Johnny Cat would ignore other potential offers. And then she would drag it out for as long as she could without garnering any suspicion. If Mr. Sharp googled Ann Travis, he'd find she was quite the player in the real estate world. And there wasn't a remote chance he could link her to Sylvia.

She took her own phone and called Jonathan's number. He answered on the first ring. "I'm surprised you didn't call the day the sign went up. I thought it would conjure some excitement among all of you."

"Indeed. Everyone's talking about it, Jonathan. Was that your wish? To surprise us?"

"Nah, things just moved faster than I anticipated."

She bristled but forced a smile as she spoke. "I suppose I can understand that. You seem like someone who seizes a good opportunity when he sees it. And to be honest, as much as it might not be ideal for me, I respect your savvy business skills."

"Thank you." She could practically see him preening. *Blergh.*

"I understand I may need to find a new place to live, but I don't want to start the search prematurely. If you have a serious buyer, do you mind letting me know so I can have a heads-up?"

"I can do that. Matter of fact, my real estate agent just texted me about something he set up for Tuesday."

"Wow. So soon?"

"The property is a hot commodity."

She giggled flirtatiously. His ego would certainly assume she was imagining *him* as the hot commodity. "Obviously. Thanks for letting me know, and please do keep me updated. If I can stay abreast of things, it'll help with the timing of when I start seriously looking for a new place."

"I can do that. Happy to help."

"Thanks," she cooed before ending the call. Now Ann Travis could always be one step ahead of the game.

~

Riki wiped down the last table with a disinfecting wipe and moved to the sink to scrub her hands free of green paint and germs. St. Patrick's Day was officially over for Room Fourteen. Thank God. She'd decided to pass out prizes to every child. It felt like the only fair thing to do. How could anyone compete with Darcy Trainor's trap? Everyone knew her parents had done the entire thing. And thanks to the box of auction prizes Mrs. Fitzsimmons had left behind, she hadn't had to spend a penny. Riki dusted her hands on her jeans before gathering her bag. With any luck, Mrs. Trainor wouldn't find something to complain about next month. They could celebrate rain showers and flowers. And endangered animals, of course. Mrs. Trainor couldn't complain about that. What was upsetting about a panda? As Riki walked to her car, her phone rang. She looked at the name on the screen and increased her pace.

"Hey, Brandon!"

"You'll never guess what happened!"

"What? Tell me!" she said as she fumbled to move the phone to her shoulder so she could unlock the door.

He cleared his throat. It made a rumbling noise that Riki found irresistible. She pressed the phone closer to her ear. "I got a *second* producer callback! They just told my agent. I'm still trying to wrap my head around it."

She could feel his excitement flowing through the phone line as she sank into the driver's seat. It was almost like he was next to her. If he were, he'd grab her into a delicious hug. "Oh, Brandon, that's awesome! I'm so happy for you." Her heart pounded as she said his name.

"Thanks. Can you imagine if I get this? God, I need this. I need it for Em," he said, lowering his voice. It made him sound wistful, like he was picturing her face as he spoke. "She's stuck by me through this crazy ride, and I want to be able to tell her I finally did it, you know?"

"Yeah." She licked her lips, trying to battle the sudden dryness that overtook her mouth. "She would be so happy."

"I know. Well, I had to tell you. You've been my one-woman support team through all this. If I get this part, I'll have you to thank for it."

"Hey, I just gave you a contact. You've done this all on your own. Be proud of that."

"Thanks, Riki." His voice softened. "Thanks."

She knew he was grateful to her. It's the kind of guy he was—the kind of man she wanted for herself. "You're welcome. And good luck with the next callback. When is it?"

"Monday. I'll definitely keep you posted."

"Thanks. Have a great weekend. Bye."

She ended the call and started her car. The way he loved Embry was nothing short of magical. Maybe that was part of his appeal. He was such an amazing husband. And seeing him interact with Kylie and Carson always made her heart flutter. She bit her lip as a sudden sadness swept through her. If they were forced to move, what were the chances they'd still be neighbors? It wasn't like their priority would be finding a place with an opening next door for Riki. Besides, Embry wanted a house. There was no way Riki could afford rent on a single-family home. Even if she could, living in a house with empty bedrooms would make her miss her family more. Doors would gape open from the hollow spaces, questioning why no one was there. How awful. The thing she loved about the apartments at Mockingbird Lane was all the people. As she drove home, her mind shifted to her upcoming trip with Chris. Maybe this weekend together would be the thing that pushed their relationship forward. She wanted him to be the perfect guy for her. He really was a wonderful person. Most of the time.

Ugh. She was going to drive herself crazy with the push and pull of her feelings. It was like the needy and vulnerable part of her heart wanted to chase after Chris, but her brain kept pulling back the reins. And she could never let anyone know where her mind had been with Brandon. That was something she had to keep locked inside. Forever.

CHAPTER
TWENTY-EIGHT

Sylvia removed her wrist brace and tossed it onto her bed. She'd worn it long enough, and besides, her wrist felt close to fine now. "Naughty Girl" by Beyoncé blared in the background as Sylvia spritzed a fine mist of Black Orchid into the air. She stepped through it, rolling her shoulders to the sultry music. The perfume was bold, so just a hint was enough. The key was to intrigue, not dominate. She'd chosen a wine-hued DVF wrap dress for her date. The beauty of the wrap dress was that it had a sophisticated appearance but could be downright sex in silk if she moved the right way. By leaning forward ever so slightly over her glass of wine, she could present him with a peek of her lacy bra and full breasts. She would maintain a neutral expression, as though she had no idea it was happening, and thus, it would give him the thrill of seeing something he shouldn't have. Men were so easy in the beginning. It was keeping them on a line that became more challenging.

She ran a finger down her neck and let it trail between her breasts. Her thumb touched her nipple, causing it to peak. She would repeat the move later tonight when she excused herself to use the restroom. Sal wouldn't be disappointed. Men were such visual creatures. Yes, Sal was a lucky man. If he only knew she'd saved him from Dowdy Sarah. What would that one wear on a first date? Cotton underpants and a sturdy bra? Sylvia laughed. And a wool dress, no doubt. She probably didn't own silk. Or know who Beyoncé was. The best she could probably do was missionary-style sex with her eyes squeezed shut.

The restaurant Sal chose was on a quaint street full of shops and restaurants. Sylvia had insisted on meeting him there. If he had picked her up, he would already be making plans for how to get her to invite him in when he dropped her off. Or at least, the idea that it was a possibility, however remote, would be in the back of his mind. It was just how males thought. But if she drove, he'd have to work harder. She'd upped the stakes for him without saying a word.

Now they were seated across from one another. She hadn't been sure what to expect—she'd only seen him in his work duds. Tonight, though, he was wearing a lovely black crewneck sweater over a plain white T-shirt and jeans.

He snapped his menu shut and sighed. "I checked twice—no blueberry muffins here. But," he said with a smile, "word on the street is they make some killer cocktails if you're inclined to order one."

"Ooh . . . I do enjoy a good cocktail." She shifted her menu and picked up a narrow card beneath it, skimming a finger down the list with a sexy swipe.

"Do you see something you like?" he asked.

She could've taken the bait and said something flirtatious, but she'd learned years ago that overt flirting was an amateur move. Make the guy work for it, want it, need it with every fiber of his being.

"Yes. Three down," she said, pointing. "The Paloma. It's made with tequila, lime, simple syrup, and mezcal. If there's a cocktail made with mezcal, that's the one I always order."

He nodded as he flipped the menu to face him. "You like smoky; I like spicy. I'll get the jalapeño margarita." He slid the menus to the edge of the table. "What else should I know about you? How do you spend your free time?"

She twisted her lips, feigning deep thought. Then she slowly licked her bottom lip, giving it just a hint of a bite. "I've just taken up golf. I'm terrible, mind you, but I like the mental aspect of the game." It was a lie, of course, but he had been at a golf course in his Facebook photo, so she figured he must enjoy it.

"Really?"

"Yes. Have you ever played?"

"As a matter of fact, I love the game. I've been playing since I was a kid."

"So you must be pretty good."

He smiled easily. "I'm not bad."

"Handicap?" she asked.

"Ah, you know the right questions. It's an eight."

She laughed. "Not bad? I'd say you're great."

"We should go hit balls sometime. I'll give you some pointers."

"I'd like that. So tell me about you, now that you know all about me."

"I know one thing. Well, two. Make that three."

"Three?"

"You like mezcal, you're learning golf, and you're beautiful."

She leaned forward just a bit. He deserved a little peek after those kind words. "Well, thank you."

The server arrived at the table and took their drink orders. He was young and handsome. *Probably an actor,* Sylvia thought. She wondered why Embry hadn't told Brandon the baby news yet. It was strange that she was so obviously nervous to tell him. The man was madly in love with her. She could tell by the way he looked at her. It was something she noticed every time she saw the two of them together. It was fascinating, like watching a hummingbird fly backward.

She studied the server's face as he recited the specials. The delivery earned him a three, maybe a three point five. Shouldn't he be selling the special, making it sound like the most delicious thing on the menu? Instead, he sounded like a second grader reciting the Pledge of Allegiance. "Do you need a few minutes to decide?" he asked robotically.

"Yes, thank you," Sal said with authority.

Once he left, Sal leaned close and whispered, "It's hard to make a peppered rib eye steak with roasted potatoes sound bad, but he did. How about we share some of the small plates? You mentioned you like doing that."

"I do. That way I can try a little bit of everything. It's so hard to make up my mind when it all sounds good. Pick whatever you want." She smiled. "Minus the boring special."

"Fair enough. And I'm saying no to the tin tin noodle dish. Poached egg and pork is a tough sell for me."

She laughed. "Agreed. I overlooked that one." Leaning forward, she said, "Tell me about your daughter. She's seven?"

"Yes. Seven going on twenty-five." His sincere brown eyes were warm, like hot cocoa by a roaring fire. "Her name's Ruby. Can I show you a picture?"

"I'd love to see one."

He pulled his phone from his pocket. Thankfully, he hadn't set it on the table when they'd arrived, eyeing it like a ticking time bomb. With a few flicks, he found what he was looking for. He smiled as he handed her the phone. "This was at her dance recital back in January. She's started hip-hop, hence the alternative outfit."

"She's rocking that outfit. I love it. Do you have more?"

"Scroll through. There's a ton."

Scroll through a man's phone on the first date? This was more exciting than molten chocolate cake with fresh cream. With a light touch, she swiped to the next photo and turned it to him. "More dance recital?"

"Yep. There's probably a bunch of those."

Sylvia looked closely at the picture. The girl—Ruby—had her hands on her hips and was mugging for the camera. She had her dad's brown eyes, but her hair was golden blonde. And she was tiny! Was this the size of all seven-year-olds? It would be rude to ask. She wondered if his ex-wife was a petite little thing. Was she a hip-hop dancer too?

"She's adorable." She glanced up at him.

"Thanks. She's a great kid." He reached for the phone, and Sylvia passed it back. "If I get started, I'll talk about her all night and bore you to tears."

Bore her to tears? *Hmm.* Had he dated other women who were intolerant of the fact that he was a father? She was intrigued by his feelings for his little girl. She wanted to know more. Did she have a favorite stuffed toy that she took with her on the trek from Dad's house to Mom's? Did she lie in her bed at night, hugging the animal tightly to her chest as she whispered her wishes and fears to it? Though maybe this tiny little girl—Ruby, whose name made her think of sparkling red slippers—was fearless. Maybe her parents didn't scream curses at each other, making her wish she could disappear. She couldn't imagine Sal throwing a bottle of Jack at the wall as he yelled, *You fucking bitch. I wish I'd never married you!*

The server delivered their drinks and took their order. He seemed disappointed they didn't order the special.

"Hey, we need to toast."

She smiled, blinking. "Whoa. This is strong. But yes, a toast." She lifted her glass.

"To our first date."

"Cheers to that." They clinked glasses. "So," she said coyly, placing her glass on the table, "have you dated a lot since your divorce? How does that work?"

He chuckled to himself. "How does it work? I have no idea. I thought I'd be married for life. That's the idea, right?"

"You should know you're asking a potential nonbeliever that question."

"You don't want to get married one day?"

"I don't know." She was treading on shaky ground here, that much she knew. It was always such a delicate topic. After what had happened with Hugh, she wasn't certain that marriage wouldn't end in murder if her spouse cheated on her. But could she go through with an actual murder? The thought of living within concrete walls and metal bars made her shiver. She'd seen those screaming inmates on TV, and if they didn't kill her with their criminal hands while she slept, their wailing would cause all the blood vessels in her brain to burst, resulting in her bloody jailhouse death. Although hypothetically speaking, if she *were* to murder someone, she'd be smart about it. No one would ever know it was her. "I suppose it would take the right person."

"Not a cheating bastard."

Well, that summed it up, didn't it? Sal was an astute man in addition to having nice arms. "Not a cheating bastard." She smiled easily. "So why did you and your ex-wife divorce? Or is that too personal a question?"

He spun his cocktail glass in a full circle, like he was opening a combination lock. His jaw was tense, but a half smile appeared. "Have I told you I like how direct you are?"

"Yes." *And I just did it again. Did you notice, Sal?*

"Good. Uh, so the divorce." He picked up his glass and set it back down again. "Short version is she wanted me to be someone else—more successful, richer, you name it. No matter how much more I did, she continued to put me down. I felt like I'd never live up to her expectations. So," he said, his lips tight, "I told her I couldn't do it anymore. *Go find someone who makes you happy, because I sure as hell don't* is what I said."

"Oof. I'm sure that went over well."

"We ran out of tissues, and she resorted to using a dish towel. She didn't want a divorce. Or at least, if we were going to divorce, she wanted to be the one to initialize it. Control issues or whatever." He took a hefty swig of his jalapeño margarita.

"People suck."

He sat back and laughed—a wholehearted burst. There was something empowering in knowing she had caused it.

"People do suck. Except us." He looked her in the eye.

"Damn right." She lifted her glass to his and offered a smile. What would his ex-wife say about him? That he was a worthless sloth with no upward mobility? *Hmm . . . But he's an accounting exec at Stone-May,* she mused. Well, maybe he found his way after breaking free from the one who was unknowingly holding him back.

Then again, he could be a sloth. It didn't matter. He was only a means to an end.

Shifting in his seat, he went for a casual tone. "Speaking of people who suck, how's the ex? Is he still pestering you?"

"I don't think so." She frowned but said nothing more.

"What do you mean by that?"

She took a slow, intentional sip of her drink. It was important to appear unsettled by the question. Setting her glass back on the table, she attempted a smile. "I'm sure it's nothing more than a strange coincidence, but I've had the feeling that someone is following me." Laughing, she said, "I'm sure it's just my imagination."

He sucked in a breath, causing his shoulders to rise up to his ears. It made him look very masculine, like a linebacker. Would he like that comparison? Probably so. "Tell me what's happened."

Peering at him from beneath her lashes, she said, "Promise you won't think I'm crazy?"

"I promise."

"Yesterday after work, I had to run some errands at the Coffee Cart shopping center."

"Okay," he said, nodding.

"When I was in the market, I kept seeing a guy who was dressed in black jeans and a hoodie. He literally appeared in every aisle I was in. It didn't bother me. Sometimes that happens, right? Like you're on the same path. But when I was in the parking lot, a car started to back up. I thought the driver saw me because I was a big target with my cart, but he obviously didn't, because he bumped into me."

"What? Oh my God!"

"It's fine. He wasn't going fast. It really was just a bump. But then the guy in the hoodie was right there. He grabbed my arm," she said, gripping her upper arm with her good hand. "He acted like he was trying to help me, but it felt like he was trying to knock me over. And then the driver got out of the car."

Sal's eyes were dark with worry, and he inched forward in his chair. "I don't like the sound of this at all."

"The driver apologized, but it felt like they were surrounding me. I don't know. It was all so weird." She shook her head. "All I could do was plow past them with my cart. He tried pulling me back, but I twisted and pushed the cart away from me." She laughed. "That got the attention of another woman in the lot. She grabbed the cart and came over to help. By then, the guys were both gone." She waved a hand. "Anyway, it was probably nothing."

Sal's arms were now crossed, and the look on his face reminded her of a frustrated television police officer. "I'm having a hard time understanding how this is nothing. It sounds like these two guys were trying to take you in plain sight and claim they were helping you. Did either one look familiar to you?"

"No." She shifted her eyes upward, seemingly lost in thought. "The one guy had his hoodie pulled up, and he had dark eyes and facial hair. And the driver was wearing a baseball cap. I can't even remember what he looked like. But my ex wasn't a bad guy. I can't imagine he'd have shady friends who would agree to scare me. It's ludicrous."

Rubbing a hand on his neck, Sal said, "I hate to point this out, but he lied about being married. He's not a good guy."

She looked down at the tablecloth. "I hadn't thought of it that way."

"Hey," he said, reaching for her hand. "I don't mean to frighten you. I just think you need to be very alert when you're out. Look, it could be a strange coincidence, as you said, but what if your ex is paranoid that you'll talk to his wife? It's possible he'll stop at nothing to prevent you from doing that. Do you get what I'm saying?"

Slowly, she looked up to meet his gaze with watery eyes. "Yeah. It makes me so mad that I didn't see through him. I feel so stupid."

"Don't blame yourself. Has he texted you again?"

"Just a few times. He wants to talk in person."

"You can't do that."

Before she could respond, the waiter arrived with their food. While his speaking abilities weren't great, his timing was. She was ready to move away from talking about Hugh. It was best to let Sal mull things over. People often created worst-case scenarios in their minds, given enough time.

~

An hour later, Sal slid his arm around Sylvia's waist as they left the restaurant. "Do you want to walk a while, maybe find a place to get some dessert?"

"I'd love to." She infused the right amount of warmth into her voice.

They headed up the street, passing two storefronts before he spoke again. "Do you like ice cream?"

"I'm allergic."

He stopped, turning to her. "To ice cream?"

"Kidding! I love it. Are you thinking the Cream Shoppe?"

"You know it. Best place in town."

The night was cool, but the patio had heated seating. They ordered cones. Sal had asked if she wanted to share a sundae, but Sylvia was quick to refuse the offer. "Ah. One thing I never share is ice cream." She looked down, smiling, before turning her eyes to his. "Sorry. I like to have my own so I can savor it." And there it was. One more challenge for Mr. Sal. It would become a victory for him if he could get her to share ice cream one day. It was all about creating opportunities for him to succeed along the way.

She took the last bite of the cone and dabbed her lips with a napkin. "Perfection. There's nothing like a good french vanilla."

Sal leaned back in his chair, a look of admiration on his face. "I would've pegged you as a chocolate lover."

"I am. But sometimes a pure vanilla is what I want." She took her lipstick tube from her purse and reapplied the dark coral color to her lips. She could do it perfectly without a mirror. Even though etiquette dictated she should do it in the restroom, she bent the rules. Men loved to watch women do anything with their mouths. It was a proven fact. As she capped her lipstick, she said, "It's subtly decadent. You should try it sometime."

He paused, checking her face for any indication of flirtation. Was he hoping she was making an innuendo about other types of decadence? Other things he should try? She could imagine his boy's brain adding *in the bedroom* to each sentence. *You should try it sometime* in the bedroom.

She rounded her lips and widened her eyes. "What? You don't like vanilla?"

"No, no. It's not that at all. I'm still working my way around *subtly decadent*. You know how to sell things."

She smiled. "It's my marketing background."

"Whatever the case, I'm getting vanilla next time." He stood. "Shall we go?"

"Yes, but I'm going to use the ladies' room before the drive home." She stood and, from the corner of her eye, confirmed that her phone was resting facedown on the chair.

Once enclosed in the bathroom stall, she took the burner from the zippered pocket of her purse and began typing.

This is bullshit!!! Stop ignoring me. Did you block my other
number? WTF?

She pressed "Send" and started a second text. It would feasibly take
a few dings to get Sal curious enough to pick up her phone and take
a look.

Answer me, Sylvia!

After waiting a few seconds, she sent the grand finale.

I didn't want it to come to this, but if you don't agree to talk to
me, I'm posting these on the internet.

Attaching the selfies she took at Sammy's apartment, she pressed
"Send." Before leaving the stall, she typed one more message.

Don't be stupid, Sylvia. You have one hour.

She stepped out of the restroom before hitting "Send." Then she
quickly replaced the burner in the pocket of her purse and headed for
the table.

As she eased into her seat, she was thrilled to see her phone was no
longer there. She smiled at Sal, and the concern in his eyes was palpable.
"Your phone kept beeping. It must've fallen when you got up, so I took
it from your chair." He slid it to her. "I didn't mean to read it, but the
text appeared when I had your phone in my hand. I think it's from your
ex. Is his name Hugh?"

Hooray for his curiosity! It had been a solid move to label the
burner as "Hugh" in her contacts, causing his name to appear with each
nasty text. She began reading, scrolling slowly until she stopped on the
first scandalous photo. "Oh no!" She smacked her phone on the table

and covered her face with her hands, allowing her shoulders to shake. It was tough to conjure up the tears, but after pressing her fingers into her eyes, she managed to get them going. Slowly, she looked up. "He's going to post photos of me on the internet. I have to respond to him. But oh my God . . ." She huddled into herself. "I feel so violated."

Sal's eyes were dark with rage. "What he's doing is illegal. It's called revenge porn. You have to report this, Sylvia."

Shaking her head, she spoke in a frightened whisper. "He won't stop. I don't even know what he wants anymore. I've promised him I won't tell his wife."

"If you're scared to go to the police, I'll go with you. Would that help?"

"I just don't know." Wrapping her arms around her middle, she said, "I'm so embarrassed. This isn't how I envisioned our first date. You've already seen me naked," she added with a bitter laugh.

"Hey," he said, reaching to smooth a hand down her cheek. "Our first date has been amazing. I'm not going to let your ex ruin any part of it. If anything, I've learned just how strong you are. You're an amazing woman."

Well, all this flattery was unexpected. Sal was proving to be quite a find. Luring him into bed wouldn't be difficult. "Thank you." A tentative smile crept to her lips. "I think you're pretty amazing too. Thanks for not making me feel bad about those pictures. I wasn't even aware he'd taken them."

He nodded and gave her shoulder a comforting squeeze. "Which is exactly why you need to report this."

"Okay. I think you're right." She drew her gaze to his. "Thank you for being so nice."

"I'm just being human. You deserve better than your ex." His lips quivered like he wanted to say more. How sweet. He rubbed a hand on her arm as they stood. "You're shivering. I'd offer you my coat if I had one. I thought we were on a warming trend."

She slid her hand to his as they reached her car. She'd found a great spot on the street a block from the restaurant. "This is me," she said, giving his hand a squeeze.

"VIP parking, huh? Lucky you."

"Someone was pulling out just as I was pulling in. Sometimes I get lucky."

He chuckled, and she hoped he was imagining getting lucky with her. "I was the lucky one tonight. Thanks for having dinner with me." He paused, circling his arms around her waist. "I can honestly say this was one of the best dates I've had in ages."

She was wearing heels, so she didn't need to stand on tiptoe. She closed her eyes and brushed her lips against his. It was a light touch, more of a sweep than a kiss. She caressed a hand down the side of his face as she did. There was magic in the right touch. She pulled back, and his mouth was still slightly open, and his eyes were hooded, sexy. "I had a wonderful time with you."

He touched a hand to his mouth. "I'll call you soon. And be safe, okay? I mean it. If he texts you again, I want you to call me."

She nodded and slid into her car, turning up the music on her favorite jazz station. Relaxing into the seat, she took out her phone and responded to "Hugh's" text. The key was making things appear real, even when they weren't. No loose ends.

Don't! I swear I won't tell Lily. I wish I had never met you.

That done, she pulled onto the street toward home. All in all, the night had been a success.

CHAPTER

TWENTY-NINE

It had been years since Riki set foot in the snow. The last time was on a family trip to Park City.

Chris's hands were suddenly around her waist. "It's beautiful here, isn't it?"

"Yes. I was just thinking that." They stared out the condo window, watching the falling snow. "Thanks for bringing me with you."

"No one I'd rather spend the weekend with." He brushed her hair to the side and kissed her neck. "Why don't you get unpacked, and I'll go with the guys to pick up food."

She turned to him. "It's really late. Is anything still open?"

"The pizza place is."

"Perfect! I'm starving."

He kissed her nose. "Me too. We'll be back soon. Cal already called in an order."

After their bags were in the room, Chris shrugged on his jacket and headed out with the guys. Riki watched as they left. Should she have gone with them? Evelyn and Shannon were settled on the sofa looking at something on one of their phones, their heads close. She knew Shannon only casually and had met Evelyn just the one time at the Lantern, but the two of them seemed, as her mom would say, "thick as thieves." She headed for the kitchen as though she had a plan. *Is everyone this awkward?* Taking a glass from a cupboard, she inspected it before rinsing it under the tap, just in case invisible germs were clinging to it.

"Hey, Riki," Shannon called casually. "I brought a couple of bottles of pinot. They're chilling in the fridge. Open one if you'd like. I know I'm ready for some wine."

"Sure. That sounds great." And it was just that easy. Why couldn't she be more like Shannon—totally comfortable in her own skin and seemingly not at all awkward around girls she didn't know well?

Rowan would give her such grief if she knew Riki was worried about a social situation. *You're such a little dork,* she'd say, even though Riki stood two inches taller. Every time she was near Rowan, she felt smaller. Littler. *Dorkier.* She found three wineglasses, giving them a quick rinse and drying them with a paper towel before setting them on the counter.

Shannon shuffled into the kitchen, readjusting her ponytail. She'd changed her clothes since they'd arrived and was now clad in black leggings, an oversize sweatshirt, and fuzzy socks. "Hey, I'll help."

For a moment, she was reminded of Embry. It wasn't because they resembled each other—they didn't. Shannon had thick brown hair and dark eyes compared to Embry's pale hair and light eyes, but the clothing was similar. Well, sort of. Maybe she was just wishing Embry were here instead of the others. It would be much easier sitting with Embry in front of a roaring fire sipping tea rather than drinking wine with women she barely knew. She could practically see her here, bustling in the kitchen as though she owned it, her ponytail bouncing as she chatted happily about the snow outside, the kids . . . it didn't really matter. She was just invigorating to be around.

Riki sat across from Evelyn, sighed, and tucked her legs beneath her in the oversize chair. If she looked cozy and casual, maybe she would feel that way.

Shannon settled into the sofa, wineglass in hand. "Sorry Cal was acting so weird about making a mess when we first got here. I think he has a little crush on his boss."

Evelyn, who had been leisurely sipping her wine, set her glass on the table. "Seriously?"

"It's not a big deal. She's married and has a kid. Maybe *crush* is too strong a word. It's more like he admires her. Maybe he wants to be *a-male-version-of-her* kind of thing. Bottom line is, he doesn't want anything to go wrong here that'll screw things up at work."

Riki nodded. "I can understand that. The *not-wanting-to-screw-things-up-at-work* part, but I absolutely do *not* have a crush on my boss," she said with a laugh. Maybe she could do this. If anything, it was good practice.

Shannon leaned forward to set her glass on the coffee table. "Remind me what you do."

"I'm a second-grade teacher."

"That's right. Do you not like your boss?"

"Oh, he's fine. I work at a private school, and he lets the parents have way too much influence, if you ask me. Just this past week, a parent complained about making leprechaun traps." Riki went on to tell them about the flurry of emails and the threat Mrs. Trainor made to contact Principal Rosenkrantz. She was so involved in her story, almost high from feeling like she was really fitting in, that it took her a minute to notice their eyes were starting to glaze. She needed to wrap things up. Evelyn and Shannon both worked in the entertainment industry, so hearing about the trials and tribulations of teaching was undoubtedly dull. "Anyway, I completely forgot to give him a heads-up that she was going to contact him and—"

"He was pissed," Shannon finished.

"Yes." She wasn't going to say any more about it. She had driven the conversation into the ground, and she hadn't even mentioned the red wagon yet. *Anecdotes, not dissertations,* she reminded herself. No one wanted to hear details anymore. Unless it was about guys.

"It blows my mind how legit adults—like people in their thirties—act like such babies. There's this actress on one of our shows who acts like a toddler every freaking time something doesn't go her way. The other day, she didn't get the revised pages before everyone else, and she was stalking around set in her nude bodysuit complaining. She grabbed our PA, who's, like, nineteen, and yelled, 'Who do I have to blow to get my pages?' The poor thing looked like his balls crawled up into his stomach. He probably won't be able to get that nasty visual out of his head for a while."

"That's hilarious," Evelyn said. "But terrible. Which actress was it?"

"Mia Marie. But I didn't tell you that. She's a nightmare."

"Aren't they all?" She turned to Riki with a broad grin. "Well, maybe not all. Your guy is amazing."

Adrenaline buzzed through Riki's body. *Your guy.* She was referring to Brandon. And for a moment in time, he was *her* guy. Oh, how she wished it were true. "Chris?" she asked, faking a confused look. She wanted to hear Evelyn say it.

"No. Your neighbor. Brandon Taylor." She said his name like she'd just licked whipped cream from a mug of decadent hot cocoa. "Our producers loved him. He's coming in Monday for a second producer callback."

"He told me," she said casually, wanting Evelyn to know they were *close.* "He's really excited about it."

"Yeah." She leaned her head against the sofa cushion and sighed. "And can we talk about how freaking hot he is? Seriously. I see hot guys all the time and I'm like, whatever. But Brandon Taylor? Totally TDF."

"TDF?"

"To die for."

"Who is this guy?" Shannon asked.

"Oh, trust me. You'll know that name soon."

"He's my neighbor," Riki said. "And one of the nicest guys I know."

"You're so lucky you live near him. Although, if I did, I'd probably end up stalking him or sneaking pictures of him with my phone."

The stolen headshot flashed through her mind. Maybe taking it wasn't as big of a crime as she'd made it out to be. Plus, she'd returned it. No harm, no foul. Not once had she snapped a photo of him, and the stalking thing—she certainly wouldn't stoop to that. Watching him mow the lawn hardly counted as stalking. He was just right there outside her window. Glancing at him was as innocent as noticing the mail carrier.

She'd started to feel stiff and dull when she told them about her work woes, but now she felt fluid and interesting. She wasn't a freaky robot but someone fascinating with a good story to share. "He's married, and his wife is a doll, so you probably wouldn't stalk him."

"I think I would. That southern drawl and those eyes." She slapped a hand to her heart. "He was practicing his lines near my desk when he was waiting to go in, and then he was like, *I've been working on my Baton Rouge accent. How does it sound, sugar?* For real? I die every time he talks to me."

Riki tried to keep her expression neutral. He'd called her sugar? Embry would hate that. A feeling of protectiveness shot through her. If Brandon ever did anything to hurt Embry, she would . . . well, she wasn't sure what she'd do.

The door rattled, and Calvin stepped in, pocketing his keys while balancing three large pizza boxes. Chris, Eddie, and Liam followed, loaded down with cases of beer and bottles of wine.

"Need help?" Evelyn asked, not moving from her spot on the sofa.

"Nope. You ladies relax. We've got this covered," Liam said with a smile.

Riki sat up, not feeling relaxed at all. She wasn't done talking about Brandon yet. She wanted to know more about what he'd said to Evelyn.

If he was being an overt flirt, she *had* to tell Embry. She leaned closer. "He's a cutie. What else do you guys talk about?"

"Not a lot. I just imagine all the conversations we *could* have. He's just there to audition, and then he leaves."

Riki relaxed a little. *Of course Brandon isn't hitting on women at his auditions.* He wouldn't hurt Embry that way. A wobbly new feeling tried to force its way to the surface, but she couldn't pin it down. She flashed a conciliatory smile at Evelyn. "To be honest, the first time I met him, my mouth went so dry, I could hardly talk. But now I can sit and have tea with him and his wife at his kitchen table while he's shirtless and holding his baby. Talk about the sexiest thing you've ever seen." *Whoa.* Maybe she shouldn't have said so much, but she wanted to prove to Evelyn that she knew him best *and* that he was married. It was stupid and immature—she knew that. But to be fair, she'd had more wine than usual. Alcohol had a way of talking for her. *Kind of like Chris,* a little voice said.

He was suddenly standing behind them with three plates, passing one to each girl. "Sexiest thing you've ever seen? My ears are burning." He kissed Riki on the temple.

Shannon laughed. "Nice try, champ. We weren't talking about you."

Riki's face flamed red as a nervous laugh fell from Chris's mouth. "What?"

Shannon winked at Riki, clearly unaware of the tension that was piled on the table in front of them.

Chris's jaw tightened. "Who were you talking about?"

"Evelyn was telling us about a part her boss is casting. We were just discussing actors." She gave Shannon a warning look, hoping she'd know to drop it.

He forced a laugh. "Who's your idea of the sexiest actor alive?" He touched a hand to his chin and thrust his hip. "Noah Centineo? People say I look like him."

Riki held in a smirk. He looked nothing like Noah Centineo, well, except that they both had dark hair and dark eyes.

"Ha! Good try. Her neighbor," Evelyn said.

Riki flinched. She scrambled to come up with something funny to say to fix things, but Chris fired a response before she could.

"Great," he snapped. "I'm getting a beer."

"Oops. I didn't know he's so sensitive. Sorry."

"He'll be fine. He gets weird about Brandon. His wife, Embry, too, for that matter. But whatever. It's fine."

She walked to the kitchen, wishing she could concentrate hard enough to transport herself back to her own apartment. Chris was being a jerk. After pouring herself more wine, she fished her phone from her pocket. *What the hell?* She clicked on Brandon's name.

Hey, I know it's super late, but I thought you might still be up. I'm with my friend who told me about the pilot. She is so excited about you! I'll fill you in more later.

She smiled and hit "Send."

~

Embry woke with a start. The front door rattled, and she sat up slowly, rubbing a hand across her face. She'd fallen asleep on the couch. Brandon walked in, his movements gentle so as not to make noise. "It's okay. I'm awake."

"Hey, darlin'," he said. "What are you doing up?"

"I was reading, and I fell asleep out here." She rose from the sofa and leaned into him for a hug. "You feel nice," she said softly.

He closed his arms around her and breathed in. "You feel even nicer. And you smell so good."

"Anything's better than a bar," she joked.

254

"True that. But even in a rose garden, you'd smell the prettiest." He kissed her forehead and smiled. "I'm gonna take a quick shower. And why don't you go get into bed. It's late." They walked to the bedroom, hand in hand. He set his keys and phone on the nightstand and headed for the bathroom as she snuggled beneath the covers. As much as they had argued lately, things always seemed better under the haze of sleepiness and the quiet of the night. She would share her news soon, and everything would be okay. A buzzing sounded, and she rolled over, slightly annoyed but also curious. It was the sound of a text, but it wasn't her phone. No one would text her this late at night, short of there being an emergency. Stealing a look at the closed bathroom door, she jolted to his side of the bed. His phone was faceup on the nightstand, and she could see the text was from Riki. Frowning, she read the bit she could see.

Hey, I know it's super late, but I thought you might still be up . . .

There had to be a reasonable explanation for it. Another light bulb? Her face grew hot, and an uncomfortable feeling slid through her. She grabbed his phone and typed in his passcode. Nothing happened! Her heart raced as she entered the numbers again, typing carefully. It remained locked. Oh, this was bad! He'd changed his passcode and was getting texts from Riki in the wee hours now? She looked up. The bathroom door was still closed, and the shower was running.

Grabbing her own phone, she held it tight, her mind spinning back to the headshot in Riki's purse and to him walking out her door.

She had to know. She wasn't going to sit by and wait for something to happen. No way. She began typing.

Hey, I saw that you were trying to reach Brandon. Is everything okay?

Embry watched the screen, her heart thudding uncomfortably.

Hi, Embry! Yeah, everything is fine. It was probably dumb to text so late. Oops! I'm with a bunch of friends and one of them knows Brandon. I thought it was a funny coincidence. I'm out of town with my boyfriend until Sunday. I can tell him about it then! Hugs. :)

Okay, have a good weekend. :)

She reread the text from Riki, searching for clues that she was lying. But if she was out of town with her boyfriend, it wasn't like she was texting Brandon for some late-night rendezvous. And she wouldn't do that! She was their friend. A trusted friend. Embry shook her head. Was it her own secret that was making her think Brandon was being deceitful? She stared hard at the bathroom door. It was true that Brandon hadn't been himself lately, but maybe they were just reacting off each other's energy. He wouldn't cheat on her. She knew that in her heart. And he certainly wouldn't cheat on her with Embry's good friend and their kids' babysitter, would he? She tried to force the hint of doubt away, but it kept reappearing. Tears leaked from her eyes.

She turned off her phone and replaced it on the nightstand before shutting off the light and saying a prayer.

You have nothing to fear, nothing to fear, nothing to fear, the angels whispered. She clung to the words and prayed again. This time, for the sweet escape of sleep.

CHAPTER THIRTY

Saturday, March 18

This is it, Embry thought. She'd woken with an amazing clarity and had decided today was the day to get things done. Riki's text was nothing to fear. She was certain she was feeling so jittery because of the baby and the financial worries the news would bring Brandon. Getting matters under control was the only way to gain some peace of mind. She closed her eyes and pictured Auntie Boots in her mind. *Yes, this is it.* She might not make millions, or even thousands, initially, but this was the start of something big. Opening her eyes, she carefully stacked the individual folders that were filled with three neat sheets of information on Hart's Honey Pops, along with her brand-new business card, and slid them into her tote bag. The boxes of samples were already packed in her car. "Ky, let's go on our adventure," she called as she hauled Carson's infant seat from where it sat on the kitchen table. He'd fallen asleep in it, just as she knew he would. Like Kylie, it seemed he preferred sleeping all hunched up in the carrier rather than in his spacious crib.

"Mama! Look at me!" Kylie zipped from her room, arms out like she was flying.

Embry's heart lurched. Her sweet girl just might be the one to close the deals. She was dressed in a T-shirt that Riki had insisted on making when she'd asked her for advice on how to put together a bee costume back in October. She'd crafted it with yellow duct-tape stripes across a plain white T-shirt. Paired with Kylie's bright-yellow tutu, black tights, and white fairy wings Riki had found at a craft store, she was the cutest little bee on the planet. As they headed for the car, Embry turned at the sound of someone calling her name. Shading her eyes, she looked down the driveway to see a woman with a stroller.

"Hello?"

The woman waved. "Hi! It's Lily. From the park?"

She walked toward her, balancing Carson's infant seat on her arm. "What a surprise! How are you?"

"Great. We're going over there now, and I thought I'd stop by and see if you wanted to join us."

"Well, isn't that sweet. We're just on our way out. Maybe another day?" Lily nodded and smiled, but Embry could see her disappointment. She knew all too well how long the days could be with a baby. Lonely too. "How about you come here on Monday? We can chat over a cup of tea while the babies look at each other."

This time, a wide smile emerged. "That would be great."

"Perfect. Come on by around four thirty."

"See you then."

As she walked to the car with Kylie by her side, she reassured herself that Sylvia hadn't come up with a crazy, elaborate scheme to put Lily in her path. She was just another mom who was finding her way, same as Embry. And besides, it felt really good to befriend Lily. For the first time, she was the one who could offer advice on motherhood. It was exactly the burst of confidence she needed.

~

Embry gripped Kylie's hand tightly and paused outside of Soul Candy. Kylie's wings sagged, and Embry felt limp herself. The visits to the grocery stores had left her hopes wilted. At the last one, the clerk hadn't even let her speak with a manager. She'd simply said corporate handled products. This was her last shot. "Ky, this is a small store with a lot of fragile things, so you need to stay close to me, okay?"

"We go home soon, Mama?"

"Yeah, as soon as we're done here." She tried to stand tall, but she felt like a pack mule loaded down with a shopping bag full of honey pops hanging from her shoulder and Carson in the sling. She wondered if it was even worth it to try.

The pops are delicious, a voice insisted. *Go in there and get it done.* This time, she didn't hear her mama or Auntie Boots. It was her own voice.

Head held high, she pushed through the door. An immediate sense of calm overtook her. Peaceful spa music played, and the same woman she had met before swept over to her.

"Hello there." She smiled serenely, and her eyes grew bright. "I remember you. Have you come back because something spoke to you after all?"

"Hi. As a matter of fact, yes. Is there a manager who I might be able to speak to?"

She nodded slightly. "I'm her." Gently extending her hand, she said, "I'm Abby Berman, the owner. How can I help you?"

"Hi, I'm Embry Taylor. When I was here last, I noticed you sell products from local vendors here."

She nodded. "We do."

She took a package of cellophane-wrapped honey pops from her tote. They were tied with a pretty yellow ribbon, and she'd added a cute tag with the printed logo she'd created on the computer. On the back, she'd written, Hart's Honey Pops are made with love by Embry Hart Taylor. Wife, mommy, daughter, sister. Thanks to my auntie Boots for creating the very first honey pops recipe. ♥

"I had a bit of an epiphany after I was here, and I was inspired to make Hart's Honey Pops. They're honey candies that can be swirled into tea or coffee or," she said, holding them up, "eaten like a sucker. The best part is, they're naturally sweetened and infused with real lemon and vanilla." She took a folder from her tote. "Here is the information sheet, which includes pricing options and ingredients." She held her breath as Abby flipped through the pages.

Abby finally nodded. "Manuka honey. That's becoming quite popular now. It's from New Zealand, right?"

"Yes," she responded eagerly. "And please try one if you like."

"Mama, I have one too?" Kylie asked.

"Sure," she said quickly. As she handed one to her, she gave her a firm look. "Just one."

Abby smiled at Kylie before biting the entire pop off the stick. She chewed, her brow furrowing as she did. "Oh my God. These are amazing."

"Thank you." Embry beamed. This felt right. Sharing her food with others was one of her favorite things. Carson wriggled in the carrier and tried grabbing for the honey pop.

"No, Carsie!" Kylie shouted. "No honey for babies!" She grabbed on to his little foot, and he let out a loud cry.

Oh, goodness. This wouldn't do. She was so close to making this happen. In a swift move, she took a pacifier from her pocket and eased it into his mouth, bouncing gently. If she'd learned anything from her pageant days, it was to turn a negative into a positive. And most important, don't let anything throw you. She wasn't about to let this slip from her grasp. Taking another sheet of paper from her bag, she passed it to Abby. "Here's a copy of my Class B CFO permit."

"Wonderful." She eyed Carson, who was now grabbing Embry's hair into his tiny fists. "You have your hands full, don't you?"

"Because she's holding Carson!" Kylie said with a loud giggle.

Abby grinned. "That's very true." Focusing back on Embry, she said, "I would love to give these a try. They're full of wonderful flavors, in addition to being a nice alternative sweetener. I'll email you our consignment agreement this afternoon, and you can send it back in at your convenience."

"Thank you so much." She untangled Carson's hand from her hair. "That's wonderful."

"I should mention this is just one of four shops we own on the Westside. We're also in Playa del Rey, Brentwood, and Westwood. I'd like to sell your honey pops in all of them."

"Wow. Really? I mean, that's fabulous." A smile broke out across her face, and for the first time in a long while, she had the good feeling that everything would be okay.

"I think so too. I'll be in touch. Have a blessed day."

"You too." As she headed toward the door, she leaned down to kiss Carson's head. She'd done it. With two babies in tow and a near meltdown, no less. Four stores! It was a better start than she could've imagined.

Brandon would be at work, but this was worth the interruption. His phone rang only once before he answered.

"Hey. Everything okay?"

"Yes. As a matter of fact, I have some great news."

"Really? Well, lay it on me. I could use some good news."

The smile in his voice added to her excitement. "Hart's Honey Pops are going to be sold in four stores in the LA area."

"Wait, *your* honey pops? The ones you make?"

She laughed a soul-cleansing, carefree laugh that she hadn't experienced in weeks. "Yes," she said, her voice sparkling.

"Wow! I, uh . . . wow. How'd you . . . They're for sale? Like, for profit?"

"Yes! They'll be at a new-age store called Soul Candy. There's one in the same center as the market."

"Holy cow. How did you manage this? I mean, I noticed you were making a lot of them, but I chalked it up to stress relief."

"That was the motivation." A little voice sidestepped in, blocking her from telling him *why* she was so stressed. Maybe it was those angels again. Whatever the case, she felt compelled to listen. But would there ever be a perfect time, or would she falter at every opportunity? Well, it would be stupid to tell him over the phone. The baby news had to be shared in person, face-to-face. "I wanted to surprise you."

"Well, you succeeded in doing that. I'm so proud of you, Em. I wish I could jump through the phone and hug you. My mind is kind of blown."

"Mine too. I'll let you get back to work, but I had to let you know. I love you."

"I love you, my sweet darlin'," he said softly. "I'll see you soon."

CHAPTER

THIRTY-ONE

Riki turned hard and forced her bottom ski to push against the snow, frantic to prevent herself from picking up speed on this hellish run. It was Chris's fault she was here alone. He'd gotten all bent when Evelyn mentioned Brandon again while they'd been on the chairlift, which now felt like hours ago. The silence that followed had made Riki sweat despite the freezing cold.

And even though he'd promised to help her off the lift at the right time, Chris had pushed ahead of her. She'd tripped—her timing not quite right for a clean dismount—and the chair operator had had to stop the whole show. Chris and everyone else had gone ahead. They were specks on the mountain, and despite trying to catch up, she couldn't. When she'd reached a spot where the run broke off into two, she'd followed what looked like the easier of the trails, but the group was long gone.

For all she knew, Chris was already back on the chairlift, buzzing with the anticipation of a second adrenaline rush. And Riki was clinging to her poles as if they were her only grasp on safety as she inched across the mountain, her heart racing every time she had to make a turn. The fear of losing control as she pointed her skis down for a brief second was relentless. Even though the crisp air bit at her exposed nose and cheeks, the rest of her body felt like she was wrapped in a muggy wet blanket.

She eased to the side of the run near a barrier of trees and paused to catch her breath again. With a shaking hand, she pushed her goggles to her forehead—a simple move made awkward by her puffy gloves. The lenses were fogged, making it so she could hardly see. She tugged at the collar of her jacket and gulped for fresh air. It burned her lungs, and the biting wind made her face feel like it might crack from the cold. Moisture dripped from her nose. She dabbed at it with the sleeve of her jacket, which only made things worse.

The beauty of her surroundings was at odds with how she felt. The trees stood like royalty, their sharp pine needles made soft by the blanket of snow—princes in fine coats. It'd be a nice spot for a quaint hut. Something private and cozy, where she and Brandon could lay a thick blanket and snuggle, mugs of cocoa and cookies in their hands. *Oh, jeez!* Did she really just think that? She sniffed. It was too easy to imagine him. He would be furious if someone left his wife up on a mountain, alone and cold. He'd even be pissed that Chris had left Riki. She imagined the conversation they'd have. His blue eyes would go wide, and then he'd shake his head and say, *Sweetie, I think you need to dump his sorry ass and find yourself a nice guy.*

She shivered. Brandon wasn't here, and the truth was, she probably wouldn't ever tell him about this. But she would certainly tell Embry. What a stupid move it had been to text Brandon last night. What had she been thinking? Well, she hadn't been. She'd been buzzing off too much wine. And now she would have to wait to tell Brandon the real reason she'd texted. It felt wrong lying to Embry, but she'd promised not to say a word about the pilot.

Turning her glassy eyes to the run ahead, she wondered how she was going to make it all the way to the bottom of the mountain. Chris shouldn't have gotten pissed and gone ahead. Instead, he should've made big *S* turns across the mountain as she followed his trail, shouting words of encouragement that would've made her feel all warm inside.

But in reality, was there anything he could say to make her feel that way? She shivered against the cold. As much as she was trying to conjure all the right feelings for Chris, they kept slipping from her grasp. He wasn't stupid. And she wasn't good at masking her emotions. Maybe he'd done the only thing he could in that moment. Hearing about Brandon again, no matter who brought his name up, might've been more than he could take. Jealousy had a way of clawing reason to shreds when it was invited in.

She thought for a moment about curling up in the snow and waiting for ski patrol. *But I'd probably die of frostbite,* she thought. *My feet will turn blue, and they'll have to amputate them. It'll be my punishment for crushing on my friend's husband.*

She shook her head. Nothing would have to be amputated. She pulled her goggles into place and gripped her poles, turning downhill in a large arc. If she started to make shorter turns, she'd be able to reach the bottom sooner.

Crisp flakes of snow pelted her as she traversed the run. Heaving a breath, she turned again, picking up speed. She automatically went into a snowplow position as fear that she would fall took over. It brought her to a stop, but she was facing straight down. She would have to pick up her left leg and move it perpendicular to the mountain. Planting her pole, she swung her leg and toppled over, but it wasn't a big fall—more like she'd just decided to sit down for a moment. She pushed up and inched forward until her right leg was perpendicular to the mountain too. The powdery snow took up residence in the tops of her boots, chilling her legs through the thick wool socks.

Clenching her poles, she forced herself to remain calm as she started down again. She could barely see the sign for the next run ahead, but it was there, and that meant she was one step closer to ending this torture.

I'm fine, I'm fine, I'm fine, she repeated to herself. Turn after turn, she crept down the mountain, each second she remained upright a breathtaking victory. She executed one more turn and heaved out a sigh. This was exhausting. Maybe she could just rocket down and hope for the best. It was snow, after all. What was the worst thing that could happen? She'd land face-first in the powder? It would certainly be faster, like ripping off a bandage.

Squeezing her eyes shut, she asked the universe for a sign. Three skiers whizzed by, causing her eyes to spring open. They were swishing along the hill, their bodies nimble, making it look easy. Fun, even. She looked down and noticed for the first time that the run swelled upward at the end, and beyond that was the small hill packed with tiny skiers that meant the bottom was near! A natural stop and then the end. Was that the sign she'd been hoping for?

Whatever the case, she couldn't stay here all day. Pressing her chapped lips together, she pushed off and headed straight down. Wind whooshed in her face as she gathered speed. The trees were no longer individual entities but a blur of white and green. A sickening mix of fear and excitement coursed through her veins as she neared the upward slope.

"Slow down!" someone shouted as she sped past.

She startled and pressed hard into a snowplow as the rickety fence at the edge of the run seemed to race toward her. But her legs were nearly in a split position, and she couldn't slow herself. There was no time to think. She forced herself to topple to the side and fall onto the snow. But the momentum dragged her toward the fence. The world around her was a blur of white. *I'm not dying on this mountain!* It was a fleeting thought, but it reassured her as she crashed into the fence, tumbling as though she were attempting a somersault.

And then the heart-stopping roller-coaster ride slammed to an abrupt halt.

As she lay in the snow, her mind worked fast, as though it'd been taken over by a trained medic.

Feeling in arms?

Check.

Legs?

Check.

Helmet?

In place.

Skis?

Gone.

She rolled to a sitting position. Her neck ached, and she pressed a gloved hand to it. It was then that she noticed the blood. The sticky red smeared across her glove and marred the pristine snow with garish drops.

A tall skier dressed in black slowed to a stop near her. He pulled up his goggles and looked down at her. "Are you okay? That was quite a fall."

She pulled off her gloves and swiped a hand beneath her eyes. "I think so, but I must've cut my neck when I landed."

He peered at her skin, amazingly stable on his narrow skis. "We've gotta get you down the mountain." As if she were a pop-up attraction at an amusement park, two kids breezed to a stop next to her, followed by a woman in bright blue, who swished down to where Riki's skis had landed. The children gathered Riki's poles. "My family," the man said. "I'm Brady, by the way." He reached down to hoist her up by the arm.

"I'm Riki. Thanks for helping me."

"No problem. Are you skiing with your family? Some friends?"

"Yeah, but they got ahead of me."

He nodded and turned to his wife, who had lined Riki's skis up next to her. "Thanks, hon. I'll help her down. Why don't you take the kids and start with lunch? I'll meet you there in a minute."

"Sure." She looked to Riki and pulled a package of tissues from her jacket pocket. "Take these to press against your cut—at least for now. They'll have bandages down at the lodge. Or I can alert ski patrol if you'd rather. I have an app on my phone for them."

"If you don't mind, I'd rather just go now. Getting hauled down by ski patrol would be mortifying." She pressed the tissue to her neck and was surprised at how it immediately clung to the moisture. *Please let it be wet snow, not blood,* she thought as she zipped her jacket up to her chin—where it should've been all along. When she'd put it on that morning, it had rubbed uncomfortably, so she'd only zipped it to her neck. Brady held her arm while she clicked back into her skis and put on her gloves.

"It's not a long way down now, but we're going to take this slow, okay? Follow my trail. Can you do that?"

"Yeah. Thanks." Shifting her goggles into place, she kept her eyes on the black-clad figure in front of her. His path was easy to follow. With each turn he made, he watched to make sure Riki was doing okay.

"Good!" he called. "You've got this!"

What a nice man. They came to a slow, uneventful stop near the lodge. "I'm worried about that cut. You're going to need to get it looked at. Can you reach one of your friends?"

"I'll call now. Thanks for all your help."

"Sure thing. And take an easier run next time, okay?" He smiled in the comforting way that seemed unique to dads.

"Yeah. I will."

He patted her on the back. "Take care, Riki."

She jabbed the ends of her poles into the snow and fumbled with the zipper of her jacket pocket to get her phone, but it was futile with her gloves on. Using her teeth, she ripped off the glove and slipped out her phone, careful not to drop it in the snow. She dialed Chris and pressed the phone to her ear. But the words she heard made her heart sink.

It's Chris. You know what to do.

She hit "End" and moved to take off her skis. As she walked into the lodge, people's curious eyes followed her, but she ignored them. And who knows? Maybe she was only imagining it. For all she knew, the cut had bled only a little, and there was nothing to see. But the sticky warmth on her neck told her otherwise. After returning the rental skis and boots—she had no interest in using them again—she padded in her thick, damp socks to the locker room. If only Chris would walk in and take her back to the condo where they could sit in front of the fireplace. *Ha!* She collected her Uggs and purse from the locker. Before sliding on her warm boots, she removed her socks and rolled them into a ball, stuffing them in her purse along with her gloves. It was time to check the damage.

People shuffled in their wet gear, patiently waiting for a turn at the hand dryers in the restroom. She slipped past them and made a beeline for the mirror.

Blood was smeared on her chin. She unzipped her jacket and gasped. The tissues were soaked bright red. Her reflection swirled and blurred in front of her as she gripped the sink. *I can't pass out.*

"Oh!" a woman at the neighboring sink said. She ripped paper towels from the holder and wet them before passing the wad to Riki. "Press these against your cut. There's a first-aid room at the lodge."

A gaping wound was revealed as she eased the bloody tissues away. It looked like someone had tried to slit her throat with barbed wire. "Thanks," she said, taking the paper towels.

"Sure. Do you need help getting there?"

"No, but thank you." Riki clamped the towels to her neck as she found a bench outside the bathroom. She tried Chris again.

No answer. This time, she left a message. As she was about to shut off her phone, it struck her that she had Evelyn's number. She scrolled through her contacts and clicked it, pressing the phone to her ear.

It rang once and went straight to voice mail.

As she stood, wondering what to do next, Brady's wife and kids walked by. "Hey there. Did you reach your friends?"

"Um, I left a message." She mustered a smile upon seeing the woman's concerned look. "It'll be fine. Do you happen to know where the first-aid room is?"

She frowned at the paper towel pressed to Riki's neck. "I do, but you might want to skip it and go to the urgent care. I think you'll need stitches, and if it were me, I'd rather have it done at a doctor's office, but it's up to you."

The thought of a potentially unsterile little room made Riki's stomach ache. "Yeah. I think you're right. I'll grab an Uber."

"Not up here. There aren't any."

Riki faltered. "No Ubers?"

"They're not allowed. But I can run you down there if you'd like. We do it all the time. Folks are nice here."

"Oh! Thank you. But I'm fine. My boyfriend will want to take me." She hoped he would. As nice as the woman was, Riki didn't love the idea of trying to make conversation with a stranger while sitting in the passenger seat of her car. Especially when she was about to freak out.

"Are you sure?"

"Yes, thanks." As she walked away, she called Chris again. Panic tried to settle in when it went to voice mail. He wasn't going to answer. Maybe he was in the middle of a run and couldn't hear it. Or he could have his ringer off. Maybe she *should've* said yes to the offer. Pushing through the door to the slopes, she scanned the area for Chris or Calvin—anyone she knew. Her neck throbbed, and blood was seeping through the paper towels onto her fingers. *Dammit!* Where were they? As if the weather were incensed right along with her, the snow fell harder. These weren't the lovely snowflakes of fairy tales—no, these were akin to getting sandblasted.

She headed inside and stopped at the returns desk, where a shaggy-haired guy sporting a pom-pom snow hat stood behind the counter. "Whoa. You're bleeding! The first-aid room is—"

"I know," Riki said, adding more pressure to her neck. "I want to go to the urgent care. Is there a shuttle?"

"Nah, man. Sorry." He stole a look at her bleeding cut. "But hang on a sec."

He returned a moment later. "My coworker just finished his shift. He'll be right out and can take you." Motioning to Riki's neck, he said, "What happened there? Did someone whack you with a ski?"

"I crashed into the boundary fence."

"Whoa. You've gotta be careful out there." He turned as a tall guy with a boyish face and kind eyes approached.

He tipped his head in greeting—*a cool-guy move,* she thought, though he looked more like someone's sweet older brother than an egocentric hipster. "Are you the one I'm taking to town?"

Riki swallowed hard and nodded, keeping her hand pressed to the side of her neck. *It's not hitchhiking.* The woman said people were nice around here. Besides, this was urgent, and the guy looked harmless. She gave him a hesitant smile. "Yeah. I'm Riki."

"I'm Cody. Let's do this."

She buckled the seat belt in his SUV, surreptitiously checking to make sure the locks worked on her side. There was no way she was going to walk directly into a trap. *Trust no one*—that's what her dad always said. *Until they prove themselves trustworthy, right, Greg?* her mom always added. *We don't want our girls to live in fear.*

"It's coming down now." He turned to her, keeping a casual hand on the wheel. "Are you just in for the weekend?"

"Yeah. There's a whole group of us who came up."

He nodded. "What'd they do—bail out when you crashed?"

She looked straight ahead, scouring the streets for the first sign of the town, because if she stopped to think too much, she might cry. "We got separated."

"You've gotta keep a buddy on the mountain, okay? Especially on a day like today."

A buddy. Wasn't that the truth? She rested her head against the passenger seat. "I know. They thought I would keep up, I guess."

He flicked on his blinker, and the steady *tick, tick, tick* reassured her. They were almost there now. Was this how Sylvia had felt when Riki had driven her to get her wrist checked? Like she just wanted to rush from the car and get on with the healing part? No wonder she'd blown off the books. There was no way Riki could get lost in a book at the moment. But she could use a hug. Or her mom.

Why hadn't Chris called back? She wrapped her arms around her purse. There was no use checking her phone again. The ringer was on, so she'd know if he had. He was probably in the lodge by now, his clothes dry and his beer cold. Would he even notice Riki wasn't there?

"This is it," Cody said, pulling into a parking spot. "You cool?"

"Yeah." Riki unbuckled. "Thanks so much for the ride."

"No prob. Good luck."

"Thanks." She hopped down from the truck and walked as fast as her slippery-soled Uggs would allow. The waiting room was empty, and a sigh of relief whooshed from her lips.

A woman wearing a pink scrubs top with a purple unicorn pattern looked up as Riki approached the counter. A name tag pinned to her shirt said SAMANTHA. "Take some of these," she said, pushing a box of tissues toward her. "Apply pressure, but don't press in." She adjusted the digital clock on the counter. "We close at three, and we've already taken our last patient." She pursed her lips and tapped the desk. "That looks bad. Let me see what I can do. May I see your insurance card?"

"Yeah." She dug her wallet from her purse and took out the card. "Here it is."

"Okay. I'll see if the doctor can squeeze you in when he finishes with his last patient. In the meantime, you can fill out these papers." She slid a clipboard to her. "Have a seat."

"Thanks." Riki settled into a chair and focused on writing answers to the questions. Her neck throbbed, but she was too scared to pull away the old tissues. She just piled the new ones on top. Blood—especially her own—was something she didn't want to see. If only Chris were here with her. She shivered. What if he didn't call back? She'd be stuck here all night. Stealing a glance at the receptionist, she wondered if she'd be nice enough to give her a ride back to the condo. Not that Riki could give her directions. Oh, this was bad. But she couldn't get ahead of herself. Panicking wouldn't help. It wasn't like she'd have to find a Starbucks where she'd set up camp while she waited for her parents to drive here. She let out a small laugh. Things weren't *that* bad. Picking up the pen, she resumed filling in the form. *Have you ever had or do you currently have: allergic rhinitis, anemia, aneurysm, anxiety . . . ?* Ha! Not previously, but maybe now.

CHAPTER THIRTY-TWO

Sylvia was restless. It was Saturday, and she would be looking forward to a lovely evening with Hugh if he hadn't turned out to be a complete and utter loser. It was despicable that he thought he could use her and toss her aside as soon as Sammy returned. *Well, that and the fact that he's married,* she thought grimly. She picked up her phone and tapped on his name. Today would be the perfect day to send him the news. She began a text.

> Guess who's going to be the daddy of Irish twins? You, that's who! Congrats. :)

After adding the video, she hit "Send." A sigh whooshed from her. God, it felt like she'd been in a frantic prizefight, but now she'd been declared the winner, and she could finally catch her breath as she leaned in to the ropes, letting them support her.

Stretching her arms above her head, she moved them down slowly, her palms toward the floor. She could almost feel herself pushing the negativity to the ground. She padded to the sofa and lit the gardenia-scented candle on the coffee table. Settling into the cushions, she watched the flame and wondered how far it would burn before her phone chirped.

Closing her eyes, she pictured Hugh pulling his phone from his pocket when he felt the buzz of a text. He would be seated across from Lily as she fed the baby, and he'd sneak a look at the text. *It's work,* he'd say apologetically. She would nod, a peaceful smile on her face, thinking, *Oh, my hard-working husband. He deserves a break on the weekends!*

Hugh's face would burn red. His palms would itch, and he'd dash to the kitchen for a glass of water, gulping the cold liquid until he choked. He'd motion to his throat. *Wrong pipe,* he'd utter as he rushed for the privacy of the powder room. He would watch the video with the volume down, his stomach screaming with each passing second.

Her phone rang, and she jumped. She hadn't expected such a quick response. She slid her finger across the screen and tucked her hair to one side before pressing the phone to her ear.

"Hello, Hugh."

"What the hell, Sylvia?" he hissed. "What is this?"

"I'm fine, thanks," she said pedantically, as though she were a manners teacher modeling the correct response. "And how are you?"

"No way! I'm not playing games. Tell me what the fuck is going on."

She waved a hand above the flame of the candle, daring it to reach her palm. It sounded like spittle had flown from his mouth as he spoke. That was so unlike him.

"You're going to be a daddy again." She could hear him breathing heavily. Smiling into the phone, she said, "If you don't want to tell Lily right away, I understand completely. But," she said, adopting an optimistic tone, "if you think she'd want to know about Hunter's half sibling, I'm all for it."

"Oh, you're not talking to Lily. I'll tell her you're crazy and unstable. I'll tell her to call the police if you show up again."

A poisonous laugh trickled from her lips. "Oh, Hugh. You're so funny. Do you even hear yourself? She knows I'm not crazy. We already bonded when I brought the gift over."

"The hell you did."

"Okay," she said with a pitying laugh. "Whatever you say."

He grunted, and she seized the moment.

"It would be so easy to go through our calendars together over a nice lunch. I'm sure she'd find it odd that the weekends I spent with you match up perfectly with your fake work trips."

"You wouldn't."

"What? Defend myself from your pathetic lies?" Her voice turned harsh. "Don't test me, Hugh. By the way, how did your conversation with Sammy go? He was so surprised to see me at his place."

A crash sounded, and the call ended. She hoped the screen of his phone didn't crack when he threw it. But there'd be more. He would come back, trembling and afraid, seeking reassurance.

~

Riki finished filling out the documents and fidgeted with the pen. After what felt like an eternity, the nurse appeared. "Come on back. Dr. Hart will see you."

She bounced from the chair and rushed to the open door. "Thank you so much."

"Sure thing. Follow me."

The exam room was small, and Riki sat on the edge of the paper-covered bed. Even though she was bundled in her ski jacket, a shiver ran through her. She wished she were back at home, sitting at her kitchen table grading papers, not in this sterile room with her hand pressed to her neck. Before she could take a breath, the doctor walked in.

He was much younger than she had imagined—thirty at most—but it was his eyes that grabbed her. They were pale hazel, almost gold, against dark lashes. Mesmerizing. "Samantha told me you were an emergency, but don't worry," he said, his voice sincere. "We'll get you fixed up, okay?"

Riki nodded, and her eyes filled with tears. *Oh, jeez.* A few kind words and she was falling apart. She pressed a hand to her face. "Sorry. It's just been a rough day."

"No need to apologize. I'm Dr. Hart." He stepped forward and shook her hand.

"I'm Riki."

"Nice to meet you, Riki. Are you visiting for the weekend?"

"Yeah, we came up from LA."

"Nice. It's a great city," he said with a smile. "And don't worry. You're in good hands. Go ahead and take off your jacket, and I'll have a look." After scrubbing his hands with a vigor she appreciated, he tugged on gloves and removed the tissues that were sticky with blood. Riki tried not to wince as he dropped them into the waste bin. Using a gentle touch, he dabbed her neck with a damp gauze pad before shining a light on it. "How'd this happen?"

"I ran into the fence on a ski run."

"Well, the good news is it's a clean cut. It looks like the impact caused the skin to split, but just in case, have you had a tetanus shot within the last ten years?"

Riki racked her brain. "I can't remember."

"We'll get you one today, then."

"Is that the bad news?"

"No bad news," he said, inspecting her wound. His face was so close to hers that she averted her eyes, focusing on the poster that listed warning signs for the flu. Doctors weren't supposed to be so cute. "You'll need stitches, but you shouldn't have much of a scar when it's healed." He smiled at her. "I'm good with a needle and thread."

Riki covered her face with a hand. "Please don't say those words again. I'm barely past hearing about the shot."

He laughed. "You're squeamish when it comes to that kind of thing?"

She peered at him from between her fingers. "Terribly. Can you knock me out or, better yet, just slap some glue on it and call it a day?"

He shook his head and sat on the swivel chair next to her. "The cut is too deep. We'll get you nice and numb. You won't feel a thing."

She looked at her hands, wishing she could believe him. He seemed so certain, but what if he was adept at lying to comfort his patients, and once he got started, it was too late for them to back out? "I'm scared."

"Don't be." He peeled the gloves from his hands and dropped them in the trash before spinning back to her. "Like I mentioned, I'm a great seamstress."

"Seriously?"

"Yep. I grew up surrounded by strong women who felt it was their duty to teach me how to sew. I can make one hell of a pillow." He smiled—not with just his mouth but with his entire face. Even his golden eyes seemed to be smiling. As much as Riki had wanted to dart from the building just moments ago, he was making her want to stay.

She met his gaze. "You're not like other doctors I've seen."

"Should I take that as a compliment?" he asked, his brow arched.

"Yes."

"Good. You had me worried. Okay," he said, standing. "I'll have the nurse come in to prep you, and we'll get started. It won't take much time at all."

She squeezed her hands together on her lap. "Okay."

"Don't look so concerned. I haven't lost a patient yet." He winked and left the room.

Riki laughed to herself. If he was this unconcerned, maybe it would be okay for her to let go of some of her fear.

Thirty minutes later, Dr. Hart was sporting special magnification goggles and stitching up her wound. There was a little pressure, but that was it. Tom Petty played in the background. When he'd come back in after the nurse left, he'd asked if she was okay with classic rock. "I work better with music in the background," he'd said.

"I love classic rock," she'd replied. If there was ever a sign that things would be okay, this was it. Her dad had introduced her to the Eagles, Bruce Springsteen, Fleetwood Mac—all the greats. It was almost like he was here with her now.

"Favorite classic song?" he asked as he worked.

She was positioned on her side with her hair tucked into a glorified shower cap and couldn't see his face, but it sounded like he was smiling. "Too many to count."

"Okay. Top three."

She wanted to smile, but she held it in. "'Beast of Burden,' 'Gold Dust Woman,' and 'Sister Golden Hair.'"

He blew out a low whistle. "'Sister Golden Hair.' Now, that's one I haven't heard in ages. I'm with you on 'Beast of Burden.' One of The Stones' best. Are you an expert skier who was showing off on the mountain when you crashed?"

"God, no. I wish."

"What happened?"

She told him about the group being fired up to start big and how she had been scared. He listened intently, or at least it seemed that way to her. "And then a nice man helped me down, since I couldn't find my boyfriend. I still haven't reached him."

"Did you try again? He's probably worried. I know I would be."

"I've called three times," she said quietly.

"Do you think he lost his phone on the mountain?"

She bit her lip. That hadn't occurred to her. What if his phone was buried in snow? It wasn't like he could borrow someone's and call her. No one memorized phone numbers anymore. "Maybe?" She clung to the idea, because the thought of Chris not caring hurt more than she could've imagined. Even though she wasn't 100 percent sure where their relationship was headed, it was important to know he cared. The fact that he wasn't there for her when she needed him most was making her feel a little crazy.

Dr. Hart patted her arm. "We're done. You can sit up now."

"That wasn't as bad as I'd imagined."

"It's going to be sore. Expect some swelling, but it'll heal nicely. You'll need to get the stitches removed in ten days."

"Okay. Do I just go to my regular doctor for that?"

"Yep. I'm guessing you're not staying here that long."

"No." She touched a hand to her neck. "Can I see it?"

He took a hand mirror from the counter near the sink. "Here you go."

She stared at her reflection. Mascara was smeared beneath her eyes. Her hair was plastered to her forehead, and the two-inch gash in her neck was held together with black thread, making it look like spiders were crawling along her skin. "Frankenstein's monster," she said in a strangled voice. She wasn't sure if she wanted to laugh or cry, but she forced a laugh. "If there's a snow-queen pageant up here today, I'm thinking I'm a shoo-in for the winner."

"You'd get my vote. That's one beautiful bit of wound care. Whoever sewed you up has some mad skills."

This time, her laugh was real. "A doctor and a comedian. That's a great combo."

Taking a bandage, he said, "All right. Let's get this covered, and you are free to go."

As he gently covered her stitches, her phone blared, and she startled. Pulling it from her pocket, she looked at the screen. *Evelyn.* "Hey."

"Riki! Where are you?" Chris was shouting into the phone.

"Didn't you get my messages? I called you," she said, holding back a sob.

"My phone's dead. I'm using Evelyn's. Where the hell did you go?"

"I'm at the urgent care. I crashed into a fence."

She waited for his reaction—a gasp or rushed words of concern—but he was too busy talking to someone else.

"No, dude. Get me another beer. I don't want to mix my alcohols." He was still shouting, and Riki could hear the buzz of a large crowd in the background. He was at a bar.

"Chris? Did you hear me? Can you come pick me up?"

"Wha? I can't freaking drive right now. I've had, like, three beers. Where are you? If you're at the condo, just walk over here. It's close."

Biting back angry words, she said, "Never mind. I'll grab an Uber," and ended the call.

Dr. Hart had busied himself making notes in her chart while she took the call. He glanced at her now. "There aren't any Ubers up here."

"Yeah. I know. He was drunk, so telling him would've been pointless."

He nodded, but she couldn't tell what he was thinking. His golden eyes reminded her of a lion's, all-seeing and in control but revealing nothing. "I'm going to come right out and say it. Chris sounds like an ass."

She sniffed. "He's really not. It's just . . . I think he had an idea of how this trip would go, but he forgot he was bringing me, not some super-athletic and spontaneous girl. I'm clumsy and a planner."

A smile tugged his lips. "Do you want me to take you back to your condo?"

"That'd be great. Thanks."

"And I apologize for sticking my nose in. I just . . ." He shook his head.

"It's okay. You've been really nice."

He tapped a hand against the door. "Let me tell Samantha up front we're done here, and I'll run you to your rental."

This time when Riki buckled her seat belt, she wasn't worried about checking the locks. Dr. Hart had changed from his doctor's coat, and he suddenly looked like a guy. Like a *hot* guy who'd jumped right off a

Hollister ad. *Oh my God,* she thought. *He's just spent an hour seeing me with makeup smeared down my face and messy hair.* She snuck a look at him as he turned on the engine. His hands were strong but somehow elegant as they rested casually on the wheel. No white-knuckle driving for him.

"Are you staying near the slopes?"

"Yeah. I can't remember exactly where the condo is, but maybe you can drop me at the lodge bar? That's where my friends are." She paused to take a breath. "It's really nice of you to do this."

He stole a glance at her and grinned. "You've had a tough day. I'm just trying to help it end on a good note."

What a nice guy, she thought. He was so much more of an adult than a lot of guys she knew. Confident and capable. "Thanks." She leaned her head against the soft leather of the seat. "You've accomplished that. In fact, listening to music with you while you . . . well, while you *stitched*—that word still grosses me out—was strangely the best part of the day."

He laughed. "That is strange. But good. Makes me happy."

A warm feeling ebbed through her as she gazed out the window. The light of day had been replaced by a blanket of darkness. "It's so pretty. I could look at the falling snow for hours." She clasped her hands in her lap. "You're lucky to live up here."

"It is magical. That's for sure. You said you live in LA?" he asked as they pulled into the lodge parking lot.

"Yeah, I . . ." She stopped midsentence and leaned forward. A group of guys, hands shoved in pockets and heads down, was crossing to the bar. It was hard to determine if it was her group or not, but as they drew closer, she could tell it wasn't them after all. "I thought those guys were my friends, but I guess not."

"Do you want me to help you find them?"

Yes! Stay. But an image of an annoyed look on Chris's face popped into her mind, forcing her to decline his offer. "Thanks, but I'm okay."

She bit her lip, wondering if she should say, *If you're ever in LA, give me a call. Here's my number.* The thought alone made her heart race so fast, she knew it was a bad idea. What if he looked at her like a child and gave her a pitying smile? He was clearly just a nice guy. So instead, she said, "Have a good night."

"You too. And keep an eye on your stitches. Take it easy, okay?"

She let herself out of the car and walked into the lodge. Calvin spotted her first. He waved a hand high above his head and called her name. Riki straightened her jacket and strode toward the table. Evelyn hopped from her seat and rushed toward her. "Oh my God! We were so worried. I saw I had a missed call from you when I finally was able to charge my phone. Where'd you go?"

"I was at the urgent care. I texted Chris and called him too. I guess his phone died."

Evelyn gripped her by the arms and scanned her up and down, looking for a sling or cast, Riki presumed. "What the hell? Are you okay?"

"Yeah. I had to get some stitches." She pulled down the zipper of her jacket enough to give Evelyn a look.

"You poor thing!" She led her to the table, a firm grip on her arm. "Chris! Did you know your girlfriend was injured?"

He looked up with a droopy gaze. "Huh? Oh, hey, Riki!" He scrambled off the barstool and tripped his way to her. "Where'd you go? I checked the condo, but you weren't there."

Riki sighed. Evelyn glared at Chris before wedging her way back to the empty stool next to Liam. "I tried telling you, but you were too busy ordering drinks." She revealed her puffy bandage, half hoping he'd pass out.

A nervous laugh fell from his lips. "What?"

"I got hurt, and I tried calling you, but you weren't there." The entire group was now leaning forward over their drinks, edging in to hear. She felt like a circus freak.

"Dude, you suck," Eddie said loudly. "I told you that you should've waited when she didn't show up after that run." He shook his head and turned his eyes to Riki. "If I were dating you, I would've waited."

Chris eyed him, and for a scary second, Riki thought a fight might break out. But then Chris eased out a chuckle. "A girl like Riki would never date a guy like you. And, dude, we got separated in the snow. It happens." He grabbed Riki by the hand and led her to the semiquiet foyer of the bar.

Relief and rage stormed inside Riki. Rage won. She pulled her hand from his. "A stranger had to take me to the urgent care. And the freaking doctor brought me back here. I kept telling everyone that you would call, that it would be fine, but you didn't. And it's not fine, Chris. You just left me because Evelyn mentioned Brandon. What the hell is that about?" He shifted his feet and hung his head like a contrite little boy. "Can't you even say something?"

"I'm sorry, okay? It pissed me off, and I needed a minute. I thought you would be right behind me! And when we got to the bottom, I realized you weren't with us."

"But you kept skiing."

"I—"

"Never mind. You're drunk, and I want to go back."

"I'll walk with you."

"You know what? Don't bother." She pushed past him and headed back to the table. "Hey, Calvin? Can I have the keys? I'm going back to the condo."

He tossed them to her.

"Um, how do I get there?"

Shaking his head, he said, "I'll walk with you."

Ten minutes later, Calvin opened the door for Riki and poured her a glass of water. "Do you need anything else?" he asked.

"I'm okay. Thanks for walking with me." The walk had been a quiet one, but Riki hadn't been in the mood for idle conversation. The only thing she wanted to talk about was what a jerk Chris was being, but that would've put Calvin in an awkward position.

He nodded. "Give us a call if you need anything, okay? You have your cell?"

She held it up. "Yep. Thanks again. Don't let Chris get too hammered."

"Might be too late for that, but I'll keep an eye on him." He raised his hand in a wave and left.

Riki tucked herself into a corner of the sofa, wishing she could close her eyes and wake up at home. *Or transport myself back to the passenger side of Dr. Hart's car.* What if he had suggested taking her to his place when she admitted she didn't know how to get back to hers? *Why don't you come home with me until you can reach your friends? I live alone and would love a dinner companion. I'm making pasta primavera with buttery garlic bread.* Because of course he could cook. This was her fantasy.

Are you sure? she'd ask.

Very. He'd smile, and his eyes would shine.

And when they arrived, his house would be big and pretty, with sweeping views of the snowy mountain. He'd start a fire and get her settled on a sofa—not unlike this one—and then ease her Ugg boots from her feet.

If only. She shook her head. What a stupid thought. She'd never see the guy again. And if he was that nice to her, chances were he had loads of women vying for his attention. He probably had a darling girlfriend who was also a doctor. They would ski and rock climb together. And Riki was a hopeless klutz. She thought about calling her mom but instead began scrolling through her emails. Two from Elliott Johanson, Dane's dad. Her happy thoughts about the doctor were washed away by a bitter dread.

She opened the first one in the chain and began reading.

Dear Miss McFarlan,

I have tried to remain impartial as things have cropped up in recent weeks. However, your complete and utter lack of discretion in passing out prizes deeply concerns me. How can you justify giving a seven-year-old such a prize? My only hope is that this was something that belonged to you, and it accidentally ended up in the prize box.

However, before dispensing any sort of prize, previewing the said items would be prudent. The fact that you didn't (and I'm assuming you did not, based on the prize) shows a wanton disregard for your students' mental health. I've attached a photo below. My wife and I haven't decided what our next step is, but we wanted to give you an opportunity to respond first.

I hope to hear from you soon, as I am deeply concerned.

Regards,
Elliott Johanson,
Senior Managing Partner
Johanson and Wolfe, LLP

What had she given Dane? She tried to remember, but it had gone so quickly with kids grabbing toys from the box of prizes Mrs. Fitzsimmons had left behind. What could be so bad? An outdated book? She scrolled farther and opened the photo.

It revealed a round fabric dartboard with three little Velcro balls stuck to it. *Huh.* What was so wrong with that? It wasn't like it had real darts that could hurt someone. She zoomed in on the photo, and gooseflesh sprang across her arms. Words were in each spot instead of numbers. BLOW IN MY EAR, HUG ME, TELL ME A HOT SECRET. And in the center—the winning heart-shaped spot—were the words HOME RUN.

Despite her horror at the thing, nervous laughter consumed her until she was swiping tears from her eyes. The absurdity of it all. How did this get in the box? She couldn't imagine sweet old Mrs. Fitzsimmons buying this. It had to have been a donation that she'd never looked at.

She began her response.

Dear Mr. Johanson,

I'm so embarrassed and terribly sorry! The teacher whose class I took over left the box of prizes for me, and I assumed they were all fine for the children. I'll know better to check each and every one carefully next time. From the wrapping, I assumed it was an innocent dartboard. My deepest apologies. I will let Dane pick a new prize on Monday. Thank you for bringing this to my immediate attention. Again, I'm very sorry.

Best wishes,
Miss McFarlan

Before hitting "Send," she remembered there had been another email. She opened the next one, skimming quickly. Mr. Johanson wondered why she wasn't responding. The time stamp was from yesterday at four o'clock. *Oh, jeez.* More than twenty-four hours had passed. Nonetheless, she hit "Send" on the email. She would say that she was out of town and her Wi-Fi was acting funny—that she'd tried to send it Friday afternoon. Besides, they couldn't possibly expect her to be on the clock seven days a week.

But a little voice in her mind said, *Yes, they do!*

She scrolled to her most recent emails, and just as she feared, there was another that caused heat to creep through her. This one was from Ms. Hammacher, the head of school.

> Miss McFarlan,
>
> Principal Rosenkrantz has forwarded me some very alarming emails from some of our most dedicated parents. To say you've created a big problem is a grave understatement. In all my years here, I've never had a teacher distribute a sex toy to one of her students. This is an absolute disgrace to Ocean Avenue Academy. The fact that you did not respond immediately shows further questionable judgment. Please meet me in my office on Monday morning at seven sharp.
>
> Regards,
> Pamela Hammacher
> Head of School, Ocean Avenue Academy

Riki's face burned, and her head began to throb. Curling herself into a tight ball in the corner of the sofa, she slammed her phone onto a cushion and began to cry.

CHAPTER
THIRTY-THREE

Sunday, March 19

Chris had both hands on the wheel, and his face was stony as he sped down the freeway toward home. Riki snapped her eyes shut and hoped she would fall asleep, but her mind whirred relentlessly, forcing her to analyze her feelings as the silence sat between them like a coiled snake. She knew she should feel something like sorrow for the way they'd fought, but it wasn't there. Another feeling nudged and prodded her, asking to be heard, and it terrified her. The weekend had created big cracks in their fragile foundation. She found herself clinging to those cracks, yanking on them, wanting to make them bigger until they both fell through. She wanted this to be over.

As Chris exited the freeway, Riki clicked off the radio and sat up straight, readjusting her seat belt.

He stole a glance at her. "Are you still mad?"

"No."

"I'm sorry I wasn't there, okay? It's just—" He slammed a hand against the steering wheel. "All the guys made me feel like a total dick.

And I get that you were upset, but it was a mistake, okay? You wouldn't let it go. I had to hear over and over about how you were alone."

"Not from me."

"I know! But you were pissed. You can't deny that. And you're still pissed. I can tell by your body language. You're all rigid."

She flopped her head against the leather seat. "All I really wanted was for you to apologize and to tell me you wished you'd been there for me."

"I did!"

"But in an angry way." She turned to him. "Look, I don't want to argue with you. With all this time in the car, I've had a lot of time to think about us."

"Oh God. Do I want to hear this?"

"Yeah. It needs to be said. I think you weren't able to be there for me because you don't really know me."

He turned to her, his mouth twisted in a scowl. "What?"

"You only know the surface."

He shook his head as though he had water in his ears. "That's totally untrue."

"No, it's really not. I feel . . ." She looked out the window, summoning the words that needed to be said.

"What do you feel?"

She twisted a lock of hair into a knot. "You like the ocean, right?"

"I have no idea where you're going with this, but yeah, I like the ocean."

"So do I. But here's the thing. I don't want to float on a raft on the surface, catching a gentle wave here and there. I want to go down deep, where it's dark and a little scary, where there might be eels and those little thingies that hide at the bottom. You have to look carefully to see particles of sand drifting in the water to notice them, but they're there. And I want to see the pretty things too—the parrotfish and angelfish. I want it all. But you want to stay on the raft and pretend that nothing exists below, because the surface is so nice." She slid the knot from her hair and turned to Chris.

"Riki, come on. I get what you're trying to say here, but what I feel isn't on the surface." He took one hand off the wheel and grabbed for hers.

She felt exposed, like she was in a tiny interrogation room. "It's not your fault. It's mine. I kind of just went along with things. Maybe I was scared, or . . ."

"Or what?" he asked in a measured tone.

"I just sometimes feel like I can't be myself around you the way I can around—"

"*Brandon?* Is that what you were going to say? Fuck! He's married, Riki."

"I wasn't going to say that! You didn't even let me finish."

"Who, then? Calvin? Did you have a good heart-to-heart when he walked you back?" He sneered. "Don't think I didn't notice. And even fucking Eddie was all up my ass. God!" His car swerved toward the next lane, and Riki braced herself against the seat, pressing her foot on an imaginary brake.

"Slow down! You're scaring me!"

He ignored her and punched the accelerator, his jaw clenched. "I've got it, okay! I know how to drive."

Her heart pounded, and her pulse raced. Arguing with him wouldn't help. She sat silently gripping her phone in her hand, wishing a highway patrol officer would roll up behind them. If he didn't slow down soon, she would call 911.

Seconds passed, and a car darted in front of them, forcing Chris to slam on his brakes as the light ahead turned from yellow to red. He blared the horn, but cross traffic had started into the intersection, and he was forced to stop.

She exhaled. "Will you please stop driving like that? I'm literally going to vomit."

He whipped a glance at her. "I'm done, okay? Give me a freaking break already! This isn't how I wanted this weekend to go." He banged the steering wheel with his fist. "But I get it. We're done."

"Yeah." She worried her bottom lip, wondering what words she could use to make him understand. *It's not you. It's me,* she wanted to say. But the truth was, nothing she could say would help him understand. She pressed her cheek against the cool window and touched a finger to the puffy bandage.

He pulled into her driveway but didn't turn off the engine. "I guess this is it. See you later." He turned to her. "Or not."

"I—"

"Just go. Can you grab your bag?"

Without a word, she hoisted her bag from the back seat and quietly shut the car door. She looked to the Taylors' apartment, wishing Brandon would rush outside to help her. Just as she was imagining him wrapping his arms around her, Embry appeared in her mind, comforting her too. She lugged her bag up to her apartment. Alone.

~

The bartender slid a tumbler of scotch across the bar, and Jonathan lifted it to his nose, breathing in the smoky goodness. He sipped the amber liquid, savoring the immediate calm it produced.

Next to him, a man in dark jeans and an expensive white dress shirt adorned with silver cuff links lifted his glass. "Cheers." He drained it in one swig.

"Celebrating?" Jonathan asked, nodding at the empty tumbler.

The man pushed it toward the back of the bar and held up a hand, beckoning the bartender. "One more. Vodka neat." Turning to Jonathan, he said, "Opposite. The jaws of defeat snatched what should've been an easy victory." He raised a bushy gray eyebrow. "I got outbid on a condo development. Sucks."

Well, well. The night was already looking up, and he hadn't even met a nice young gal yet. "Sorry to hear that." He sipped his drink slowly, contemplating how to play this. "The real estate world is a wild game."

"That it is. You in it?"

Jonathan raised his glass to eye level, assessing the rich color as though it were more important than what he was about to say. "I just listed my apartment complex. It's on Mockingbird Lane. Prime real estate."

"No shit."

The bartender delivered a fresh drink, and the man thanked him with a nod.

Jonathan shrugged. *No big deal that I own prime real estate.* "I've had a few developers express interest. It currently houses four bungalow apartments on a twenty-thousand-square-foot parcel. Could be great for someone who wants to tear the place down and build up."

"Do you have a card on you?"

Shit. He'd been meaning to make some up. He patted his shirt pocket and frowned. "I usually keep a few here. You interested in seeing the property?"

"Why not? This could be my lucky day after all. Cheers once again." They clinked glasses and finished their drinks. "Can I swing by tomorrow night around six or seven?"

"How about six thirty?" He slipped his phone from his pocket. "What's your number? I'll text you the address. I'm Jonathan Fisher, by the way."

"Frank Overland." They shook hands, and he rattled off his number. "I'll see you tomorrow."

CHAPTER

THIRTY-FOUR

Monday, March 20

When Riki had fallen into bed last night, sleep had come quickly, but dreams tossed through her mind all night. She was trying to run through the snow, but her boots sank deeper and deeper with each step. She'd eventually tugged them off and tossed them behind her, breaking into a run again. With each step, the snow sparkled and transformed into warm sand.

And now it was Monday morning, and as she walked to the head of school's office, it felt like she was sinking into quicksand.

Ms. Hammacher's assistant greeted her with a stoic gaze. But as she led her to the office, she patted her shoulder and whispered, "Good luck in there."

She stepped inside, and her breath caught in her chest. Ms. Hammacher sat behind her desk, and four chairs in a semicircle were occupied next to it. She looked from one person to the next: Principal Rosenkrantz, Mr. and Mrs. Johanson, and Mrs. Trainor. A lone chair sat opposite theirs.

Ms. Hammacher motioned to it. "Please have a seat."

Riki sat, the feeling that she was facing a firing squad pounding through her. She was thankful she'd worn a turtleneck sweater to hide her wound, because her neck was certainly turning red and blotchy. "Thank you for giving me the opportunity to explain."

Ms. Hammacher raised a brow while the occupants of the other chairs shifted eagerly, like they were ready to pounce. "We have had some lengthy conversations over the weekend, Miss McFarlan. As you know, the families seated here today sit on the board of directors at Ocean Avenue in addition to being parents of students in your class. Their concerns as both members of our board and as parents are warranted. Ocean Avenue has a long history of quality education. We rely on our teachers to set a positive example. That being said, the list of complaints you've received in your short time here is staggering. How would you respond to that?"

Her hands shook with nerves, and her wound suddenly burned. She licked her lips. "I'm so sorry for what happened, Mr. and Mrs. Johanson. All the prizes in that box were left for me by the previous teacher." She didn't mention Mrs. Fitzsimmons by name, showing that she wasn't trying to place the blame on someone else. That should score her some points. "I absolutely should've checked them in the same way I preview videos or books I share with the students. Nothing like this will happen again." She exhaled quietly, hoping she would be free to go soon.

Mrs. Trainor spoke next. "Isn't that what you said after the leprechaun-trap fiasco? That nothing like that would happen again? And now we have a more egregious situation. How do you justify that?" Her eyes were slits, and Riki felt like she was being pinned to the chair under the harsh gaze.

"The leprechaun traps were meant to be a fun way to end our unit on folklore and fairy tales. But that was overlooked when you accused me of wanting to perpetuate lies. I wasn't. And as for the prize box, it was one hundred percent my fault. I trusted what was there, and I shouldn't have. But the bottom line is, I adore my students. They are all flourishing in my class. I care about each and every one of them."

No one spoke for a moment, and she felt she would choke on the silence.

Finally, Ms. Hammacher chimed in. "Miss McFarlan, I understand you care for your students. That is evident. However, your lack of judgment is a problem. I believe we're all sitting here wondering what's next from you, and we simply can't have that." She placed her hands firmly on the desk. "I have a sub in place for you today. I'll review everything, taking into account your responses from our meeting, and I'll let you know by the end of the day what my final decision will be as to whether you will remain on staff here."

Mr. and Mrs. Johanson exchanged pensive looks.

Mrs. Trainor smirked. "I want her gone. That's my vote."

Mr. Johanson nodded in agreement.

Images of the emails, the cattiness, and the many disapproving glares flashed through Riki's mind, creating a storm of anger. She stood abruptly. "That's your vote? You want me gone, so I'm gone? I'll save you the trouble." Flapping her hands to her sides, she snapped, "I quit. And you know what? I feel sorry for your kids. They're going to have a tough time in life if they're expected to be perfect all the time."

The parents exchanged knowing glances, as though she'd just proven how unfit she was. Riki half expected Mr. Johanson to heartily shake hands with everyone in the room. *Well done, people. Well done,* he'd say. It was pathetic.

Ms. Hammacher rose from her seat. "In that case, I'll expect your written resignation." She turned to the parents. "I believe we're finished here. Thank you for your time."

"Good luck in finding a teacher who they'll approve of," she said, flicking a hand at the group of sour-faced parents. "Oh, wait! You can hire a robot. That'll solve everything." With that, she stalked out the door. *No running on campus,* she thought to herself as she jogged across the quad, but what could they do, fire her? She giggled. It was all she could do to stop herself from shouting, *I'm free!*

~

Sylvia arrived at the office early on Monday morning. As she fired up her computer, a pale-blue envelope caught her eye. It was propped against the monitor, her name written in small, slanted letters across the back. *A man's writing,* she thought. It had to be from Sal. No other man at the company had reason to leave a note. Although it could be a female's printing, but her boss wasn't one to leave notes. And what other female . . . ? Well, it could be from Dowdy Sarah.

As she contemplated the note, her cell phone rang. She checked the number. *Jonathan.* She closed her eyes and took a breath, forcing a smile as she answered. "Hi, Jonathan. Good morning."

"Yeah, I wanted to let you know I've got a guy with deep pockets, a Mr. Frank Overland, who's really interested in the place. Things are moving quickly. I told you I'd keep you informed, and I keep my word."

What the hell? Ann Travis was supposed to be the big player, not some other guy. She quickly wrote the name down on a sheet of paper. "You're a good man. Thanks for letting me know. Has he made an offer?"

"Not officially. He's coming by tonight at six thirty to check the place out."

"Well, as much as I don't want to move, business is business."

"Yup. That it is. Bye now."

She ended the call and began making a list. Suddenly, her day had become very busy. She grabbed the blue envelope and ripped it open. A smiling coffee mug with heart-shaped eyes was pictured on front. Inside, it read, *Can I take you to lunch tomorrow? Please respond via text, email, phone, or carrier pigeon. Warmly, Sal*

Carrier pigeon. Clever. She turned to her computer and typed *carrier pigeon* into the search bar. One of the first images was of the bird holding a note in its beak. She printed it and proceeded to cut it out. On the small note in its beak, she wrote, Lunch tomorrow sounds great in tiny print. She placed the pigeon in an interoffice envelope and placed it in the pickup box. He'd have her answer within an hour. Maybe less.

That done, she typed a name into her phone. *Frank Overland.* Results appeared immediately. *Good Lord.* The man could buy ten apartment complexes without noticing a dip in his bank account. At least, according to Wikipedia. His stated net worth gave her chills. That made him a real threat. She sent a text to both Embry and Riki.

Hi, it's Sylvia. We have a situation that needs to be dealt with.
It has to do with Jonathan's plans to sell. Please respond ASAP.

Seconds later, her phone rang.

"Hi, Embry. Thanks for getting back to me."

"What's going on?"

"Jonathan just called, and he has an investor coming over tonight who's made a fortune buying old properties and turning them into big complexes or condos. Bottom line is, we have to find a way to stop him or else we're looking at moving boxes and bulldozers."

"What can we do? He won't care if we come up with faults about the place if his intent is to tear it down."

"No. He won't. It will require something more. Are you in?"

"Yes. Whatever it takes."

CHAPTER
THIRTY-FIVE

Riki let herself into her apartment and locked the door behind her. The euphoria she'd felt earlier had been swallowed by fear. She'd *mocked* the head of school and criticized powerful parents. And worst of all, she'd quit! What had she been thinking? She gently banged her head against the closed door.

The voice of reason edged in, and she stopped. *Your sanity is more important.*

That may be true, but how would she earn any money? She fumed as she stormed to her bedroom. Questions swarmed her mind until she felt dizzy. She yanked the tote from her shoulder, and both straps ripped clean through in the process. She chucked it across the room and watched as her papers spilled out across the floor. What a mess. "Just like my life," she whispered. She wished she'd paid more attention to Amelia when she'd warned her about the parents. But even if she had, would their watchful eyes and critical words ever have felt okay? The answer was no. Maybe she could ask Grandma Willet for some tips on how to solve word puzzles. She could try out for *Wheel of Fortune*. Who knows? Maybe she'd end up making more in one night than she made in a year. Wouldn't that be great? She shook her head. That was just another stupid fantasy. She'd have to find something.

Even though it was only just past eight, she took her phone from her purse and flopped onto her bed as she dialed her mom.

"Hello?"

"Hey, Mom." It was all she could manage before she burst into tears.

"Riki? What's going on? Talk to me, honey."

"I'm okay. It's just—I quit my job."

"What happened? Why?"

Pressing her fist to her forehead, she swallowed her tears and told her mom everything, from Mrs. Trainor and the emails to the scandalous sex toy and the early-morning meeting.

"Couldn't you have reached out to this Mrs. Fitzsimmons to ask if she knew anything about what was in that box?"

"It wouldn't have helped. People loved her, and I'm certain she had no idea it was in there. I'm guessing some parent cleaned out a closet and donated all the unopened games, not realizing that one was totally inappropriate."

"Oh, sweetie. I had a bad feeling about you moving down there. Maybe it's time you come home. I'm sure you can find a job at a school up here."

Tears threatened again, but she forced them back. "Yeah, but you and Dad would get sick of me after about five minutes. I'd be over for dinner every other night."

"We'd love having you back. You know that."

Do I? Her mom spent so much time talking about how much she missed Rowan that it felt like she didn't mind that Riki was far from home too. Not as far as Australia, but still. "I guess."

"Uh-oh. What's that I hear in your voice? What else is going on?"

She swallowed. "Nothing. I'm okay. It's just a lot to process." Taking a breath, she said, "And I ended up in the urgent care after a ski accident this weekend. I had to get twenty-five stitches in my neck."

"What! Why didn't you call sooner? Are you okay?"

"I'm fine. Really. The doctor said I shouldn't have a big scar."

"Well, that's a relief."

"I'm like the good-news queen today."

"Do you need me to come down there? I can get Grandma to join me. We can take her new car. She got the Lincoln, by the way. It's bright blue—not the color I would've chosen—but she says the sparkle makes her happy. Anyway, how about I call her right now?"

"It's okay. Really. Everything happened so quickly, and I haven't had a chance to sort out my feelings about all of it. But I'll find another job. I know I will, even if I have to work as a sub for a while." She bit her lip before continuing. It wouldn't help if her voice came out shaky. "And the cut will heal." She rested her head against the pillow and touched where her wound was hidden beneath the thick turtleneck sweater.

"Keep the positive attitude. And check in with me tomorrow. The job situation will work out. From what you've told us, you'll be better off at another school. They sound like a bunch of blowhards there."

"Yeah." She chuckled softly and sat up. "I might have told them off. As things go," she said, crossing her room, "it felt good."

"That's my girl! Sometimes people need a little drink of reality."

Taste of reality, she thought as she looked down at her phone. A text had just come in. "That's the truth," she said absently, her focus now on the text. "Tell Dad I said hi, okay? I love you."

"Will do. Love you too, sweetie. And hang in there! Bye."

She ended the call and read the text from Sylvia.

Seconds later, Embry called, talking rapidly. "I just hung up with Sylvia. Have you heard what's going on?"

"No. I—"

"Here's the deal. An investor is coming over tonight. Sylvia wants me to show up to Nadine's place when she alerts me and ask if Nadine is home." She lowered her voice. "It's downright morbid, if you ask me, but she says it's the only way it'll work to put a stop to Jonathan."

"Are you going to do it?"

"Yeah. I feel like I have to."

"Okay, let me know if I can help." She frowned as she ended the call. This was just weird. A noise sounded outside, and she peered through the window. Brandon was closing the short picket fence behind him, keys in hand. Hurrying outside, she called to him.

"Hey."

"Hey yourself." He crossed to her, and she fell into step with him as they walked toward the carport. "I've got my callback today."

She had planned on asking about the weird plan for tonight, but his perfect appearance jolted her train of thought. "Wow! Okay. You look amazing. You're going to kill it. I just know it."

"Thanks. You're always cheering me on. My agent says if I go through on this one, the next step is a chemistry test with the handful of actors who are also up for series-regular roles. And then they'll decide if I'm it or not."

They stopped near his truck. "I was with Evelyn this weekend. I texted you, but I'm not sure if you got it. Anyway, she had really good things to say about you and your audition."

"Really?" His eyes lit up. "What'd she say?"

"Just that you were great and they're rooting for you." Those weren't her exact words, but it was how she'd taken them. And what was so wrong with giving him some hope? He needed it.

"That's really good to hear. Really good," he repeated. "Is she a close friend of yours? You were with her all weekend?"

"With a big group, yeah." Riki's eyes suddenly burned and filled with tears. She pressed her hands to her face. "Oh my God. I don't know what came over me. I mean, I do, but—"

"Hey now. What's going on?"

"I'm so embarrassed." She shook her head and forced back the stupid tears. "We were on a trip with friends. The guy she's dating is a friend of my boyfriend. Ex-boyfriend as of yesterday." She blew out a breath and met his eyes. For the first time, she didn't want him to drop everything and kiss her. It was more of a wish that she could find someone like him. Someone funny and kind and handsome.

His eyes were soft, compassionate. "Aw, man. The guy's an idiot, okay? You're a great girl. The right guy is out there for you."

She searched his eyes, wanting to see a flicker of truth in them, as though he were a fortune-teller. "How did you know with Embry?" she finally asked.

"Ah." He swiped a hand across his mouth as though hiding a private smile. "I didn't really come to know she was the one for me. It was more like I was struck by a bulldozer. I met her and never wanted to leave. We just fit. Now, I don't know if that happens with everyone—in fact, I got damn lucky—but if you know what you want in a partner and are open to it, I think your person finds you."

She wrapped her arms around her middle. "That's a good way to look at it. Thanks." Smiling, she said, "It makes it pretty clear that Chris wasn't the one for me. Some strangers were nicer to me than he was." She bit back her desire to tell him about the accident. About Dr. Hart with the big heart. He had an important audition to focus on.

"Well, it sounds like you're better off. Don't take crumbs when you deserve the whole cake."

"I'll remember that. Break a leg."

He smiled and climbed into his truck. As she jogged back toward her apartment, a feeling pushed its way to the surface, fighting to be recognized until it was in full bloom. *Oh my God,* she thought as his truck trundled past her down the driveway. *I haven't really wanted Brandon all this time—I just want to be loved in the way that he loves Embry.* She lifted her hand to wave, even though she knew he couldn't see her, and she watched as his truck grew smaller and smaller in the distance until it disappeared completely. "Bye, Brandon," she whispered. Her mind crept back to her epiphany, poking and prodding it to see if it was real. *Yes. It's always been that.* She startled at the new adult-sounding tone that emerged as the voice in her head, and she walked into her apartment. Everything was exactly as she'd left it, but *she* was different. The uncomfortable guilt that had clung to her for so long began to evaporate, and a refreshing clarity took its place. She knew she'd always think Brandon was hot—that was simply a fact. But the truth was, he was so attractive because of the way he treated his wife. His family. Chris was handsome too, but his features had been quick to turn ugly when things didn't go his way. Maybe one day she'd find a great guy who liked her no matter what—even if she was a clumsy germaphobe and a homebody. She smiled to herself. *One day.*

CHAPTER

THIRTY-SIX

Sylvia pulled into the lot for the neighborhood pet shop. A banner hung in the window that read Cat Adoptions Saturday! Good thing it was Monday, or she might have been tempted. A cat would be nice. She hadn't been joking when she'd told Hugh she wanted one. If all went as planned, maybe she'd come for a visit on Saturday. A bell jangled when she pushed through the door.

She headed straight for the counter, where a man who resembled an old basset hound sat. How fitting. "Hello."

He raised his eyes from the newspaper he had been reading. It was in a foreign language that Sylvia couldn't begin to decipher. "How can I help you?" he asked in choppy English that sounded like he was swallowing each word.

"I'd like to purchase a fish that's easy to care for. One that lives in a bowl, not a tank."

He pointed to an aisle behind her. "Halfway down, you see the bettas. That is what you look for."

She thanked him and turned down the aisle. Stacked one on top of the other were small cups, each holding a single brightly colored fish. "Why are they in individual cups?" she called.

He peered over his round glasses. "The males. They will kill each other. They are the fighting fish."

She grinned. Beautiful little killers. How perfect.

"I have this one." He wagged a finger toward a shelf at the front of the aisle. "It is in a bowl already if you like to buy it."

Even better. It was a bright-blue fish with a top fin that resembled a peacock's plume. Tiny pink rocks rested on the bottom of the bubble-shaped bowl, and a plastic green leaf was anchored in the middle. She took it to the counter along with a container of food and paid in cash.

When she returned to her office, she placed the fish on the corner of her desk. "Don't get too comfortable, buddy. This isn't your new home," she muttered. In the center of her desk, the same carrier pigeon printout sat with a new note taped to its beak. She removed the tape carefully and unfolded the single page.

Excellent! Do you like Nona's Chicken and Waffles?

She tucked the note into her drawer and pulled out her phone.

Love it! Can't wait.

Seconds later, he responded.

I'm pleased to see you're utilizing a variety of the modes of communication I suggested.

I aim to please.

Lol. Counting down the minutes until tomorrow.

~

Two hours later, Sylvia was home. There was too much to do to stay at work until five. She'd told Miriam, her boss, she was feeling sick. She kept green concealer in her makeup kit for such occasions. It was meant to counteract redness, but she found if she applied a thin layer to her entire face with a makeup sponge followed by a dusting of loose powder, it had the effect of making her look pasty and ill. Of course, she used a shade of nude lipstick instead of her usual Lady Danger. With a tissue wadded in her hand, she'd gone to Miriam. There was something about a crumpled tissue that spoke volumes. No one wanted to get near it. She didn't have to explain whether it was a cold or the flu. The tissue did the talking. Miriam told her to get some rest, and that was the end of it. She was free to leave.

She walked down the long driveway to her apartment. A half-naked Kylie was hunched over the handlebars of her tricycle, pedaling toward her with fierce determination.

"Whoa! Slow down, there, speedy!"

Kylie laughed and skidded her feet to the ground, stopping the little trike. "I go fast, Miss Sylvie!"

"Yes, you do! I thought you were going to mow me over for a second there."

She slid off the tricycle and rounded it proudly, as though it were a fancy sports car. Sylvia held back a laugh. The little girl was clad in *Finding Nemo* underpants, light-up sneakers, and a plastic gold tiara. Nothing else.

Embry flew from her yard. "Kylie! Did you run into Miss Sylvia?"

"No, no," Sylvia called. "She came to a full and complete stop upon seeing me. I believe she deserves a good-driver award today. And perhaps a fashion award."

Kylie giggled and resumed riding her tricycle, making big circles in the driveway.

Embry smiled. "It was so nice outside, I figured I'd let her get a little sunshine on her skin." She was dressed in yoga pants and a basic T-shirt, but she positively glowed. Pregnancy agreed with her. Lucky woman.

"It is a nice day."

"You're home earlier than usual, aren't you? Is everything okay?" Her tone was loaded with worry.

"To be honest, I wasn't feeling well." She patted a hand to her stomach. "Though it very likely could be stress."

"You poor thing. I keep thinking about that ex of yours. Is he still bothering you?"

"I wish I could say he stopped, but it's only gotten worse. I may have to file a restraining order." It was so easy to lie about Hugh. In fact, it felt good to talk about him like he was someone to fear. She was acting as karma's right-hand gal.

"Oh no! We're here for you—however we can help." She looked down and twisted her hands. "Speaking of helping, do you still need me to do the thing tonight? Asking about Nadine and all?"

"Yes. I think it's the only way. You don't mind, do you, being that our homes are at stake?"

"No! It's just a little weird. But as long as you think it'll work."

She crossed her fingers. "Let's hope so."

"All right, then. Um, by the way, Lily is coming over in an hour or so. You should stop in and say hi."

Sylvia kept her expression neutral, but her mind was racing ahead. Of course she would stop by. The timing couldn't be better. "Thanks. I just might do that."

As she walked to her apartment, her phone chirped. It was a text from Belinda.

You left work early. Everything okay?

How nice that she was concerned.

Yes. I was feeling sick, but it must've been something I ate this morning. I'm feeling much better now.

Oh, good. :) I wanted to tell you I have a date tonight! And he's not from the internet, LOL! I met him at my niece's ballet recital on Saturday. He's divorced and a dad, but we're at that age.

Sylvia's radar was up. Divorced and a dad? There had to be hundreds of thousands of divorced dads in Southern California alone, so it was downright ludicrous to think for a second that it was Sal. He hadn't said anything about his daughter doing ballet, only hip-hop.

That's great! Details? How old is his daughter? Is she a friend of your niece? And what's his name? Wouldn't want to refer to him as "the ballet dad"!

Ha! Yes, my sister says he's a good guy. His name is Jason. :)

Of course his name was Jason. Not Sal.

Have a great time with Jason. Details tomorrow.

U got it. Fingers crossed he doesn't turn out to be a freak show. And funny enough, Sarah is going out with her guy with the good arms. I can't believe she had the nerve to ask him out!

What the actual fuck? Sylvia resisted the temptation to throw her phone against the wall. How had that even happened?

How cute. The one she was gushing about from accounting or some such?

Yes! They're only meeting for coffee after work because he has to take his kid somewhere or something, but she's freaking out. You should text her. That girl needs all the moral support.

LOL. Have fun tonight.

This was no laughing matter. How the fuck had Sarah conjured up enough courage to ask Sal out, let alone convince him to say yes?

She wished she'd strangled Sarah in the bathroom when she'd had the chance. This upcoming coffee date would put a wrench in her plans, but no matter. She was up for the task. Unexpected challenges only made things more interesting.

A smile tugged at her lips. Snagging Sal away from Sarah would be all too simple. For God's sake, he'd probably scorch his tongue from downing his drink too fast and claim he had to rush off for a family emergency.

First things first.

She headed back to the bathroom and assessed her face. She really had done a first-rate job of creating a sallow complexion. Embry hadn't said a word about it, but she was probably too polite to be honest about something like that.

Now it was time to revert to her vibrant self. She washed her face with an invigorating cleanser and patted it dry. Thanks to the abundance of high-quality skin-care products on the market, her skin had a youthful glow. Complemented with the right makeup, she could pass for twenty-nine. She opted for a daytime look even though it was nearing the evening hours. The goal was to appear like she was heading to the gym.

Lining her lips and filling them in with a muted plum was the final step. She pressed them together. Perfect. If she hadn't pursued marketing, she certainly could've found success in makeup artistry. And now for the wardrobe. Low-rise yoga pants were in order. It was imperative that her tattoo peeked out from the waistband. She decided upon a cropped black-and-white color-block sports tank. It allowed for a better view of the web. She chose a cropped zipper hoodie to wear over her ensemble and evaluated her look. Not bad. The spider crept out from beneath the waistband. It really was hard to ignore, with its vibrant jeweled body. Lily wouldn't be able to look away. On the way out, she shoved the plastic bag holding the burner phone into the pocket of her sweatshirt, along with Hugh's camera.

She knocked on the Taylors' door, taking note that an unfamiliar stroller was parked on the porch. It had to be Lily's. A large floral-print diaper bag hung from the handle. As she stood outside the door, she leaned down to ease open the bag's zipper before she resumed a waiting stance.

Embry swung open the door. "Hi! Come in."

"Hi!" she said in a girlish voice. Waving toward Lily, she said a polite hello and made a beeline toward Hunter, whose infant seat sat on the kitchen table. "Hi, you little cutie," she said, leaning over him, allowing the unzipped hoodie to fall open. She turned toward Lily. "It looks like he's already bigger. They grow so fast," she said, spreading her arms to the side. A dorky move at best, but it allowed for a great view of her tattoo. "Thanks for returning my license, by the way. I was going crazy trying to figure out where I'd left it."

"You're welcome. I found it on the sofa." Sylvia noticed Lily's eyes went to her hip, but then she forced her gaze upward.

"What a stroke of luck that you met Embry and figured out we know each other. Kooky coincidence." She watched Lily's face, searching for any hint of deception.

"Very much so." She smiled timidly.

Before Sylvia could respond, Kylie looked up from where she was sorting crayons by color on the table. "Miss Sylvie, you color?"

"Oh, I wish I could stay and color, but I'm off to try a yoga class." To Embry she added, "I hope it helps with the stress."

311

Kylie pointed toward her. "No, you colored your tummy, silly!"

"Oh, this!" Sylvia smiled as she motioned to her tattoo. "Yes, I suppose I did draw on myself."

"Use lots of soap in the bath to scrub real good," she said, nodding affirmatively.

"Thanks. I'll do that." Turning to Embry and Lily, she said, "Good to see both of you. Here's to hoping my yoga class is all it's cracked up to be. I could use some calm in my life."

"Amen to that. Thanks for stopping by. We'll see you later."

"Bye." She wiggled her fingers and headed for the door. She wanted to hug Kylie for drawing attention to her tattoo. Kids were so delightfully observant! And she had planted just enough hints about stress to make Lily question Embry about it. They would talk about her in hushed voices, and Embry would reveal that Sylvia's ex was a horrible person. Someone to fear. And when Lily discovered Hugh was the ex in question, she would have piles of evidence proving he was a very bad man.

Outside, she paused by the stroller, bending down to tie her shoe. At least, that's what anyone would assume she was doing. She took the burner phone from the pocket of her hoodie and shook it from the small Ziploc into the diaper bag, followed by Hugh's camera. She jostled the bag, making sure the evidence swam its way to the bottom. How long before it was discovered? Well, it didn't really matter in the end. Lily would learn of his deception, and that would serve as a final blow to Hugh.

What would timid little Lily do with the knowledge? Sylvia envisioned her bursting into tears and pounding her birdlike arms to Hugh's body as he stood there, unable to defend himself because the truth would be right there in vivid color. He would know it was Sylvia who had gathered all the evidence, but he wouldn't be able to prove it. And that would drive him crazy. She chuckled to herself and pictured him among a herd of mad cows. *No laughing matter indeed, Hugh.*

Embry smiled at Lily from across the table and kissed the top of Carson's head. "I don't know how she does it. That ex of hers is plain scary if you ask me, but she just keeps on going."

"Scary? What do you mean?" Lily asked, setting her teacup on the saucer.

Embry looked to Kylie, who was busy scribbling a blue crayon across her page. "Hey, Ky. It's been a while. Why don't you try to go potty?"

She slid from her chair. "I go potty right now, Mama!" She skittered to the bathroom.

Embry placed a hand on her chin as she looked at Lily. "I don't like gossiping, but her ex has sent threatening texts. I feel so bad. She had no idea the guy was married, and now it seems he's blaming her anyway."

Lily lifted her teacup and set it back down again. "How awful."

"I know." Shaking her head, she said, "It makes me wonder who you can trust."

Kylie bounded back into the room and resumed her spot at the table. "All done, Mama! I wash my hands," she said, holding them up for inspection.

"Great job. Do you want to build a super-tall tower with your blocks now?"

She clapped and dashed across the room to the basket of blocks.

Embry made sure she was out of earshot and said, "It's easier to talk without an audience, if you know what I mean."

Lily smiled, and Embry wondered what she was thinking.

"So how did you meet your husband? Have you been married long?"

"Almost three years. We only dated for a month before we married."

"Wow! That's fast. How is he with the baby? It's an adjustment, isn't it?"

Lily looked away, her focus on the kitchen counter, the window, the linoleum floor, before returning her gaze to Embry. "Well, um . . .

You know how it is. Was your husband—I don't know—a little off at times after the baby?"

"In what way?" Embry asked, bouncing Carson gently on her knee.

"I don't know." She laughed uncomfortably. "It seems like Hugh has the pregnancy hormones now. He's up one minute and down the next. And angry," she said quietly, more to herself than to Embry. "He's angry about the house not being as clean as before and how tired I am. He thinks I sit around doing nothing all day, but—"

"For goodness' sake! Having a new baby is a full-time job. It's feeding and changing and rocking and trying desperately to get them to sleep. And, I might add, doing all of that on minimal sleep ourselves." She could picture all the women in her family stepping forward, arms crossed and determined looks on their faces. Hart women didn't stand for ignorant men. "You're not giving yourself any credit here."

"I've tried to explain that, but he doesn't get it." She attempted a smile, but it crumbled from her face.

Embry studied her, taking in her fragile hands and cracked expression. One harsh word could knock such a sweet woman over. "I can imagine that's a cause of tension." She couldn't say she knew exactly, because as stressed as Brandon had been, he'd never once said that Embry did nothing all day. A comment like that would've gotten him a tongue-lashing like he'd never seen.

Lily nodded. "It is. Sometimes I feel like I'm walking on eggshells." She shook her head. "But he's great most of the time. I shouldn't complain. I have so much to be thankful for."

Embry fixed a stern look on her. "It's okay to vent. Us moms have to be able to let off steam in a safe place. Goodness knows we need stockpiles of patience stored up to deal with each and every cry or tantrum. You haven't hit the meltdown stage yet, but taking care of babies and toddlers requires fortitude. It's exhausting. There's no way around it."

Lily's eyes became glossy with tears, and she dipped her head. Embry waited, knowing all too well the tumultuous effects of postpartum hormones. But as Lily's shoulders began to shake, worry rushed in. Something wasn't right. "Is he making you feel bad about yourself? Is that what this is about?"

She nodded. "Sometimes I wonder if he's starting to hate me."

"Oh, honey," she said, patting her arm. She couldn't say it would get better, because at this point, she wasn't sure how bad it was. It could be that her husband was being verbally abusive. Oh, how she hated that word. It was so ugly and accusatory. Not a term to be used lightly.

Looking up, she said, "And Hugh seemed angry that Sylvia stopped by, which is so weird." She traced a line along the table with her finger before continuing. "He says she's a big drama queen."

"Oh, dear, I wouldn't call her a drama queen. She honestly doesn't talk about her personal life much, but she's always very contained and together."

"Don't tell her I said anything. Please."

"Of course not. And know that you can confide in me at any time. We really do need to stick together. Maybe it would help your husband to understand if you leave the baby with him for an entire Saturday. Let him see for himself how much time he has to sit around and do nothing."

Lily offered a feeble smile. "That would be nice." She stood. "I really should go. It's getting late. Thank you for having me. And I'm sorry for blathering on."

"You don't need to apologize, okay?" Embry said gently. "We should do this again. We can have weekly tea."

"I'd like that."

"It's settled. Monday afternoons are good for me. Maybe around four thirty again? I call it the 'witching hour,'" she said with a laugh. "All of us are cranky by then, so any distraction is welcome!"

"Next Monday is great. Thanks, Embry."

As the door closed behind Lily, Embry waited, unmoving. Her instincts were talking to her loud and clear. Lily was in more distress than she'd let on. Something about her situation just didn't feel right.

CHAPTER THIRTY-SEVEN

The drive took longer than usual thanks to some inconsiderate drivers who were probably still hungover from a weekend filled with green beer. Sylvia didn't mind, though. No amount of horn honking could ruin her mood. After analyzing the situation, she'd decided it was a stroke of luck that Sarah had asked out Sal. Nothing said fun like a little healthy competition. Well, maybe the competition was more pathetic, less healthy, but it was there nonetheless.

She finally turned into the shopping center parking lot and found a spot smack in the middle of it, equidistant between the grocery store and the coffee shop. It was a gamble to assume they'd end up here, but she was banking on Sal wanting to be as close to his ex's house as possible so he could pick up his daughter on time. And it worked well for Sylvia, because this was *her* neighborhood. *Her* coffee shop. It couldn't be considered unusual for her to be here at all. The one rogue possibility was that Sal would've offered to let Sarah pick the place. But then again, knowing Sarah, she'd defer to him. The poor thing probably had a hard time deciding which sock to put on first.

She zipped her hoodie to just below her cleavage, leaving a tiny peek available. A twentysomething guy pushing a train of shopping carts rolled slowly toward her. He smiled as he passed and gave her a look that said, *Yeah, I know my job sucks.* She chuckled as she made her way to the coffee shop. His life surely didn't suck as bad as Hugh's.

But no time to dwell on him. She needed a moment to clear her head and imagine all possible scenarios. Preparation was key. She'd checked the time as she parked and noted it was five thirty. If Sal and Sarah planned to meet directly after work, chances were good that they'd agreed to meet around then.

This could be all for naught, but she had a feeling she was onto something. Sarah had no game, no mystery.

By the time she opened the coffee-shop door, her plan was solidified. A damn bell rang as she entered, and she tipped her head toward her phone as though concentrating on a text. She'd forgotten about the stupid bell. Strike one against her.

But the music was loud enough to blot out the noise. She snuck a subtle look to her left, scanning the tables. No sign of them. She tightened her grip on her phone and moved to the counter, doing a sweeping glance of the right side of the café.

Well, holy hell in a handbasket.

At a two-top pushed up against a window sat her targets. It was almost like she had visualized them so clearly, she'd manifested their appearance. Well, not really. Not *realistically.* The idea of manifesting anything was nothing more than a way for needy people to have something on which to focus their attention. Children were said to be better at it than adults, and if there was any truth to that at all, her dad would've rolled up in his blue Chevy, parked it, and walked in a straight, sober line to the tiny apartment, his arms loaded with groceries. She had never wished for anything so hard.

So no, she'd manifested nothing.

She was simply very good at discovering people's motivations. If you knew what they held dear, they became quite predictable. In this case, Sarah was motivated to pin down Sal, so she'd agree to any meeting place he suggested. And Sal, of course, needed to be close to his daughter so he wouldn't be late picking her up.

Wearing a friendly smile, she greeted the barista—this time, a youngish guy with a scruffy beard and eager green eyes. "Hi. What looks good to you tonight?"

She let a hand drift to her chin and ran her fingers down to her neck as she focused on the menu with a furrowed brow. "Hmm. It's so hard to decide." She looked away from the menu and focused on his eyes. "I'm in the mood for something hot. Do you have any recommendations?"

He cleared his throat and ran a hand across his mouth. Unlike the brooding girl with the bleeding-heart tattoo, his skin was tattoo-free. The only adornment was a thick silver band on his thumb and another on his middle finger. The sign of someone who was trying too hard. It was fine—she had no use for him other than to make sure he was looking at her with interest in case Sal looked up and spotted her. Jealousy was a consistently reliable ally. "The caramel latte is good if you like your drink sweet."

"Umm. I love sweet. I'll have it to go, please."

She stood to the side, where a few people were congregated waiting for their drinks, and turned her head, her eyes fixed on Sal. As though feeling the pull of her gaze, he turned. Feigning a surprised look, she smiled and walked toward him.

"Hi there! Fancy meeting you here."

"Hi!" He stood to greet her with a friendly peck on the cheek before resuming his seat. "What a nice surprise."

With a broad smile, she said, "Nice to see you too. I usually only stop in early, but a big night awaits me, and I need the caffeine."

Before he could ask what she was up to, she turned toward Sarah. "Why, hello! I had no idea you two were friends."

"Hi. Um, we sort of just met. You know each other?"

Sylvia met Sal's eyes with a smile before turning back to Sarah. "We do."

Sal cleared his throat. "I guess introductions aren't needed, then." He looked to Sylvia. "What are your big plans for the night?"

She waved a hand and sighed. "There's a Diana Krall concert tonight. It's sure to be amazing. I'm just feeling a bit tired after my power yoga class." Flicking her gaze to Sarah, she said, "I left work early because I wasn't feeling well. I'm afraid it turns out it was just stress. The yoga did wonders." That should cover her bases. And it was a good thing she had heard an ad for the concert on the radio this morning. She hadn't lied, had she? She'd only confirmed that there was indeed a concert. She never once said she was attending.

"Diana Krall," he said, his eyes brightening. "Are you a fan?"

Sarah interrupted before she could respond, her squeaky voice as annoying as an animated chipmunk. "Who's Diana Krall?" she asked, leaning so far forward, a strand of her hair just missed her foamy latte.

"A jazz singer," they said at the same time. Their eyes met again, and they shared a quiet laugh.

"She's great," Sal said.

"The best." So Sal liked jazz too. Interesting.

"What do you think of Dave Koz?"

"One of my favorites." Sylvia smiled. It was lovely how Sarah was blocked out of the conversation.

"Mine too. I might have a connection for tickets to his concert. It's at the Bowl in June. You interested?"

"I love the Bowl, and I love Dave Koz. Count me in." She wondered if they would still be in touch in June. It probably wouldn't take her that long to get pregnant. And whether she decided to let him know and stick around? Well, that was something she'd feel out later.

"I'll keep you posted."

She glanced at the counter and saw her cup sitting there. "Looks like my drink is waiting for me. So great to see you. Sarah, a pleasure as always."

Sarah looked like a kicked dog wearing a frilly collar. It was sad but funny at the same time.

Sal's entire body was pointed away from Sarah and toward Sylvia. She could hardly blame him. Her company was so much more dynamic than the lacy lump sitting across from him. She strode away, smoothing a hand down the back of her sleek yoga pants.

With any luck, he would be so distracted that in his mind, he'd follow Sylvia home and press her up against the door as he kissed her with wild abandon.

She collected her coffee and left the shop without a backward glance. Time was of the essence. There was a lot left to do tonight.

Fifteen minutes later, she was home. She bustled to the kitchen and shouldered her reusable shopping bag, which was packed with all the essentials, before picking up the fishbowl. Grabbing the key to Nadine's apartment from her catchall drawer, she headed for the door, moving carefully so water didn't slosh from the bowl. She paused to scan the carport. Empty. *Here we go,* she thought. She crossed the driveway and climbed the stairs. The air in Nadine's place was stale. Jonathan had been by a few times, but other than that, it had been untouched for four months. A fading flicker of sunshine lazed on the floral-patterned sofa. If this had been anyone else's apartment, Sylvia would've cringed at the ruffles and rosy tones. The place looked like an old English tea shop, complete with hobnail milk-glass table lamps and vintage crystal candy bowls, but admittedly, it was quintessential Nadine. She scanned the room, looking for the perfect spot for Fishy, as she had taken to calling him. Someone who paid less attention to detail might've elected to simply bring fish food over. But questions could arise. Everything had to be in place. A small glass-topped side table sat between the sofa and matching upholstered rocker. She shifted the lamp to one side and used a tissue to wipe away the dust before placing the bowl next to it. Perfect.

That done, she walked to the kitchen and deposited the shopping bag on the counter, plucking items from it. Moving swiftly, she dumped half the bottle of prune juice down the kitchen sink and flicked on the faucet to wash the putrid purplish liquid away. Recapping the bottle, she placed it in the fridge along with a six-pack of water—minus one—a loaf of wheat bread, a bag of green grapes, a jar of jam, and a box of butter. All the items were hers minus the prune juice, which she'd picked up from the store. After shifting the items around to make the fridge appear fuller, she stood back, assessing her work. Satisfied, she moved to her next task.

Taking the small plastic bag from the pocket of her blazer, she placed it on the counter and began opening drawers until she found a mallet used for tenderizing meat. Smoothing the baggie, she centered the round white pills and brought the mallet to them, effectively turning them to a fine powder with one solid strike. She emptied the powder into one of Nadine's prized champagne flutes. The cut crystal was a stunning shade of red and perfect for the role it would play. Once every last speck of the crushed pills was in the glass, she positioned it back on the shelf and closed the cupboard.

Tucking the empty bag into her pocket, she smoothed her blazer, snatched the shopping bag, and left the apartment. Now she only had to wait. She walked down to her car and placed a large canvas bag on the passenger seat. She adjusted the rearview mirror, making it so she had a view of the entire driveway, and turned on the engine. When Jonathan arrived, it was important that it appear she had pulled in moments earlier.

A minute passed.

Then another.

A sickening feeling crept into her stomach.

She'd done this before—waited and watched for a car.

But this was different, she reassured herself. She clenched her jaw and ordered the bad feeling to retreat. There was nothing to fear now. She was an adult. And Jonathan wasn't her parent. He was a bully who needed to be stopped. Nadine would approve. No one would lose but the loser himself.

She saw the lights before the actual car and made a silent wish that it was Jonathan, not the investor. Because Jonathan needed to arrive first. If not, her plan would fail.

The car rolled into Nadine's old spot, and she shut off her engine. It was time. She shouldered her purse along with the large canvas bag and exited her car.

Jonathan waved as he rounded his Camry. "Hi there."

She wore a confused look. "Hi. I'm surprised to see you here."

"I have that meeting with an investor."

"Oh, right! You did mention it's today." She cleared her throat and infused her voice with the right amount of admiration. "Well, you look great. Low-key power mogul." *If the power mogul were a slob kebab.*

"Thanks." He straightened his limp linen coat.

She pursed her lips in thought. "It's funny I ran into you. I've been struggling with a business matter and have been hoping to talk to someone who can give me some solid advice. Do you have a moment?"

He glanced at his watch. "Uh, yeah. Only a minute, though. Walk with me?"

"Thanks. I appreciate it."

"What can I help you with?" he asked, unlocking the door to Nadine's apartment. He flicked on the lights and set his briefcase on the round pedestal kitchen table.

She stood near the table, not moving to set down her bag just yet. "A friend has started a side venture. It's direct sales. Are you at all familiar with those?"

"Of course. Back in the day, it was Tupperware. Now it's something chef."

"Right. Pampered Chef."

"Seems to do pretty well. What's your question?"

She tucked a lock of hair behind her ear. "I'm not considering Pampered Chef. This is where I need some guidance. To give you some background, the start-up kit costs one hundred fifty. But the payoff is great. My friend has made enough money for a week's vacation in Hawaii by what boils down to hosting parties."

"So what's the product?" he asked impatiently.

She placed the big canvas bag on the table and stuck a hand inside, knowing she'd have to work quickly to keep his attention. She pulled out a pair of pink marabou handcuffs. "It's an adult toy and lingerie company. That's where I need advice."

"Uh-huh. What can I do for you?"

"Well, she's had more success at couples' parties. The men spend two to three times as much as the women. My concern is, will guys like you—you know, sharp, successful guys—think it's cheesy?"

He shrugged, eyeing the bag. "Hard to know. What else does the company sell?"

"She gave me her starter kit to borrow for a few days so I can get some feedback." Sliding a hand into the bag, she lifted a slinky piece of red silk and passed it to him. Next, she pulled out a black bra that was really nothing more than two patches of silk with lacy straps, along with a bottle of sparkling wine. Reading the rose-colored label, she said, "This is called Orgasmic Pink. Cute, huh?"

He cleared his throat again as he inspected the bra. "Yeah."

"In fact, she said I can keep the wine. We should do a toast to your new business venture. We'll only pour you a tiny glass, though, since your meeting is tonight." Without waiting for his response, she expertly removed the cork with only the slightest *pop*.

He took the bottle from her, reading the label like it mattered. "I can hold my liquor, thank you very much."

"Okay, then. Take a look at the other items in my bag while I find some glasses." She knew exactly where they were, of course, but she opened the cupboard that housed water glasses first, just for show. "It's been a while," she said with a grin. "Cupboard above the knife block is where your mom kept the wineglasses." Setting them on the counter, she felt a slight tremor of guilt about what she was going to do next, but the truth was, she'd researched extensively if the sleeping pills Nadine's doctor had prescribed her had any deadly side effects. None was listed. There were tales of strange behavior and binge eating while sleepwalking, but it was a risk she'd have to take. Besides, she would give him only two pills. It was more than the recommended dose, but she needed quick results. They were already crushed in the glass. Forethought was the best thought.

"What's this?" he asked, his finger hooked along a string of pearls that was attached to a snip of lace.

She turned. "A thong." Tilting her head, she said, "Well, the string of pearls attaches the front to the back."

His neck flushed a bright shade of red, and he exploded his hands open near his head. "Mind blown. I've seen a lot, but nothing like this."

Crossing the kitchen, she took the bottle and filled their glasses, keeping his in her left hand. Thanks to the red crystal, nothing suspect was remotely visible. She passed one to him, and he gulped it like water. "It's well made too," she said in an even voice, as though they were discussing salad spinners. "That's what made me think this company might be worth a look."

"I think you could make a killing if you do couples' parties. Any guy would love to buy stuff like this for his girlfriend."

"Wine's not bad either," she said, pouring a touch more into her glass. "Care to have another little slug?"

"Sure, just a bit. And then I'm going to have to ask you to go. My meeting." His lip curled in what she supposed was his attempt at a seductive smile. "Or you could stay in the bedroom and model these for me when we're finished." He held up the undies with a finger. "I see what you're doing here."

Her mind raced. *Shit.* She should've known he would assume she wanted to seduce him. In a quick move, she filled his glass almost to the top and looked at him from beneath her lashes. "Is it that obvious? I really treasure your advice. You're one of the smartest men I know." How long was it going to take for the pills to kick in? If the investor arrived when he was still up, her plan would fail. She should've tripled the dose.

He gulped down the wine. "Let's cut the bullshit. You want me. I've seen the way you look at me."

It was stupid on her part not to have considered this outcome. Now she was treading on shaky ground, and her usually keen mind was stuck. She lowered her eyes to the table and began sweeping the items into the bag, buying time. "You're so smart, Jonathan," she said in a low voice. "And way out of my league. I really just wanted your advice. When I have a party, will you come? I'll invite some of my niece's friends to model the lingerie. You would like that, right?"

"I didn't know you have a niece," he said slowly. "I'll come to the par . . . party. Lem . . . Lemme know."

Pretending not to notice his slurring, she said, "Sure. You'll be the first on my list."

"I've go a lot of frenz . . ." His head bobbed forward and jerked back.

"Yes, I'm sure you do." She waited, watching him.

"Are you my fren?" he asked, his eyes drooping. She had to work quickly now, or he'd pass out on the floor. And the investor would be here any second.

She took his arm, keeping behind him, and ushered him to the bedroom. "I'm your friend."

"Thanz, Syl—Syl-vi-a."

"Let's just go lie down for a few minutes. A quick nap will have you feeling a lot better. It looks like you're coming down with a cold. Maybe you caught a virus during your travels."

"No, nooo. I'm zokay," he slurred.

She didn't argue. It wouldn't do any good. She'd learned that from an old boyfriend who'd taken to mixing vodka with Ambien, so she simply pushed him onto the bed. Just as she'd predicted, he was out cold in seconds, his feet hanging off the side of the bed. In a quick move, she hoisted them up with the rest of his body. Thank goodness he was thin. Lugging that ex of hers had always left her breathless and her shirts marred with ugly sweat stains.

A loud knock sounded, startling her. *Dammit!* She hadn't had a chance to clean up. But she couldn't wait. She rushed from the room, pulling the door closed behind her. She eyed the kitchen and grabbed Jonathan's wineglass, rolling it beneath the sofa on the way to the door.

"This is it," she said to herself. "Showtime."

The bell chimed as she yanked the door open, and she winced, hoping it wouldn't wake Jonathan. "Can I help you?" she asked in a not-too-friendly tone.

"Hi, I'm Frank Overland. I have a meeting scheduled with Jonathan Fisher about the complex." He smiled politely. "Is he here?"

Her heart was racing, but she had to pull this off. It would be best to let the man think she was upset about Jonathan. "Well," she said with a grimace, turning her head to the interior, "he's here, but he's sleeping at the moment. I think he's had too much to drink. I came by to feed his mother's fish, and he was a mess. Do you want me to pass a message to his mother? She's the owner."

"I'm sorry. Did you say Mrs. Fisher is the owner?"

"Yes," she said, eyes wide. "She's in the hospital for a few days, but I'm her neighbor. Well, neighbor and tenant. I've been stopping by to feed her fish." She took the small container of fish food from her pocket and held it up for him to see before motioning to the bowl on the table.

"Were you going to discuss renovations? She's mentioned wanting to get the windows retrofitted."

"No." He frowned. "Are you certain Mrs. Fisher is the owner? Because Jonathan told me his mom was dead and he wanted to sell."

Sylvia's jaw dropped. "What? Come in for a moment, will you?" It was a risk, but she had to make him believe. She marched to the kitchen and opened the refrigerator. "Does a dead woman need prune juice?" She slammed it. "For God's sake, do you think he's planning on killing his own mother? Or he's just that eager for her to die?" She touched a hand to her mouth. "I've been the one caring for her, and he's just . . ." She pointed to the wineglass. "A wreck." She took a breath and gave him a brave smile. "I'm happy to wake him and he can tell you himself that his mom is alive." She took her phone from her pocket and subtly hit "Send" on the text she'd prewritten.

"No, that's not necessary. I'm really sorry to have bothered you."

"To be honest, I'm glad I was here. I'm just not quite sure how to handle this. What do I say to his mom?"

"That I don't know. I'll leave a message saying the spot isn't right for me after all. I'm not interested in whatever game he's playing."

Sylvia shuddered. "His poor mom."

Embry appeared at the bottom of the stairs. "Hi, Sylvia. I heard some commotion. Is Nadine back home?" she called.

Frank shook his head. "What a supreme waste of my time. Good night."

"I'll follow you out," she said. Gathering her bags, she walked behind him down the stairs. She smiled when she heard him leave a message for Jonathan.

"Thanks, Embry," she whispered once Frank was out of earshot. "We've effectively gotten rid of one investor."

"Where's Jonathan?"

"Oh, he's fine. He's up there sleeping."

She raised a brow. "Really? How—"

"The less you know, the better, okay? You've done your part, and I'm thankful. It will all work out. Trust me."

Twenty minutes later, she was back in Nadine's place, keeping watch over Jonathan. His breathing was steady, and his skin showed no signs of pallor. He would be just fine. She rinsed both wineglasses and put them back in the cupboard. She gathered the groceries and the fish and headed for her own apartment.

Jonathan probably wouldn't wake until morning, but to be on the safe side, she set her alarm for four thirty. She'd go back and check on him then. As she set Fishy on the console table, she picked up the book Nadine had given her. "I hope you understand why I did what I did," she whispered, fingering the cover. A feeling of sadness ebbed through her. Strange. She certainly wasn't one to form attachments, nor was she someone to become overly sentimental. But Nadine had been different. An individual whom she had trusted. Not a bad bone in that woman's body. Cracking the cover, she headed for the sofa. If ever there was a time to escape in a good book, it was now. As she pulled a throw blanket over her lap, her phone rang. Slipping it from her pocket, she sat up straighter as she read the name on the screen. *Hugh's Phone.*

It was the burner phone.

Adrenaline pulsed through her. She certainly hadn't expected it to be discovered so quickly.

"Leave me alone, Hugh!" she said in an exasperated voice.

The response was a gaspy breath. *Not gruff,* she noted. It had to be Lily. She waited for her to say something, but the call ended.

Well, well. Had she snooped through all the texts, pausing in horror at the photos of the naked woman with the spiderweb tattoo across her hip? Would Kylie's words drift through her mind? *No, you colored your tummy, silly!*

Sylvia placed her phone on the table and let her eyes fall shut. It was so easy to imagine Lily in the kitchen, taking pots and pans from the cupboards with trembling hands. Would she go through the motions of preparing dinner as anger nipped at her? Perhaps Hugh would walk in, and she'd throw a plate at his head. But no, poor Lily would most likely fall into a chair and cry. And that would be the worst torture for Hugh. The man hated weakness. Detested crying. Yes, Lily's tears would drive him out of the house in a fit of rage. With any luck, he'd crash his car into a tree and end up with two broken arms.

Regardless, it was out of her hands now. And if he tried to blame Sylvia for anything, the burner phone, listed under Lily's name and Sammy's address, was full of evidence proving *he* had been harassing *her*. Not to mention the scores of people who would confirm that Sylvia's ex was tormenting her. All in all, a success. She padded to the kitchen and poured herself a glass of wine. "To you, Hugh. I won."

She resumed her spot on the sofa and picked up the book. A few pages in, a note fell out, but before she could open it, a knock sounded at the door. *Good Lord.* Setting the note on the table, she crept to the peephole, her mind racing with what she would say if it was Jonathan.

But it wasn't him.

It was Lily.

Exhaling, she opened the door.

Lily stood in front of her, draped in the horrible tunic she'd first seen her in at the Coffee Zombie. The poor thing resembled a zombie, with her colorless face and wide eyes. "It was Hugh." Her voice sounded like her throat had been scrubbed with sandpaper. "The man you cried about is Hugh."

Sylvia only nodded. Lily had a firm grip on her keys, as though she might decide to use them as a weapon. And the crazed look in her eyes? Well, there was really no telling what she was capable of. Best to handle this tactfully. She opened the door, and Lily stepped inside. Tension flitted through the room, darting here and there, as though wondering whether to crash-land or simply drift out the door. It wasn't emanating from Sylvia, of course. Her feelings were tucked casually in her pocket. Revealing the truth to Lily was as uncomplicated as righting a fallen chair. What would be uncomfortable was righting a fallen Lily. Sylvia prayed she wouldn't do something dramatic, like faint.

"There are no words to express my regret at not discovering he was married. I am truly sorry," Sylvia said.

Lily's expression tore into a grimace. "I found a phone. There were pictures," she said, her voice growing louder. "They were of you!" She shook her head wildly, the keys still tight in her grasp. "I should hate you!"

Sylvia stepped toward the kitchen table and pulled out a chair. "He lied to me, too, so directing any hate toward me is useless. Here, sit. We should discuss this like adults."

She pressed her hands to her temples, her keys knotted through her fingers. "I don't know! I don't know! Someone is lying!" Dropping her hands to her sides and letting the keys fall to the table, she said, "I texted him before I came over. He knows I'm here." Her voice was fragile, and she sank into the chair Sylvia offered. "I told him you invited me over for a glass of wine. The baby is at my mom's house. I needed to know the truth." Her lips quivered.

"I hate to say it, but you know already. He lied to both of us. He cheated on you."

Lily's face twisted and contorted—the quiet before the storm of tears that rained down her face. She gripped the edge of the table and opened her mouth to scream, but the noise that emerged was nothing more than a croak. It was then that she slid from her chair in a heap onto the floor. Her body shook with sobs.

There was really nothing to do but wait it out. Sylvia knew better than to offer a comforting touch. If she were married, she wouldn't want her husband's lover to touch her. As her wails softened to whimpers, Sylvia said, "When I came to your home with a gift that day, it was so I could see for myself that what I suspected was real. I needed to know the truth also." She spoke calmly, hoping Lily would listen. "And I wanted to hate you too. I really did. It would be so much easier if I could hold on to the idea that Hugh was in a bad marriage with a crazy wife. But you were sweet and genuine. I couldn't help but like you. When I left, you felt like an ally. Another victim of his lies."

Lily slowly curled herself to a sitting position, tucking her knees to her chest. She met Sylvia's gaze with red-rimmed eyes. "Why should I believe you?"

Sylvia folded her hands on the table and began calmly. "He led me to believe his name was Hugh Martin. We would meet at an apartment that I trusted was his. Turns out, it belongs to some guy named Sammy. When we saw you at the coffee shop, he told me you were an unstable ex and he had to pretend we were coworkers or you might come unhinged. And then he told me Hunter was a Pomeranian." She eyed her carefully, knowing those last words had the power to sway Lily's beliefs.

"What?" she spat. "He said our baby is a *dog*?" She leaped to her feet and gripped the back of the chair. For a second, Sylvia thought she might pick it up and chuck it across the room. Such a powerful move for little Lily.

"The things he has done sicken me." Sylvia looked up, her eyes searching. "He's a skilled liar. To be honest, the man terrifies me."

"Well, he's on his way here. Either that, or he'll buy a one-way ticket to Mexico. I don't even know him anymore." Lily shook her head, a vacant look in her eyes. "What will I say to him? I don't know if I want to kill him or beg him to fix things. Go to a good therapist."

"Murder is never a good option, though I don't know that counseling will work either. Once a cheater, always a cheater." Sylvia met Lily's eyes with her piercing blue stare, punctuating her point. With a hesitant shrug, she added, "But I've been wrong about people before. When confronted with the real threat of losing you, he may change, right?" She scrunched up her face apologetically.

"It's getting dark outside. It looks like it might start to rain again," Lily said in a hollow voice.

A chill ran through Sylvia. Lily seemed more fragile than ever, though not like she would crack, more like she would burst.

They sat in a cold silence and waited.

The trilling of a phone cut through the quiet, and Sylvia grabbed for her cell, spinning it toward her. "Hello?"

"It's Embry. Something's happened at Nadine's. I just sent Riki there. Can you go too? I'm scared."

"I'll be right over." She looked to Lily. "I need to help Embry. You should leave."

"I need a minute."

Sylvia studied her face for a moment but was met with a vacant stare. Part of her worried for Lily, but she had to go. If Jonathan was somehow awake and chatting with Embry, she needed to be there to perform damage control. "Fine. I'll be just across the way if you need me. And if Hugh shows up, stay out of the kitchen."

"Huh?"

"It's where the knives are." Sylvia left, letting her words hang in the air for Lily to grab on to.

CHAPTER
THIRTY-EIGHT

Riki twisted her hands as she stood over Jonathan. He was facedown on the floor next to the bed. Embry had called her in a panic, describing a strange thumping noise she'd heard in the apartment above, and she'd begged her to take a look, since she couldn't leave her kids unsupervised. Riki fished her phone from her pocket and called Embry back. "It was Jonathan," she rushed to say as soon as Embry answered. "He must've fallen off the bed." She lowered her voice as she looked at his body, splayed in an awkward position. "I'm scared, Em. He doesn't look good. In fact, he looks really bad."

"Like he's sick? Or is he . . . ?"

Riki nodded, even though she knew Embry couldn't see her. "Passed out? I don't know."

"Sylvia's on her way. I should've just called 911 when I heard the noise," she said, her voice shaky. "But what with her odd request to have me ask about Nadine . . . Oh, I just don't know!"

Did Sylvia kill him? Riki willed herself to check for a pulse, but she couldn't move. All she could do was stand there and stare. Footsteps sounded, and she turned. "Sylvia's here," she said into the phone. "I'll call you back." She ended the call and looked at Sylvia. "What did you do to him?"

Sylvia smirked. "Well, I didn't do a thing. The man was inebriated, and I helped him to bed." She marched toward Jonathan and touched her foot to his leg, jiggling it. He didn't move. "Oh, for God's sake."

Riki cried out. "What?"

Sylvia raised a brow. "Calm down. It's not like we're going to have to roll him up in the bedcovers like a burrito and pitch his body off the pier. He's not dead. Can't you see his chest rising and falling?"

She looked down at him. "I guess I can now. It was just so scary to see him like this."

"Well, he *is* dead asleep." She moved so she was near his head and reached her hands below his shoulders. "Come on. You're going to help me lift him back onto the bed. We can't leave him here."

Riki rushed to grab his legs. He muttered something, and her hands slid.

"Please, Riki. My wrist is literally going to break."

"Right! Sorry." She bent her knees before attempting to lift, the way she'd been taught to do at the gym, but he wouldn't budge. "I think we're going to have to wait for Brandon."

"Concentrate. We can do this. On the count of three." She counted, and they tried again. This time, they were able to deposit him back onto the bed, and Sylvia rolled him to his side. It was miraculous he didn't wake up.

Riki rubbed her hands down her jeans. "What do we do now?"

Sylvia exhaled. "Leave him. I'll check on him in the morning. And for all of our sakes, please don't let him know you saw him like this. Who knows what he might think?"

"I won't say a word," she whispered. "Can we go now? I'm totally creeped out."

"Don't be. He just had too much to drink. It happens. Let's leave him to sleep it off."

Riki rushed out. It had started to drizzle, and she shivered as she let herself into her apartment.

~

Sylvia marched toward her apartment, attempting to crush her annoyance with each heavy step. Why couldn't Jonathan just stay put and let her enjoy her victory? The fact that he'd fallen right off the edge of the bed was a little worrisome, but at least he'd stayed asleep. Now, he just needed to make it through the rest of the night. She opened her door to find Lily sitting at the kitchen table like a statue. There was no sign of Hugh. "He's clearly not coming," she said flatly. "And to be honest, I'd like to take a shower and get some rest. I'm exhausted."

Lily turned her head slowly to look at her. "You seem like a smart woman. How is it that you didn't know?"

Sylvia frowned. "I could ask you the same thing. How come you didn't suspect anything?" Footsteps pounded the stairs, and she cursed under her breath. "What now?" A knock sounded, and Sylvia headed to the door. She startled as Lily suddenly flew past her.

Yanking the door open, Lily stepped onto the landing. "How could you, Hugh? How could you?" she shouted.

Sylvia watched from the doorway, a sick thrill rushing through her as she absorbed the pained look in Hugh's eyes.

"What did I do? You told me you were here," he said, his hands raised as though pleading his innocence.

She stepped forward, suddenly larger than life. "You're lying! You had an affair, Hugh," she said, jamming a finger at him to punctuate her words. "How'd you even know where Sylvia lives? I never gave you her address. You're a liar!"

"It's not like that. Let me explain."

Well, this is interesting, Sylvia thought. How could he possibly worm his way out of this? She inched forward as Hugh stepped closer to Lily.

He reached for her hand, and as if his touch were searing poison, Lily flung out her arm, knocking him away.

Hugh teetered backward, his arms flailing wildly. "Lily!" he screamed.

Her face was an eerie calm as she lifted her hand to help. Sylvia tried to make sense of her calculated movements. Everything was too slow. *Move faster,* she wanted to shout. It was as though time hurtled to a stop, only ticking to life again when Lily's scream pierced the air—a shrill accompaniment to the sound of Hugh tumbling down the stairs like a crash-test dummy.

Ass over teakettle, Sylvia thought. He'd end up with more than a sprained wrist. *Poor Hugh.* Although it could've been worse. The mental anguish of Lily's tears would cause deeper, longer-lasting cuts. Maybe that would come later. There was nothing more agonizing than poking nearly healed wounds until they were raw and open again. And Lily didn't seem like the type to let things go. With any luck, as his bones were mending, she'd nag at him until his brain felt like it would explode.

Lily flew down the stairs, tripping on the bright-orange tape, but miraculously, she landed on her feet as graceful as a ballerina. Sylvia puzzled over her sudden rush to action, watching curiously as she fluttered to her husband, who lay in a crumpled heap. Blood seeped from beneath him. Had he scraped his skin on the rough ground?

Bile rose to Sylvia's throat as the realization hit that his injuries might be more than a few bruises. She raced down the stairs, holding on to the banister like her life depended on it.

"He's hurt! Help me!" Lily screamed.

Sylvia dialed 911. "A man fell down the stairs," she said into the phone. "Send an ambulance right now! 1054 Mockingbird Lane." Squeezing her eyes shut, she recalled Hugh's head bouncing off the concrete wall with a grotesque *thud.* And then he'd spilled down, down, down before smacking the hard asphalt with a sickening blow.

She'd been so transfixed by the look on Lily's face that she hadn't fully absorbed the fall.

Lily looked at her with a shattered expression. "Was this my fault?"

Sylvia didn't respond, but her brain kicked into high gear as she watched blood pool beneath Hugh's head. *Oh, Hugh. It shouldn't have come to this.* If he died and Lily went to jail, Hunter could become an orphan. That had never been part of the plan. The little boy deserved a loving parent. Everyone did. Then again, maybe she was getting ahead of herself. Her eyes drifted to the ghastly red pool, and she knew in her heart it was bad. "He fell," she said firmly. "I saw the entire thing. He must've misjudged how much room he had when he stepped back. It was an accident."

Lily nodded wildly. "But I watched him fall! I didn't stop him!"

Interesting choice of words, Sylvia thought. But she would never say that. "It happened too fast," Sylvia assured her. "There was nothing we could do. I saw you reach your hand out to help. You tried."

Lily flinched, then fell to her knees near her husband and took his limp hand. "Hugh, please! Please don't die," she begged. Sylvia stood silently. Suddenly Lily fixed a steely gaze on her. "You can't tell anyone about the affair. If he doesn't make it," she started, a sob hitching her speech. "If he dies, I don't want his name ruined."

"What about the phone he was using to call me? He posted pictures of me online."

"Anonymously!" she hissed. "No one knows he did it."

Sylvia spoke in a whisper. "You'll need to destroy the phone. Back over it with your car and dispose of the pieces in several public rest-rooms where there are no security cameras. And we have to tell the same story."

Lily nodded as tears spilled down. "I stopped by to say hi to you and lost track of time. I called him to pick me up. It was getting dark, and I thought it might rain. I didn't want to walk home."

"You walked here?"

"It's not that far."

"Yes. It looked like rain, and you didn't want to walk."

"Thank you," she whispered. "But he'll be okay, right? He'll be okay," she said, rocking like a broken doll by his side.

Back when Sylvia was a kid, a pomegranate tree grew outside of a house near her school. She and some of the kids used to shake the branches until the hard-skinned fruit fell, collecting as many as they could. Then they would take their haul to her neighbor's house, where they would hurl the fruit at the garage, slapping high fives all around when one finally broke. Hugh's skull had to be stronger than a piece of fruit. Should she mention that to Lily? It was strange how she wanted to comfort her.

The other tenants appeared suddenly, swarming from their apartments.

"What happened?" Brandon called as Embry rushed to Lily's side with Carson in her arms.

"Don't touch him! He's hurt!" Lily said through sobs as mascara-tinted tears streamed down her face.

Embry scurried back. "Brandon! Call 911!"

"I did already," Sylvia said firmly. "Docs anyone know CPR? Riki! You're a teacher. You must know how to do it."

Riki's arms flapped helplessly at her sides. "I don't know how! What happened to him?"

Lily turned, her face a horror film. "He fell. He slipped, and then he fell down the stairs. He'll be okay," she said, stroking his hand gently. "He'll be okay."

"Is that her husband?" Embry whispered as she tucked Carson close to her body.

Sylvia moved beside her. "Yes. Lily stopped by to say hi after she left your place, and she lost track of time. It was getting dark, so she called him to take her home. He was at the top of the stairs, and then he just—" She flung an arm in front of her. "He just slipped." Shaking her head, she said, "I don't know. With the busted stair . . . It all happened so fast."

And so it began. The new story. The one that would effectively eradicate her connection to Hugh. And if he lived, well, he would only have to answer to Lily.

Sylvia stood between Riki and Embry, her arms crossed loosely at her chest. Their small semicircle was casual, like spectators at a parade. "Well, a body at the bottom of the stairs is sure to draw a crowd." She coughed and cleared her throat. "Sorry. I shouldn't make bad jokes. I just don't know how to react in situations like this."

Embry gripped the gold pendant that hung from her neck, her usual rosy cheeks turning a ghostly shade of white. She opened her mouth to speak, but nothing came out.

Riki slapped her hand to her eyes, covering them. "You don't think he's . . . ?"

"Dead?" Embry whispered.

"I wouldn't know," Sylvia replied.

Moments later, two police cars careened into the driveway, the red and blue lights cutting through the air. Sylvia watched as they spoke with the ambulance driver, and then she stole a subtle glance at Nadine's place, praying Jonathan would sleep through the chaos.

"It sounded so bad," Riki said as her face grew pale. "I heard the thumping from my apartment."

Embry nodded, looking like she might barf. "How strange that two men fell here tonight."

An officer, intimidating in his pressed blues and impressive physique, walked authoritatively toward them. "Did any of you witness the fall?"

"I did," Sylvia said quietly.

"Come with me. I'd like to take your statement."

"Of course." She touched Riki's arm. "I'll be right back." As she walked with the policeman, she told herself to play the role of the frightened witness. Concern about Hugh would be important. She needed to come across as shaken but helpful.

He directed her to a spot away from all the action, which was quite a relief. Watching the emergency workers hunkered over Hugh was enough to make her stomach churn. She'd wanted him to suffer, but she hadn't wanted him to *die*. She forced herself to think of smashing pomegranates. *Skulls are thicker.* He would be fine. Perhaps divorced soon, but fine.

"State your name for me."

"Sylvia Webb," she said, wrapping her arms around her waist.

"And you live here?"

"Yes, in apartment D, the one he . . ." She raised a trembling hand to her mouth.

"Okay. I know this is difficult. Why don't you tell me what happened?"

She kept a neutral look on her face. This one would be a bit tougher to explain, now, wouldn't it? Best to stick to the facts they'd agreed upon.

"He came over to pick up his wife. We're friends. It looked like rain, and she didn't want to walk," she said, her tone measured. "We were chatting at the top of the stairs, and he stepped back." She paused and looked upward to the left. If he knew body language, he would perceive the movement as a truth indicator. Looking up and to the right was what liars did. "He must've misjudged the space. It was so horrible," she said, moving a hand to cover her eyes. "I can't stop seeing it in my mind."

"Do you know the man well? Does he come here often?"

"No. It was his first time. I know his wife."

"Uh-huh. And were he and his wife having any troubles that you're aware of?"

She gaped at him. "Lily and Hugh? No! They're adorable together. They have a new baby. As far as I can tell, their lives are perfect."

He cocked his head to the side. "You'd be surprised. Not everything is as it seems."

"Yeah, but they're happy," she stated firmly. "You can tell by the way they look at each other. And he made the drive over here just to pick her up. They're sweet like that."

"Okay. Thank you. It appears it was an accident, but we have to ask questions."

She nodded. "I understand. Do you think he'll be okay?"

He shook his head. "I don't know."

As she trudged back to Riki, a bloodcurdling scream sliced through the night. She darted her eyes to where Lily stood. The paramedics were covering Hugh's body with a white sheet.

CHAPTER
THIRTY-NINE

Tuesday, March 21

The sun wasn't up yet when Sylvia's alarm blared. She slapped the bedside table in search of her phone, wondering why it had gone off so early.

Reality punched her in the gut, and she lurched upright. Hugh was dead. Her mind eagerly showed her clips of the tragic evening, but she forced them away. Hugh had been a terrible person. No need to attempt any sentimental thoughts about him. She gripped her sheets. None of this was her fault. Sure, she had led Lily to the truth, but she hadn't killed him. No one could accuse her of a thing. And if anyone found the burner—well, it could be traced back only to Hugh. She was free of guilt.

Exhaling, she showered and dressed quickly. It was time to visit Jonathan. Armed with a box of tissues, a sleeve of saltine crackers, and a quart of orange juice, she let herself into Nadine's apartment once more.

All was quiet.

Setting her groceries on the kitchen table, she summoned her courage and headed for the bedroom. Jonathan was on his side, slumped like a corpse. *Blergh.* Her mind was certainly morbid today. She couldn't blame herself after all that had happened. The man wasn't dead. He was only sleeping, just like he had been last night. "Good morning!" she called.

Jonathan stirred, and her body went limp with relief. She hadn't realized she'd been stiff with tension.

"Wha's . . . Where?"

Channeling her mother, whose bedside manner had been efficient rather than warm, she strode to the window and threw open the curtains before turning to him. "You must've caught a nasty bug. How are you feeling?"

"Huh? Did I sleep here?" he asked, his voice sounding like he had a mouth full of cotton. Glancing at his body, he said, "Looks like I did. What happened?"

She gave him a pitying look. "Don't you remember?"

"Not really." He rubbed the side of his head as he sat up, touching his feet to the ground.

"I brought you some orange juice and crackers. Based on how you seemed last night, I wasn't sure if it was a cold or the flu that hit you."

"Right. Yeah. We were talking and had that wine . . ."

She frowned. "You did have two glasses. I know you said you can hold your alcohol, but if your immune system were already compromised, it might not have been a good idea."

He suddenly jumped from the bed. "My meeting!"

Holding up a hand, she said, "It's okay. After you fell asleep on me, I waited here for your guy to show up, but after an hour passed and no one had stopped by, I tucked you in and left. Your phone rang while I was here, but I didn't want to answer it. Maybe it was him who called?"

He stuck his hands through his limp hair and turned to her. "Thanks. You've been really helpful. I just don't know what came over me. It's true I've been going hard and fast. Maybe I picked up a virus in Europe."

She frowned. "Or on the plane. The incubation period can be a week or more." She looked around the room. "Is there anything I can get for you? Do you want me to pour you a glass of juice before I go? I have to get to work."

"Uh, no. I'm okay." Standing, he said, "I'm embarrassed you had to take care of me like that."

"Don't be. And maybe the investor had to reschedule anyway, so it will all work out, right?"

He patted his pockets for his phone and slid it from a front one. "Yeah. I'll just check my messages."

"One last thing." She softened her voice. "I hate to tell you this, but a friend's husband fell down my stairs last night."

"What? The broken step?"

She nodded, even though it wasn't true. He should have had that stair fixed when she'd asked him to. "He fell from the landing. It was horrifying." Her eyes drifted to the ground as she tried to block the vile memory. "He's dead."

Jonathan flinched. "Dead? Someone died here last night?"

"Yes. It was a terrible tragedy. I'm so sorry to have to share this, but I thought you should know."

"Yeah. Thanks. This isn't my fault, you know. They didn't say anything about liability, did they?"

"No, they didn't." *Always looking out for number one, aren't you,* she thought. "I'll leave the juice and crackers here for you. Make sure to stay hydrated." She gave him a sad smile and walked down the stairs.

Back in her apartment, she sat on the sofa and wrapped a throw blanket around her shivering body. The morning sky was layered with ominous clouds, and she couldn't escape the feeling that Hugh's ghost was storming through the sky. She reached for the note from Nadine. She needed some comfort to slough off the sorrow of the previous night. She unfolded the pages and began reading.

Dearest Sylvia,

If you're reading this, it means I've passed on to the great hereafter. I'm hoping the letter will be frayed and soft with age by the time you do, but we never know when our time is up, do we? Over the last few years, you have become like a daughter to me. I'm so proud of all you've accomplished with your life. I know you keep your childhood secrets close to your heart, but from what you've shared, I know you grew up without much. If you had been my little girl, I would have loved you every second of every day. It's what you deserve—what any of us deserve, really. I loved Jonathan that way, but for reasons I still can't comprehend, he wasn't able to love me in return. Some days it makes me quite sad, to the point where I look at old photo albums and cry. But then I dust myself off and look at the person who's not related by blood but who is here for me every day, whether it's something small, like loaning me a stick of butter, or something big, like taking me to the doctor and sitting by my side. You, Sylvia, have been here for me unconditionally. I love you for it. And I love you for the wonderful person you are. Don't forget that, dear. As I told you once before, this book by Maya Angelou is one I've treasured. Read it when you're ready. My hope is that it will mean as much to you as it's meant to me. It is the best gift I could think to leave you with.

My other gift to you is the property at 1054 Mockingbird Lane. Please see the accompanying page for my trust and will. (You would be proud—I learned how to do this on the internet.) It's all legal and binding. And of course, I've had it looked at by an attorney

friend. Her name is Lianne Wallis. Contact her with
any questions. (424) 555-9800.
   With love and best wishes always,
   Nadine

Sylvia set the letter aside, her mind whirring. The place was hers. Nadine was surely smiling at Sylvia's surprise. Too bad for Jonathan that she hadn't read the letter sooner. It would've saved him from what was certain to be a slamming headache today. On second thought, he deserved it.

～

Riki spent the day going through notes and pictures her students had made for her throughout the year. It gave her comfort from the horror of last night. She had been afraid to go outside and see the spot where that man had fallen. Now it was almost five.

She sighed as she smoothed a note from Jeremy into her stack. Would the parents have rallied so hard against her if they knew how much she loved their children? How much time she'd spent fostering their strengths and patiently working through their weaknesses? All because she cared. But those parents were too self-important to see it. A tear slid down her cheek, but she shoved back from the table and headed for the bathroom. *It's not like anyone I love died last night,* she reminded herself bitterly.

She splashed cold water on her face and dabbed antiseptic cream along her stitches. Bags looked like bruises beneath her eyes, but only time would fix that. She smoothed her hair into a ponytail and resumed her spot at the kitchen table, where she began piling the papers back into a box. As she picked up a card from Penelope covered in colorful Crayola hearts and the words, *I love you so so so so so much, Miss McFarlan!* the tears spilled over. She tossed the card into the box and shoved it across the table before pushing back her chair. This could be dealt with later. She needed fresh air. A walk would be nice. Grabbing her keys, she went outside.

The low, late-afternoon sun greeted her, and she blinked a few times, the tears and light blurring her vision. As she reached the driveway, she nearly fell over as a giant creature rushed her. It took a second to recognize it was a dog, not an escaped polar bear. It wriggled and wagged and licked her face, as though understanding on some intuitive level that she was upset. Despite herself, a smile emerged, and she wrapped her arms around the giant fluff ball, pressing her face into the soft fur.

The sound of rushed footsteps caused her to look up, and she shaded her eyes with a hand. "I'm guessing she's yours?"

"Yes. Sorry she darted over here," he said, attaching a leash. "Are you okay?"

Their eyes met, and he blinked back surprise as she slapped a hand to her chest. "It's you," she uttered. "The doctor."

He laughed. "Dr. Hart. And you're the very brave Riki."

She rose to her feet. "I wasn't that brave. I was kind of a wreck."

"You were great." He moved his mouth to say more, but no words came out. Smiling, he tried again. "You live here?"

Realization hit her, and she slowly nodded. "I do. And you're Embry's brother. The urgent-care doctor."

"She's watching Gracie for me until I get settled. I'm moving down here."

"That's great!" It came out too quickly and too eagerly, but he didn't seem to notice.

"I'm happy to finally settle down somewhere. I've been working locum tenens, meaning I've been moving from one urgent care to the next, following the seasons. It's been a great way to see a lot of the country, but it's time to be near family. See my sister's kids grow up."

"They're awesome. So is your sister, for that matter. She's a great friend."

"Is that so? You must be 'the sweet gal who lives across the way.'" A big grin emerged, and she tried not to pass out. "I've heard a lot about you. Just didn't know it was you she was talking about. How is the wound, by the way? Are you taking good care of it?"

Touching a hand to her neck, she nodded. "Thanks again for being so nice to me."

He rubbed his dog's ears. "You're welcome. Do you have a minute to say hi to Embry? I think she'll get a real kick out of this."

"Okay. Avoid that spot there, though," she whispered. "A man died there last night."

"Embry told me. How sad," he said, mirroring the wide arc Riki made as they crossed the gravel driveway.

~

Embry held the phone in her hand, a silly grin hanging on her face. "Brandon!" she shouted as she sank onto the sofa. "Can you come here for a second?"

He stepped out of their room with a freshly changed Carson in his arms. "Yeah, babe? What's up?" He stood in front of her and smiled at the look on her face.

She lifted the phone in her hand. "I just got off the phone with Daniella Stefani's manager."

"Daniella Stefani? Are you kidding me?"

"Nope." Her smile took over, and a laugh burst out. "Daniella was at Soul Candy in Westwood, and she loved my honey pops so much that she wants to give away packs of them in her birthday-gala favor baskets next month."

"Shut the front door! That's amazing, Em!" He ran a hand down his mouth. "I'm floored."

She stood and wrapped her arms around Brandon and the baby. Kylie rushed over from where she had been filling a basket with plastic fruit and grabbed on to Embry's leg. "I hug you, too, Mama!"

Embry laughed. "Thanks, Ky. We're going to be making a lot of honey pops in the next little bit here."

"I help, Mama." She rushed into the kitchen and opened a cupboard. Embry didn't try to stop her.

Brandon looked into her eyes. "This could be huge, Em. Her social media following is in the millions."

"I know! And her manager was so nice. She said that Daniella strives to help female-run businesses. She read the tag and loved my story."

"I love your story. You're amazing, darlin'."

She bit her lip. Now was the perfect time to tell him. "There's one—"

"Hey, Em!" Evan burst through the door with Gracie in tow. Riki stood next to him. "We have a funny story to tell you."

She smiled at Brandon. Her news could wait just a little while longer.

~

Sylvia set her phone on the kitchen table, her mind spinning. Lianne Wallis had just returned her call, and she'd confirmed what Nadine had written. The place belonged to Sylvia. Lianne had warned that Jonathan might try to dispute it, but she assured her that the documents were ironclad. There was no way he could fight Sylvia and win. Pressing her hands to her face, she sighed. How could something so wonderful happen the day after something so tragic had occurred?

Her stomach rolled as her thoughts turned to Hugh. It didn't ache the way it had last night, causing her to curl into a ball. But it felt like she had a nasty hangover. She had called in sick. And, of course, she had to cancel her lunch with Sal.

"A friend's husband died last night," she'd said. "He fell down my stairs. It was horrible. I'm a giant bundle of nerves."

"Oh man, Sylvia. I'm really sorry. That's a lot to handle. I'm here if you need me, okay?"

"Thanks, Sal. I appreciate it." Standing, she headed for the door. Riki and the Taylors would be interested in her news, to say the least. She stepped outside and was surprised to see the black Camry still parked in Nadine's spot. Had Jonathan stayed all day? Well, if there was ever a sign to break the news to him, this was it. She stepped back inside and collected Nadine's letter along with the holographic will. Inching down the stairs, she tried not to picture Hugh's tumbling body, but it was useless. She raced down the last steps and jogged across the driveway. Once this was all said and done, she was going to move.

She knocked. Footsteps sounded before the door swung open. Jonathan pressed a hand to his neck and yawned. "Hey."

"Hi. I wanted to see how you were feeling. Better now?"

"Yeah. Thanks."

Sylvia didn't wait. "Good. There's no easy way to break this to you, but I came across a document from your mom that directly affects us both."

His eyes came alive. "Do you want to come in for a sec?"

"It's fine. We can do this here. It might be simpler if I show you." She handed him her copy of the holographic will.

He scanned the page, his brow furrowing more deeply as he neared the end, and he laughed uneasily. "What the hell is this?"

"Something your mom left behind. I just found it in the book you gave me."

Glancing at the page again, he said, "I don't know what you think this is, but I'm pretty sure it's fake." He crumpled the page in one hand.

"It's not fake. Nadine left me a letter, and I had the will checked out by an attorney."

"It's bullshit," he said with a tight grin. "Call it what you want, but I call it bullshit." Without waiting for a response, he shoved past her. She grabbed for the railing and held tight as a wave of nausea rolled through her. *Jesus.* He could've knocked her over. She regained her composure and headed slowly down the stairs.

Trekking back up to her apartment, it became crystal clear she didn't want to live here any longer. She shivered as she let herself inside. All this belonged to her, so she could do with it what she wanted. Kicking off her boots, she slid her feet back into her bunny slippers and sat at the table in front of her open laptop, but her stomach complained loudly. The date caught her eye. March twenty-first. Her mind sped through the calendar, and her mouth went dry.

She hadn't lied to Hugh about being five days late. But it wasn't unusual for her periods to fluctuate. But what if the nausea she was experiencing wasn't stress related?

She crossed to the bathroom and took the second test from the box.

Five minutes later, she stood in the kitchen, the test on a paper towel, just like before.

And just like before, a second pink line washed across the screen. She was pregnant.

Sinking to the floor, she pressed her hands to her head. It was everything she had wanted. Still wanted. But she would be attached to Hugh for eternity.

No! She stood abruptly and swiped her hands across her face. She would not let the fact that Hugh was the father of this baby change a thing. Her baby would have a wonderful life. But she needed to get away from this place.

Lianne had said she would introduce her to a real estate agent friend. So yes, she would sell. She couldn't imagine the others would want to stay either. At least, not for long. She would let them live rent-free until she sold. It was time to start making new plans. She began typing into the search bar on her laptop. It was amazing how much information one could gather in two seconds flat. And with the profits from the sale of 1054 Mockingbird Lane, a world of opportunity awaited her and her baby.

CHAPTER FORTY

The sky was getting dark, without a star in sight. The fog had rolled in, and the streetlights shone down, lighting the sidewalks. Riki felt safe next to Dr. Hart. *Evan.* He held Gracie's leash as they strolled down the block. The night air felt good on her skin. Refreshing, like it could cleanse her of the cloud of death that hung in the air outside her apartment. Turning to Dr. Hart, she said, "How do you get through the day without worrying about everyone you see?"

He smiled at her. "It gets easier with time. Some patients stick with me more than others."

"Makes sense, I guess. I would get too attached to my patients."

"You'd be surprised. Some can be downright mean."

Laughing, she said, "I hope I wasn't mean. That day is kind of a blur. I do remember how nice you were, though. Thank you, if I didn't say it at the time."

He touched an elbow to hers. "You did. Thank me, that is. And you weren't mean. In fact, I was thinking about you as I drove down today. Wondering how you were doing. I'll admit I was hesitant to leave you there with your boyfriend. What happened with him?"

"Long story short, he's now an ex-boyfriend. We didn't even date that long. It never felt right."

"Still tough, I imagine."

"Not so bad." Gracie stopped to sniff some bushes, and they slowed. "I have a question. Do I call you Dr. Hart or Evan? Because I've been calling you Dr. Hart in my mind, but now that seems too formal. But I'm fine with it if—"

"Call me Evan."

"Right. Evan. Okay." He was crazy cute. And sweet.

He smiled at her as they resumed walking. "We should get back. I have to be in Torrance early tomorrow."

"Is that where you're moving?"

"Manhattan Beach, but I'll be working at a family practice in Torrance. It'll be nice to be able to see Embry and the gang more often. Without traffic, it's only a twenty-minute drive."

"Yeah." She laughed. "But there's always traffic."

As they reached the long driveway, he stopped. "True, but it's still not that far. It'd be great to be able to see you again."

She swallowed hard. "I'd like that. A lot."

He grinned, and his hazel eyes were bright. "Good. Now, in the meantime, try not to take out any fences or otherwise injure yourself."

"Right. Good night, Evan."

"Good night, Riki. Sweet dreams."

CHAPTER

FORTY-ONE

Wednesday, March 22

Embry shuffled from the bathroom, swiping a wet cloth across her mouth.

"Mama, you okay?" Kylie asked. She was wearing her Supergirl cape and had been spinning circles across the room. The sight had caused Embry to lose her lunch.

"I'm great, sweetie. Just a little tired. Maybe a little dizzy from watching all the spinning. How about you come sit on the couch and read with me?"

The door rattled, and Brandon walked in. "Hey there. How are my favorite girls?"

Kylie wriggled down from the sofa, her cape flowing behind her as she plowed into him. "Daddy!" Embry sighed with relief. Maybe now she could crawl back into bed for an hour until Carson woke up.

Brandon scooped Kylie into his arms and kissed her forehead. "Hey, sugar!"

"Uncle Evan had to go, Daddy. And Mama barfed!"

Setting Kylie down, he walked over to Embry. "You okay, darlin'?"

"Nothing to worry about. The last few days have really gotten to me."

"I know. I'm so sorry for your friend."

"I barely know her, but it's just so sad."

He rubbed his hands across her shoulders. "Would some good news help, or should I save it for later?"

"What good news?" She arched her neck so she could see his face, and he sat next to her.

"Really good news. Amazingly great news," he said, his blue eyes sparkling. "You're looking at the newest series regular on *Baggage*, a brand-new legal drama starring the one and only Sandra Bullock. And me," he added with a grin.

"Brandon!" She took both his hands in hers. "Are you serious? When did you audition? I didn't know a thing about this!"

"I've auditioned over the course of the last few weeks. In fact, Riki is the one who gave me the contact. One of her friends works on the show."

"Riki?" she asked slowly. She bit her lip as she thought back to the headshot in Riki's purse and the late-night call. It was all so innocent. A twinge of guilt shot through her for having thought badly for one second about her.

"Yeah. She's been great. Anyway, it's an ensemble cast," Brandon continued. "I'll play a young cop, and Sandra Bullock is the DA. I'm the only unknown. The others have all been on series before, so I got really lucky. Adena is hammering out the deal as we speak. It's looking good. Really good." Gazing into her eyes, he said, "It sounds like it'll be an eight-episode deal with an option for more. Adena says we can get somewhere near thirty grand per episode."

She stared back at him, her eyes wide. "I think you need to pinch me so I know this is real."

"It's real, Em. We did it. You and me, babe." He brushed the hair back from her face. "I wanted to tell you so badly when I got the audition, but I was afraid to get my own hopes up, let alone yours." He met her eyes. "I'm really sorry I've been a pain in the butt the past few weeks. The pressure . . ."

"It's okay. I get it. More than you know. We just have to remember to be honest and stick together when things get tough. We're a team." She exhaled, accentuating her point. Had she been holding her breath for weeks? It sure felt like it. Even with trying to be mindful and positive, she had been struggling.

He smiled. "Team Taylor. I like it."

"Are you ready for some more good news?"

"Lay it on me. Does another pop icon want to buy some honey pops?"

"No, not that."

"What is it?" he asked, a smile hanging on his lips.

"Team Taylor is going to be a team of five this fall."

He gaped at her. "Five?" Shaking his head, he looked to where Gracie was sprawled on the kitchen floor. "We're keeping the dog?"

"No." She smiled.

"Wait a sec. You mean . . ."

She nodded and placed his hand on her belly. "Meet Baby Number Three."

"Baby Number Three?" A tear leaked down his cheek as he cupped his hands on her shoulders. "I . . . Wow. This is the best news. Did you just find out?"

"I took a test on our anniversary. And I really wanted to tell you, but it's been so tense and—"

"I get it." Drawing her into a hug, he said, "I love you so much. Damn, babe. You're amazing. How did I get so lucky?"

"We're both lucky."

He stole a look to the window. "We've made some wonderful memories here, but what do you say we start looking at some houses? We'll finally have enough to buy something real soon."

She shuddered in his arms. "I'm ready to move far away from this place."

"It's settled, then. Now, why don't you go catch a nap, and I'll get Carson when he wakes up." He looked at her in awe. "A baby? You're one hundred percent positive?"

"Yeah. We're having another baby." She walked slowly to her room, her mind drifting from Brandon's beautiful smile to homes with big yards and shade trees with plenty of space for her kids to run free.

CHAPTER

FORTY-TWO

Sylvia had taken another sick day. She would go back tomorrow, but today was going to be a busy one. *Busy, busy, busy,* she thought. First on the list was meeting with Lianne, the lawyer. It was crucial she gather all the information on the potential time line for selling the place so she could inform the neighbors. With any luck, she would be able to sell within the next month. She'd already decided she would give Riki and the Taylors $15,000 each from the profits. That should help them get along until they found new places. It was what Nadine would've wanted. And what was $30,000 when you had millions?

There would be more, though.

Finding a simple man who would be her partner and the father of her future child had failed miserably. And Sal? Well, she had to scratch him from the list, since she was moving far from here. A nice man, indeed, but she had a new plan.

Scrolling down the open page of her laptop, she reviewed the details she'd gathered last night. It had been so easy. The idea had emerged organically with a search for a new place to live. A fresh start. Real estate websites were chock-full of interesting information. There were homes listed for $40 million! $50 million! One was even listed at $165 million. Who on earth had that kind of money?

Turns out, the answer was a click away. How fun it had been to research the people behind the For Sale signs! She'd never once considered finding a man through real estate, but it had proven to be quite a treasure trove.

Grant Hardcastle, owner of a lovely craftsman off the coast of Massachusetts, was the man she'd decided upon. Wikipedia had been oh so helpful in telling her exactly who he was: a developer of a new GPS technology whose net worth was $70 million. And sadly (or ideally), he was a widowed father of two young children. And soon, he would be a daddy-to-be again.

Grant was often spotted at Red Sox games. Well, that would be simple enough. She had plenty of time to learn about baseball. Of course, she would claim to be a Dodgers fan, so they could have a friendly rivalry.

He was hosting a charitable event on April seventeenth in Boston. How ironic that she would be there too. By then, she would be prepped and ready. She would enrapture him. *A virtual whirlwind romance,* he would tell his friends.

She would deliver the baby news over a romantic, candlelit dinner. She'd laugh, rubbing her tummy. "With my luck, this little darling will arrive late," she'd say. And when he or she came early, they would giggle at the irony. "Already a pleaser, this one," she'd say.

She looked at a photo of him with his son and daughter on her computer screen and smiled.

"Hi, honey," she said. "I'll see you soon."

ACKNOWLEDGMENTS

Thank you to my agent, Beth Miller, who responded with "I'll read whatever you send my way!" when I told her I wanted to try something different. I'm so grateful for her unwavering support, guidance, and her belief in this project from the very start.

Thank you to my editor, Alicia Clancy. Her enthusiasm for this book encouraged me to work even harder, and I'm so thankful for her keen insight, sharp eye, and clever sense of humor. To the entire Lake Union team, a huge thank-you for your dedication and hard work. You have surpassed even my highest expectations, and I feel very lucky to be part of this family.

Thank you to Marisa Reichardt and Elise Robins, who endured reading way too many versions. I'm so happy to have you both in my corner.

Thank you to Officer Vela, Officer Garkow, Officer Zuber, and Stephanie Swartz for sharing your time and wisdom to help me with details along the way and for patiently answering my many questions. Thank you to Pappy for your inspiring words.

Thanks to my mom and dad, Nancy and Don Wise, and to my sister, Stephanie Nalick, for all your love and support.

Thank you to my amazing kids, Kelly, Madeline, Cameron, and Jake. No one else can make me laugh to the point that I'm coughing my water across the dinner table. I love you guys to the moon and back.

ABOUT THE AUTHOR

Photo © 2015 Liz Lonky

Stacy Wise is the author of *Beyond the Stars,* winner of the 2017 YARWA Athena Award, and *Maybe Someone Like You,* winner of the 2019 YARWA Athena Award. She lives in California with her husband, their four children, and three dogs. For more information, visit www.stacywise.com.